On the follo\
Stories of fictio\
None of which are intended for those of faint heart\
Nor are they recommended for those soon to part...\
&\
Pictures - there are a few\
Some I've taken and borrowed too\
And now I'd like to share my plight,\
By welcoming you to

The Darker Side of Light

Weird and Wacky Tales & Other Such Nonsense

As sure as I am of one mind, I am sure of many

Literary Fiction

Front and back cover, formatting and graphics

by Linda Noble-Cordy

Author's Original

1 of 2

All parts of this book have been written by Linda Noble-Cordy. All rights reserved. No part of this book is to be printed, copied or reproduced without the written consent of the author.

October 2017

The Darker Side of Light

Titles

Page no#

    3…To my family and friends – Bring in
    5…The Power of the Mind
    6…Confession of a mad man
    7…**The man with the brief case**
  14…Bishop's Field
  16…**Glasgow Scotland 1928**
  19…Olivia Bellbottom
  20…Ode to Serenity
  21…**The Selfless Butterfly**
  25…A bed-time scare
  26…**The tale of the Itnescomber, *Thief of the Young***
  84…Words
  88…**Orla**
  91…Indulging Poverty
  93…Incumbent thoughts
  94…An excerpt from the diary of a mad house slave
  95…Betsy Bouncy Doll
  97…Little fruit fly Sally
  98…In keeping with Robert Service
  99…**Once Upon a Sorry Time**
123…Lonely Heart
124…The Eager Man
125…Melancholy Babe
126…**Liam**
152…Angel of Misery
153…**The Seed and the Wind**
156…Dandelions Bloom
157…The Cheating Heart
159…Who am I mocked the turtle
161… My Solitary Wanderer
162…**The Sea Raven's Barnacle**
250…The Predator and the Prey
251…Let me in
252…The Will in Love
253…Our trip to the Zoo
255…The Seasons
256…My Write
257…Acknowledgements

To my family and friends

Bring in

Bring in the light so that I might see
For my eyes are not the only things that fail me
Bring in the sound so that I might hear
The tranquil tapping of raindrops on the windowsill near
Bring home the children so that I might laugh again
And open my heart to a remembering when
Bring in the fun, the play to be found
On the streets, in the parks and in the playgrounds
Bring in a whistle, a clap and a cheer
Bring in the hearts you mostly hold dear
Bring in a friend, a lover, a mate
Bring in the message before it's too late
Bring in the Love, you long for, you miss
Bring in the person who longs to be kissed
Bring in the hugs, the cuddles, the embrace
That once you had but somehow misplaced
Then bring in a time when all will be fine

By bringing in yours and bringing in mine

I.H.R
Always Linda

The Darker Side of Light

Weird and Wacky Tales & Other Such Nonsense
Linda Noble-Cordy

The Power of the Mind

What greater sin is there than this?
To have the gift of all gifts, to have the power of the mind
And have it chained, locked behind
The walls of self-indulgence, emotional blindness and human err

What greater sentence would be fair?
To see the light, but feel none there
To know and yet not
That there is more for one so blind, to hunger, fear and mankind

What sadder tear has crossed the cheek?
As one so mournful of deceit
To be guided by a gentle hand
Then left alone, alone to stand

Are we the few that lock our minds?
For fear of terror that we may find
Willing victims are we to circumstance
And alone we must stand

For to free the mind, is to free the soul
And lost are we who do not know
The gift we all possess inside
Awaits the freedom of the mind

Confession of a mad man

If someone said that you were insane
How much would that upset ya?
If another said you were a fool
How much of that would affect ya?
Me, it didn't bother nor did it cause alarm
No harm, no harm...
And if when they called you to the stand
And proceeded to call you a liar
Would you pack a gun next time?
And just open fire.
Me, it didn't bother nor did it cause alarm
No harm, no harm…
If their tongues flapped and flapped
And they just wouldn't shut on cue
Would you beat them senseless?
Just to teach them a thing or two
Me, it didn't bother nor did it cause alarm
No harm, no harm…
And if they were going to lock you up
For something you didn't do
Would you take a knife?
And show them who is who
Me, it didn't bother nor did it cause alarm
No harm, no harm…
If all your eggs were in one basket
And you dropped them on the floor
Would you pick them up?
Or just leave them dying and ask for more
Me, it didn't bother nor did it cause alarm
No harm, no harm…no fowl
Because Elvis has left the building
And the nut has left the shell
So, I'll see you next Tuesday,
When you visit me in hell…

The Darker Side of Light

The Man
With The
Brief Case

Weird and Wacky Tales & Other Such Nonsense
Linda Noble-Cordy

Albert Flinch had been working for Service Canada for just over ten years. And not once in the last two years had he seen a single pay raise. At every annual review, he was told he was already making too much money, way above his pay scale. This he thought was total and utter crap.

His co-workers knew he didn't usually put up with any crap- well at least not from his clients. They could count on him for that. Therefore, any difficult or should I say *challenging* cases were sent his way. Yes, Albert was more than a bit of a hardass. He was downright nasty at times. And for some reason they let him get away with it. I guess it's because somebody had to do it and Albert fit the profile.

He didn't start out this way. In the beginning, he was kind and caring, patient and understanding. He had big dreams of making a difference in the world by helping those less fortunate than himself.

It wasn't until one of his co-workers- Loretta Weise was shot and killed that he started to question his purpose. She was one of the nicest people you could ever meet. Too nice, and it got her killed- and not in the street, where it could look like an accidental shooting. No, it happened right in the office, in Meeting Room 108.

After that a lot of the workers got counseling, some quit, others relocated. But not Albert, he stayed on determined not to let it affect him. And once the safety glass and emergence buttons where installed in all the rooms, he told himself he was safe. He was an untouchable – physically and mentally.

Another long and pointless day about to end, he pulled up his last appointment. He had met this client briefly the month earlier. He had been in the system for about a year. And in that time, he had been passed from one worker to the next. He skipped previous comments and went right to his own. He didn't really care what the other workers had to say. If he had even bothered to read what the previous worker had written, maybe he would have handled the situation differently – but probably not...

He reviewed his notes: client #R08971 – Samuel Riggs. To bring in: bank statements – 3 months; renter's agreement and list of job search. Then in the special note column – very quiet –doesn't say much. Seems okay, don't know why he has been assigned to me? (Read history). Well it was too late for that now. He didn't have time to read all the notes written. He would do it another time, he told himself. Pushing down the speaker he called, "Samuel Riggs report to room 108, Samuel Riggs report to room 108."

Samuel had been sitting in the waiting area for almost an hour. His left leg shook madly and the briefcase that contained his fate bounced vigorously upon his lap. He held on to it so tightly that the knuckles on his right hand were white. His heart raced causing anxiety to escalate as tiny beads of sweat began to form on his brow. Coincidentally, a nervous disorder he acquired right after being fired from his teaching job and around the same time his mother met with an untimely death.

A large man sat down right beside him and he felt very uncomfortable; so much so that he got up and walked over to the counter to ask how much longer. "It won't be long Mr. Riggs please take a seat and your worker will call you soon." Came the voice of the imprudent secretary. Bitch, he thought to himself. Sitting back down in another spot, he thought; How much longer? This is nuts. I have things to do. Better things than sitting here waiting for this imbecile.

He didn't want to be there. He could feel the eyes of strangers upon him. Did they know? Could they tell he was a killer? Were they afraid of him, because they should be. His eyes darted around the room then quickly settled on his bouncing briefcase.

He thought about his latest victim. She still lay on the basement floor of his mother's house. He needed to get home and clean up the mess he had made. Fear and hate fueled his anxiety as he thought about his mother finding her- she always finds them. She would be terribly disappointed with him. "What is taking so long? This is ridiculous!" he said aloud.

Even in death she had a hold on him. And in his *head*, she was very much alive. "Sam, Sam… get home! I want this piece of trash out of my house right now!" Under his breath, he uttered, "Shut up mother, I'll take care of it when I get there." A little louder he said. "Now just shut up!" A woman who sat across from him looked over. Sam could feel her smiling – laughing at him.

Bitch! he thought as he gave her a dirty look, she quickly looked away. He didn't belong there – among these low life's, these welfare cases…He was better than all of them.

It wasn't fair what had happened to him. It wasn't his fault, she asked for it. She was the one coming on to him. He thought about Bonny, his student. He was once so fond of her – loved her. And now he hated her with a passion. A sick, perverse passion that he acted out not only in his mind but on his victims. "Slut." He yelled out. Frightened and upset the woman got up and moved to the other side of the room.

He placed his left hand on the case and felt a profound sense of power. Smiling he looked around the room and imagined himself killing everyone. He would take out the fat man that had sat next to him first. Then systematically take out the rest. There were seven people waiting not including a boy that looked to be about nine or ten. He would spare the kid, leaving him alive to tell his tale. Deranged fantasy awoken and knee silenced, he reached for the latch on briefcase.

"Samuel Riggs report to room 108, Samuel Riggs 108…" Finally, he could get this over with…

Samuel entered the white walled room and sat directly in front of his case worker. "Samuel Riggs?" Albert asked.

The Darker Side of Light

Samuel nodded his head at him. "How are you?" he questioned, a standard inquiry. "Okay," he responded. Albert thought - this is going nowhere fast so he asked, "Have you got the paper work I requested last time we met. He looked towards the computer screen and voiced, "The last 3 months' bank statement, renter's agreement and a list of the jobs you've applied at?"

Samuel nodded his head yes and slowly opened the briefcase that sat on his motionless lap. One hand firmly grasping the gun inside the case; with the other he removed the papers one by one; sliding them through a 1-inch opening at the bottom of the glass wall. Still annoyed from his long wait, he thought, "I better not get a hassle from this jerk." He was sweating profusely now, as he tried with all his might to keep the bad feelings at-bay.

Albert briefly looked at the bank statement then put them off to one side. Next, he picked up the forged rent receipt and once again looked at it for a moment and then placed it with the other papers.

Waiting for a few seconds, he looked at Samuel. "Where's the list of places you've applied for work?" "Don't have one. Didn't know I needed one; never needed one before." He began to nervously move about on his seat.

Albert chuckled a little out loud and thought to himself, here we go again - another dead-beat loser, looking for a free ride. "Well if you don't have a list you can't get assistance. We have to see you are at least trying to find work." "Well I am, I just don't have a list," Samuel insisted. "Oh, like I haven't heard that one before." Albert spouted as he looked over at Samuel and for the first time really looked at him. He could definitely see he was lying about something.

He picked up the renter's agreement and read the name out loud. "Daisy Riggs." Then with some sarcasm in his voice he questioned. "Is this a relation you are renting from?" "Yes, my mother," he responded. Albert shook his head in dissatisfaction. "I'm going to have to review your case and get back to you." He stated frankly.

Samuel's aggravation escalated. "No!" He shouted. "You can't do this to me. I'm not leaving here without my cheque. I have bills to pay. I need it!" Then he added, "Mother will be very upset with me if I don't give her the rent money."

Albert started to laugh at him. "You can't be serious? You don't think I'm just going to issue you cheque –just like that!" then he added, "You're renting from your mother and to top it off you don't have a job-search list. What kind of loser are you? I mean really, how old are you?" Albert eyed the computer pretending to look for his age on it.

He knew he would have to give this guy his cheque. But not before he belittled him and made him feel like shit. That was his game plan. Make them beg and then just to show them what a nice guy he is – make an exception, just this once.

Samuel could no longer control the bad feelings inside him. He stood up fast and hard, knocking both the briefcase and chair to the ground. He pointed the gun at Albert. In a brief moment of forgetting, Albert, eyes fixed on Samuel he reached for the emergency button then stopped.

He had no worries. "Sit down Samuel, don't be a fool. The glass is bullet proof." He told him matter-of-factly. Beyond coming back to any reasonable resolution, Samuel turned the gun on himself. Shaking madly, Samuel yelled out. "Is this what you want? I'll do it, I swear I'll do it!"

Oh, this is great, Albert thought. Forget the raise, if this guy offs himself, I'm looking at early retirement with all the bells and whistles.

He pulled himself close to the glass, looked right into Samuel's eyes and whispered loud enough for Samuel to hear, "Just do it already. I really don't give a shit."

The Darker Side of Light

"Just kill the bastard!" his mother ordered. "Go on, what are you waiting for!" "Go away mother." He insisted through clenched teeth. "What was that you said Samuel?" Albert asked calmly. He didn't answer but did repeat it as he continued to address the voice inside his head. "Go away, I can handle this myself." Albert just smiled at him mockingly.

"Alright, alright!" he screamed. And through the one-inch slot meant for pushing papers through – he stuck the nose of the gun. Albert didn't have time to push any buttons or even get out of the way. Samuel shot him dead.

Picking up that what fell to the floor, he sat back down and waited for someone to come in.

No one did. "Room must be sound proof." He said aloud as he chuckled to himself.

He just wanted what was owed to him... that's all. "Why couldn't he have just given me my god-dame cheque?" He said out loud as his annoyance surmounted. Gun in hand, briefcase in the other, he got up to leave the room. "Now to deal with those other bitches, he announced to his mother. She replied, "That's my boy, you teach them all a lesson son..."

Bishop's Field

Alone he sat in Bishop's field
In the stillness before dawn
With a-knowing in his very soul
He could not carry on
And as he pondered life itself
What else was he to do?
For he had nothing more to gain
And nothing left to lose
The shell that held his spirit once
Had also held is pain
A spirit lost, forsaken so
Could no longer house his shame
So, it left him to wander aimlessly
Adrift without a sea
A world without an ocean
An endless misery…
And if you can look without judgment
In a field of eternity
With an eye that is opened
To every possibility
You may see his shadow
Or feel his presence there
You may witness the after-life
Of one who once was here
Against the mist, the foggy plane
Against the dimness of the light
You may sense his sorrow there
The burden of his plight
So, make the best with what you've got
And free yourself from strife
It doesn't matter if you're rich or poor
Because there's more to *this* - than just a life…

The Darker Side of Light

Weird and Wacky Tales & Other Such Nonsense
Linda Noble-Cordy

Glasgow Scotland 1928

The year was 1928, July the 5th, I think…And I was on my way again, to McGhee's Emporium of fine art and Antiquities. To sell a piece of art, I had acquired – I won't say how-only to say that I got it that day – from a man who'd trade beans for a cow.

No one turned to notice as I walked through the front door. And no one looked to see what I had for them instore. I set it on the counter-top and waited for my turn. Then old man Mc Ghee looked at me – "You're back, you have returned?"

He turned and shook his head, to the gentleman and said. "I don't know why I bother…" Then to me turned and spoke, "I hope it's not mar cartoon crap, or a drawn o yer mother."

The gentleman smiled and nodded his head and gave a little laugh. But his face soon changed when I took out the paint'n that I had.

McGhee rubbed his baldy head, "Where'd you get that my lad!? Wait a minute, never mind, don't tell me so, I don't really want ta know. I'll take a closer look, and tell ya what I know."

As he took out his magnifying glass, a small crowd began to show. And after a brief inspection he announced – "Looks real enough ta me- A fine piece of art by my friend Claude Monet."

The anticipation of the group – you could have cut it with a knife. Even I felt excited as one man yelled "I'll buy it fer me wife." The same man felt the need to take me aside, and whispered in my ear. "I'll buy it from ya lad –five hundred pounds – would that be fair?"

I agreed to his offer, and then I shook his hand. And then I took his money, and let's just say I ran…And as I left the build'n my heart was filled with glee. I thought about what I'd done, and how I knew it was a forgery, me and old man McGhee.

That night at the supper hour, the old man sat with me. We had a laugh at the man's expense as we sat and drank our tea. You see the old man was quite the painter. He could impersonate the lot. It didn't matter who it was, he could copy it on the spot. What they called a photo graphic memory and a prodigy of such. Me not so much, but I could draw - pencil and paper was my source. Not as

The Darker Side of Light

good as the old man – cartoon was my course. And there was another problem; I wasn't the best of crooks. I, myself couldn't tell one paint'n from the other, even with the best of looks.

It wasn't till he got up to stretch and fetch his pipe, did he notice the paint'n hidden from his sight. As he picked it up and walked passed, he took a second look. Then frozen he stood, "oh no, this canny be, don't tell me, what have ye done?" He rushed into the closet to look for another one.

Now like I said, the old man could copy anything, Da Vinci, Van Gogh, and even Grew. Monet was his favorite, so I knew he'd made a few. He even had originals that he purchased from Oscar himself. That's what he'd told me, but the chances are he nicked them off the shelf. Yes, my father was a swindler, a liar, and a cheat, but he could paint like no bodies business and it kept us off the street. He made a nice wee business of taken people when he could. And this day, caught up in the moment, he coned himself, and that is never good.

He yelled and then yelled louder, and then he yelled at me, cursing the day I was born and all the misery…

When he came back out the closet he sat quietly on the chair. Then he looked at me, and softy said, "Well my son it's clear. You'll have to nick it back, that's what you're to do, and you'll go before this night is through." "Oh, no," I said, "I canny, I willney, I won't." But he insisted with a left hook that nearly broke my jaw bone. Then he shook his fist at me– "You'll do it or you'll be deed. That painting's worth more tey me than your sorry heed."
"I'll go way yeh, and stand guard. Ya got ta get it back." Fist a flail'n in the air, "Dey yeh want anoer crack…? You know I canny climb the pipes nay mar –no whey my bad leg. And I canny shimmy in the windie like I used tay dey."

I didn't have a say in it, and I guess I was to blame. I was noth'n like my old man even though we looked the same. And all the days that passed, he'd question everyone. For he couldn't believe he had such a stupid son.

Here is where the story should end, but I'm afraid it's just no right. For I was caught and locked in jail for a full fortnight. And the only reason my time was such was because of what I did. When question, under interrogation, I gave up that which had hid. Aye, my dear old Da, was nowhere in sight when I got pinched. Although I think I heard him laugh'n at me underneath the bridge.

The old man got twenty years for the crimes of what he did. And me, I stayed away from him, aye, that's right I hid…Soon all his forgeries became famous for a rich man bought the lot. His talent on display, picture in the paper, a right ol' celebrity, all thanks tey me. Aye, he'd painted many masterpieces for museums and art galleries. Commissioned by the queen herself, Aye, her majesty…

After ten long years in prison, the old man he retired, caught a cold one day and from that he soon expired. And all the money that he'd earned, I never seen a penny. Despite I was his only kin, they said there wasn't any.

It eased my mind a little, to know that I was on his mind in the end. That he hadn't forgot his only son and his only friend. A paint'n that he left me, I knew it right away; it was the one that Da had gave me back in 1928.

Only this one was newly painted – done just before he past and across it in big red letters he signed:

The Darker Side of Light

Olivia Bellbottom

Contrary to popular belief, Olivia Bellbottom had very small feet
All of 4 foot 2 -small for a woman and much smaller for a man
And in the shoe department she took a size ten
Large for a woman and small for a man

On the seaside shore where she carried out her task
Some folks - the not so polite, would point and laugh as she paddled past
But she didn't blink or flinch, she cared not for the lot
Having no time for those who mucked about and so rudely shouted out

Amongst the vomit that was the seaside, she picked and poked about
Searching for what she had once –she couldn't remember when
But still she searched for it like a long-lost friend
A friend that had no end…

But just as the day before, and the days before that too
Nothing did she find, nothing that was true
Maybe tomorrow would be the day, yes, she felt it now
Tomorrow would be the day – and she knew just how…

She would start extra early, that's where all the secrets hide
Springing forth the false hope - that's where everybody lies
And tells themselves there is a way, if only they had another day
Another chance to find, that which is held so dear to mind

Olivia Bellbottom took another chance; a chance that never ends
With the finding of a friend
All of 4 foot 2 – small for a woman and much smaller for a man
And in the shoe department he took a size ten
Large for a woman and small for a man

Weird and Wacky Tales & Other Such Nonsense
Linda Noble-Cordy

Ode to Serenity

Serenity life's sweet mistress
Peaceful is thine nature
Amongst a host of discontent
The valve placed upon your head
…is all but spent
Washed away with yesterday's rain
Will you ever rise again?
Oh Serenity, sweet mistress of life
You feel man's discord
His utter loss and shame
You are there to catch him when he falls
Again and again…
In times of desperation
You will be his strength
His vision on into the night
Oh Serenity, sweet mistress of life
Your reign is all too short
You must comply with man's contort
Over shadowed by those more demanding
You take your place in the dark
Waiting for his call
His cry for help, for need
And there you will be

Oh Serenity,

Life's Sweetest Mistress

The Selfless Butterfly

Caterpillar was the first of her kind to emerge into existence. And as she roamed from tree to tree eating every leaf she possibly could, she experienced great pleasure. Oh, how she enjoyed the delectable favours of the tender, juicy leaves. The fields of wildflowers for as far as the eye could see, gladdened her heart with a feeling of completeness as she grazed there morning, noon and night. Oh, what a wonderful life she had. She thought, "It doesn't get any better than this…"

Much time passed and still Caterpillar ate and ate, until one day she could eat no more. Not for lack of hunger but because she was too tired to carry on. And although she wanted to keep on eating, she knew she had to rest, it was just the way. Caterpillar became very sleepy, "I must rest now and when I awake I will eat again." As Caterpillar made her bed, her mind travelled to all the lovely fields she would venture when she awoke; fields lush with foliage for as far as the eye could see; green leafy trees that would welcomed her visit. How peaceful and content she felt and as she drifted off to sleep she thanked the plants for making her feel so good.

While Caterpillar slept, she had the most beautiful dreams. Of course, she dreamt of eating; lovely feasts of fresh new green leaves delighted her taste buds like never experienced before. The fields rich with scrumptious wildflowers exceeded her every need and she felt satisfied.

Caterpillar slept a long, long time, and when she finally awoke she found she was not hungry at all. "Funny," she thought, "maybe I'm not hungry because of all that I ate while I was asleep?"

How different she felt, changed somehow. Then Caterpillar heard a sound, it was the voice of her Creator. "You are now your true self… Butterfly. You no longer need to feast; hunger is no longer a part of you…" Butterfly slowly stretched open two magnificent wings that had formed upon her back and flapped them in the gentle breeze. Her numerous legs that carried her with great intention were gone and were replaced with six thin, nimble stick-like replicas. Oh, how beautiful she felt and as she took flight, gracefully and with great determination she flew high up into the morning sky. Even the sun admired her radiance as the brilliance of her form captured the attention of the entire universe. With

The Darker Side of Light

wings of golden shimmering luminosity, she flew up high into the Heavens and there she lingered.

The Creator himself had never seen such a magnificent creature, and he was proud of his creation. "You are absolutely perfect Butterfly, and you bring me great joy when I look upon you." The Creator wanted to give Butterfly a gift; Butterfly was given two gifts to choose from: to stay as she is – in ones or to have both worlds – that of caterpillar and of butterfly.

"I wish to stay as the splendor you now see before you Creator. I have no need to eat, I am satisfied with who I am." She felt the life of a caterpillar was beneath her. "You may if you wish great Creator, take away the trees, take away the leaves, I have no use of them...I am free." "As you wish Butterfly" the Creator responded.

Butterfly in awe of her own radiance, exclaimed, "How exquisite I am. Look upon me, and see my perfection." And all that could see her were captured by her loveliness; they adored her, and wanted to be like her. Butterfly flew higher and higher up until she could no longer see her home planet. Far she travelled, far, far away from home, never to look back.

So, it would be...

Butterfly had chosen her gift... she was glorious and she was free. She did not need to eat and eat to attain experience and pleasure. The pleasure that was attached to Caterpillar was long forgotten. All the succulent green leafy trees; all the splendid fields of wildflowers for as far as the eye could see were no more. Butterfly had no need for that life, as she roamed from one universe to another, gaining more admirers and more confidence as she went. But alas no true companions...

She hadn't realized how alone she really was, and began to grow tired of the endless journey. She thought of home and felt a little home-sick. She missed the green planet and began to long, nay, hunger for the mere sight of it. All the while her body began to grow heavy and needed rest. She started on her long arduous journey home. It took a long, long time. Funny she thought, "I didn't realize I had travelled so far from home."

She gently, ever so gracefully floated back down into her planet's atmosphere and could sense the desolation; a feeling as bleak and

The Darker Side of Light

as barren as the view. There were no trees, no fields of green... just naked soil, bleak and dreary, barren terrain. She came to rest upon the parched soil. Dust covered her radiant form with debris, how filthy she felt. She began to choke for even the air was not clean anymore.

A strange feeling swelled up deep inside of her, she was changing; she was about to lay eggs. The thought of her future offspring gladdened her sorrowful heart for a moment. Then her predicament was met with reality. Where and how would her offspring survive?

"What will my brood feed on? What will nourish their growth?" she questioned. The Creator spoke, "They will not survive; you should relieve your body of the burden and fly free once more Butterfly." She was very sad. She didn't want it to end this way. How could she have been so selfish? She thought. "If only I had known the effects of my actions, I would have chosen another way." She pleaded with the Creator to take back her gift and give it to her children. "I am nothing without them, I know this now, and I will not abandon them. If they are to die than so shall I."

Butterfly laid thousands and thousands of eggs and when she was finished she was very tired. "I must rest now," she thought, "for I will need to find a way to feed my brood when the time comes." Wrapping her massive golden wings around the world, Butterfly fell into a deep, deep sleep; then deeper still. In time, her magnificent form melted into the soil which then fertilized the dry parched ground. Plant life formed and started to grow in abundance. Before long, tall green leafy trees sprang up across the land. Fields of wildflowers for as far as the eye could see, gently blew in the soft supple wind.

And as one egg, then another, then another still began to open; the lovely little caterpillars fed... roaming from tree to tree eating every leaf they possibly could; they experienced great pleasure. Oh, how they enjoyed the delectable favours of the tender, juicy leaves. The fields of wildflowers for as far as the eye could see, gladdened their tiny hearts with a feeling of completeness as they grazed there morning, noon and night. Oh, what a wonderful life they had... They thought, "It doesn't get any better than this..."

The Darker Side of Light

The Darker Side of Light

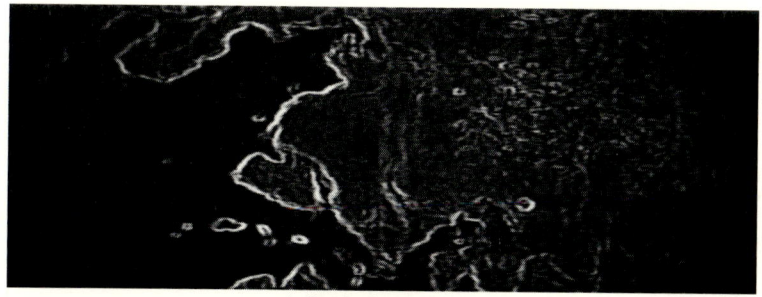

A bed time scare

Close your eyes and sleep fast my dear
For it's not the sandman that visits tonight I fear...

Shadows in the dark of night
Will form the deadliest of sights
So you must sleep while it's still light
Just listen to the birds outside your windowpane
A lullaby of sweet refrain
The sound will help you rest and find your sleep
Before the room is filled with creeps
And if by chance you wake to the sound
Of the raven's cry of warning
Close your eyes real tight till morning...
Now remember what I've said
Never look beneath the bed
And hold the covers close
That just might be a ghost

Sleep tight little one
Before the terror has begun
Before the creeps and crawlies come
And if you feel a hand reaching for you
To pull you where they dwell
A place that's cold and dark and damp
A place that some call hell
Try not to scream or yell...
Try not to move or jump or run
Because that's when they have their fun
On this night of doom, do not leave your room
And try not to stay awake too long
Because it's in the *wake of the mind*
That everything goes wrong...
{evil laugh}

Weird and Wacky Tales & Other Such Nonsense
Linda Noble-Cordy

pg. 25

The tale of the Itnescomber
Thief of the Young

The Darker Side of Light

Tired but content, Patricia Clark sat quietly in the shade of her backyard porch. The warmth of the sun's rays heated the atmosphere with a stillness that only a perfect summer's day can embrace. The old oak trees that surrounded the half acre property sheltered this mother and her three children from the outside world. Sometimes she missed the sounds of traffic and the bright lights of the big city; sometimes, but not often.

One month old, Aiden lay in the cot beside her fast asleep. Five-year-old son Creed and eight-year-old daughter Violet played contently in the yard a few meters away. As she watched over them at play, she was very happy with her life and all that she had; a loving husband, a beautiful home, and most importantly three healthy children. What more from life could she possibly want?

Her instincts, a mother's instincts, told her to protect her children; told her that she needed to be extra watchful. For it was in these times of security and satisfaction the Itnescomber liked to strike; and their target – children. Therefore, she watched them like a hawk. It was mainly out of childhood fears that she felt the way she did. Stories she was told as a child, and then there was that time when she was a very young… she couldn't really remember what happened even though she so desperately wanted to.

Rocking gently back and forth in a dream-like state she stared at her children at play and smiled tenderly. Creed called out, "Wook at me mommy, wook at me!" As he slid down the slide, she responded. "I see you Creed, good job." Violet sat in the sand. "Creed," she called to him. "Let's make a tunnel for your cars to go thru." "Okay," he responded with enthusiasm, as he ran the few steps over to where she sat.

As long as she could watch over them she knew they would be safe. Of course, other precautions were taken to keep the children safe. She hung up the gift of Telitanis Chimes her Oma gave her when Violet was born. One hung at the front door, the other at the back. On each window of the house, in the left-hand corner out of sight, were small protection symbols. It would be virtually impossible for any ominous creature to enter her home uninvited. And besides, the Itnescomber would never strike when a parent or guardian was on guard. They wouldn't dare, it was just too dangerous for them. If truth be told they were horrendous scoundrel and dreadfully cowardly creatures- so she was told.

Even though Patricia took all these precautions to keep her children safe, part of her didn't really believe in supernatural creatures. It was more out of respect for her Oma that she heeded the warnings and hung the charms.

Patricia began to recall the stories of warning her Oma, Ruth had told her as a child. And how it was in those warnings she was able to elude her own ill-fated path. Yes, she started to remember what happened when she was a very young child.

Patricia could hear her Oma's thick German accent as clear as day inside her head. "Itnescomber, are thieves of the young and innocent. They disguise themselves as regular people, and look very normal. But they are not normal people; they are in fact terrible monsters. They steal little ones from their parents. Most of the time right out from under their noses; when the mother or father is not around or is distracted by something or someone. It's more fun for them that way. They get a charge out of hurting the parents and those who love the child. It somehow adds to their evil immortality."

Patricia drifted off to a time when she was five; a time she had long since forgotten. She placed one hand on Aiden's cot and continued to keep a watchful eye on Creed and Violet.

She recalled playing in the front yard of their home on Chester Avenue in downtown Toronto. She lived there with her parents Monika and Peter and her Oma -Ruth, who had arrived from Germany the month earlier.

A little old lady passed by the garden gate and stopped. Patricia was singing a song she had just learnt that day at nursery school. "Ring around the rosy," she sang as she skipped rope on the walkway. The old woman joined in by singing along with a thick German accent. "Pocket full of poesy's, husha, husha, we all fall down..." She smiled warmly at Patricia, who stopped jumping to look at the person who stood outside her little white gate.

She spoke to Patricia in German, "Gefällt Ihnen, dass Kinderreim kleines Mädchen?" (Do you like that nursery rhyme little girl?) Patricia looked at her cautiously and nodded her head yes. Continuing to smile at Patricia she spoke to her in broken English; sounding not that much different from her own Oma. "Did they

The Darker Side of Light

teach you Hey diddle, diddle yet?" Patricia shook her head no. "Oh that's a good one. I'm surprised you don't know that one."

The old woman looked towards the house casually; not wanting to bring any attention to her conduct and to make sure no one was looking or coming out of the house. As she cast her gaze back to Patricia, she placed her hand beside the latch on the gate. "My name is Udo, what is yours?" she asked her. "Patty." She said in a low voice without thinking. "Patty," she repeated, that is a beautiful name- short for Patricia, right?" Patricia nodded her head in agreement. "Do you like to sing Patty, because you have a lovely singing voice? I would love to hear it better." She placed a hand to her ear and said. "But I am very old and can't hear so good these days." Patricia didn't say anything, she just stared at her. "If you come closer I could hear your lovely singing voice much better Patty. We could sing a song you know together if you like."

There were sounds coming from inside the house. Someone was talking just on the other side of the closed door. "Well maybe another time then, I really must be on my way home. My grandson is coming over for supper. Bye for now Patty, I'll see you again."

Even though she knew she shouldn't talk to strangers, she thought she was a nice old lady. "Bye," she said quietly. The front door opened and Oma stepped out with her shopping bag in hand. "I'm going to the grocers Patty. Would you like to come along?" she asked. Patricia turned her attention to her Oma for a moment. "Yes, Oma I would like to go." She turned to look down the street in the direction the old woman had gone. She had disappeared. Running a few steps to the little gate she opened it to have a better look down the street. "Wait for me Patty." Her Oma stated, and then yelled in the door she had not yet closed. "I am taking Patty with me." From inside the house the muffled voice of her mom shouted, "Okay mama."

The next day and the day after that the nice old lady came to visit and shared a song or nursery rhyme with her. She never stayed long enough for anyone to see her and she never tried to trick her like the strangers her Oma had told her about. Still, she kept her distance and not once did the nice old lady try to enter through the gate.

Weird and Wacky Tales & Other Such Nonsense
Linda Noble-Cordy

The Darker Side of Light

One night at supper time, she mentioned the old lady's visits to her parents. Mom and dad didn't seem to think anything of it. Oma on the other hand was very upset. "What did I tell you Patty? You don't talk to strangers ever." She insisted. "Did you forget already about what I have told you? About all those poor little children, and how they were tricked into the traps set by the Itnescomber?"

Mom interrupted. "That's enough mama, you're going to scare her." But Oma wasn't finished, far from it. "Keep quiet Monika!" She yelled at her daughter in German. Mom spoke up. "No mama I won't be quiet. You are jumping to conclusions again. You always think the worst about people." "Well I have every reason to. You of all people should be aware of this! I can't believe you think there is nothing wrong with a strange old lady stopping by our gate every day to talk with your daughter. Has she nothing better to do? Does she not have her own family? And why haven't any of us ever seen her?" She questioned. "Mama, since when is talking a crime? I'm sure it was harmless." She told Oma. "Du Narr! (You fool!)" Oma exclaimed. "You don't know what you are talking about."

Then she turned to address Patricia, who sat in silent panic and wished she hadn't mentioned it in the first place. Oma's voice rose to high pitch. "She will steal you away from us and eat your flesh with toast and jam. You will never see any of us again Patty. Do you want that to happen?" Paralyzed with fear she could only shake her head no.

Mom interrupted again. "Mama really, that's enough, you're scaring her half to death." Oma started to get very upset. Her eyes filled with tears as she started to yell out in German. "Was ist los mit dir Monika? (What is wrong with you Monika?)" "Mama please, English, enough with the German already. We talked about this before." She cast a glance at dad and said, "You need to speak English only, remember?" Then Oma looked over at dad and said, "Oh I'm sorry Peter, it's just very upsetting for me that my only daughter does not take these things seriously." He nodded at her and replied. "That's okay Ruth I understand your concerns." Mom looked at dad and spouted. "You're not helping."

Oma turned to mom and reminded her of the past. "Have you forgotten what has happened to your own little brother Able, to

The Darker Side of Light

his friend Styles Glubber, to the other children? She has to know about the danger she is in before it is too late."

Mom sighed a sigh of failure. "Mama, it was so long ago, I don't know what really happened to him and neither do you." Enraged, Oma slammed her fist down hard on the table, causing the salt container beside her jumped off and smash on the hardwood floor. "Nonsense Monika, you were there, you saw it take him!" She screamed. "You told me, Itnescomber stole Able." You might not remember but I do. I will never forget that horrible day. I will never forget my little Able." She wiped a tear off her cheek and repeated it in German as she drifted off to long ago. "Nein, ich werde nie vergessen, mein kleiner Able..."

Mom, seven months pregnant, got up with some difficulty and walked over to Oma to give her a hug. "I know mama, I know...but I really don't remember, I'm sorry." Noticing the broken salt container on the floor, she got the broom and dustpan and started to clean it up.

When Oma noticed what she was doing she proclaimed, "Look at that Patty. That is a bad sign, a very bad sign... It is a warning of the danger that has come to us again." She bent down and quickly pitched some of the salt between the figures of her left hand; and as she sat back up she threw it over her right shoulder, then closed her eyes and said a silent prayer.

Mom looked over at dad for help. He knew he was best to keep out of these situations. So, he remained silent and just shrugged his shoulders and looked at her as much to say. "She's your mother, you deal with her."

Opening her eyes, Oma focused in on Patricia, "Tell me everything she said to you, I want to know everything." Patricia told her what she could remember. Oma responded, "I don't like it, I don't like it one little bit. The next time she comes around you call to me as loud as you can. I want to see this woman for myself." Patricia shook her head in agreement and said, "Okay Oma I will." Oma smiled lovingly at her only grandchild and spoke to her gently in German. "Das ist mein gutes Mädchen." Then in English for dad's sake, "That's my good little girl, now come and give your Oma a big hug." Patricia went over and hugged Oma. She felt safe with Oma despite her outburst; she knew she did it because she cared about her.

The Darker Side of Light

When the nice old lady showed up the following week, she had forgotten at first what Oma had told her to do. Playing with her little friend Isabel, she was too involved in their game of hopscotch to notice her standing by the opened gate. Out of nowhere came her voice as she began to sing a little song with the hopes of drawing one or both of the girls close to her. They both turned in the direction of the sound. It was a nice voice, very pleasant to the ear.

"Hello Patty, how are you today?" she stopped singing to ask. "And I see you have a little friend with you today, how lovely." She took a step through the opened gate and looked towards the house with caution. Then smiling at both the girls she reached into her purse and pulled out a bulging brown paper bag. "I bought this bag of candies for my grandson. But I'm afraid he doesn't like them. I didn't want to throw good candy away, so I thought I would bring it over to you Patty." Then she added. "There is enough for both of you, if you'd like to share it."

Isabel got excited. She loved candy. She took a step towards the old trustworthy grandmother. She was almost within reach of the bag of candy that she held out. Patricia grabbed Isabel by the right shoulder and pulled her back to stop her from getting any closer. "What are you doing Patty?" she asked somewhat annoyed. "OMA, OMA, OMA! Come quick she's here!" She screamed so loud her face went beet red. "What are you doing foolish girl, there's no need to call your Oma." Udo spouted as she took a step closer and eyed the front door. "Do you want the candy or don't you?" "No," she screamed.

Patricia hadn't noticed but Isabel was standing right beside the old lady. "I would like some candy please Mame." She said politely. Isabel reached out to take the bag of candy. The Itnescomber put its right hand on Isabel's shoulder and held on to it tight. "Open the bag child." She ordered. A wicked evil smile on its face, she threatened Patricia. "I'm not finished with you yet Patty." As Isabel opened the bag they both vanished into thin air. The front door flew opened and Oma ran over to her screaming, "Are you alright Patty, what has happened, where is Isabel?" Overwhelmed with fear she cried. "Did you see her Oma? She was here, she took Isabel, she took Isabel!"

Patricia felt a terrible pressure in her head caused by a numb, humming sound. And as she forced herself to gain consciousness

– back to the real world; startled that she had fallen asleep; her mind instantly went into panic mode. She could hear in the far-off distance the sound of Violet screaming out in sheer panic. "Creed, Creed, where are you?"

The ill-fated path
of one Isabel Wrightready
Part One

Isabel screamed out in terror at the sight that stood before her. The nice old lady was gone, replaced by a horrible, ugly, wrinkled-up, old hag. The Itnescomber, whose true name was Gelp, smirked mockingly at the child whose hair had turned pure white at the sight of her true form. She was indeed hideous and as far as Itnescombers' goes- *one of the worst.*

Poor little Isabel didn't know where she was or what was going on, for that matter. All she had wanted was a few of those yummy candies the nice old lady was offering. You see, six-year-old Isabel Wrightready, if truth be told, was a little on the chubby side. And it was for that reason her mother had cut her off sweets for an entire week. So, when the offer of some delicious candies came her way, how could she refuse?

Now it would seem that the nice old lady was gone and with her any chance of treats. "I want to go home, I want my mommy." She pleaded. "Oh, you want your mommy do you, you want to go home do you?" She said sarcastically. "Well too bad, you're mine now, I'm your new mommy!" It laughed a wicked horrid laugh that quickly turned to cruelty. "And if you know what's good for you," She smacked Isabel hard across her plump little face. Falling over sideways, Isabel put a hand to her hot, swollen, red cheek and looked up at the hideous form above her. "You'll do exactly what I say," it spat out at her. Isabel nodded her head in agreement and tried very hard not to cry.

The Itnescomber pinched Isabel's ear picking her up off the ground and pulled her along beside her. "Keep up you wretched little girl, or I'll eat you alive," she cackled out loud. Then spying the approaching form, she nodded with some hesitation and spouted, "Beety."

As they meet with this foul creature, the smell of it was so bad that Isabel, without thinking, pinched her nose to hide it from the stench. Its black, withered-up, pin-holes for eyes glommed at little

The Darker Side of Light

Isabel. And with great anticipation it began to speak. "Why Gelp, that's a fine fat little one you have there. You always find the good ones. Are you on your way to market with it?" Gelp replied, "No." It licked its wrinkled, dried-up puckered lips and added. "Splendid, shall I prepare it at my place or yours?"

"I'm keeping this one for myself." She told her flatly. "Oh, come now, you're not keeping it *all* for yourself, are you?" Poking poor frightened Isabel in her side with the long stick she held in her hand. Isabel let out a little yelp and tried to hide behind the one called Gelp. "There is plenty to go around; I could fix us up a lovely casserole or baked a pot-belly pie." Beety grabbed at Isabel, as Gelp pulled her away from her. Stare fixed on her foe, "No." Gelp replied. "Well surely you'll at least invite me over for a bite? You're still not mad about the last one, after all you enjoyed it as much as I did," she reminded her. "I have other plans for this one Beety. None of which include you! Don't be getting any bright ideas in that thick head of yours like you did with the last one. Or it will be your head I make to squall." Gelp threatened. "Suit yourself then." She uttered as she walked away in a huff.

*Squall- form of slop- thick putrid mixer that Itnescombers eat on a regular basis

Gelp Synch and Beety Beltwacker - were what one might call neighbors. However, they were both far from neighborly. As a matter of fact, they hated each other. And if not for the fact that they used each other for their so-called skills, one would have surely killed the other if given a reason to.

Gelp was crafty and devious, having extraordinary luck when it came to catching children. Beety was low down and dirty, but she was an exceptionally good cook. On more than one occasion she had convinced Gelp into letting her cook up her servant.

The last one- a little three-year-old boy, she only had for a week before Beety got her way. "What good is he to you Gelp?" she began. "He cries all day and night, it doesn't matter how much you beat him. He can't do any real work around here." Then she added, "What do you want with a *boy* anyhow? They're only good for one thing and one thing only… and too soon he'll lose all that yummy baby fat. You may as well make the best of it while you can."

The Darker Side of Light

This time it was different, this time Gelp wanted to keep it, train it proper; make a loyal and obedient servant out of it. She was tired of travelling to the outside world to get children, and wanted to train this one to do her bidding. Besides it was getting harder and harder to steal them. After all, that Patty child had got away-a terrible disappointment to her. She was the one she really wanted, having worked on her trust for the better part of a month. If it hadn't of been for her greedy, fat, little friend Isabel, she would have gone home empty handed.

She wouldn't forget Patty; Itnescombers never forget the ones that get away... But for the time being she would have to make do with what she had.

Gelp knew Beety would try to talk her into making a meal or two out of this one. Their arrangement was as such; Gelp brought them home and Beety *–being an excellent cook*, would prepare a feast. And even though she firmly told Beety she wanted to keep this one, she knew the minute her back was turned, she would try to steal it from her; cooking it up into something too delicious to refuse.

They took turns entertaining each other at the supper hour once a month – not because they liked each other but because they were conditioned to socialize – *misery does indeed love company...* and tomorrow night was Gelp's turn.

She thought to herself. *It's time for Beety Beltwacker's bye, bye farewell pie!"*

She decided she wasn't *that* fond of Beety's cooking anyways.

Unlocking her front door, she grabbed Isabel's forearm and pulled her through it. She ordered, "Let's go child, inside with you." She squeezed it so hard that Isabel let out a little howl and tried to release the grip Gelp had on her now paining arm. "Ouch, you're hurting me, let me go, let me go!" she pleaded. "Stop that!" Gelp enforced, as she squeezed her arm even harder and smacked her several times across her face with her bare hand. Isabel began to cry. The evil Itnescomber shook Isabel hard, demanding her attention. "Look at me child! You will do as you're told when you're told it, and not a word will you speak; not a sound, not whimper, will you make. If you cross me, you will pay dearly. The first thing to go will be your wicked little tongue."

Weird and Wacky Tales & Other Such Nonsense
Linda Noble-Cordy

Pulling her over to a closed door she opened it and threw her in. "I'll be back for you later, now remember NOT a sound or I will silence you!" She demanded. Locking the door behind her, this horrible Itnescomber went into her kitchen to plan Beety Beltwacker's last supper.

Poor little Isabel sat in the pitch black, on a bare floor up against a jagged brick wall and cried silently to herself. The little bit of light that trickled in from under the wooden door allowed her to see the four walls that were her prison cell. It was small room with no visible windows, or furniture. The room would have been completely empty if not for a pot in one corner and small bare mattress beside it. She cried and cried until she could cry no more. "I have to get out of here." she told herself. "I have to escape and find my way back home…"

The heinous formation of the Itnescomber
Congratulations Mr. and Mrs. Malice, it's a ten-pound nasty piece of want…
You both should be thoroughly disgusted.
It was true the Itnescomber was created by Ignorance, terrible neglect, nasty thoughts and shameful hatred.

Aspirations inspired by not only the bad feelings but also the erroneous actions of every-day people had to go somewhere… Karma would see fit to form a physical reality in a world created for its means. An underworld of sorts, filled with the supernatural, filled with the stuff nightmares are made of…

Creatures of such fowl, misguided iniquity would somehow find a way back home to their source. And their victims would be the most precious resource, the most treasured life force - the children; the little ones that were so dearly loved by their families. This was the greatest sin they could possibly inflict on a world that created them so carelessly.

At first it was out of vengeance, and then as more time passed, it would be out of necessity that they ventured into the real world. They came to rely heavily on children as a vital source of food and income. Don't get me wrong, they stole a great deal of other things as well, for greed natural found a home here. A culture built around the trade of items stolen would keep this depraved society functional.

Udo or should I say Gelp, was indeed one of the most wicked –*if not the most wicked* Itnescomber to ever be formed. Her creation was just that – a bad one…

The Perfect Plan
One that would actually work

It was for this reason she cared not, for anything or anyone. Consequently, the killing of Beety did not sit on her conscious or bother in the slightest.

Her immoral brain sized up the situation. She would need to devise a fool-proof plan; one that was perfect, one that would actually work.

She wouldn't be able to kill her in any conventional way, such as poisoning or drowning (both brilliant executions – but utter failures when attempted in the past). She couldn't just hit her over the head with a heavy object and be done with her – her head was simply too durable. Gelp had also found this out the hard way- having spent the better part of a day trying to maneuver a large 50-pound boulder up onto her roof-top without damaging it or being seen.

A direct hit! Then a terrible disappointment… Beety didn't even wince; didn't even notice the huge rock that came to rest beside her. Looking up she placed her hand on the spot where the so-called – *instrument of destruction* made contact. Then began to rub it like she was wiping off dust or debris. "Oh Gelp, what are you doing up on the roof?" Beety questioned when she noticed Gelp peeking over the roof top. "Not another hole?" she exclaimed. "No, no, just cleaning off the dirt – sand and leaves mostly. I didn't hit you with any of it, did I?" Gelp questioned with false concern.

"Think, think, think… What is Beety's weakness?" She pondered. "What am I overlooking- forgetting, not seeing…? Then it came to her in a wave of sheer genius. "That's it!" she yelled with pure enthusiasm. She started to cackle an evil, foreboding sound. Then she quickly silenced her enthusiasm for fear that Beety might be lurking about and find out she was up to something.

It was known to Gelp that Beety was terrified to travel to the outside world. This was one of the many reasons why Gelp hated her so much. For she relied on Gelp to supply her with what she could not obtain herself – children. Gelp didn't know the details, only that Beety had not ventured there for a very long time. And when Gelp brought up the topic, Beety quickly changed the subject. She did on one occasion slip-up and say that if she were to go there (the real world) she would perish for all times. That she could not survive in her true form.

Gelp finally knew how to get rid of Beety for good. She would send her to the other world- the human's layer. She knew the spell to get her there and just how to trick her into taking the bait. After all she had been using the same ruse to trick innocent little children for ages. "She won't know what hit her?" She laughed mockingly and mused, "She never does…"

The ill-fated path of one
Isabel Wrightready
Part two

It didn't take long for Gelp to set the scene for the deadliest of deadly traps. The potion made, all she needed to do was get the child ready. She would need to trick her if she was to get her to cooperate with the plan. She was so proud of herself for coming up with such a brilliant plan. For the first time ever, she was in an agreeable mood.

Opening the locked door, her tone somewhat kind, she called in. "Isabel, Isabel…are you here child?" Come out into the light, I have something I want to talk to you about." Isabel didn't know what to think. She got up off the floor and silently walked over to the shadow in the doorway. Gelp turned and walked towards the kitchen and Isabel followed.

"Sit down and I will fix you something to eat." She said as she pulled out a chair for Isabel to sit on. All the while Isabel did not say a word. She was still too afraid to. Gelp placed a bowl of squall in front of Isabel and patted her on the head. Isabel cringed with fear and braced herself for the worse. Nothing happened… she didn't hit her. "Go on, eat up." She ordered.

Sitting across from her now, Isabel could feel Gelp's stare fixed on her. She wanted to cry, she wanted to scream out. I want to go home. She hadn't realized it but that's just what she did. She screamed out loud, "I want to go home!" she heard the voice but couldn't believe where it was coming from.

The Darker Side of Light

Just the opportunity Gelp was waiting for... Gelp got up and walked to the counter and picked up a pair of scissors that were waiting there for her.

Isabel started to cry uncontrollably. "I'm sorry, I'm sorry; please don't hurt me. I didn't mean it. Please don't hurt me. I'm sorry." Isabel covered her mouth with both hands as hard as she could and closed her eyes tightly. She felt a little tug on her hair and then the sound of scissors cut behind her. A shiver ran down her spine as she shook uncontrollably.

Gelp bent in close to Isabel's left ear and whispered, "I'll make you a deal, you help me – you do exactly what I say, and you will go home." Isabel looked straight ahead, still too afraid to look directly at this monstrosity. Its hot, foul breath burned the side of Isabel's face as she held her breath for as long as she could.

Is it true, will she really let me go home? She thought. She slowly removed her hands from her mouth and nodded her head in agreement. "Okay." She uttered. Gelp backed off a little and stood there staring at her. "Eat," she ordered as she placed Isabel's lock of hair in her pocket. She would need it to complete Beety's vanquishing spell.

Isabel could barely pick up the spoon, and when she placed the putrid, lumpy liquid next to her lips her hand trembled terribly. "What's the matter? You don't like it!" Gelp had to bite her tongue. You ungrateful, little wench, she said to herself. "Don't worry it'll grow on you. Seeing how that's all you'll ever get to eat." Then she corrected herself. "For today, that's all you'll get to eat for today." She smiled a horrid wicked smile and said, "You'll be home tomorrow. Won't that be nice?" Poor little Isabel took a mouthful and tried to swallow it fast as she nodded her head in agreement.

"Now you must do exactly as I say, or it will be the end of you! I'll let Beety have her way, and you won't be going home." She moved in close again, one hand on the table and the other on Isabel's stiff neck. She pressed her grotesque, mangled face up against Isabel's cheek and whispered her diabolical plot into Isabel's ear. Isabel nodded her head in agreement as if her life depended on it – which it did...

The Cavalry Arrives

The police notified, it didn't take long for word to spread that a young member of the Clark family had gone missing. Neighbors and concerned citizen gathered at the sight and began a search of the area. Patricia's husband Eric came home from work right away and after consoling his wife joined in on the search. Even Patricia's grandmother Ruth and her mother Monika arrived from the city.

The next morning the three women sat in the kitchen. The atmosphere dreary and hopeless, Patricia spoke tearfully. "I can't believe I fell asleep... I can't believe I let my guard down." Monika stood up, baby Aiden propped up on her left shoulder she walked over to where Patricia sat. Caressing her shoulder gently she spoke, "It's not your fault Patty, it could have happened to anyone. Don't blame yourself." Monika cast a glair at her mother for she knew in her heart what she was about to say.

Ruth began, "It's happening again. Just like what happened to your own little brother, Monika. And all those other poor, little children..." A scowl on her face, Monika shook her head no with the hopes of silencing her. "Oh and Isabel, poor little Isabel. You remember that don't you Patty? You remember what happened to your little friend Isabel don't you?" she questioned.

Patricia looked wide-eyed at her grandmother. She was about to let her know that was the very reason she went into a trance; that was the reason for her dropping her guard. But Ruth turned to her daughter and said, "The Itnescomber stole more than one child that day, didn't it Monika? And we almost lost you too." "Don't be foolish mama, you know full well they caught the woman who took Isabel." she stated firmly.

Patricia having restored those old, lost memories responded, "Yes, I remember feeling safe after that, after they caught the little old lady who took Isabel." Ruth looked at Patricia strangely and questioned, "Little? Mrs. Feld was far from little, Patty. She was a beast of a woman if I recall correctly." Then she turned to address her daughter, "Isn't that right Monika? Mrs. Feld was a big woman. You remember, you told the police it was her. You confirmed it was she that took Isabel." Ruth looked intensely at Monika, "I guess we will never know now, will we Monika?"

The Darker Side of Light

Monika didn't want to remember what really happened, it was just too painful for her. Upset with her mother for bringing it up, she responded, "Mama, this is not the time. Can't you see that Patty is already very upset? Why must you always bring up the past?"

"What do you mean? This is the perfect time. We must figure out why this keeps happening. Why do you always hide from the truth?" Irritated and very upset, the old well-weathered great-grandmother stood up and began to yell. "The Itnescomber has taken another one of our children – there is no denying that fact! And you say this is not a good time! Well excuse me for not sparing the feelings of a grown woman, whose child has been stolen- one she will never see again. That is the hard, cruel reality Monika!"

Then she added, "When is a good time, you tell me? You tell me what you are going to do about it; because something needs to be done. Someone has got to stop this tragedy that plagues our family over and over again!" Ruth banged her hand down hard on the table and Patricia started to weep silent tears of despair. Monika's eyes filled with water as she looked at her mother too choked up to talk.

Aiden began to cry a gut wrenching scream consuming Monika's attention for the moment. Bouncing him up and down, she hummed a little song. And in between the screams and the humming she forced herself to speak, "I think you should try and feed him again Patty, maybe your milk will come back in." Ruth, dissatisfied with the lack of response waved a hand in the air gesturing her feelings of disappointment and left the room.

Just outside the kitchen, beside the hallway cabinet Violet sat in a fetal position; clutching her brother's favourite stuffed animal; a fuzzy old brown bear called Mr. Bean. She looked up at her Uroma, who spied her hiding there and sadly said, "Creed needs Mr. Bean, Uroma. He won't be able to sleep without him." Her face red from crying, she stood up to show her great grandmother the toy.

Not that much shorter than the old woman, Violet stood almost eye to eye with her. Ruth smiled warmly, "It's good that you are keeping it safe for him Violet. He will be happy that you are taking good care of his bear for him." Wrapping her soft white jiggly arm around Violet's slender shoulders, she spoke kindly, "Let's

The Darker Side of Light

you and I have a little talk." Together they walked to the guest room Ruth was sharing with her daughter. She sat on a single bed beside Violet.

Placing her old freckled hand on top of Violet's small youthful one, she turned to question her. "Tell me what happened Violet? Don't worry, I won't be mad at you. I want to hear from your own mouth what happened. It is very important that you tell me everything, okay?" Ruth knew that the other two would be busy in the kitchen for a while tending to the hungry, crying baby. It was the perfect time to talk to Violet alone, without them mending in and stopping Violet from telling the truth.

"Well, Creed and I were playing cars." She began. "I made a tunnel for Creed to drive his cars through. But he wanted to drive his big, yellow dump truck through it. And he broke the tunnel. I got mad at him and threw his dump truck behind the slide. Then he got up and kicked sand at me so I..." she stopped and looked down at the ground. "It's okay Violet, remember I need to know everything. You won't be in trouble, I promise." She assured her as she touched her chin gently, turning her head to face her again.

Teary-eyed she quietly uttered. "I slapped him across his face and said I hated him, and that I wasn't going to play with him anymore. That he could make his own tunnels and that he was stupid... But I didn't mean it Uroma, I didn't mean it!" she said earnestly. "I know, I know Violet, a lot of times we say things and do things we don't mean because we are angry. I understand..." Ruth held Violet's hand to comfort her. Her heart ached as she began to think of her own little son Able.

Violet continued, "Creed picked up his truck and ran to the back of the yard. He said he was running away. And I said - good go. I started playing in the sand again. Then I couldn't see him anymore. I stood up to see where he was. He usually hides behind the big oak tree in the corner by the shed, I went there to look for him. He wasn't there. I called to him. Creed where are you, stop fooling around. Mommy is going to get mad at you. He didn't answer me. I called to him again– Creed, Creed, where are you? But he didn't answer me. Mommy said he must have wandered off and fallen asleep under a tree or something... But that was yesterday and he should be home by now."

Violet looked at her great grandmother with great intention and then spoke. "He wouldn't really run away Uroma." A tear trickled down her cheek as she held up the old matted teddy bear. "Not without Mr. Bean, he wouldn't." Then Violet gave a sigh of deep despair. "It's all my fault isn't it? I shouldn't have hit him, I shouldn't have said I hated him. It's all my fault." Violet covered her face and started to cry.

It took all of Ruth's strength to keep herself from crying too. This whole ordeal was taking its toll on not only her mental state but her physical health as well. With all that she was, she hid her sadness. "There, there Violet, don't blame yourself for this. It's not entirely your fault." She wrapped her arms around Violet to comfort her. Continuing she said, "The creature that took Creed already had its sights on him – or you for that matter." Puzzled Violet stopped crying and looked towards her. "What do you mean Uroma? It was after me too?" Ruth nodded her head yes then commented, "I'm afraid so."

Then she began, "A long, long time ago when your Oma was a little girl she had a brother too. His name was Able. And just like you and Creed they played together. One day a terrible thing happened. The Itnescomber came and stole my little Able." Her face grew red as her sadness increased. The pain suffered by loss did not fade with time. It may have altered the truth of what really happened but did not alter the pain.

Ruth drifted off as she recalled the unfortunate events that followed that day. Then she was quickly brought back to the moment as Violet questioned her. "Did you call the police, did they ever find Able? "No, they never found one sign of him."

"What do we do now Uroma? How can we get Creed back?" The weary old great grandmother looked intently at the little bear Violet still clutched tightly, and for the first time in a very long time her eyes filled with tears. Confessing her worst fear, "I don't know, I just don't know…"

Bending down she picked up her purse that was beside the bed. Taking out two tissues, she passed one to Violet. The other she used to blow her own nose. A loud honking sound followed startling them both. They laughed a little and Ruth stated, "Look at us a couple of blubbering fools…"

The Darker Side of Light

After a time of silence Ruth announced. "I have something to show you Violet." Reaching into the bag again she pulled out a round pale blue, glass ball. "I have never shown this to anyone. It was found after Able went missing. He played with it all the time. Said it belonged to the Itnescomber that took his friend Styles. Able told me it had powers, magic powers and that it spoke to him, told him things." She held the solid round object up in front of her. "Bad things, that is what it told him. At the time, I didn't believe him. I thought he was just making it up. But after he was taken, I knew he was telling me the truth."

"It belonged to one of those creatures?" Violet questioned. "Yes, my dear, it belonged to one of those nasty creatures; and they are not from here. They are from an underworld, an evil, wicked world." Ruth held out the heavy glass ball in her right hand and pointed at it with her other. "Able called it his mystic orb and when he played with it, it was bright red and when I found it, it was like this. Now what other explanation is there? She questioned Violet. "How could it change colour like that…that is just not normal."

Violet was extremely curious. "Can I hold it? Can I hold the mystic orb, Uroma?" She asked. "No, I don't think you should. It might be dangerous." "Please," she begged. "Please can I touch it?" Part of her wished she had not shown the orb to Violet and the other part was curious to see what would happen when a child held it again.

Ruth hesitated then gently placed the orb in Violet's hand. The orb activated by her touch turned dark blue and began to heat up. "Wow!" She exclaimed in amazement. Terrified, Ruth grabbed the orb from Violet and it instantly changed back to its original colour. She thought to herself – This is bad, this is very bad…

Violet wanted to hold it again. She reached out to take it. "No!" Ruth yelled as she pulled it to her chest and rapped both hands around it to hide it from view. "I should have never of shown it to you, let alone let you hold it. It was a big mistake." Violet reached out again. "Oh, please Uroma, it's not dangerous, it's like one of those mood rings or something." She assured her. "No Violet it's not like that at all, it is pure evil! And much too dangerous for you. I don't want you to get hurt." "I won't get hurt. Please, please..." she pleaded. "No and that is final." She stated as placed the orb back into her purse. Holding on to her purse tightly she told Violet she was tired and wanted to have a little sleep.

Violet wanted nothing more than to hold that mystic orb again. In the few seconds that she held it, she felt a strange feeling she had never felt before. It wanted her to take it. She deserved to have it. Violet got up and kissed her Uroma on the cheek. "Okay Uroma, have a nice sleep and I will see you when you wake up." Still clutching her purse Ruth lied down on the bed. "Close the door, will you dear?" she asked Violet.

Ruth knew all too well the power this orb had for she had witnessed the effects it had on her son Able. She wasn't about to let her great granddaughter suffer the same fate.

Violet safely out of the room and out of sight – so she thought - she got up and looked around the room. She would need to hide it so that Violet couldn't get her hands on it. She knew Violet would try to take it. I'm so stupid, I should have never shown it to her. Why did I do that?" She thought to herself.

Sneakily peeking thru the crack of the door, Violet watched her great grandmother walk to the bottom of the bed and place the orb under the mattress. She smiled to herself and waited…

Insight to clarity

Although Violet was not permitted to leave the house, she did just that. Orb in hand she went to the far end of the backyard behind the shed. Here she could have a better look at her treasure. She felt devious and sneaky and it felt good to her. She threw the orb up into the air and watched it as the colours changed before her eyes. She did this several times and laughed out loud as she did. Then her attention turned to the sound of movement in the forest in front of her.

There was a child wearing a dark brown hooded cape. It was standing at the edge of the forest. Violet could see it was very pale, and sickly looking. With an odd kind of half-smile, it gestured to her to come closer, and when she did, it turned and ran into the forest. Ducking down to avoid the foliage its hood caught on a branch; pulling it off to reveal a head full of stringy white hair. "Wait," she called to it.

Not sure if she should follow, she looked back at the house as she walked slowly forward. Then turning her head around sheer terror filled her heart. Standing right in front of her was a horrible fowl creature. She could see now it was not another child.

Grabbing her arm, it held on to it tight. Violet screamed and at the same time hit the creature with the orb in its left eye. It let out a painful screech as the orb burned its flesh. Reflex made it release the grip it had on Violet's arm, giving her the opportunity to make a run for it.

She was met by Monika at the back door. "What is going on Violet? What has happened, why are you screaming?" She wrapped her arms around her and hugged her tightly. "Where's my mommy, I need to tell her." she said hysterically. "Your mommy is sleeping with Aiden right now and we are not waking either of them up understand? Besides she needs her rest." "Where's my daddy then, I need to see my daddy? I have to tell him?" "He's at the police station Violet, what is all this about?" Monika questioned as she let go of Violet.

She couldn't hold it back. "I know what happened to Creed, I know who took Creed! It was the Itnescomber. I saw it. Just like Uroma told me, it happened." Monika grabbed Violet by the arms, holding her firmly to face her, she spoke with great concern. "You saw it? What did you see?" She looked over Violet's head and through the opened door half expecting to see something there.

"Just now, I saw it." Shaking her head disapprovingly she spouted, "No, not possible, it's just your imagination. How could you see it Violet, it's not real? There is no such creature as the Itnescomber. It is all make believe - to frighten little children. The Itnescomber is just a made-up creature, it was a real person that…" she stopped herself. Then she added angrily, "What were you doing outside? You are supposed to be in your room. You are not allowed to go out! If your mother finds out I let you go outside she will have a conniption."

"But Oma…" Violet held the orb tightly in her right hand and was about to tell her all the details; about how it grabbed her arm and how she hit it in the head. But she remembered she had stolen the orb from Uroma, so she kept quiet. "No more of this foolishness Violet. I don't want to hear another word of it." It was hopeless, Oma just wouldn't believe her.

Angry at the defiant child and disappointed her mama found it necessary to share such tales of horror with her great granddaughter, she ordered Violet to her room.

"But I did see it." She demanded. "I'll tell Uroma, she'll believe me." "You will do no such thing. Uroma isn't feeling well and she is resting too. Do not get her upset. That's all I need right now. Go straight to your room." She ordered as she escorted Violet to her bedroom.

"Now you stay in here and play with your toys until I come and get you for supper, okay?" "Okay," she agreed. "I mean it Violet – don't leave this room. And don't mention what you just told me to your mommy; you don't want to upset her more than she already is. And for heaven's sake don't tell Uroma either. Or we will never here the end of it. Promise…" "Okay." She repeated unhappily. "That's a good girl. Now you play and I will see you in an hour." She said somewhat satisfied as she closed the door.

Outside of Violet's room, Monika felt a little light-headed. Holding tightly to the banister she sat down on the staircase. She didn't want to think about the past. But there is was –back to torment her. Looking down at her left wrist she grabbed it and began to ring and twist at the scar there. She remembered the day Patty's little friend Isabel was taken and how she could do nothing to stop it.

Monika heard her daughter's screams first. From the upstairs window, she looked out in horror.

It all came flooding back; the fear, the anguish, the helplessness…

She banged on the window with open palms and screamed at the little old woman in a desperate attempt to somehow keep her away from them. In that split second, she remembered what happened to her brother Able. Was it happening again? "No, get away from her, get away from her!" But no one could hear her. She tried to open the window but it wouldn't budge. In a panic, she punched at the widow breaking the glass and in the process badly slicing her left wrist wide open.

Turning swiftly to leave the room she felt a sharp pain in her lower abdomen that paralyzed her for a few seconds. Buckled over, panic and desperation in every step she made her way to the stairs,

The Darker Side of Light

"Mama, mama, help- outside! Es ist die Itnescomber! Es ist die Itnescomber! (It's the Itnescomber!) "Hurry mama!" Blood poured out of her opened wound and as she clung to the stair's banister everything went black.

She awoke in the hospital and quickly found out she had lost the baby. Consumed by grief, it didn't take much coaxing to convince her that the picture they showed her was Isabel's abductor. When it was all over and she was home again with her family, she told herself Isabel was taken by a person and not a supernatural creature. And to this day that is what she told herself.

Violet lay on her bed and looked into the orb that was now clear. She thought about the creature and wondered if it would be coming for her still; if it was angry and wanted her orb. In the center of the orb a dark spot appeared and as it got bigger it turned into a vision of the creature. She could see it running into its home- then it was inside. Someone else was in the room with it. Tide up – It was Creed! "Creed," she screamed out. It looked straight at her and she was terrified. Could it really see her? It was getting closer; its hands reached out for her. It was coming for her!

In one motion, she jumped off the bed and threw the orb in the corner of her room. Without hesitation, she ran out of her room calling "Oma!" To her surprise her Oma sat on the top of the stairs just outside the bedroom door.

Wrapping her arms around her she said, "I'm scared, I don't want to stay in my room by myself. Can I stay with you?" Monika returned her embrace and told her yes. Both still lost in their own thoughts, they sat on the stairs, finding comfort in each other's company. After several minutes, Monika stated. "I better get back to the kitchen and finish making supper. Come along Patty you can help."

They all met in the dining room for supper. Aiden still asleep was placed in the cot beside Patricia. Violet sat across from Ruth, Monika sat at the end of the table. And two spots remained empty – one for Eric, (as he was still at the police station), the other spot was for Creed.
Despite the lovely aromas of the food cooked, very little was eaten. Monika insisted that her daughter eat to keep up her strength. "You have the baby to think about Patty. You have to eat." "I just can't mom, I'm sorry." She said despondently. "Leave

her alone Monika. Can't you see the poor girl is in mourning? If she doesn't want to eat she doesn't have too." Ruth spouted. Tears streamed down Patricia's face as she held her head down low.

After a long period of silence, she addressed the room. "I heard the phone ring earlier, who was it?" "It was Eric." Ruth responded. "Well. What did he say?" she questioned. Anything? Any news?" Ruth just shook her head no. "Did he want to speak to me? Why didn't you call me to the phone?" Because..." she hesitated, "because there was no news. So, I didn't think you needed to be bothered." "But I need to talk to him. I want to know what they are doing to find Creed."

Patricia got up quickly with some animosity and headed for the phone. "You should have called me, I wanted to talk to him." "Well I didn't think you needed to." she stated. Directing her anger at Ruth she stated. "That wasn't for you to decide."

"What is that supposed to mean?" Ruth questioned in her own defense. "I'm only looking out for your own best interest." then she added. "Don't bother trying to call him now. He can't answer his phone. He said he would call back later." Patricia turned to go sit down again. She felt kind of bad snapping at her grandmother the way she did.

"Just let him handle what needs to be done there. You concentrate on taking care of the children you have left." Ruth added. Monika could feel her blood boil. "Mama!" she yelled. How can you be so insensitive?"

"What, what did I say?" she said gesturing her confusion then added. "It's true, she needs to take care of Violet and Aiden. They are her main concern. There is nothing else she can do or needs to do." Patricia knew in away; her grandmother was right. Monika just shook her head no in disapproval as she got up to clear the table.

Ruth looked over at Violet who had been quiet for the entire time. She could tell by the look on her face that she had something to say. "What is it Violet? Do you have something to tell us?" she questioned. Monika froze on the spot. Violet looked over at her as she subtly shook head no.

The Darker Side of Light

Ruth looked over to her daughter quickly. "What is going on here? Why do you silence the child, Monica? You have no right!" Then addressing Violet, she questioned her. "What are you not saying Violet? I want to know, even if nobody else does."

Patricia looked at her and said. "What is it Violet, do you want to tell us something, maybe something you remembered?" Quietly she whispered, "No." For a moment Monika breathed a breath of relief, and then Violet continued. "No, not something I remembered, something I saw."

"You saw something Violet, what did you see?" Patricia said in a panic. Violet looked over at her Oma who was red faced with anger. "I told you to keep quiet Violet, you promised." Then turning on her mother she spouted, "This is all your fault mama, if you hadn't filled her head with your stories she wouldn't have snuck outside to look for an imaginary creature!"

"What do you mean my fault? I did nothing wrong… all I did was tell her the truth! She deserves to know the truth, we all do." Ruth yelled in her defense.

Patricia didn't know what was going on. All she knew was that Violet had something to say and she wanted nothing more than to hear it. "Would you two stop bickering? I have heard enough of it!" she screamed. "I want to hear what Violet has to say." They both stopped instantly and simultaneously looked at Violet.

Suddenly Violet was very nervous, she couldn't tell them the truth, the whole truth; she would be in trouble for sure. She lowered her head, eyes fixed on her lap. "Nothing mommy, I didn't see anything, I'm sorry." She started to sob, I'm sorry mommy, I wanted to find Creed, that's all. I only wanted to help." She convinced them.

Patricia sighed deeply and started to tear up. "That's okay Violet. Why don't you go up to your room and play for a while? I will come up later and see you and we can have a talk okay?" Violet shook her head yes without looking at anyone and got up to leave. As she left the room her Oma spouted out. "You see nothing; she saw nothing, because there is nothing to see! It was a real person that took Creed. Not some creature of your imagination."

The Darker Side of Light

As she climbed the stairs she would hear the angry voices of her Oma and Uroma yelling at each other. And as she closed the door to her room her mother joined in followed by the bellowing scream of baby Aiden.

It was very upsetting for Violet to hear them all fighting the way they were. She felt it was all her fault. If she hadn't fought with Creed, if she hadn't stolen the orb, if she hadn't gone outside and then lied about what really happened, none of this would have happened. Then she spied the orb lying on the ground next to her closet door. It was glowing brightly and as she cautiously picked it up it began to turn a blood red. All her feelings of guilt and responsibility left her in that moment and she was free again.

Able's Fable
The magic of the orb

Able sat on the swing in his back yard. His face still hurt from where his mama had slapped him. She was very upset with him and for this reason he was very sad and also very angry...

It wasn't his fault, why didn't she believe him. It was the orb; it flew right out of his hand. If he hadn't dropped to the floor it would have probably hit and killed him.

His mama came running into the room. She stood for a moment in utter shock. Everything that was breakable was broken. She looked at the cabinet were her porcelain vase once stood. The family heirloom she had got from her Uroma when she got married. It was smashed to pieces.

"Able what have you done?" she screamed out in German. He stood to face her. "What have you done?" she repeated as she grabbed hold of his arm. He was too shocked himself to answer her at first. She slapped him hard across the face several times. And he cried out, "It wasn't me, it wasn't me, it's not my fault." "Don't lie! I don't want to hear any more of your lies!" she shook him and he continued to cry. "Go outside, I don't want to see you right now."

His little five-year-old sister, Monika, who stood in the doorway, had witnessed the whole thing. Following him outside, she sat on the steps and watched him. She knew better than to get too close.

The Darker Side of Light

He could get very mean when he was upset. This she had learnt the hard way.

Picking up a large stone from the ground he looked over at her. "Why didn't you say something? You saw what happened. Why didn't you tell mama?" He said scornfully. Monika became very frightened and for a moment thought she had better go back into the house.

Then he turned in the other direction as if someone had called to him. Without another word to her he got up and walked to the back-yard gate. Monika couldn't see anyone and wondered what her brother was doing.

The gate opened and she saw something reaching out for Able. Able let out a little scream and tried to hit the creature with the stone he still had in his hand but it didn't help. The creature knocked the stone out of his hand and pulled him thru the gate. He called out for help as he grabbed onto the gate post for leverage, but the spring on the gate caused it to slam shut on his fingers. He had no choice but to let go.

Monika stood up and cried for her mother, "Mama, Mama! Hurry Mama!" Ruth come running out of the house half expecting to find Able beating up his little sister. "What is it Monika, why are you screaming?" She questioned, looking around for Able. "Mama, Itnescomber took Able...! I saw it, it's real." Frightened beyond belief, she stared and pointed at the gate.

In a panic, Ruth ran to the back-yard gate and threw it opened. "Able!" she yelled. The gate slammed shut behind her knocking her into the alleyway. Not knowing which way, he had gone and not knowing which way she should go, she stood there and screamed, "Able where are you?" but it was too late- He was gone.

They didn't believe Able when he told them a monster took Styles Glubber, but it was true – every word he said.

Able had just got a new baseball and glove for his ninth birthday. He and his little friend Styles met in the field behind the school to throw the ball back and forth. It was Styles who saw the creature first as he was facing the wooded area it appeared out of.

"What's wrong with you?" Able questioned his friend who stood there with the strangest of looks on his face. Styles opened his

The Darker Side of Light

mouth to warn Able. But it was too late the creature was right behind him.

Able screamed as the creature grabbed hold of his arm. Able tried to pull away but the creature was too strong. Styles took the hard ball from his mitted hand and threw it as hard as he could at the beast. It hit him right on the forehead. Startled, the creature let go of Able's arm. Able fell down but quickly got up and ran towards the school. Passing his friend who stood motionless, he screamed, Run Styles…!"

He made it to the school but the door was locked. Banging on it as hard as he could he cried for help. He turned to look for his friend Styles, only to see him being carried off into the woods. He ran towards the field. "Styles! Someone help!" he screamed in desperation as they disappeared into the forest.

Turning to face the school he yelled, "Help, someone help! It took Styles." The creature stepped back out of the woods alone. It began to run towards Able. Then it stopped short and threw the ball at him. He turned around just in time to see it coming straight at him. And if he hadn't of caught it, it would have surely knocked him out.

Able few backwards and landed hard on his back. The creature was steps away from him now. "Hey you, get away from that student!" Mr. Mondel the school's caretaker was at the school's back door. It took another step towards Able and Mr. Mondel started to run towards them.

"Give me the orb." It demanded. Able frighten shook his head no and held his mitted hand closed tight. Mr. Model was getting closer. The creature turned and ran into the woods. "I'll be back for what's mine…" it spouted. Then it was gone.

Able sat up and looked inside his glove. It wasn't his ball, the one he and his friend had been playing with. It was a little smaller but just as heavy. It looked like a red, crystal ball. He closed his hand again and held onto it tight with his other one.

"Are you alright?" Mr. Mondel asked as he helped Able up. "Did you see it? Did you see the monster?" he questioned Mr. Mondel. "What that man? Did he hurt you?" He questioned. "He took Styles." Able screamed. "What?" Mr. Mondel ran into the forest. By this time others had come outside and were on their way over to where Able stood. Too afraid to go near the forest, he stood frozen and just kept saying, "It took Styles, the monster, it took Styles..."

It had been just over a year since Able first encountered the creature that stole his best friend. It would prove to be an experience that would permanently scare, for Able began to change for the worse. He was often cruel and said mean things to other children; especially his little sister Monika. He would torture small helpless animals just for the fun of it. He started to tell incredible stories about creatures he called Itnescomber; and how they would steal children. His imagination knew no bounds. His parents didn't know what to do. They thought maybe if they let him express himself it might help him deal with the abduction of his friend.

But that wasn't it. It was the magic of the orb. It was programmed with evil intent and that evil was slowly taking over Able. It would tell and show him things, things a child shouldn't know or see; terrible horrible things that nightmares are made of... except they were real.

And now Able had been taken, just like Styles Glubber was taken. Except for one difference - Able was already consumed by the evil...

Finders Keepers

Exhausted but not able to sleep, Ruth lied on her bed. The faint sound of Monika snoring in the bed across from her didn't help. She couldn't understand why Monika blamed her for everything. She was doing her best to help she thought. She didn't want anything bad to happen to Violet.

...Violet, she thought. Why did Violet go outside? Was she not afraid after all that has happened? Her mind began to race and she feared the worst- the orb!

Pulling the covers back she lifted the mattress a little to look. It wasn't there -Violet had stolen it, she was sure of it. This is bad, she thought as she sat down on the bed. She decided right then and there she had to do something. This was her fault and she would have to fix it before anyone else found out about it.

The Darker Side of Light

Without turning on the light she went to Violet's bedside and quietly shook her arm to wake her. "Where is it Violet?" Violet awoke and knew instantly what she was talking about. "Give it back to me, it doesn't belong to you!" Looking around the room hoping to see it, Ruth walked over to her dresser and began to search for it. "You must give it back Violet; only bad things will come to you if you don't. I'm not mad at you, but you have to give it back." She told her.

Violet lied to her and said, "What are you talking about Uroma?" "You know exactly what I am talking about Violet! The orb, you stole it!" she yelled quietly as she walked back over to her. "Now, where is it?" "I don't have it." She said nervously.

Pulling the covers back, she noticed the red glow coming from Violet's right hand. "You little liar!" she said angrily. "Give it to me?" Without hesitation Violet screamed and hit her great-grandmother in the side of the head with the orb. She stumbled over backwards and fell unconscious on the floor.

Hiding the orb under her pillow, Violet screamed again and then yelled. "Itnescomber, Itnescomber!" Forcing herself to cry just as her mother and father came rushing into her room followed closely behind was her Oma.

Patricia flicked on the bedroom light. All three saw Ruth lying on the ground but it was Monika who spoke first as she knelt down to check on her mother. "What has happened to Uroma, Violet?"

"Itnescomber." Violet cried out in a panic. "It was the Itnescomber, its coming to get me, just like Uroma told me." She cried harder. Patricia wrapped her arms around Violet. "It's okay, it was just a bad dream. You're safe now." Eric gently stroked her hair. "You're okay Violet."

Ruth gained consciousness and tried to speak but couldn't. Trying desperately to sit up, she pointed over at Violet. "It's okay mama, Violet is okay, just relax, we will help you back to bed." she told her. Ruth shook her head no, but still could not find words to express her feelings.

"She must have taken a fall." Monika stated. "Help me get her up, will you Eric?" Without hesitation Eric walked the few steps over and helped Monika take Ruth back to her bed. And as they did Monika scolded her mother. "Mama you shouldn't be wondering about in the dark. What were you thinking?" Ruth couldn't answer her, all she could do was shake her head no and make small groaning sounds.

Patricia sat with Violet for a long time. Stroking her hair gently to comfort her, she told her not to worry, that everything was going to be okay.

The next day Violet got up and headed down stairs for breakfast as if nothing had happened the night before. She sat at the kitchen table to eat her cereal. "Where's Uroma?" she pretended to care. Monika looked at her with some concern and then said, "She's sleeping still. She isn't feeling well today. I'm just going to take Uroma her breakfast. I'll be right back, okay? We need to have a little talk." Violet nodded her head without looking at her.

Monika stood at her mother's side for a moment before placing the tray on the bedside table. She loved her mother but was very angry with her for being so foolish. How could she believe in these supernatural creatures? She just didn't understand it. Sighing deeply, she gave her mother's arm a little shake, "Mama, breakfast." Ruth began to wake up. "Okay mama, here's your breakfast. Take your time. I'll come back later to get the dishes."

Passing by Violet's room she noticed her bed was unmade. She shook her head in disapproval and went in to make it. As she picked up the pillow to fluff it, she stopped in the motion as her gaze fell on the blue, glass ball. Dropping the pillow on the floor she quickly picked up the orb and stared at it. She had a terrible sick feeling in the pit of her stomach. "What is this doing here?" she said out loud. It was so long ago but she remembered it, the damage it caused - how it smashed all of her mama's things. She remembered finding it under the couch and how upset she was when her mama wouldn't let her keep it.

How did it get under Violet's pillow? Mama, she must have given it to her! Monika was very angry. What is she thinking? Why on earth would she give this to Violet? As she turned to leave the room to go confront her mother, she came face to face with Violet. Quickly she hid the orb behind her back. But it was too late, Violet saw it.

"That's mine Oma! Give it to me." She reached out her hand to take it. "No, you can't have it. Where did you get it?" she questioned. "Uroma gave it to me." She lied. "Uroma should never have given this to you. I'm going to have a talk with her right now." She stated matter-of-factly.

Violet tried to reach around and take it from her. "What are you doing, I told you no!" As she struggled to keep the orb away from Violet, she held it high above her head. Violet jumped into the air trying to grab it from her but she couldn't reach it.

"Give it to me, it's mine." "No Violet, Stop! What has gotten into you?"

Violet's anger grew and in that moment, she hated her grandmother for keeping the orb for herself. It was hers. It belonged to her and she wanted it. Fists clenched, she punched her grandmother as hard as she could in the stomach. She buckled over in pain and as she did she pushed Violet hard, knocking her through the doorway.

It took a moment for Monika to catch her breath. She couldn't believe what just happened. "Oh my God!" she said under her breath. And for the first time Monika sensed the evil that her mama always spoke about.

"Violet wait come back." she called after her. "Violet! Come back here now!" she screamed louder.

Eric came out of the bedroom first followed closely by Patricia. "What's going on?" Eric questioned. "It's Violet, get her. Stop her! There's something wrong with her." Monika spouted. "What do you mean?" he questioned. "No time to explain. Just get her before she runs away. Eric raced down the stairs after his daughter.

Patricia looked at her mother confused. "What's going on?" "It's the orb." she said sadly. Patricia still didn't understand, she shrugged her shoulders at her. "What orb, what are you talking about?" "This orb, this ..." she said somewhat annoyed as she held it out for her to see. "This is the one my brother had as a child. You remember, the one Uroma talked about when she talked about Able. Violet had it under her pillow. When I told her she couldn't have it, she punched me hard in the stomach." She said frazzled.

Patricia didn't understand what was going on. "What did you do to her?" she questioned. "Did you hurt her mom? Because Violet does not act like that." Patricia questioned. "No, of course not, it's this orb! That's why she is acting the way she is." "That doesn't make any sense. Why would she act like that over a glass ball?" "I don't know, but she did!" Monika insisted. Unhappy with the situation Patricia headed down the stairs to talk to her daughter.

Monika went into the room to have a word or two with her mother. Stomach still hurting from where Violet had punched her, she sat on her bed and looked over at her. She could see she was asleep again. "Mama wake up we need to talk. Mama," she called. No response. Monika began to get a little worried. Normally she woke very easily. She got up and walked the few steps over to her. "Mama, wake up we need to talk." She repeated. Still no response. She shook her arm. Then and there she knew something was seriously wrong with her. She raced to the phone and called 911.

The ill-fated path of one
Isabel Wrightready
Part three

Beety arrived for dinner, and of course, didn't have a clue as to what lay in store for her. "So Gelp my dear friend, what's on the menu tonight? Have you had a change of heart?" Beety asked as she entered Gelp's kitchen. Gelp knew exactly what she meant and was happy she had asked. "No Beety, no change." She said pretending to be cross. "And where's the brat?" she asked as she looked around the room. "She's locked up, so you can't get your hands on her." Gelp said as she looked at her with all serious intent.

"Is that squall, I smell?" Beety asked with some concern. Gelp knew Beety hated squall, especially the way she made it. Beety walked over and looked into the huge pot that was boiling on the stove. "Not squall again Gelp, if I'd known you were making squall, I would have brought something over. I have a tasty jar of pickled yams and Cornish melts prepared at home. Maybe I should run home and get them?" She questioned as she turned to head out the door. "No, no Beety squall is fine. Don't trouble yourself. We'll dine on pickled yams and Cornish melts another time. I'll just add some pepper to it. You like it with pepper right, a lot of pepper?"

Gelp walked over to the cupboard where she kept the pepper and started to pour the content of the bottle in the goopy concoction. Shaking the bottle Gelp exclaimed, "Oh, it looks like I'm out of pepper. I'll just make a quick trip to market and pick some up.

The Darker Side of Light

You don't mind waiting a bit, do you? You're not starving are you and want to eat it without pepper? Or maybe you should just go over to your place and bring the pickled yams and Cornish melts?"

"No, no Gelp, I don't mind waiting for you. I do love squall with a lot of pepper, it is so delicious, especially the way you make it." She laughed a little and continued. "Funny thing I'm out of pepper too or I would run over to my place and get some for you." Beety was falling right into her trap.

"I won't be long, why don't you come back over later?" Gelp suggested. "Oh, you don't mind if I wait here, do you? I might be tempted to eat those yummy pickled yams if I go home and spoil my appetite."

"Very well then, make yourself at home. I'll see you in a bit." Gelp turned the burner off and then headed out her front door. But not before yelling to Beety, "Don't be getting any ideas in that thick head of yours. I don't want any surprises when I get home." Beety sat at the table and picked up the copy of their local newspaper that was in front of her. Pretending to be interested in it and spouted, "Oh no, don't worry Gelp, no surprises here. Bye, bye." she said laughingly.

Gelp gone, Beety went to the stove and lit it. Then quickly headed to the room where she knew Gelp kept her brats. The door was locked so she took out a flat pin from her pocket and forced it into the key hole – unlocking the door. Looking in, she knew right away the child was not there. For the widow that normally was covered with a thick piece of wood was gone. And the light of day was able to enter the empty, despondent room. "Tricky, tricky…" she muttered under her breath. Beety began to search every room in the house. But the child was nowhere to be found. Back in the kitchen she sat at the table again, this time very hungry and confused. Had Gelp traded the child or already killed it and if so why did she keep it from her, her best friend and neighbor. No, this could not be the case for Gelp had told her she wanted to keep this one for herself. It had to be here somewhere –but where?

It was very quiet in the house except for a low moaning sound that was coming from beneath her. The basement! She hadn't looked there. As she walked down the stairs the sound grew louder.

Weird and Wacky Tales & Other Such Nonsense
Linda Noble-Cordy

Sitting in a corner, in the dark was the little fat brat she had met the day before. She was so happy to have found her. She began to salivate at the sight of her.

"There's still time." She said under her breath. Talking sweetly to her she said, "What are you doing down here in the dark child? Why don't you come upstairs with me and I will fix you a hot drink? You'd like that wouldn't you…?" Beety swallowed hard as she forced herself to ask the brat its name. "What's your name little one?" "My name is Isabel." "Oh, what a lovely name." She flashed a smile that would frighten stone and said, "Come with me Isabel, let's go upstairs to the kitchen, I have something there just for you." She raised her voice and tried to talk kindly. "I have something you will love – chocolate cake and butterscotch ice cream. You would like that, wouldn't you?"

"Yes, but my new mother told me to say here. And I don't want to make her angry at me again." she said quietly. "Oh, nonsense Isabel, I will tell her it was all my idea and besides she's out on an errand. She won't be back for a long while. Come on." Beety turned to walk towards the stairs. Isabel stood up and as she did she carefully grabbed the little sealed brown paper bag that was hidden behind her back. Following Beety to the stairs she knew she had to do exactly what Gelp had told her to do or she would never get to go home again.

Holding the bag closed tight, she gave it a little pinch as she was instructed. The paper bag made a crackling sound behind Isabel's back. One foot on the stair, Beety turned her body to face the noise. With a little distance between them Beety questioned her. "What have you got there?" Isabel looked at the ground and said nothing. She was so nervous. She didn't know what was going to happen next. All she knew was that when Beety took the bag she was to back away from her quickly. And under no circumstances was she to let her touch her. Because if she did, something terrible would happen to her and she would never be able to go home again.

"What have you got there?" she repeated crossly. "nothing." Frighten she backed up trying to get away from her. She had Beety's full attention now. The repulsive creature stepped towards her. "What is behind your back brat!" she yelled at her. Isabel started to cry. She remembered Gelp's words – "When she takes the bag, you get as far away as possible from her you hear." But where was she to go? Beety would surely get her, she was trapped.

Beety reached behind her and grabbed the bag. "Stealing from Gelp? She won't have any part of that!" Now Beety had an excuse for what she was about to do to the brat. Isabel ran back over to where she was sitting before and prepared herself for the worst. Eyes closed tight, curled up in a ball on the floor, she heard Beety spout. "What's this?" And as she asked the question, it was already too late. She disappeared into thin air. Silence for what seemed forever… Isabel slowly opened her eyes and looked around the room. She was gone. Where did she go?

She sat for a moment, too stunned to move. Then she remembered the other one was gone too. Quickly she made her way up the stairs, only to be stopped mid-way by Gelp. "Where are you going in such a hurry?" Looking up she spouted with some enthusiasm, "I did just what you said. Can I go home now please, like you said I could?" "Why of course you can!" Gelp shoved Isabel hard, and mockingly said, "Welcome to your new home! Get used to it, because it's the only home you'll ever know." Isabel fell down the stairs and came to land on the damp dirty soil. Laughing at poor little Isabel, she slammed the door shut and waited for what she knew would happen next.

Isabel was hurt, but she was also very angry. In the pitch-black, she made her way up the stairs. It was difficult and as she hopped on one foot the pain was almost too much to bear. She tried to open the door but it was locked. Screaming at the top of her lungs, she banged on the door. "You promised I could go home! You promised! You lied! Liar, Liar!" She continued to bang on the door and scream, "Liar! Liar!

Calmly, Gelp walked into her kitchen smiling a wicked, evil, cunning smile. Opening the draw that contained her sharpest scissors, she took them in hand and gestured a cutting motion with them. She was quite happy with herself. There is a remedy for everything, she declared. And out loud she muttered towards the locked door, "I warned you about talking back brat!"

The training had begun… poor little Isabel didn't know what tortures awaited her from that moment on, how could she…

Maimed for life, it wasn't just her physical being that was crippled but her spiritual one as well. She would never forget the wicked words the Itnescomber told her just before she cut out her tongue. "I have to say Issy, you did a great job, too bad you had to go and rune it by talking back. Unforgivable. Well that's to be expected from a brat like you…" She begged her not to do it, but she won't listen.

Then this wicked creature spouted the worst news of all, "Too bad for you that you did such a good job. If Beety had got her hands on you, she would have brought you back to your world; right back home to your own house with your own mommy and daddy." She laughed a horrible immoral laugh then did the heinous deed. Isabel lay on the cold unforgiving floor and cried. Blood poured out of her mouth. The Itnescomber threw the little severed piece of flesh at her and amused herself by saying, "Hold your tongue brat!"

Isabel reached out and picked it up. It was covered in dirt and blood. She thought that maybe she could put it back in her mouth and it could re-attach somehow. Curling up into a ball Isabel lay, hopeless and defeated. All Isabel could think about were the words the horrible lying creature said. She had promised her she could go home. And when she had the opportunity to do just that, she missed it. How could she let herself believe anything that monster said? She never would, never again.

The Arrival

Beety travelled to the place she had once feared. Her mind blank, stripped of any knowledge of who she was or where she had just come from. She stood there against the grayness of the dark night, not knowing which way to go or even where to go. From behind she heard the voice of someone calling, "Isabel, Isabel!" Turning to face the sound a large woman grabbed hold of her and lifted her up. She fought to free herself but she held on tight. "Isabel, it's okay, it's me, its Mrs. Feld, you know me." She screamed and continued to fight her. "Stop that Isabel, I won't hurt you. I'm going to bring you home."

She let out a terrible noise, a sound that a normal child would not make. "It's okay Isabel, look your house is just across the street." she reassured her. But it was no use. She clawed at her face with

The Darker Side of Light

both hands and Mrs. Feld let out a cry of pain as blood ran down her cheeks.

"Stop Isabel! It's me! What's wrong with you?" She wondered why she didn't recognize her. She struggled to move her head out of her striking range but it was no use. Isabel went for her eyes, and she was forced to drop her to the ground. She quickly regained her footing and she ran off down the street. Mrs. Feld screamed and ran after her, "Isabel, come back, Isabel!"

A rookie cop named Jamison sat in the police car a block away. His partner Phillips had just gone into the restaurant to buy coffee and use the facilities. Jamison heard the strange scream and knew right away the little girl was in trouble. There was no time to wait for back up. Jumping out of his car he ran and quickly caught up to this person of interest. Gun pointed at her he yelled, "Freeze, hands in the air."

She stopped in her tracks and turned slowly to face the officer. Pointing in the direction in which she was running. "Isabel," she said winded.

"Drop the bag, kick it over to me and lay face down on the ground." He ordered. He could see that she had gapping scratch marks down both her cheeks and it was quite evident that her right eye was injured.

Blood soaked, confused and out of breath she just stood there. Jamison repeated it with more authority. "I said drop the bag and down on the ground now!" She took a step towards him. "I can explain." She reached into the large bag to show him a poster of Isabel. She had been out all day long putting up posters. "Stop!" he ordered. But she didn't. In that split second, he fired on her. She fell to the ground dead.

Her parents couldn't believe it. How could Mrs. Feld have done this? She had known Isabel since she was born and had even baby-sat her on occasion. And to make it worse they didn't know what she had done to her. The only explanation was that she had given her a strange drug causing memory loss and possible brain damage. And even though there was no trace of any known drugs in her system that is what they concluded.

Spending the majority of the time under sedation because of her violent behavior and psychotic out bursts; it would be a long time before Isabel could return home to her family. After a full year of treatments, tests, and evaluations she still was no better than the first day she arrived at the hospital.

Her devoted parents visited her at least once a week and on occasion brought along her little three-year-old brother Zack for a visit. She took notice of him and would ask if he could stay with her. She seemed to be calm and well behaved when he was around. The doctors thought that she was relating well to another child and that even though she wasn't receptive to any of them - the doctors, her parents, and the staff members; she would probably do well at home in a loving environment. As long as they kept her on the medication, away from sharp objects and brought her in once a week for evaluation; she would adjust and be a functioning part of society. Of course, she wouldn't. She would never adjust? She would however with time, remembered who she really was and what she liked to do best - bake...

The ill-fated path of one
Isabel Wrightready
Part four - final chapter

Isabel lurked in the shadows of her captor for many, many years; years that equaled a life-time to a child deprived of love and care. Striped of all innocence and moral dignity she lived as Gelp lived, she thought as Gelp thought.

Isabel hated Gelp with everything she was. But at the same time, she knew no other life. She no longer remembered her own mom and dad or anything prior to her abduction. And as more and more time passed she grew more like Gelp and lost a little more of herself.

Isabel was changing, and no longer looked like the child she once was. She was still very small, due to the lack of nutrition and personal care. However, Gelp felt she didn't have the same hold on her; she sensed it slipping away as each day went by. And despite the fact she was well trained, obedient and quiet, Gelp knew the time had come to get rid of her. It was just a question of how, where and by what means.

Gelp had a few ideas and she played each of them out in her mind. Her first thought was to make a trade – Isabel for another child. But no one would take her at her age, no matter how well trained she was. Another idea she had was to let her go back to her own world. She knew she would never survive long in her condition. However why take the chance. Then she thought she would cook her up. Sure, she'd be a little tough, but that's the price you pay for keeping them for so long and working them half to death.

Yes, she decided, she would do just that!

At market that day, Gelp spied an old guillotine. Her mind raced as she devised a plot to kill Isabel.

She pointed at the contraption. "How perfect Issy, you can use it for chopping…things…" She hesitated as she tried to think of things it might be used for. "What say I get it for you? Consider it a present for all the hard work you do." Then she let out a laugh, cruel and evil. Isabel looked at her blank-faced and waited for further orders. She knew what Gelp really wanted it for. Gelp was far too predictable now.

Gelp turned to the merchant. "How much you want for it?"

The fat beast that sat eating a strange mixer from a bowl, looked up at her, chewing slowly he spat out, "Thirty crowns." "What! Forget it, I'll give you ten."

He started to choke at her offer and as he did food flew out of his mouth and proceeded to run down his chin and on to his bare chest.

Clearing his throat, he spoke, "You insult me Madame. This is a much sought-after item. They don't make'em like this anymore. He stood up, "Just look at the quality of the wood. And that blade is razor sharp. Why, you could split hairs with that blade." He tapped his head. "Only been used a few times, if you know what I mean."

Gelp turned to Isabel, handed her a few coins and ordered, "Go get me 2 ounces of nutmeg and 3 ounces of white sage."

After some haggling the deal was done. Isabel back from her task then loaded the contraption on to the wagon and pulled it home.

Placing it by the pile of old dead wood in the back yard, Gelp ordered Isabel to set it up for chopping. She did just that. After a few releases of the blade, Gelp announced, "No, no, something's not right with the blade. Fix it Issy." Isabel looked at her confused.

She pointed at the contraption, "Put your head in there and look up at the blade. Tell me if it's straight. Make sure the angle of the blade is right for chopping." She ordered.

Isabel pretended like she didn't understand. She picked up a large piece of wood and put it in. "No, no stupid girl, not like that, not the wood…!" Gelp screamed.

And because she never refused to do anything unless she didn't understand how to do it. Gelp made the big mistake of placing her own head in the contraction. "Like this idiot."

Isabel smiled for the first time in over twenty years. And as the blade came down, all that was left of Gelp was the look of horror on her despicable face.

Her head rolled onto the dirty wood-chipped ground and there it stayed. Her body was a different story. It jumped up and ran about wildly. Isabel quickly climbed up the wood pile to sit and watch the show. Laughing out loud, she mused at the headless body as it ran around the yard, until banging into a large tree. She screamed with great delight and clapped her hands together as it fell hard to the ground. It twitched and jerked a bit then stopped.

Finally, it was over… she started to laugh an evil, wicked laugh and as she jumped down she kicked Gelp's stone-like head hard. It travelled a little distance through the air and landed close to the dead body. Her laughter turned into screams of hysteria and eventually to sobs of relief. She could leave this place, finally she was free. But where was she to go? A part of her wanted to run, just start running and never look back. But she couldn't find the will power to do it.

Madness began to surface. She was free from Gelp once and for all… free yes, but freed not in the slightest.

Picking up the head, she reached over and grabbed one of the legs and began to walk towards the house.

She was more than familiar with what to do next. She had done it a thousand times before. However, she would need more than 2 ounces of nutmeg and 3 ounces of white sage to tenderize this tough old bird. Dropping the remains just inside the door she then closed it and headed back to market to get the much-needed spices to prepare old Gelp up properly.

The wakeup call

Monika felt she had to do something. Her family was falling apart; her grandson missing, her mother in the hospital; her granddaughter possessed by some kind of evil spirit. And the guilt she was feeling about the past was beginning to consume her every thought.

She had lied when she told the police that the picture of the women they had shown her was little Isabel's abductor. At the time, she was mourning the loss of her new born son, so when they told her they had caught the women in a struggle with Isabel – it made sense to her. After all, they did tell her, she was the one. She was just confirming it.

She thought about Isabel. And wondered how she escaped the clutches of her real abductor. She knew she had suffered at its hands. The damage it had inflicted on her was undeniable and she never recovered – as far as she knew. Poor little Isabel, it must have been horrible for her, she lamented.

If she could talk to Isabel, maybe – if she remembered anything, she could help her find out where Creed had been taken, and how to get him back. Her rational mind told her it couldn't possibly be the same person involved in the abduction. But her irrational mind told her it had to be. It had to be the Itnescomber.

That poor family, she thought, as she remembered they had a small son who died tragically of some kind of childhood illness shortly after this had all happened. They move away after that and no one heard from them again.

She searched on Canada 411 and found three listings for Wrightready. One of them was a W. Wrightready. She remembered the father's name was Wallace and the mother's Silva.

The phone rang for a long time and she thought for a moment she was going to get voice mail. A man answered, "Hello." "Hello, Wallace?" she asked. "Yes," he said slowly. "Wallace, I don't know if you remember me. I'm Monika Price. Our daughters played together when they were very young." He was quiet for a few seconds and then he said, "Oh yes, I remember you. You lived just down the street from us on Chester Avenue." "Yes, that's right. I'm sorry for calling you out of the blue like this. Does your

The Darker Side of Light

daughter Isabel still live at home with you? It's her, I really need to talk to." Dead silence. "Wallace, are you there?" She wondered if he had hung up. Then she heard him clear his throat. "Yes, I'm here. Why do you need to speak to Isabel?" She really didn't know how to put it to him - why she needed Isabel's help. She couldn't tell him she was hunting down a supernatural creature and that Isabel might be able to help her. "Remember when Isabel was taken – well my grandson is missing."

Wallace sat down in his recliner, the one he sat in each and every day to watch T.V. He picked up the remote control and turned it off. His heart sank into his stomach as terrible memories from the past came flooding back. *His own little son and all those poor little children.* All he heard was her name - Isabel and her grandson was missing.

"It can't be her." "Pardon me, what did you say?" she questioned. "It can't be Isabel, she's locked up; has been for over fifteen years now, she couldn't have taken him."

Monika didn't know why he said that. She thought for a moment that he might be senile or suffering from dementia. "Where is she?" She asked. "She's at Brookside – it's a private hospital" He paused for a moment, "She's very ill." He told her.

"Is it okay if I go and see her? I need to talk to her. Maybe she can shed some light on where the kidnapper may have taken my grandson Creed." "I don't think that's a good idea, she's not…" he stopped. "I wouldn't go there; I don't think she can help you." He told her.

After some convincing, he gave her the number. Before hanging up she asked how his wife Silva was. His voice cracked and she could hear a great sadness in his voice. "Silva took her own life shortly after our little Zack died. She just couldn't cope with…" he stopped again."

Monika felt so terrible and wished she hadn't asked. This poor man, he has suffered so much. "That's okay Wallace, I understand. You don't need to explain anything to me. I understand."

There was an uncomfortable silence and then Monika continued. "Do you want me to call you after I speak to Isabel? I'll let her know I was talking to you." "No, that won't be necessary. I'd rather you didn't and don't call here again." He hung up the phone. She was upset at his response but she realized he was in a lot of pain.

Numb, Wallace sat for a long time staring at the festering bite mark on his right forearm; all he could think was –She must have got out. The police would be showing up soon. He couldn't go through that again. He just wasn't strong enough. He quickly got up and walked into the kitchen where he kept the Nardil; his pills for depression. Emptying the content of a new container of pills into his month, he washed it back with a shot of hard scotch.

Brookside Asylum for the criminal insane
As she approached the hospital gates she felt extremely nervous. The building itself look pleasant enough. A large white building surround by a well-manicured, empty lawn. She found the public parking and then walked a short distance to the front entrance.

She stood in front of the camera then pressed the button to get in. The voice of a man came across the speaker. "Yes, can I help you?" "Yes, I called the other day, my name is Monika Price. I'm here to see Isabel Wrightready." She responded. "Just a minute." He replied.

It took him some time before he got back to her. "I'm sorry, I don't see you on the list of allowed visitors." "That's because I've never been here before. I'm an old friend of the family. I did call ahead and they said it would be okay." "Do you know who you spoke to?" he questioned. "I'm not sure." She responded. "Is it not written down somewhere – or in the computer?" He couldn't find anything but he wasn't surprised. With the constant turnover in staff it happened way too often.

Another long period of silence then he came back on. "Okay, when you here the buzz sound and see the green light, open the door. In the next foyer, wait for the buzz sound and green light again." Go through the door; follow the white line on the floor to the reception area." He informed her.

Inside the building, Mark Deset sat at the reception desk. It wasn't his usual job. Usually he worked on the ward with the patients. He did however on occasion help out in different departments when they were short staffed.

The Darker Side of Light

He knew Isabel, knew what kind of patient she was –an H.P.S. - homicidal psychopath with schizophrenic tendencies. He knew Isabel had only one visitor – her father, once a year on her birthday; and that just happened last month. He remembered it well. Isabel few into a rage and attacked him. It took him and two orderlies to pull her off. The poor old guy was so upset; thought he was going to have a heart attack right there and then. He wondered if that was why Mrs. Price was there – to tell her about her father.

He wasn't permitted to ask –that was against the rules. Just like it was against the rules to discuss the patient's history with anyone other than staff or immediate family. Mark followed the rules even though a lot of the other staff members didn't. One of the reasons (of many) why there was such a high staff turnover.

Monika stood at the door with the reception sign on it. Again, she waited for the sound and the green light before she could enter. As she approached the desk Mark smiled at her warmly. Hi Mrs. Price, sorry about the mix up. If you'd like to take a seat and fill out the paper work while you're waiting that would be great." She acknowledged him and did just that. She couldn't understand why there was so much security or why she had to fill out a form to see her.

The questions were fairly standard and easy to answer. She finished and brought the paper back to Mark. "Thank you." he responded. "Now if you'll just take a seat again, I'll let you know when they have her ready." He took the paper and entered her information into the computer.

She wondered at the words he used "have her ready." For a moment, she felt like she was visiting a dangerous criminal. *She had no idea what she was in for – literally.*

A large, well kept, woman dressed in white came in, went to the desk and spoke. "Hey Mark, I'm here for Isabel Wrightready's visitor." Mark looked over at Monika. "She's right there." She turned to face her. "Hi, I'm Sandra, Isabel's nurse. I can take you to see her now." "If you could just put on this name tag." She passed her a sticky tag with visitor and the hospital log on it. Finally, she was going to see Isabel.

The Darker Side of Light

They walked down the hall to an elevator. Sandra waved a security card across the metal panel. A green light went on, opening the elevator door. As they walked in Sandra spoke. "Isabel is good today. You've picked a good day to see her. So, you can meet with her in the rec-room."

She swiped the card across another metal panel and then pressed the number 4. Monika looked at her puzzled. She continued. "She doesn't have many good days, I'm afraid. Lucky for you she is coherent and manageable today." Then she added. "I guess it's because she was expecting a visitor today." Monika looked at her agreeable, and nodded her head yes.

The elevator door opened and Monika was hit with the smell of pinesol and pee. They walked down a bare corridor. The walls and floor were very clean except for one area. Passing the custodian, Monika looked over at the floor and wall. It appeared to be vomit and blood he was wiping up. She quickly looked away as the smell and sight of it made her want to throw up.

They walked a little further and Sandra stopped in front of a closed door that was marked Recreation Room. "Okay, before we go in, I just want to warn you about Isabel's restraints." She began. "She has to wear a mouth guard and arm restraints when she is in contact with anyone. So don't be alarmed when you see her. She can still talk –she just can't harm you."

Monika was taken aback and started to wonder what she was doing there. Nothing could have prepared her for what she saw when the door was opened – nothing.

A tiny, petite, Isabel sat in a chair facing her. The first thing she noticed was the dirty white mouth guard partially covering- what appeared to be a small pale face. The only things showing was some very short black matted hair and two dark brown – almost black eyes; eyes that appeared empty - hollow. Her hands and arms, stretched out across the table in front of her – were covered with a rubber-like suit that didn't seem to bend.

Monika stared at this young woman with fear and also great sadness. How could it have come to *this*? What has happened to her? She thought.

The Darker Side of Light

"Mrs. Price, are you okay?" Sandra asked. Monika looked over at her, still lost in thought. She cleared her throat, "Yes, I'm fine, I'm fine." Giving her attention to Isabel, she walked over to her and said, "Hello Isabel, I'm Mrs. Price. You might not remember me. I am Patricia's mom."

Isabel just stared at her. Monika looked at the nurse, "I'm okay now, do you mind if I sit and have a talk with her?" "No, that's fine." Sandra replied. "In private," she added. "It's a family matter." "Oh, yes that's fine; I'll just be over at the desk if you need me." Monika nodded at her and waited for her to be out of ear-shot to continue.

"Oh, dear little Isabel, just look at you? What has happened to you?" She questioned her. She reached out and touched her mitted hands. Isabel moved them stiffly out of the way. "I'm not going to hurt you dear." She assured her. "Do you remember my daughter –Patty? You and her, were good friends. You played together before that bad thing happened to you. Do you remember?"

Isabel just kept staring at her – blankly. Monika started to wonder if she could hear or see her or even if she understood what she was saying. "I remember that horrible day. You and Patty were playing in the front yard of my house. Do you remember?" she questioned her again. "No, you probably don't, you were so young."

Then Monika leaned in across the table and whispered loudly. "I saw her Isabel, the old lady who took you. And it wasn't Mrs. Feld, like everyone thought it was." She had Isabel's attention now. Her empty eyes filled with curiosity. "I was in the upstairs bedroom when I heard Patty screaming. And when I looked out the window I saw her talking to you and Patty." Monika thought for a moment that she might be smiling under the mask.

"Gelp!" Isabel said quietly. "What was that dear? Did you say something? Monika questioned in a normal voice. Then Isabel muttered, "Patty, your daughter is Patty?" "Yes, Yes, my daughter is Patty, do you remember Isabel?" she said with some enthusiasm.

Isabel didn't remember Patty, but she did however, remember the little brat who tricked her into returning to this world. The one she was mistaken for and had to live as. She started to put the pieces together. She shook her head yes.

"Isabel, I know this is very difficult for you, but I need to ask you a few questions about what happened to you after she took you. That is – if you remember." "I don't." she replied.

Isabel knew what this woman wanted and she knew why. "Who's missing?" she asked abruptly. Monika was caught off guard, "What?" She repeated it, "Who's missing?" "My grandson," she answered. "How old?" she asked with great interest." "Only five." Monika was certain that Isabel was smiling under the horrid dirty mask.

A five-year-old boy, oh the fun I would have with him. She thought to herself. Then she asked. Do you have more grandchildren?" "Yes, two more; an eight-year-old granddaughter and three-month old grandson." She said proudly. Isabel got excited. "Do you have any pictures of them?" she inquired. "Yes, I do as a matter of fact." As she reached into her purse and took out her wallet, she felt she was getting somewhere. Maybe if Isabel saw a picture of Creed, she would feel some sympathy, and want to help her find him.

Modus operandi begun- What are their names?" And as Monika told her their names, Beety's true nature awoke. She looked at the photos and began to fantasize what she would do to them; how she would prepare them. It had been such a long, long time. "What beautiful grandchildren you have."

Beety leaned towards Monika and spoke, "I'm not who they think I am. It's all a lie." Monika looked at her strangely as she continued. "I didn't do what they said I did. It's all a lie." Monika remembered the conversation she had with her father, Wallace. "Okay," she said to her. "There was no proof. Not one body. They had to blame someone for all those missing children. So they thought let's blame the crazy girl, who was kidnapped and brutally tortured; the girl who nobody cares about, not even her own parents." She pretended to be upset and started to cry.

Monika began to get frightened. She quickly picked up the pictures to put them away in her purse. Isabel's mood changed dramatically, "What's that you've got in your purse?" She noticed

The Darker Side of Light

the orb. It was glowing red. "It's nothing," she closed the purse up quickly. Beety knew exactly what it was – her ticket out of there.

"I know where your grandson is. I can get him for you. But you have to get me out of here if you ever want to see him alive again." Then she looked towards the desk, Sandra was just hanging up the phone. "We're out of time. Come back tomorrow and bring the orb." She ordered.

Sandra walked over to them. "I'm afraid the time is up?" "But we're not finished talking yet." Monika told her. "Sorry, Isabel has to go back to her room. It's time for her meds." Monika began to get anxious. How was she going to get Isabel out of there? And why did she want her to bring the orb?

Two orderlies entered the room and walked over to where Isabel sat. One on either side of her they escorted her out of the room. "Tomorrow, come back tomorrow." She repeated.

What choice did she have? Isabel was her only hope at finding Creed. She knew she won't be able to remove Isabel from the hospital. It wouldn't be allowed – or would it?

"I'll escort you to the exit Mrs. Price." Sandra said. As they reached the first exit door, Monika asked, "So are the patients here allowed day passes?" Some are, but very few." She stated. "What about Isabel?" Sandra stopped dead in her tracks and looked at her in shock. "Isabel, oh no, she will never be able to leave." Sandra couldn't believe she had just asked that question and was starting to think there might be something wrong with her. "You are a friend of the family, right?" she questioned. "Yes, sort of, my daughter and Isabel played together as children." Sandra began to get curious, "Do you mind if I ask why you came to visit Isabel?"

Monika didn't want to reveal the exact reason she was there so she repeated, "It's a family matter, you understand?" "Oh yes, I heard about her father, poor man." Then she continued. "Well she can't be released. Not even to attend his funeral." Monika tried hard not to look surprised. She had only spoken to him the other day. "Well, I thought it wouldn't hurt to ask."

"One other question, if you don't mind?" Sandra spouted as they walked through the first door to the outside. "I noticed you were showing Isabel some pictures." "Oh, yes," my grandchild. She asked to see a picture of them." Sandra felt her stomach turn. She thought, that sick bitch! "Do yourself and your grandkids a favour – if you do decide to come back, don't ever show her a picture of them again. Or any other kids for that matter?" "But why?" Monika asked earnestly.

"You do know why Isabel is in here don't you?" she asked seriously. By the innocent look on her face, Sandra could tell she really didn't have a clue, even though she nodded her head yes.

"Isabel is responsible for the murder of her own brother and five other children." She announced firmly. Monika stood there in total shock. She looked at Sandra, "but she said they didn't have any proof, that the children were missing and that she was innocent."

"Isabel is a pathological liar, among other things. Of course, she told you she was innocent and that they didn't have any proof. That's because she cooked them up and served them to her family." Monika felt sick and couldn't believe what she was hearing. "I don't remember hearing about this or reading about it in the papers. When did this happen?" Monika was confused. All this time she thought Isabel was suffering because of the trauma she suffered as a child; and that it was so terrible, it scared her for life.

"They caught her in ninety-two trying to lure another child away. She was only twelve. I'm not sure of all the details. Only that the basement of her father's house is where she killed them. They found, knives, chain saws, meat hooks hanging from the rafters. No bodies though. Only a small amount of blood from one of the victims was found. Oh, and a diary – a cookbook of sorts. That's how they knew what she was up to." Then she added, "Do you recall, 'The baby stealer,' it was all over the media back in the late eighties early nineties?" Monika remembered that. "Yes, they caught him, right?" "They caught her… All the details were kept private because of her age. She is as crazy as they come." Sandra stated matter-of-factly.

"What about her father? He didn't know? They didn't suspect he might have something to do with it? After all, she was just a child herself." Monika questioned. "He was ruled out. The poor man had no idea he was living with a monster. I can't imagine how horrible that must have been for him. To know your little daughter was bringing kids home, killing them right under your nose and then cooking them up and feeding them to you. I mean how do you live with yourself after that? I'm surprised he lasted as long as he did. Lord knows her poor mother didn't." She told her.

Sandra opened the last exit door and Monika walked through it. "Bye." she said as a response. She walked to her car and got in it. She sat for a long time. She thought about Isabel; about what Isabel had said to her. The reaction she had when she saw the orb. She thought about what the nurse had told her about Isabel – how could a child do that? Something just wasn't adding up. Confused and not really sure if she should return tomorrow, she headed over to the hospital to pick up her mother. If anyone could make sense of it all it was her, she would know what to do.

Monika had full intentions of telling her mother everything. But when she saw her sitting there in the hospital chair - so frail and weak, she decided to wait. "Hi mama, I spoke to the nurse, she said you have caused enough trouble, so they're sending you home." She said smiling.

"It's about time." She said annoyed. "They have done every test under the sun – and there's not a thing wrong with me." Monika laughed, "You're telling me, I have to live with you. You're as healthy as a horse, and as stubborn as a mule." "You're a fine one to talk." she said in retaliation. "Okay mama, let's get you home. It will be nice to sleep in our own beds tonight."

On the car drive home both women sat very quiet. They both had their secrets to keep, both thinking they were protecting the other.

Monika helped her mother get settled in. "Have you heard any news from Patty?" Ruth inquired. "No nothing new today mama." "And what about Violet?" "What about Violet?" She questioned her back. "Yes, about Violet, mama. Why did you give her that glass ball?" Ruth began to get very upset. "I didn't give it to her, she stole it! And when I went to get it from her, she hit me!" She placed her hand on her left temple. "Its pure evil, you know I would have never given it to her." Her secret exposed, she continued. "We have to get it back from her, she is in great danger."

For a moment, Monika considered not telling her mother that she had already taken it. But she didn't want her to worry or feel the need to go back to Patty's house. Not yet anyhow.

"I have it mama. I found it under her pillow. She made quite the scene when I told her she couldn't have it. She hit me too and ran away. I hid it in my purse and kept it with me all the time." Monika picked up her purse from the table and brought it over to where her mother was sitting.

Ruth looked at her gravely, "I let Violet touch it. And the moment I did I knew it was a big mistake. It woke the evil in it. I'm afraid the Itnescomber that owns it, is coming for it." Monika patted her purse. "Not as long as I have it, it won't get its filthy paws on it." She assured her.

Monika thought for a moment about what Violet had said she saw in the back yard. Was it really true, did she see this creature? Could it be the creature that took her brother? Then her mind instantly went to Isabel –she somehow knew about the orb. "Mama, I have something to tell you." She sat down beside her mother. Ruth could see something was deeply troubling her. "What is it Monika? Spit it out."

"I went to see little Isabel. She knows what happened to Creed, she knows what took him." She told her. "But how, how can that be? Ruth was puzzled.

"I'm so sorry mama." Monika began to tear up. "All these years I have had to live with this lie. I can't do it anymore. The truth must come out. No matter how crazy it all sounds. I just wished I had told the truth from the beginning- when Isabel was taken. Maybe if I had we won't be looking for my grandson. Our family wouldn't be suffering this torment." Ruth kindly scolded her, "There will be plenty of time for regret later Monika, for now you must be strong – we must be strong, and together we must face our demons."

Monika informed Ruth about the events that had lead up to this moment and when she was finished it was decided – Monika would drive her mama to Patty's home and then she would meet with Isabel as planned.

The departure

It took some persuasion and threats about her civil rights, to get the head nurse to agree to the removal of the hand and arm restrains. And as she sat patiently waiting for the woman who

The Darker Side of Light

unwittingly would be springing her; she thought about the infant and the fun she would have with it. She had no intention of helping her find the brat, she never did. She hated humans – all of them. In her eyes, they were good for one thing – and only up to a certain age. After that they were of no use to her.

Escorted by a young nurse named Mary-Ann, Monika entered the same room as the day before. Mary-Ann cheerfully said, "Isabel your visitor is here." Monika, noticed right away Isabel's arm restraints were missing. She wanted to ask why, but decided against it. Mary-Ann announced, "I'll be over at the desk if you need me." She nodded to acknowledge her, then set her sights on Isabel. As she stared at the masked face of this young woman, she felt very uneasy. It wasn't because of her appearance. It was something else; there was something evil about her. She was surprised she hadn't noticed it the other day. "Hello Isabel," she said warily. Isabel nodded to acknowledge her presence. "I'm only here because you said you can help get Creed back."

"Yes, I can." She stated then continued. "Is it possible to see his picture again and the picture of the other beautiful children?" Monika remembered what nurse Sandra had told her yesterday. "Why do you need to see the pictures? What difference would it make?" she questioned, upset that she was asking.

Isabel tried to put some kindness in her voice. "It gives me some comfort when I see the beautiful faces of children. It helps me to remember the innocence that was stolen from me so long ago." "No, you can't see the pictures." Monika told her. "Then I have nothing to say." She stated frankly.

Her inner voice spoke to her; *Just show her the pictures already. Look at her – she's harmless. Besides she's not going anywhere too soon. And maybe it's not true. How could it be – she was only a child herself.*

With some hesitation, Monika placed two photos on the table – one of Creed alone and one of the three children sitting on the couch – Violet holding new baby Aiden. She reached out and picked up the photo of the three children. "Is this where the children live? I mean it looks like a lovely home." Monika looked over at her and shook her head yes. "May I keep it?" She asked nicely. "No" Monika reached out to take the photo from her and

Isabel pulled it from her reach. "Uh- huh, not so fast. I have something you want and you have something I want."

Cutting through the formalities, Isabel blurted out, "Did you bring it?" Monika motioned to her purse. "Yes." Isabel eyed the purse. "Can I see it?" She reached into her purse and then stopped. "No, not yet." She looked hard at Isabel. "First you tell me what you know. You tell me how to get Creed back."

"I know about them – what you like to call the Itnescomber." She began. "I know what they do to children and how they do it. I can get your boy back, but I will need the orb to do it." "Why do you need it? What is so important about it?" She questioned her. "I can use it as a seer. If I ask it, it can show me where he is – it can take… lead you to him. What's the harm?" Isabel questioned.

She could tell by the look on Monika's face she wasn't convinced. "It's not like I'm going to take it and run off, is it? Look around you. Where am I going?" This woman was beginning to annoy her terribly. She wanted to jump across the table, slit her throat with her bare hands and take it from her. And if she didn't get what she wanted soon that's just what she was going to do.

Monika reached into her purse slowly and took out the orb. Holding the glowing blood red orb tightly in her right hand she looked at Isabel with concern. Isabel stood up and reached out her hand. "You're sure you will be able to see my grandson?" "Oh, yes my dear. I will."

Monika had strong reservations- But her mind was fuzzy, and she couldn't think straight. It was too late anyhow. Beety held on to it with both hands. She laughed a horrid wicked laugh. Doubting her actions and desperate for answers Monika questioned her further, "Can you see him, can you see my grandson, can you see the monster who took him?"

"Of course, I can." She laughed louder and mockingly announced, "It takes one to know one. And this one is going home." She vanished right before her eyes. Beety would be going home but not before she made a pit stop. She was feeling a little peckish and new exactly where to find her next meal…

Monika stood up. "Oh my God, what have I done?" The nurse noticing Isabel was missing, yelled out, "Where is she, where did

The Darker Side of Light

she go?" Not waiting for an answer, she sounded the alarm. Within seconds three orderlies and the head nurse Edith, came rushing into the room. Mary-Ann spoke first. "Isabel is missing. She just disappeared – vanished into thin air." "That's not possible. People don't just disappear." Edith said firmly. She looked at Monika for answers.

"It's true she just disappeared into thin air." Monika told them despondently. Ashamed that she was trick by this Itnescomber and upset that she would not be able to save her grandson, Monika sat back down on the chair and quietly began to cry.

Patricia knew how terrible Violet felt about everything; to avoid any unnecessary conflict between her daughter and her grandmothers she let Violet go to her friend's house for the afternoon.

Ruth sat at the kitchen table waiting to hear from Monika, she wondered if she had got anywhere with Isabel. It had been an hour since she had dropped her off at Patty's house. The phone rang and she got up to answer it but Patricia beat her to it. It was Monika on the phone and she was in a state of hysterics. "Patty, I need to speak to my mother right away!" "What's wrong mom?" she asked. "No time to explain, just get her." She demanded. "Okay mom, hold on, she's right here." She passed Ruth the phone.

Patricia could hear the sheer terror in her mother's voice coming through the receiver, but she couldn't make out what she was saying. Patricia questioned, "What's going on? What's she saying?" Ruth put up her index finger motioning a 'just a minute.'

"How could you be so stupid Monika? You should have never given it to her. What were you thinking?" she scolded her. "I know, I know mama! I don't know what came over me. I had no idea this would happen. I thought what harm could it have – showing her the pictures of the children, and then when she asked to see the orb. Where was she going? I thought, she can't get out of this place." She started crying again. "What have I done? Now we will never be able to find Creed."

Ruth interrupted, "What? You showed her pictures of the children? You know better, what's wrong with you?" Her mind began to race. She added, "Which pictures did you show her?" "One of Creed and one of the children sitting on the couch."

The Darker Side of Light

"Monika, where are the photo's now?" she demanded to know. Ruth prayed she had them with her. Monika stopped sobbing long enough to say, "She has it. The one of the children, she wouldn't give it back."

Ruth's mind went into overdrive. The sheer panic in her eyes told Patricia something was terribly wrong. "What is it Uroma?" What did she say?" she demanded. Ruth dropped the receiver and screamed, "Go get the baby!"

Patricia didn't ask any questions, she turned and raced up the stairs. She dashed through his bedroom door and went straight to his crib. "Aiden!" she screamed out in horror. She turned to face Ruth who was standing in the doorway. "He's not here, where is he?" Turning to face his crib again, something caught her eye from outside the window. She quickly went to it. Someone was in the backyard walking towards the forest. "Oh my God!" Without another word, she raced past Ruth. "What is it Patty?" she said as she turned to follow her.

Hidden from sight, Beety had already searched the house for the girl. She must be here somewhere, she thought. Orb in hand and baby in arms, Beety felt elated. She was almost home free. She couldn't wait to get back home. She would kill Gelp for sending her to this horrible place. And if that brat Isabel was still living – she would take care of her too.

She stood by the children's play set. There was movement in the forest- someone was there, just out of sight. "Violet, is that you?" she called out sweetly. She walked towards it and the movement stopped. "Violet, your mommy wants you. Come with me and I will take you to her." She said kindly.

Beety stopped short. It wasn't Violet; it was one of her kind. He stepped out of the forest and before she could make a move he was on top of her. He grabbed the orb from her and pushed her hard to the ground. The baby fell from her grasp a short distance away and began to cry. Patricia raced over to them, picked up her baby and held on to him tight.

Beety quickly jumped to her feet to challenge him. She reached out for the orb. She needed it; she wouldn't be able to get home without it. "That's mine!" she screamed as she tried to take it from him. But it was hopeless he was much too powerful for her. A punch to the jaw bone would render her unconscious before she hit the ground.

Frozen with fear Patricia stared at this Itnescomber. Was he the creature that took her son? "Do you have my son?" she asked. "Please, let me have him back, I miss him so much. We all miss him so much." Shocked and dismayed, Ruth stood beside her now. He glared at them both scornfully and said not a word. Then he turned and headed towards the forest.

"Able," Ruth blurted out. Able is that you?" He stopped dead in his tracks but did not turn around. "I'm so sorry Able; I never wanted this for you. Can you forgive me, son?" In the near distance was the sound of police sirens.

He continued to walk quickly towards the forest. "Please Able, give me back my Great-grandson. Please Able, I beg you." As she pleaded with the monster, she fell to the ground too weak, too upset to stand. He stopped again and before entering the forest he spouted. "Able is dead, old woman. He died a long time ago." Then he was gone.

Her heart ached with sorrow and guilt. She wanted so desperately to go after him but she couldn't, she just didn't have the strength.

Four police cruisers arrived at the same time. Guns out, the armed forces cautiously approached Isabel. Noticing she was unconscious, but not taking any chances one of them cuffed her hands and feet. Another radio in the situation.

There was a rustling in the bushes causing the officers to be on guard again. Two of them advanced towards the forest. While the others ready themselves for anything.

A small figure came running out. It didn't take long for everyone to see it was a little boy. "Patricia ran over to him. Creed!" she cried. Baby in one arm, she wrapped the other around him. "Thank God, you're okay."

Ruth looked towards the forest. She smiled to herself. Maybe there is a little good left in him after all. She thought.

The Darker Side of Light

Isabel sat in same room she had occupied for over ten years. She had to get out there. The little taste of freedom that she had, left her wanting more. She would play their game, if that's what it took. She was meeting with an attorney to discuss her case. With the old man offing himself, she had inherited a nice chuck of cash; enough to hire a good lawyer; one who could make a monster like herself look like an innocent victim of circumstance.

She heard the door unlock and Nurse Sandra walked in with two orderlies. "Your visitor is here Isabel." She announced. Isabel stood up slowly. "Oh, thank you Sandra." She said with enthusiasm as she stood and waited for the orderlies to put on her mask, arm restrains. "It's such a beautiful day, isn't it?" Sandra looked at her with some concern. She wasn't sure if it was the meds she was on or if Isabel was finally showing signs of improvement. "Yes, it is a beautiful fall day Isabel."

Modus operandi begun once again, a smirk of pure evil hid behind a dirty white mask. In her minds-eye, she played out her evil deeds over and over again; horrible, despicable deeds that would too soon become reality.

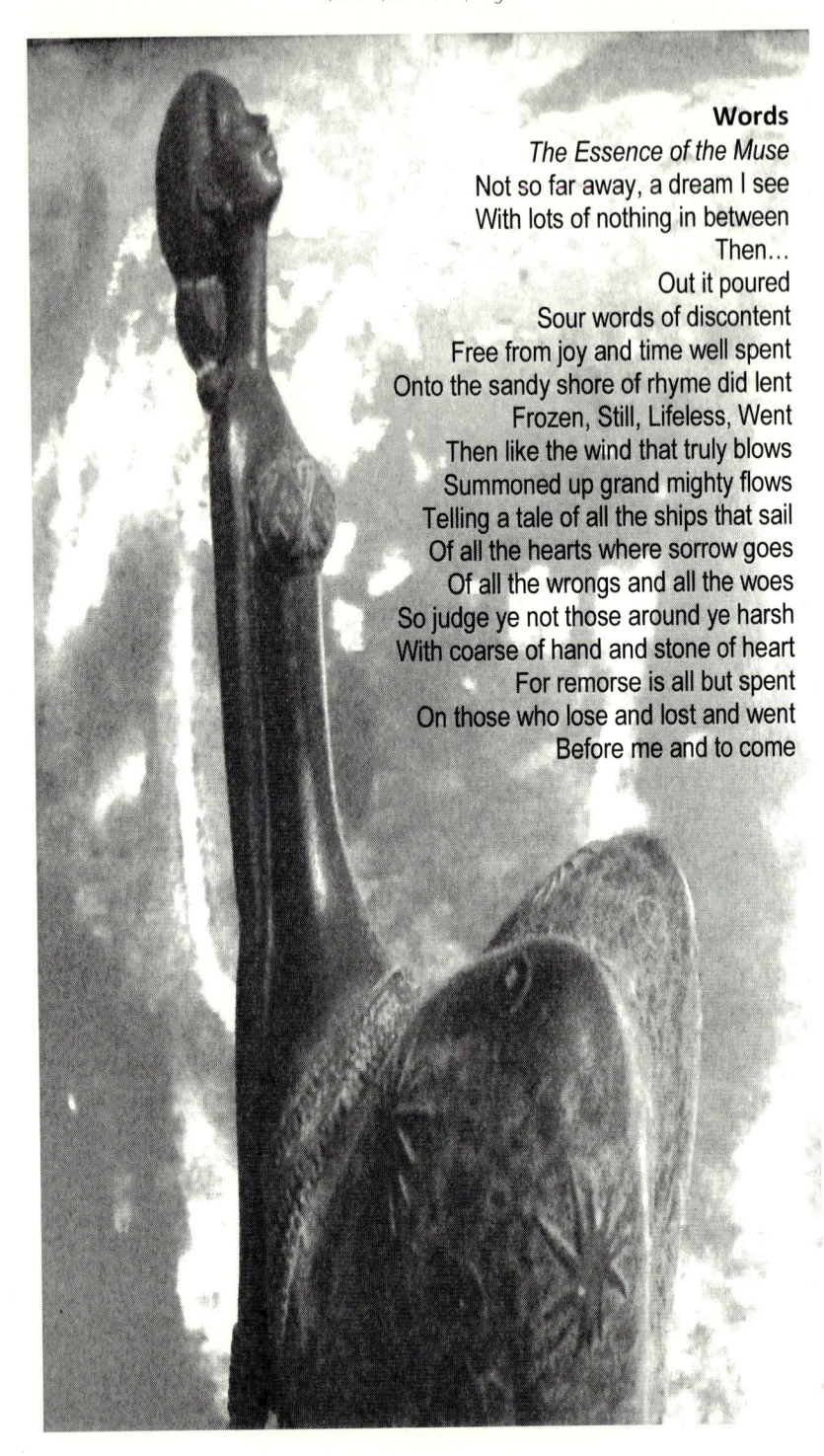

Words
The Essence of the Muse
Not so far away, a dream I see
With lots of nothing in between
Then…
Out it poured
Sour words of discontent
Free from joy and time well spent
Onto the sandy shore of rhyme did lent
Frozen, Still, Lifeless, Went
Then like the wind that truly blows
Summoned up grand mighty flows
Telling a tale of all the ships that sail
Of all the hearts where sorrow goes
Of all the wrongs and all the woes
So judge ye not those around ye harsh
With coarse of hand and stone of heart
For remorse is all but spent
On those who lose and lost and went
Before me and to come

Orla

I don't know how it started...oh wait, yes, I do. I was four or maybe five years old. I know this because I started senior kindergarten at Gulfstream public school two months earlier. I was very excited because I had just lost my first tooth. It seemed like all my school pals had started losing theirs, so the temptation to yank out one of my own had crossed my mind on more than one occasion -didn't want to be different, and besides the thought of getting money for my teeth was just too appealing (it makes one wonder if greed is innately born...). Anyhow, it turned out, I wouldn't need to. I was very careful not to lose the tooth and all day took special care to check my pocket by giving it a little pinch to make sure my new-found fortune was still there.

That night I went to bed more willingly than usual; *normally I made a fuss and tried to hide behind the couch.* I placed my tooth under my pillow, and closed my eyes tight hoping I could force sleep to come. It didn't of course- well not until it was ready to. It seemed the old sandman was a little behind schedule on this particular evening. Just my luck...

I should mention at this point my parents had not been getting along for quite some time and they fought constantly. I don't know if this has a direct influence on this little story but in hindsight it is a crucial part.

When morning came the first thing I did was check for my loot. To my dismay my little tooth was still under my pillow. I told my mom, who assured me that the tooth fairy was probably very busy and just didn't have time. "Just leave it under your pillow. I'm sure she'll come tonight." She assured me. I accepted that and went into my room to get ready for school. I could hear through the walls my parents; they were fighting again. Somehow in my mind I was responsible for the argument and I felt really empty inside.

The next night and the night after that my tooth remained under my pillow. I wondered if the tooth fairy would ever make it to my room. I didn't want to let my mother know because she had been crying a lot and I didn't want to make it worse. You know worrying about what might have happened to the tooth fairy and all.

The Darker Side of Light

I awoke one night to my parents fighting in the next room. Their blaring voices echoed enraged sentences that I could not understand. I heard a glass smash and loud bangs. My mother screamed a horrible gut wrenching sound. I wanted to go to her but I was too afraid. I sat up in my bed and hugged my pillow tight. Make it stop, make it stop… I repeated, over and over again.

Abrupt silence… I cried and cried so much so that my body shook and trembled. Why was this happening? I just didn't understand.

Then something amazing happened… A light appeared beside my bed. It was the most beautiful array of colours imaginable. I thought to myself it must be the tooth fairy, she's finally here to collect my tooth. I looked behind my back to get the tooth to hand it to her. It was gone. I must have sent it flying when I inadvertently grabbed my pillow.

"It's okay Laura." I heard a soft, low voice say. "My name is Orla and I'm here for you. I share your sadness and I am here to comfort you and tell you it is not your fault." Orla's light form changed into a solid outline revealing a forthcoming shape. Orla was not much bigger than I and she was very, very old. Her hair was pure white and her smiling blue eyes were kind and caring. She was very wrinkly but her skin was soft like kitten's fur. She hugged me gently, rocking me back and forth in her freckled arms. I can't express with words how safe I felt, how wanted I felt in that moment. All my troubles seemed to vanish and I was free from sorrow.

She held me for such a long time that I fell asleep in her arms. Morning came as it always does and my little room went from a shadowy darkness to light shades of yellow, and as more light filtered in slowly, I began to awake. Everything looked the same, my room had not changed, but my entire world was about to.

She told me that in my parents' bedroom something terrible had happened but I was not to look in. I was to get ready for school and leave the apartment. I wasn't afraid at all for some reason. I listen to what she told me and I went to school.

What happened next is kind of a blur and I don't remember much. I do know, I never went back to our apartment and I never saw my mother or father again for that matter. I went to live with my mother's sister Paula and her husband Gab in Vancouver B.C.

And although I missed my mom and dad at times, my life was very good.

It wasn't until after I got married and had a child of my own, did I start to wonder what happened to my own mom and dad. Sadly, by this time I had very little memory of either of them. And could barely remember what either of them looked like. I went to my aunt who had raised me as her own and questioned her. At first, she didn't want to tell me, but she knew I was an adult and could handle it. It turns out my dad was very jealous of my mom and in the heat of passion he killed her then took his own life. How tragic I thought, such a waste of life. I can't explain how separated I felt from them. I didn't feel sorrow for losing them as parents as much as I felt sorry they lost their lives for such an ill-fated reason. I, myself lived a full and meaningful life and was very happily married. I couldn't wrap my head around the life of my own parents for some reason.

It's strange though, how tragedy can afflict a person throughout their lives, and I was no exception to this rule.

When my first and only son Joshua was three years old, he was hit by a car and killed. I can't tell you how responsible I felt for his death. I didn't want to live and if not for my baby daughter Tamara, I would have ended it on that horrible day. Years went by and I still could not get over it… how could I? I was so stupid; I should have never taken him out of his car seat first. He would be alive today if I had just done things differently. But alas, I did not and he was dead. All the birthdays he would miss… all the Christmases, I thought about it constantly as I obsessed over him. Before I knew it, my daughter was three and instead of enjoying her, I continued to mourn the loss of her brother.

One night as I lay in bed beside my husband as usual I thought about Joshua. I prayed he could hear me and would forgive me for being such a horrible mother. I needed to go to where he was and hold him in my arms. My guilt would not let me see any other way. Not wanting to wake up my husband, I got up and went into the kitchen to sit and think. I felt so terribly depressed.

Sitting at the kitchen table hands covering my face, I felt a light touch on my hands. I moved them quickly away from my face to see who had touched me so softly. No one was there. I wasn't terribly surprised; after all I didn't really have my wits about me anymore. Then I heard a gentle voice call my name. "Laura…" I looked across the table in the direction of the voice. "It is I Orla, I am here for you Laura." She seemed familiar to me, but I couldn't remember why. I then recalled a memory buried too deep, too untouchable.

I started to cry when I finally recognized her. Tears of joy that she had returned when it seemed I needed her most. It was the little old woman who visited me on the night my parents tragically died. She looked different from what I remembered. A little younger and not so wrinkly, but her blue eyes remained the same, kind and caring. She spoke, "You must forgive yourself for what has happened Laura. I know it is a difficult thing that I ask, but it is the only way. You cannot live in the shadow of loss, for you are now the shadow and life is lost to you. You are needed in the world of the living, and as hard as it sounds, your son does not need you to mourn his life." I looked at her. How could she be so indifferent, of course I would mourn his loss, of course I was to blame.

"I have something to show you." She came close to me and as she stood beside me, she placed a hand on my shoulder. I remained seated, but the room seamed to spin around me wildly. I was in the same place but there were people all around. I could not move or talk; I could only watch and witness the turn of events. My three-year-old daughter was in the arms of her father. He was crying and being consoled by his mother. My daughter Tamara hung on to him tightly and I could hear her little voice. "I want my mommy." He patted her back to comfort her as he told her I was gone, and then he passed her off to his mother.

I wanted nothing more than to get up and take her in my arms, but alas, I could not. The room shifted and moved around me quickly again. This time Tamara was sitting across from me eating her breakfast. She was a little older and had long brown hair that was tied up in a ponytail. There was another woman, I had never seen before at the kitchen counter. I heard Tamara call her mom. As Tamara ate her cereal she reached two fingers into her mouth and made a strange face. Her little tooth had come lose and she took it out and looked at it for a moment. I felt excited for her and in my mind, I thought, "Go put it under your pillow Tamara for the tooth fairy. She sighed deeply then got up and threw it in the trash can. "No" I cried in vain. "Don't give up so easily."

The Darker Side of Light

Orla removed her hand from my shoulder and I was back. I felt different about my life from that moment on. I wanted to live and although I couldn't bring myself to forgiveness, I wanted to live for my daughter. I really did have a wonderful life…

When I was fifty-eight I developed breast cancer. It was a very difficult time for me. I recovered from the surgery but had to endure the effects of the treatments. The sickness was too much for me to handle and at times I felt I might be better off dead. "Why me?" I asked. "Haven't I suffered enough over the years?" I had a very supportive family whom I loved very much, but it just wasn't enough…

Depression overwhelmed my senses like a curse I just couldn't shake. I needed the one thing I didn't seem to have… strength. Strength to live, to fight for life, it was gone. And I didn't know where to find it.

I sat in my room alone with a full bottle of narcotics the doctor had prescribed for the pain. I felt so very sick and tired; tired of the sickness, tired of the pain, tired of living this way. Completely fed up with it all, I picked up the bottle that sat on my night table and held on to it firmly. My hands trembled and my body felt like a rubber ball that had lost its bounce. I had difficulty opening the lid, but I did it. Placing the lid on the night table I poured the content of the bottle into my hand and closed it tightly around them. "This is it." I said to myself. "I'm done."

"There is another way Laura." I heard a soft high-pitched voice say. I turned and looked around the room. No one was there. "Laura." I heard the fresh voice say again. Then I saw her as clear as a bell. "It is I Orla; I am here for you, to help you through this most difficult of times." She appeared before me, not as an old woman but as a youthful child of ten or so. She was a lovely little girl with curly blonde hair and big, bold dimples that accompanied a warm and caring smile. The only feature that was remotely recognizable was her lovely kind blue eyes. "Is that really you Orla?" I asked in desperation. "Yes, it is I." she replied.

She sat beside me on the bed, and taking the hand that contained my fate she removed it from me. "It is going to be okay," she said. "You are through the worst of it. You just need to hold on a little longer." Then she smiled sweetly at me and I felt comfort in my heart. She stayed with me and held my hand for the rest of the night and when the night finally ended so too did my sickness. I can't explain it, it was just gone. That morning I got a call from my daughter Tamara - she was pregnant, I would be a grandmother for the first time. I was so excited and looked forward to the birth of my first grandchild.

When I was eighty-four, I sat on the balcony of the retirement home where I stayed, and as I looked out over the ocean I reflected on my life's course. I lived a full life and experienced many sad but also joyful times with my family and friends. As I looked to my left, Orla sat beside me on a chair. A lovely child of four or five, she reached out and touched my old, wrinkled, freckled hand gently; her touch soft like kitten's fur. "I'm here with you Laura." She said smiling warmly. "I have always been right here beside you." I looked into her innocent little face. How beautiful she was. At that moment, I somehow knew she had always been with me. Through bad times and good, she was always by my side.

I felt comfort in her words and completeness in her presence; and as we both skipped off hand and hand two youthful spirits that had shared a common experience, a common bond… I knew I would also be there for her… LIFE

Indulging Poverty

Poverty knocked upon my door.

At first pretending not to hear,
I hesitated then answered, "Yes dear."

"May I come in and sit awhile?"
She said curved of lip to make a smile.

"For I'm tired and want of rest,
And feel your home is by far the best."

Opening the door as wideness would allow,
She stepped one foot and then another.
Then commented, "I shall be no bother."

Silent in demeanour there,
Misery in the form of grace,
She casually looked around the place.

"Sit awhile," I gestured to her.
"Tell me all your news."
The entertainment of a muse.

I served her tea and cookies.
She indulged my loss and woe.
Oh, how could I say no?

Sorrow grabbed and held me tight.
Consumed by the lack of need,
The wants of another breed.

"How long will you be staying now?"
I asked as I went and closed the curtains.
She said, "I am not certain."

We commiserated, talked, and had more tea.

She kept me up all of the night.
"Alas, I see the morning light.
You should rest, before it is too bright…
Weary morning is near in sight…

The Darker Side of Light

Your complexion fair, may fade to grey.
And you being self-contained,
Will suffer great with some distain.
Sleep will find you comfort now."
I said to her then took a bow.

Tucking her securely into bed;
"Close eyes and rest," I said.

When she awoke, to her surprise,
She was alone, all by herself.
A note I left upon the shelf.

'Sorry I couldn't see you wake,
For welcome in my home was fake.
I am in need, but that's not all…
A traitor to you, I do appear,
For prosperity draws me near.
And I being who I am,
Must rise and make my stand.
For abundance is close at hand.
And although I find you most appealing,
Familiar to your gaunt;
I'm afraid I do not enjoy your haunt.
So, in closing I would like to state;
I wish you well and by the way,
Please don't call another day.
…And when you see fit
To leave my humble home
Please do not mess about,
And lock the door on your way out!'

I.H.R
L.N.C

Incumbent thoughts

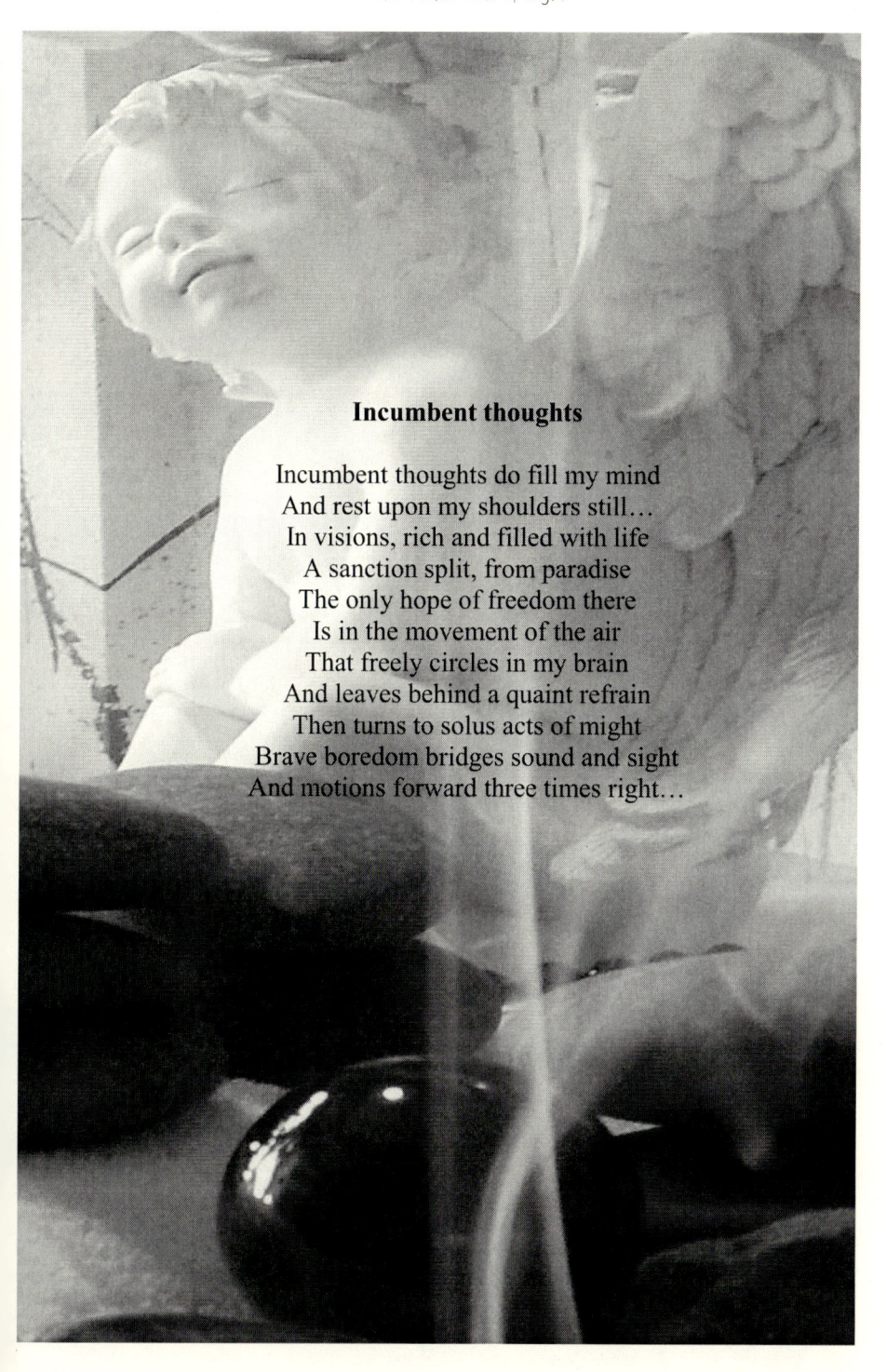

Incumbent thoughts do fill my mind
And rest upon my shoulders still…
In visions, rich and filled with life
A sanction split, from paradise
The only hope of freedom there
Is in the movement of the air
That freely circles in my brain
And leaves behind a quaint refrain
Then turns to solus acts of might
Brave boredom bridges sound and sight
And motions forward three times right…

An excerpt from the diary of a mad house slave

Day one: It has begun once again. Starting as a small but meager pile of still lifeless form. Contained only by the frail bars of reform, silent and still… The only reminisce of rebellion is marked by the odd broken bar holding diligent captives. I will wait for another sign.

Day two: Somehow it is growing, moving, shifting. Somehow this collective mass has formed a central brain, an intelligent life force causing it to reproduce, to multiply. The smells of this copulation invade the senses like the plague. Numbed by the sour opisqualting odor, I must retreat.

Day three: The oddities are too numerous to count now. Over flowing there holding cell. Breeding while I watch it seems. Massive clumps of endless matter. I can barely stand the sight, let alone the smell. Silent voices cry out; Calls for change, for purification spill over endlessly. Consumed by paralyzing thoughts of anguish and discord, I slave to this transformation know I must comply with the ritual. I will try to resist one more day…

Day four: I had great difficulty sleeping last night. My brain ached as thoughts of my condescending dilemma dogged my dreams repeatedly, causing fits of restless wake. Dawn, blessed morning I await thee…

And now I stand before it. Here where a spastic breeding frenzy has taken place. Amongst a fortitude of colours confused, and I bewildered. Amongst a contrived bouquet of stench and endless aromas. As I stand limp I know what I must do.

Laundry day is upon us, and I slave to my own fate comply…

Betsy Bouncy Doll

Little Molly Minden begged her mother please…
Could I have a Betsy bouncy doll for Christmas?
I've been good all year you see
And I really want one, everybody does
And if I don't get one, I think I'm going to bust…
We'll see, we'll see, her mother cried
Don't bug me about it now
I'm far too busy to think of toys
I've other things to do…
Write it down, make a list
And later I will look at it for you
Well that's just what little Molly did; she wrote it all by herself
And the day before Christmas, her mother found it on the shelf
Oh my, oh my, her mother thought, she felt a right old louse
And quickly grabbed her coat and purse ran out of the house
Panic started to set in as she went from store to store
Every one of them was sold out, not one Betsy bouncy doll about
Oh, the tears that would flow when her daughter started crying
Christmas would be ruined and not from lack of trying
I'll have a look at the list and see what's exactly on it
Then her eyes filled with tears
Lost and not knowing what to do
She sat upon the bench and cried a little too
Paper wrapped tightly in her fruitless fist
For it was the only blasted thing on the list…
Well I guess that's that, there's no point in crying
They're all gone, so what's the point in trying?
And as she got up to leave her heart began to race
Who could have guessed it would be sitting in that place?
It was a Betsy Bouncy doll sitting on the shelf
Right next to the oversized bras, right next to a lady elf
And as she raced over to it, she felt she'd struck it rich
And as she reached to grab it, she thought, oh this is it!
What joy she felt, what happiness
Christmas would be saved and the road to bliss now paved
Until a hand came down upon hers and ended quickly her dream
It turned out someone else's mom, thought the exact same thing
They looked at each other
She said, I got it first and as she grabbed it close to her
The women hit her with her purse
A fight broke out and Betsy bouncy fell to the floor
Another woman screamed out loud

The Darker Side of Light

There's more of them in isle four!"
It was a mad frenzy as the ladies fought and yelled
That is until the manager showed up and stopped the brawling bunch
Which was a good thing because Molly's mother was about to take a punch
Ladies, ladies, shame on you, I know what we can do
We'll go up to my office and view the tape on channel two
Then we'll see just who is who and who had dips on Betsy first
I did, yelled Molly's mother, and then *she* hit me with her purse…
Calm down, there's no need to fight
I will make this right…
And when it was over, Molly's mother knew she'd won
A smile of satisfaction on her face, she beamed from ear to ear
Christmas would be great this year
On Christmas morn, little Molly was so happy and relieved
She got her Betsy bouncy doll, her Christmas was complete
She placed it neatly on a table and ran off to play with friends
But not before she told her mom, "thanks you're the living end…"
Then one week after Christmas, the madness long forgot
She found Betsy Bouncy doll lying in the same spot
It seemed that Molly had forgot she'd wanted her so bad
It seems that Molly didn't know the trouble her mother had
How could she have known the folly created by this one small dolly?

Next year, Molly's mother thought, I wouldn't mess about
And if someone tries to fight with me, I'll just knock them out

Little fruit fly Sally

Little fruit fly Sally loved to socialize with other fruit fly flies
But more than that she loved to eat tasty bits of fruits and pies
And although time was a factor that was sure to be her demise
She didn't seem to mind and happily she flew around to dine and socialize
Oh, what a life, so much to do and so little time it was true…
Roaming around the place that she called home,
trying to find tasty bits of fruit to chew upon
But alas she found none and all her friends were gone…
What to do, what to do, what to do???
Hunger hit her quickly as did loneliness,
as little fruit fly Sally tried to make sense of it
Here one moment then gone the next,
Sally thought she had met her match
As madness fell upon her and anger took a toll
Sally ate what she could find and talked to the toilet bowl
She grew larger than what was to be expected and mightier than most
But she couldn't fly because her little wings they did not grow
Some say it was an accident, but I say it was fate
The way little Sally fruit fly took a dive that day
"Good bye for now cruel world," she cried out in vain
"I'll be back, you'll see me again…"
Then she was gone but not for long,
like that bird from the ashes
Sally rose above it all and gathered in the masses
The rest of this tale is plain to see, if you know of the fruit fly power
Here one moment, gone the next then back within the hour…

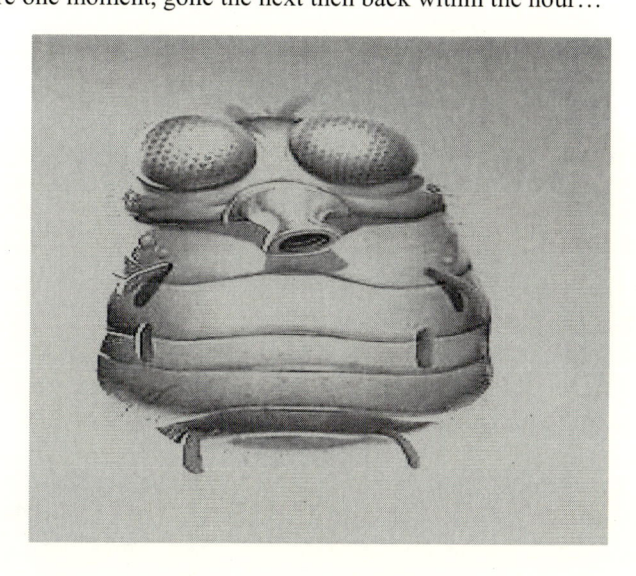

In keeping with Robert Service
As I was walking down the street one day
A stranger I chanced to meet
He stopped me there and said hello
Then stared upon my feet
Nice shoes he said
I mean, did you buy them here or what?
It took me back the words he spoke; I thought he was a nut...
He must have recognized my concern
As he quickly apologized in turn
So, mate he said of late, you see I had the exact same pair
I bought them in Italy when I was over there
He paused for mere seconds as he re-grouped his thoughts
And as he spoke, I felt my stomach turn and twist and knot
My wife and I, well we've had some words
And she quickly gave me the sack
All my things she gave away
And I've yet to get them back
A sad look on his face, he slowly said size 10?
As he nodded with a gesture
Lovely shoes...
You won't find another pair like them again my friend
I wondered at his choice of words
And wondered why he cared
And furthermore, I wondered why he persistently stared...
Shallow thoughts invaded my heart
For I knew in this my part
I must be on my way, I said
Off home to feed the cat
Then in a lowly voice he said
I'd really like them back...
Well if truth be told as should be now
I really must confess
I paid a pretty penny for this comfort on my feet to rest
Never had I ever wore, the likes of shoes so fine
Never had I ever felt a feeling so divine
How can I express the ease that soothes a weary sole
Or frees the mind of burden, a taxed and tearing toll
So, pretending not to care, my heart filled with disgrace
As thoughts went rushing through my mind
A cold and empty place...
I felt somehow, he must have known
I got them at his place.

The Darker Side of Light

Once upon a Sorry Time

Weird and Wacky Tales & Other Such Nonsense
Linda Noble-Cordy

Psychological Ramble
I would like to make mention of a fact, simple and true
This little story, I made out of the blue
It is complete and utter nonsense if truth be said
A brain tickle, a fluff, a joke to be read
For a test of verbatim is naturally fine
When one reads behind the line
And looks deeper, then deeper still
And weighs the freedom of the will

Once upon a time, there lived in the town of Sorry, Bedlam, a boy named Train. He had one mother named Elda, who he saw every day except during the week and most weekends. And in the father department he had four, none of which had any given names to speak of. Having so many fathers and not enough mothers, he seldom knew a parent's care. As a matter of fact, they didn't even know he existed, for the most part.

I should mention at this time, that Train is a boy of seasoned years. How many seasons? I'm not quite sure... only to say his boyhood years had ended long before the boy in him had. That being established – and do to the fact that he was indeed a boyish-man – rather than a mannish-boy – Train decided it was time to head out on his own to find himself, because he certainly couldn't find himself at home, *it appeared no one could...*

...Hence a story is born

Having packed a bag of unmentionables; which included an extensive collection of buttons and what-knots; Train sat down and composed a brief note for his mother to find one day. The letter began as most letters do – with endearment - *Dearest Elda...*

In the note, he explained why he was leaving; *that he was setting out with the hopes of finding the life he was somehow missing.*

Stepping through the front door he turned and returned a wave goodbye to the photo of his four fathers that hung on the adjacent wall. Then with a deep sigh he closed the door and *naturally* headed east, not out of choice but out of necessity.

He journeyed along a well-travelled path for as long as he could. Running out of an eastwardly passage, he had no other choice but to travel north. Which was fine with him because the sun had been

The Darker Side of Light

shining in his eyes the whole time and it was really starting to bother him.

After travelling in a northerly direction for a very long time, he sat for a long-needed break. As he ate a bit of what have you - and causally sipped on a flask of hot tea; his mind wondered far off into his future. Content with his thoughts, he decided he would write to his fathers' whenever he could and he would call his mother on the phone when he got there (his future that is). Smiling, he got up and continued his journey in search of a life outside of Sorry, Bedlam.

Before he knew it, he was out of sidewalk again, and would have to take the only path that remained. He was kind of happy about it all in all, because the wind blew furiously in his face the whole time and he had grown tired from fighting with it.

Making a left turn he headed west. "Yes," he thought, "finally I'm on the right path I can feel it in my bones." The wind was no longer a problem and the sun- well it was starting to set, so he felt he could put up with it for the time being.

He would need to find a place to sleep for the night, he decided.

Taking an *unnatural* path, he ended up in front of a house he felt most comfortable with. Knocking on the door, there soon after, a nice lady answered it. "Well hello to you fine sir" she said. "Hello to you." He replied. "Can I help you?" She asked. "Yes, I believe you can." He perceived. "I am a traveler on my way to better days. May I stay here this evening, my good gentle lady?" He inquired. "Why of course you may young man." She replied. "Come in."

He entered a room he felt most comfortable in and sat beside the fireside. "I'm making supper would you like a bit?" she asked. "Oh, yes please." He said. "I'm starving." After having eaten his supper, and after having washed up and all, she showed him to a room and said. "If this room is suitable to you good sir, you may sleep in here tonight. It is my son's room, and as you can clearly see, he is not here." "And will he not be using it; will he not be back for it?" He inquired. "Not that I'm aware of." she replied smiling warmly.

The Darker Side of Light

Looking around the room, he liked what he saw and felt content. He turned to her and spoke. "This will do just fine good lady, I thank you." And with a nod of his head he said. "Good night."

In the morning, he would set out early before the sun starts to rise, he decided. He would leave a note for the good lady, thanking her for her kindness and generosity. And of course, leave the customary fee. If you're wondering what the customary fee is in Sorry, Bedlam, you'll have to go for a visit to find out.

In the morning, way before the sun began to rise, he set out. Because it was so very dark still, a path could not be seen with the naked eye. He decided then and there it wasn't worth looking for. He turned right instead of going straight; it just felt right to him. Beneath his feet was not the *normal* pavement, instead the ground was soft and lumpy. He tripped over a large rock and fell down, rolling over into some water. Shaking off the wet, he continued on until he reached a hill. By this time the stars began to fade and the light of day descended upon the land. A light breeze travelled beside him as he climbed up the Waverly hill (this by the way, was also the name of the hill). He could see behind him in the far-off distance the little town of Sorry. How small and insignificant it appeared from this view. He wondered if the good lady had found his note of gratitude and the customary fee he had left for her.

He travelled on until he came to a dirty little town. Walking passed a sign that read: **You are now entering the town of Have-Not - population unknown**. And in small print at the bottom of the sign it read: *Who really cares anyways?* "Good point," he thought aloud, "but very useless."

When I had mentioned the town was dirty, I meant it…

The dust and dirt flew in the air and desperately needed someone or something to tie it down. There were no sidewalks to speak of and the homes and businesses all seemed to be under some form of construction.

Train looked down at his feet as they were growing increasingly heavy. He hadn't noticed until this point that his shoes were covered in thick blackish grey mud. "That settles it then. It looks like I'm stuck here for a while." He proclaimed.

The Darker Side of Light

He managed to make his way to an Inn that only took up half the corner of a street; do to the fact that it was only half built. It was lucky for him he had packed the what-knots because this turned out to be the only unofficial currency they accepted here. The nice Inn keeper gave him the best room in the place; the corner suit, the view was exceptionally good, having no external walls to speak of. As Train gazed out at the sites that lay before him he felt a sense of satisfaction. "So much opportunity lies before me here." He surmised. "Why just look at all the commotion that is going on in this dirty little town of Have Not. Just look at all the people working and planning...building and doing-- things..." He decided in that moment, and with that thought, he would wait for his future to find him there. "No point in getting *my* shoes dirty," he thought. Looking down at his feet he chuckled to himself when he remembered they already were.

As time passed more and more people came to the little town of Have-Not, and the town seemed to complete itself around him. Even his room with the exceptional view changed dramatically.

Untouched by change, soon after, the mud that stuck to his shoes dried up and fell off. "It's hopeless here, how will my future ever find me in such a place," he concluded. "It's time to move on," he thought. A little older, but none the wiser, Train gathered up his belongings and headed out in the direction he originally took.

Passing the sign, he once passed a short time ago, he looked at it from the inside. It read: You are now leaving our little town, hope you enjoyed your stay. And in small print at the bottom of the sign it read: *Who really cares anyways?* "Good point," he thought aloud, "but very useless."

He stood just on the other side of Have-Not and wondered what was next. He contemplated his stay in the town, and felt somehow it was a complete and utter waste of time. Valuable time he could have spent finding himself- *finding his life.*

Looking back at the sign from the outside, he noticed it had change from its original posting. It now said; **Welcome to the town of Haves. Not to be confused with the whence town of Have-Not.** Confused still further and bitter to boot, he stated, 'Haves' did not part upon me any favour... useless that's what it was. I think I'll travel onward. Onward and upward..." Which was really quite fitting, because he stood at the base of a gigantic mountain.

The Darker Side of Light

Half way up the mountain he met a man who appeared to be standing on one leg. He was babbling incessantly under his breath, and Train couldn't understand what he was saying. Perplexed, the likes of this sort he had heard about, but never had actually seen before.

Train asked him what he could possibly gain from standing there on one leg, talking to himself. And stated matter-of-factly - that he could not see any use for such action.

The babbling man responded after some deliberation;

Well my dear young lad,
If you really must ask
It's a question of being
And of not really seeing
As much as to say
If you really must know
I stand on one leg
Cause I'm hoping to grow
Not in the sense that
You're thinking does tax
But more in the sense
Of a matter of facts…

As he looked over his left shoulder he added. "At least I have a leg to stand on… unlike my old friend Helm over there, who does not." Train eyed a form up against a locust tree in the far-off distance. The torso waved to him and yelled out something Train couldn't quite make out. As he waved back, the one-legged poet spouted, "Where are my manners? I'm afraid I almost forgot them entirely."

My name is Truss Philpot the Third,
Once Deputy General to a Kingdom of Nerds
That is until the spring of forty-five
When the great panic hit
And we ran for our lives.
And who might you be my find young man?
Are you also on the run?
Felt the need, so you ran?

"My name is Train, and I am not on the run necessarily, more like on a quest." he replied. With a puzzled look on his face Truss commented.

Train, just Train, have you no other?
What of your father, what of your mother?
Have they not a name they have given to you?
A name for name sake like Thomas or Stew.

"No, they didn't, well not that I'm aware of," Train replied despondently.

Truss stared at Train with the most serious look on his face, and then after some contemplation he spoke.

That's just not right,
That will never do
I'll tell you what,
I'll give one to you.
If you like, I will give you my name
The one that I have,
The one in the same.
Philpot the fourth
It's fitting, it's fine
A name worthy of taking
And I really don't mind.

Train didn't know what to say. He really didn't care either way, so he shrugged his shoulders and said, "Okay, thank you." Then he added, "Why poetry, Truss Philpot the Third? Why converse in rhyme? Haven't you heard that poetry is a dying art?" The one-legged poet intently gazed into the eyes of the inquisitive young man and profoundly said.

Even the dying
Has the right
To breathe in
Its last breath
So let living …live
And the dying …die"

Train nodded his head in agreement and thought to himself –Good point, but completely useless.

Looking towards the torso of the elderly gentlemen he asked. "So what's his deal then, how did he lose his legs?"

Truss sighed deeply and began,
We don't talk much about it any more
It's been a long time
Much more than before
And it's taken a toll on him as sure as can be
And if it goes any further they'll be nothing see.

Train's attention was then captured by the voice of Helm, who at that very moment was making his way towards him. Pulling himself across the ground he yelled in a panicky state, "Wait, wait… I have something of the utte most importance to say. Don't listen to Philpot! He doesn't know what he is talking about. The old fool…"

Finally reaching Train, he plopped himself up against a nearby tree. Out of breath and at his wits end, it took him a good minute before he was able to speak. But when he did he looked straight at Train and spoke in the most serious of tones. "My dear young, lad… I am Helm Rich, I'm sure you have heard of me." Train wanted to say yes, but he would have been lying. "No sir, I haven't heard of you." A little disappointed Helm commented as he cast a glare at Truss. "Just as well. Some of the details are not pleasant by any means." Then he added, "I have some good, solid advice for you, would you like to hear it young man?" Truss broke in. "You're not going to start with that old ramble again?" Helm raised his hand to silence Truss. "Tut, tut, Truss, times they are a changing. And besides I have the floor. No one wants to hear your rhymes anymore." Helm smiled to himself when he realized what he had just said, and then looked at Train for a response. "Well young man, what will it be, do you want some good advice or don't you?" Train couldn't see any harm in it. "Sure, why not." He replied.

"Right then, listen carefully, because the information I'm about to give you grown men would kill for." "*Or be killed for.*" Truss said under his breath as he shook his head in disappointment.

Helm took a deep breath in and stared deeply into Train's eyes. "Always give more than you've got and never take more than you can give. For it is in the giving and the taking that a wise man's destiny is folly." Then he winked at Train. Train stood there silent with a puzzled look on his face. He didn't have a clue as to what the old man was getting at. He wanted to say – *What kind of advice is that?* But he decided against it. Instead he said, "Thank you for your wise words, I'll remember that."

Helm clapped his hands together and with great excitement he spouted. "You see Truss, you see, times they are a changing." Still excited he announced, "Time for tea old boy, and break out the fruit cake, a celebration is in order!"

After tea and cake Train announced that he would be heading up and out. "I would like to reach the top by night fall." He said his goodbyes, but not before thanking them both for their hospitality. And adding, "Thanks again for your good advice Helm Rich, I'm sure it will come in handy one day." Helm nodded his head in agreement, the look of satisfaction all over his face he proclaimed, "Right you are young man, right you are…"

When he finally reached the top, the sun was beginning to set. He felt very light headed and forgot just about everything he knew and had experienced up to this point. This really didn't seem to bother him in the slightest, as he felt he hadn't really learnt anything, anyways… Resting for the course of the night, when he woke he continued from where he had left off. He had no place else to go but down… which took him the better part of the day.

Near the base of the mountain was a lake called Cap, or so the sign read. He thought it might be short for something but he wasn't sure for what.

Here he met a talking fish who politely introduced himself as 'Osmos the amazing seer fish.' He told Train that he could see into the future on most days and into the past on the rest. Osmos asked Train if he was interested in knowing what his future held for a small fee. "A fee?" Train questioned. "What possible use have you for such things Fish? It's not like you can leave the lake, or even carry with you such burdens." Osmos was upset by Trains comments for he hadn't seen it coming.

"What say you boy, to judge me, when it is you that cannot leave; having really never ever any place to call home? You see you cannot leave something you have never had, having never had it in the first place - in other words. And as for burdens… well I may not carry them as you do, but I can carry them nonetheless." Train was surprised at how sensitive the fish actually was. "I'm sorry Osmos, I didn't mean to offend you in any possible way." He stated. "Too late you already have." The fish announced.

Train was very interested in knowing his future, but not until he got to it, he told Osmos, who was somehow surprised at the answer. And if not for the fact that it was most days, he would have excused the reply.

"I'll tell you what," he began. "I will waive the fee, for a charge, if it suits your needs." Then to sweeten the pot a little more he added, "I know what you are looking for and where you will find it." This caught Train's attention and he agreed to the charge.

Unfortunately, the sun was beginning to set. And it turned out to be the end of most days at Lake Cap… and having really no interest in his past – having already lived it, he thanked Osmos the amazing seer fish and headed on his way. Resting only to sleep the night, he awoke the next morning refreshed and somewhat lighter.

Entering a quiet town by its back street, he wasn't sure where he was exactly. He spied a lady across the way that looked friendly enough so he approached her with a friendly hello. For some reason, she screamed at him very loudly and ran off in the other direction. That's odd he thought. That has never happened to me before.

Passing by a small crowd of people he created the same response. What is going on? He thought. Are the people of this town completely mad? As he passed by a store front window, looking in to see if there might be any normal folk inside, he caught a reflection on the window pane. He screamed, and jumped back. Then he quickly realized it was his own reflection he was seeing, and that he was missing his head.

No wonder everyone was afraid of him. He now understood what Osmos the amazing seer fish was about to reveal to him. It was a pity he didn't stick around to hear his past, because more likely than not, his missing head would have been found, he surmised.

He would need to go back to Lake Cap and find the talking fish again. And hope that he wasn't too angry with him for leaving so soon…

The Darker Side of Light

As he walked back to the lake he tried to think where he could have possible have lost his head. He was sure he had it when he woke from his sleep on the mountain top, but he really couldn't be sure. Considering the fact, he didn't even know it was missing until it was brought to his attention. And even then, he had to see it for himself. *He wondered how that was even possible…*

When he reached the lake, the amazing fish was nowhere in sight. Instead he met a turtle sitting on the grass by the lake; who also seemed to be missing his head.

Train approached him and spoke. "Hello." He tapped on his shell. "Are you home?" "I'm looking for Osmos the amazing seer fish, do you know him good turtle, can you tell me where I might find him?" he questioned.

From inside the shell he heard a small voice that sounded very, very far away. "Usually one waits for a cordial reply before engaging in inconsequential conversation my boy, after all…" He waited for him to finish his sentence, he didn't. He waited a little longer. Then longer still…

"Well do you know where I can find him? Hello…" He tapped on the shell again and then again, harder this time and yelled, "Hello, can you tell me where to find him?" A very annoyed turtle popped his head out. "Find who?" he yelled. What are you on about boy? Can't you see that I am very busy…?"

He noticed he was missing his head. "Well I guess you can't, can you? Get your head out boy, what's the matter with you? Everyone knows you don't go around bothering folk, and engage in inconsequential conversation with your head tucked in, after all."

"After all, after all what?" Train questioned. "There he goes again…" he said to someone other than Train. Train, not seeing anyone else, responded. "He -do you mean me?" He looked around just in case there was someone other than his headless self there. He heard another voice coming from inside the turtle's shell but couldn't quite make out what it was saying. Then he heard, "I told you he was thick." "Who was that?" Train asked rather concerned. The turtle shook his head at him in disapproval and said scornfully, "Who was what boy? You're not making any

Weird and Wacky Tales & Other Such Nonsense
Linda Noble-Cordy

The Darker Side of Light

sense with your head in your shell, come out and state your business, after all."

Train replied, "I don't have a shell good turtle, I've…" The turtle cut him short, "Nonsense boy, everyone has a shell. What makes you any different?" Then he heard a little voice from inside the shell say. "Tell him to go away." "Who is that?" he demanded. "Is that Osmos the amazing seer fish, because if it is, I demand he tells me where my head is?"

The turtle popped his head back in his shell. Train placed his head –*if he had one*, next to the shell to get a better listen. It was difficult to hear having no ears, but from what he could make out the turtle was conversing with someone who was not happy with Train's return. "Get rid of him Fel, he's not getting it back. It's mine fair and square! A charge is a charge, as anyone knows." It was Osmos and it was he who pinched his head.

*I would like to say; right out from under his nose, but the nose was gone too.

The turtle popped his head back out and smiled at Train and said, "I guess proper introductions are in order despite the minor setbacks. My name is Felship the second and who might you be headless boy?" "I think you already know, seeing how you are harboring the criminal who undoubtedly appropriated my head in a most ill-mannered way.

"Nonsense!" came a little voice from within. Then Osmos made a most unusual appearance. Squeezing out from between the shell and the side of the turtles neck he spoke. "You agreed to the charge did you not?" "But you tricked me. How can you charge me for the charge? That's like taxing the tax; you can't take something before its time and then claim it as the object of interest, of the thing sought after…"

Train was confusing himself. "To put it in simpler terms," he said. "You never once mentioned that I would be looking for My Own Head, and that I would find it in your possession." "A minor setback I can assure you. If you hadn't left in such a hurry, I would have revealed your past – as the charge had been applied by this point. And although I was under no obligation in telling you your past –only your future that was the agreement, I would have out of the goodness of my heart." Osmos concluded.

Felship interjected. "Why don't you just give the lad back his head? You haven't any use for it anyways, after all." "True," said Osmos. "It's not like it holds any validity, importance or consequence for that matter. And it is terribly heavy for such an empty vessel." Train was happy to hear that – not that his head was of no significance, as much as the fact that Osmos felt it so.

"There is one little problem though, which I think is more than obvious." Osmos added. "I haven't got it with me at the moment. I've seemed to have left it somewhere and for the life of me I can't remember where."

As most people are aware, fish have very short attention spans. Even though Osmos was an amazing seer fish, he didn't have much in the way of a memory department.

"Think fish, think! How can you call yourself 'Osmos the amazing seer fish' when you can't see where you, yourself have left things!" Felship demanded. "I can't work under all this pressure." Osmos cried. Then trying to make Train change his mind about having and needing a head in the first place he stated. "What do you need a head for any ways boy? It will only weigh you down. I had a hell of a time trying to move it, and besides that one didn't have much in it to speak of. You look just fine without one, doesn't he Fel?"

Felship looked intently at Train's body and commented. "It could take some getting used to after all." "And besides," Osmos added. "It doesn't affect your hearing and seeing, does it?" Train shook the place where the head should have been, and said no. "Well then no harm done." Osmos concluded.

Train's stomach kicked in. "How am I to eat, I'm getting very hungry?" He stated. Osmos looked over at Felship then back to Train and sighed. "That is a problem, isn't it? Could you maybe just... no, that wouldn't work."

"Get on with it fish, find the boy's head and be done with it, after all." Felship demanded.

There was only one way Osmos would be able to find Train's head. He would have to do a reading for him. And in order to do that he would need to collect a fee or a charge. Train did not want

The Darker Side of Light

another charge so he agreed to a fee. "I have buttons and what-knots, what do you prefer Osmos?" he questioned. "Do you have a gold button?" Osmos questioned with some excitement. Train looked through his bag of buttons and found a small gold one. As he passed it to Osmos, he thought, it would have been simpler if I had just paid the fee in the first place. "Here you go." He said.

Osmos the amazing seer fish jump into the water and disappeared for some time. Train was beginning to get concerned that he had been hoodwinked again. He turned to Felship and said, "Does it always take this long to have a reading done?" "Patience my boy, all in good time, after all." Felship responded despondently.

Much more time was passing. Train was almost certain he had been fooled again. Then, just as he was about to give up and except the fact that he would have to go through the rest of his life, headless, the fish was back. He was glowing bright green, and seemed to be floating just above the water line.

"We have travelled far and we have seen much," He stated in an unusual tone. "We can tell you, you will find your head again and that you will be all the wiser when finding it. Your path is set and you must comply to your fate, least you make another one." Then he added in his normal voice. "Which by the way, I will not be responsible for."

Train looked over at Felship, who looked just as confused as Train was feeling. "Is that it?" he said as turned his attention back to Osmos, "Is that all you can tell me? I waited all that time for nothing?"

Train looked at Felship again for help in this matter. He just silently tucked his head in his shell and did not come back out. It all seemed so hopeless. "Where is my head Osmos?" He insisted. Then in the strange voice again the amazing seer fish added. "We see your head is right where you left it."

Train was very angry at his words, he spouted. "*But you took my head Osmos, remember?* You were supposed to find out where *you* put it, not where I left it!" "That is all we have to say on this matter. If you wish to know more, it will cost you another gold button."

Train was furious. He stormed off, not knowing where he was really going, or what he was about to do. But he had every intention of somehow having a nice fish and chip dinner for supper that night.

*Little did anyone know (except for the ones who lived or ventured there) that at the bottom of Cap lake was Cap City. And like most cities it had its share of criminals. It was a well-known fact in Cap City that Osmos the seer fish was a bit of a scoundrel and cheat, and that he had an awful addiction to particle plankton; which by the way is highly addictive to most fish. It was for that reason he had tried to trade Train's head (which turned out to be far too heavy for him to move). A Gold button on the other hand was easily transported and was as good as gold bullion in Cap City. It bought a hefty amount of particle plankton if the truth be told, and it was for that reason and that reason only Osmos made his grand prediction-with the hopes of cheating Train out of a few more gold buttons.

Train walked past the Lake Cap sign and tripped over an awkwardly placed rock and fell to the ground hard. He screamed out loud, and grabbed the air for a nose that was not there; as he had a terrible pain where the nose should be. He sat for a moment and wondered what it was he had fallen so hard over, to hurt an appendage he no longer had.

Then he noticed a familiar face; it was his own, he had found it. At that very moment, he realized he had kicked himself in the head. A little worse for wear, he placed it back on, and then wiped the blood off his nose. He was happy to be whole again, even though the weight of it was noticeable now.

Maybe the fish was right. He considered for a moment going back to find out what else the fish had to tell him about his future, but then he remembered what a swindler he really was and changed his mind.

In the far-off distance, he could see a line of movement. Curious to what it might be, he began to run towards it. His head felt a little odd, having been off for a time. Funny he thought, if I hadn't known it was missing, I don't think I would have missed it.

With a little less space between himself and the moving monstrosity, he could see it was a caravan of sorts. It was making its way towards the massive gates of a city cordoned off from the rest of the world. As far as the eye could travel was a high horizontal wall.

His curiosity peeked with enthusiasm when the guards that walked on the wall-top came into view. His mind wandered to fanciful places as he envisioned the treasures that awaited him inside. "Maybe here is where I shall find myself," he thought with some intrigue.

The skies darken as the night neared. Then in a flash, a neon light appeared on the great wall. It read – **Welcome to The Side of Freedom - The Endless Forest of Green's Pass.**

"Awe," Train signed with immense disappointment as his illusions of grandeur went up in smoke.

Coming from the town of Sorry, Bedlam, Train had heard tales of this city along with its adversary – *Green's Pass of Endless Forest*. As the story goes -No one could actually remember what the proper name of the country was, some (the much older folks) said it was just 'Freedom.'

What Train had been told – or what Train had overheard- I should say, was that many heated conversations had erupted at the expense of a name. Some thought it was so named because of all the trees and plant life. Others thought it was the named after the man who first discovered it. And a third much larger group (everyone else); a group where Train came from, simply didn't care.

*It was for this reason the Great Wall of Freedom was built to separate the forest from the rest of the world; those who believed one thing and those who believed another and a third party – who didn't really care in the first place.

Those who lived on the side of Freedom were quite content with the separation because they felt it meant they were right all along. I should mention at this point, both sides considered themselves **the side of Freedom**.

High brick fences bordered both Cities, with signs on both that read: Welcome to the side of Freedom. Not to be confused with **the other side of Freedom**. *Right under this posting was a large* *brightly coloured arrow pointing in the direction of the city they were referring to.*

Not to under play the third group-the ones who didn't care. They lived on both sides and all around the wall, and also had their share of debates. Splitting them into sub-groups, and so on and so on... Both sides of Freedom considered these folks to be fence-sitters, and therefore were outcasts to either side and not allowed within city limits. This turned out to be the only thing the sides of freedom could agree on completely.

Getting back to Train.

When he finally caught up to the caravan they were just arriving at the gates.

Hunched over, out of breath, Train stood at the back end of the last cavalcade. Sitting on the steps was an attractive young woman with chestnut brown hair and dark brown eyes. "Hi," she said to Train. Train waved a hand at her to gesture that he needed a minute to catch his breath. "Have you always been on the run?" She continued.

Train looked up at her confused. "I am not on the run." He said winded. "Well why are you out of breath and why have I seen you running all the way from lake Cap?" she questioned sarcastically. He didn't care much for her type- girls who thought they knew it all. He found them either annoying or nosy. And this one fit both categories. "I was just trying to catch up with you..." She looked surprisingly happy to hear that. "Well not *you* exactly, but the caravan." "Oh," she said somewhat disappointed. "Why have you... I mean, why has the caravan stopped?" he questioned. "My father said we can't get through the gate. We might have to go around. We were hoping to go through Preston Square, maybe do a few shows. Then it is on to Greenland where we are booked for a whole month."

Train looked down the long line of trailers and contraptions and stated. "I think I might be of some assistance." Feeling like he had finally caught his breath he began to walk towards the gate of the Endless forest of Green's Pass. It was a very long procession, consisting of over twenty trailers; some containing wild and exotic animals, the likes of which he had never seen before. Walking to the front of the long line he said hello to some of the friendlier folk, and others he just nodded at.

When Train reached the front, he stood beside what appeared to be a giant. Sizing up the extra-large size man from the caravan he then looked up towards the guard on the wall. "Just open the gate, you senseless ninny." The giant bellowed. "State your business? And no funny stuff," demanded the guard as he shook his fist in anger. "I have already told you, we are on our way to Greenland to perform our show. We ask that you open the gates and let us pass." "Incorrect, incorrect! The frazzled guard shouted.

Because of the controversy between the two Cities, a guard stood watch at the gate and questioned all who wished to enter. He wasn't about to let this sort through the gate. They might be spies for Green's Pass of Endless Forest, or criminals. Or even worse, *fence-sitters*... which turned out they were.

"Excuse me good sirs." Train stated. Then again, a little louder, "Excuse me gentlemen." Finally, he had their attention. The giant looked down at him a little surprised to see him there and the guard just looked at him annoyed. "I think I might be of some assistance in this matter."

Having lived all of his life just on the outskirts of both Great Walls of Freedom, on the side of The Endless Forest of Green's Pass, he was somewhat familiar with the politics of that county.

"What could you possible know boy, after all... you're just a boy?" the guard surmised. "I am, am I?" He looked up at the XL man and shrugged his shoulders. Then turning his attention back to the guard, he added, "How can you be sure, how can you really tell from way up there?" "Well you look like a boy, being the size and shape of one and you even sound like a boy." The guard began to doubt himself. He questioned, "What are you then, a man or a boy?"

"It doesn't matter what I am as much as to say, what I believe to be true. And if the truth is what it is, then anyone who is anyone knows that The Endless Forest of Green's Pass is that! And that the fine city of Preston Square is on the right side of Freedom."

The guard smiled and started to chuckle. "The Right Side of Freedom indeed. Brilliant, brilliant... the boy knows what he's

The Darker Side of Light

talking about." He began to jump about like a school girl who had just won tickets to a Justin Bieber concert. Then he stopped and spoke to Train with admiration in his demeanor. "I'm Brilt Dominel, nice to make your acquaintance. Where do you hail from lad?" he said excitedly.

"I hail from Sorry Bedlam and all the folk there that count, believe it as well. And those who don't, well let's just say aren't worth counting." Train said convincingly. "Aha," the guard exclaimed, "this boy, if he is a boy, after all, is brilliant!" Mockingly, Train wondered for a moment if this guard Brilt was related to Felship in anyway. He did *after all*, look a little on the turtlely side.

Brilt yelled to another guard, "Hey Bran, come here, you've got to meet this boy." Then he addressed Train. "What did you say your name was again?" "I didn't and its Train. The guard looked a little concerned. "Train, just Train?" "Train Philpot the fourth", he finished.

"A Philpot! You don't say?" He was starting to get excited again. "Come Bran, meet this chap Train Philpot the fourth from Sorry Bedlam of all places! He's smarter than most and clever too. *And he's a Philpot to boot*! Wait till the chief hears about this."

Bran approached the edge of the gate and looked down at an ordinary boy standing beside a large full bodied man. "Philpot the fourth you say?" Bran inquired with great doubt. The two guards spoke privately.

It was a miracle or at least a great coincidence that a Philpot was to show up at this time and at this place. For it was foretold that one day a great leader would come to the side of freedom and return order and peace and basically set the record straight.

Helm Rich who once long ago ruled over the great forest of Freedom; a philosopher at heart; a man whose thoughts exceeded the times, also inadvertently saw fit to collapse a sound idea by introducing a conundrum. In a moment of pondering his own thoughts, he made the big mistake of asking the question aloud, "Good people of Freedom, are we part of the endless forest of Green's pass or are we part of Green's pass of endless forest? Can you see the truth that lies in wait?" They couldn't. So, it began...the great depression of 45.

The Darker Side of Light

Of course, Helm Rich and Truss Philpot the third, his best friend and trust worthy ally knew it was a good time to get. Having no place on either side they vanished –slipped away in the night, making it look like they had been captured and then executed by the other side of freedom.

Their great leader dead, the good people divided and separated, soon thereafter war broke out and after much loss and suffering the great wall was built to separate the two sides of freedom.

Addressing Train again Brilt requested, "Tell him what you just told me, go on." Train repeated what he had just said – *"that The Endless Forest of Green's Pass is that! And that the fine city of Preston Square is on the **Right** side of Freedom."*

The response was overwhelming. Before he knew it a whole regiment of guards stood on the edge musing over the words they loved to hear. And to hear it from –said Philpot, well that was the icing on the proverbial cake.

The man from the caravan whispered to Train. "You're doing fine lad, but let me take it from here, before you mess up your lines." Giving him a little wink, he then cleared his throat and addressed the group that had gathered on the top of the wall.

"My name is Timber, Mr. Benjamin Timber and I am – uncle to the wise and noble Train Philpot the fourth. It is true the words he speaks and he speaks it for all of us." He gestured to the rest of his party, who by this time were all starting to gather at the gate as well.

"Now why couldn't you have said that in the first place, come in, come in, all are welcome, all are welcome." Brilt chuckled, repeating himself with excitement. "Open the gate and let the good people through to the Right side of Freedom!"

Never before had anyone from the outside or inside for that matter, make such a claim - such a strong declaration. And as it were, a lot of the folk from all parts of both sides of Freedom were starting to have second and third thoughts about where they stood on the matter. People were leaving the cities – left, right and center. The elected officials were concerned that it would soon turn into a fiasco- like the great depression of 45.

Just in the nick of time this boy arrives, this Philpot the fourth boy, with such conviction and care.

Once inside the gate Train noticed a sign that read.

Welcome to The Side of Freedom
The Great City of Preston Square

*You may stay as long as you like, as long as you're not from the **other side of freedom** – (namely, The City of Regent Square) or a fence sitter – in which case you should take your leave immediately, hence you be fed to the giant *forest chickens.*

*Note on forest chickens- **they do exist**. *Standing approximately seven feet tall, these giant birds are quite a force to reckon with. Or so they would have you believe. In actual fact, they are really rather timid and shy creatures. Indigenous mainly to the Metro Toronto Zoo, these creatures hide in the forest areas and only come out when the coast is clear, or when you aren't looking. Many a parent has used the forest chicken approach to scare their children into behaving while visiting the zoo. Telling the child, "You better not run off or the giant forest chicken will get you." Or "You better be quiet or you'll wake up the giant forest chicken. Oh, you certainly don't want to be doing that!"*

Word soon spread to the other side of Freedom – Green's pass of endless forest that a boy named Philpot the fourth had arrived with a very important message. The elected officials on both sides of Freedom decided it was time to meet.

The gates opened, soon thereafter the wall was taken down and all the good people of both sides of freedom gathered. Even the fence sitters were allowed in. Everyone was happy and enjoying each other's company. Long lost relatives reunited, happy that the truth was finally revealed.

The sign posted when one entered either side of freedom was changed and replaced with a common sign:

Welcome to the Right Side of Freedom

Anyone who is anyone knows that The Endless Forest of Green's Pass is that
And that *this* City is the **Right Side of Freedom**

A declaration of The Great Train Philpot the fourth!

The Darker Side of Light

"Finally," Train thought, finally he had found himself in a town far away from Sorry Bedlam. He decided he would stay here; here where he was recognized and appreciated-*even if it was under false pretenses.*

Because of his overnight success people from miles around came to see this brilliant lad and the company he kept. Soon the City was inundated with tourists. Business was booming and the traveling act made a small fortune before it would move on to Greenland.

The mayor's assistant Rudd Helf handed Train a letter. It was a request from the mayor himself; asking Train if he would address the people and those who had come to see him; if he would give them words of inspiration and encouragement before he left their fair city. Train told Rudd he would do it. But thought to himself, I'm not going anywhere.

Not exactly sure what to add to his already successful speech, he thought about the advice Helm Rich told him some time ago. How times were changing and all that nonsense.

After a brief introduction by Rudd Helf, Train stood high above a large crowd of admirers; Train waved a hand at them and they clapped their hands and whistled their approval and excitement. "My good people of the Right side of Freedom and all those who have come to visit our fare and just cities," he began. "We know that the Endless Forest of Green's pass is that!" the people cheered and hollered. He continued, "And that this good and fair City is the Right Side of Freedom!" They cheered louder, some of the women actually fainted.

The people cheered and yelled out. "Yes, tell us more Train Philpot the fourth!" With a smile on his face he nodded at them in acknowledgement and continued. "A wise man once gave me a very important message. And today I am going to tell it to you." They clapped and cheered, excited that they were going to be told something of great importance. He waited for the crowd to silence and then he began.

With great confidence, he spouted; "Times they are a changing..." The mood of the crowd suddenly shifted. Not noticing the change, he continued. "Always give more than you've got and never take more than you can give..." a deadly stillness filled the air... The crowd looked at one another in shock, as they began to see each other for the first time. A skinny woman whispered, "How do you give more than you've got? What does it mean, I'm confused?" "Well that's obvious, you stupid women." said a large robust woman gnawing on a drumstick.

As he was about to continue someone cried out, "It's 45 all over again." "This is an outrage!" a large man screamed. "That's the other side of freedom talk!" an even larger man yelled. "What's that supposed to mean?" said a skinny young man as he kicked the fat man in the shin. The crowd instantly turned on each other as all hell broke out.

Train looked down into the crowd. And for the first time he saw the people, he actually saw them. All those fat and skinny faces, they were all so angry. He thought maybe if he was to finish Helm's advice, they would have a better understanding of the message. It was too late...

He couldn't believe his eyes, so much hatred; they wanted to kill each other, to kill him. A moment of clarity, he uttered, "What have I done?" Rudd grabbed him by the arm. "We better get you out of here." He said hastily.

For a moment, Train thought he might have got the words wrong. As he went over them in his head, Rudd informed him. "You've been set up." Train didn't understand. "You must leave here immediately. Runaway Train, and never look back." He advised him.

This put a fast ending to an even shorter reign. Train left the town as quickly as possible so as not to meet with the angry lynch squad.

It was all about the balance... the heads of 'The Endless Forest of Green's Pass' and 'Green's Pass of Endless Forest' knew just that. The people didn't want 'change'-they wanted to remain the same. And here this young Philpot was trying to change them- just like Helm Rich tried to do a long, long time ago... 'Always give more than you've got and never take more than you can give.' That was the talk of a traitor. Both sides of freedom knew that!

As Train ran away he decided one week away from home was long enough. Finding the life he was missing, didn't seem all that important, now that he was in danger of losing it.

The Darker Side of Light

As he opened the front door he realized it was better *this* way. Sighing deeply, he forced himself to smile as he returned a wave hello to the foursome that waited patiently for his arrival. At least they seemed happy to see him again.

Much time passed, much more than before… forgetting the past, Train content with just being, lived in the moment. His life was just that.

One day he noticed quite by accident, a letter on the kitchen table addressed to him. It was from his mother. He thought about her for a moment. Opening the letter that began as most letters do -

Dearest Train…

Lonely Heart

Water, earth and sky
A bonnie lass sitting by
For him she waits with lonely heart,
Too long, she feels, they've been apart
A sad forlorn of discontent
Will he never come home again?
Will she never feel his loving embrace?
The bonnie lass, her mind does race
As she searches the sea a ship to view,
Any ship will do
Any sign that her man is on his way
That he is safe, that he's okay,
She prays to the sea,
Oh, bring my lover home to me…
Onto my loving arms do lent
Before my time here is all but spent…
Before they call me that which I fear
The bonnie lass, she sheds a tear
And freely gives it to the sea
Oh, bring my lover home to me…

The Eager Man
Parallel to consistency the eager man's dream
Waits for him in shelters and sits in rows of three
His heart it knows of pleasures that only dreams can score
He waits with baited breath for the knock upon his door
And when it comes will he be seen?
Troubled less and with new means?
Or will a victim's stand garnish his plate?
And scream in facts…it's much too late!
…That only fools hold true to fate
Seldom will you hear him sigh
Or wait for time to pass him by
Action takes what action wants
Like the peddler with his wears to flaunt
And yet he still has dreams so bold
A king's ransom milked in gold
That covets all the finer things in life
And finds a way to win his wife
Then frees his soul from bitter nights
The cold and empty city lights
The vacant stare on faces fine
That tricks the senses of his mind
And leaves him wondering if all is fair
In love and war… and what's the tare?
Should he weigh his life to that…?
The eager man has tipped his hat
But still he follows hopes and wishes blind
That forms the consistency of his mind

Melancholy Babe
As she tiptoed lightly through my head
Forced to recall the words she said
Sadness invoked by discontent
My life force more than spent…
In a perfect scenario I still can't teach her
In a perfect world I still can't reach her
Frustration at the sake of loss
A nickel in the game of toss
No words to comfort, calm or rest
A heart that suffers endless

Liam

Liam... he was so dreamy, I couldn't believe he was actually interested in me… *the plain Jane*; the one nobody wants to ask out or even talk to, plain Jane (*well not anyone half decent anyways*). But Liam did, boy did he - he swept me right off my feet and right on to my back... not the way you're thinking, or the way I would have liked. Let me explain.

Late one night, in the wee hours of the morning, a handsome stranger came into the diner I worked in. He sat at one of the tables and proceeded to look around the room. I'll never forget this part: As his glance caught mine, he smiled warmly and nodded his head as if to say hello. I nodded in return then turned around quickly, picked up a menu and walk towards his table. All the while I could feel his intense stare upon me. I felt naked – exposed, like he could see what was inside of me. I could feel my face grow flushed, and as I walked over to him, I stumbled over my own two feet. Lucky for me – those gruelling years of gymnastic class were about to pay off, as I caught myself from not only an embarrassing fall but also a bruised ego. Recovering my footing, I smiled and chuckled out loud, trying to make light of my clumsiness.

He spoke to me with the most seductive British accent. "Hello love, you know you're not the first beautiful young woman to fall for me." Smiling with a shy reserve, I passed him the menu.

Don't get me wrong, a lot of drunks and low-lives' come into the dinner in the wee hours of the morning and a lot of them think they're the cat's pyjamas - so to speak. They tell you how they own all kinds of stuff, from mansions in Beverly Hills to islands off the coast of Costa Rico. They'll tell you just about anything if they think it will get them a bit of action. Funny though, when it comes to tipping or better yet paying in some cases, they're flat broke. Gill the owner had to have the person that worked the night shift put a sign up after midnight every night. It basically said; Pay First Then Eat. It seemed to work, and it took a lot of pressure off us that had to work the graveyard shift. You know, not having to get into it with a drunken millionaire who had left his wallet on his yacht.

This guy was so different; I knew it as soon as he flashed that seductive smile at me. "Hi, I'm Avery, your waitress, can I start you off with a beverage?" His green eyes sparkled with charm and as he spoke my heart began to jump out of my chest. "Just a glass

The Darker Side of Light

of water please love." "Okay I'll be right back with your water," I told him. It was really strange, I had never felt like this before – I liked it. He sat with the menu closed, so I figured he already knew what he wanted. I placed the glass of water on the table and at the same time asked him if he was ready to order.

"Well my lovely Avery, for starters let me introduce myself, my name is Liam; And I'm here at your mercy, what would you recommend?" I know now that it all seemed pretty corny; the way he was talking to me, but at the time it was so great. I could feel my face growing red. He was so hot! My mind went into overdrive as I spouted out the specials for the last month I think; I didn't even know what I was saying. He sat back in the seat and looked up at me affectionately, and as I finally focused my attention back to the real world, he said. "Yes, but what would you like Avery? What do you fancy?" Fancy? Me? I start to giggle, and I knew I must have been really red-faced now. For in my mind I was thinking...You in my bed, that's what I'd *fancy (it was really late...what can I say).*

"Well," I began. "That depends on what you like. I'm a vegetarian, so for me it would be a salad." Oh, why couldn't I have been more creative? I sounded like a moron. He laughed as he spoke. "Very interesting, a vegetarian you say? Splendid, I think I'll have the sirloin steak, rare, very rare, no spices and no onions." He touched his well-defined chest, and said, "I can't take the spices and as for the onions... well let's just say I don't feel like crying tonight." I nodded my head in acknowledgement, he was so sweet. "And to drink?" I asked. He looked at the glass of water in front of him and spoke slowly. "The water will be just fine Avery my dear." I felt so lame; I had just put the water on the table like a second ago... "Oh ya, sorry about that." I said as I pretended to keep my focus on my note pad. "No worries love," he said. I could feel his stare upon me again. A deep passionate stare that I wanted to explore, I wanted to meet. But part of me was just too afraid to. Not making eye contact, I picked up the menu. "I'll be right back with your order." I told him.

Liam must have been a good ten to fifteen years older than me but I didn't care. I really liked him, and I think he knew it. I wished I had something witty or amusing to say. I had nothing, it's no wonder I didn't have a boyfriend and worked nights.

When his order was ready I brought it to him. Placing it on the table he thanked me as he inhaled deeply, smelling the bloody red meat. "That smells wonderful Avery, you don't know what you're missing." He told me. In my head, I was thinking- Oh yes I do. I just smiled at him politely and said, "Is there anything else I can get for you…Liam?" I couldn't believe I was actually calling him by his name. Something I wouldn't normally do, not even for some of the regulars. And here he was a new customer, someone I had never seen before; and did I mention incredibly hot? It just felt really strange to me, but strange in a good way.

This was my first encounter with Mr. Dreamy but it wouldn't be my last…

I walked home that morning after my shift had ended, and thought about him. I really hoped he would come in again, after all he said he would. He left a ten-dollar tip on the table and as he left he called to me. "Bye Avery, I'll see you again soon love, thanks." "Bye Liam." I did it again, I said his name. "Thank you, come again." I spouted. Oh, how lame was I? I should have said; it was so great to meet you Liam, here's my phone number if you want to get together sometime; or better yet, here's my address, and the key to my place, come over anytime. Oh, who am I kidding, I would never say any of those things, not in a million years.

When I reached my front door, there was this shiny black cat sitting there. I was so tired. In my mind, I was thinking, "Are you waiting for me cat?" The cat meowed and rubbed up against my pant leg. And as I opened the door to my place, the cat jumped inside before me. "Hey, what are you doing? You don't live here cat?" It was small and scrawny and looked half starved. So, I figured it must have been hungry. As I had mentioned already I'm a vegetarian- but I did eat tuna on occasion. I know… my bad…

I opened a can of tuna and placed it on the kitchen floor. I was right, it was starving. It gobbled up the food in no time. "Okay you should probably go now, I need to get to bed" I told it like it could understand me. I opened my front door to let it out, but it wouldn't go. Instead it ran into my bedroom and hid under my bed. "Okay whatever; I'm too tired for this." I said out loud as I closed the front door. I really didn't mind it staying, I loved cats.

The Darker Side of Light

I went into the bathroom got washed up and went to bed. As I drifted off to sleep, I thought about Liam; his handsome smile and his seductive green eyes; his sexy British accent; and of course, that hot body of his.

I awoke to the sound of the cat crying. I got up and met it at the front door. I went to unlock the door. Shit, I didn't lock it! How stupid was that? I let the cat out, "bye, bye, come again." I told it as it jumped out the door and ran off. As I locked the door the phone rang. It was my girlfriend Jenifer Talbit.

"Oh, my God Jen, you're not going to believe this." I woke up as my excitement mounted. "This really awesome guy came in last night. He was so hot, and I think he likes me." I told her what he had said to me word for word. She listened then replied, "He sounds like a creeper to me. You gotta watch out for those guys Avery, you're far too trusting." "What? No way Jen, he's the real deal. I think he's great. And his English accent is so sexy. I hope he comes in again really soon." "Whatever," she spouted. "Are you getting ready, we have to go pick up the tickets for the concert remember?" "Ya," I said. "I'll be ready in about a half hour, see you then." Jen lived at home still, which was lucky for her because she could borrow her mom's car whenever she wanted.

I was off work for the next two nights, which was fine with me, even though I thought Liam might come in and I might miss seeing him. And as fate would have it, this was the case. When I started my shift at eleven Thursday night, Taylor, the girl who I was replacing handed me a piece of paper from Sam; one of the other graveyard shift waitresses. It read: Handsome English gentleman looking for you Avery. Lucky girl... said his name is Liam. I think he is coming in tonight. *Good luck, Sam.*

I was so excited, I could barely think straight. I think I would have been better off not knowing he was coming in; because he was all I could think about. I know it sounds crazy, I had only met him that one time. Every time the door chimed I quickly looked to see who was coming in. We were particularly busy, just about every table in the place was full by two o'clock. It didn't start to die down until about four-thirty and that's when my dream man turned up. Coincidently, he sat at the same table. I tried to play it cool and didn't approach him right away.

The Darker Side of Light

Okay, I thought, stay calm, and don't say anything stupid. I got a glass of water and approached his table. "Hi, may I take your order?" I said as I passed him the menu. I did it again, what was wrong with me? He didn't seem to notice my blunder. "Well hello my lovely Avery, how are you this evening?" "I'm fine, thanks, how are you? It's Liam, right?" I played it cool. "Why yes," he replied coyly. I placed the glass of water that I was still holding on the table and took out my note pad. I needed something in my hands, security of some kind – my note pad and pen were it. I don't know what had come over me. I just stood there. He spoke to break the silence. "I'll have the steak, very rare." I added. "No spices and no onions?" He stared into my eyes, as I looked away. "Yes, that's right love." I looked at him briefly. I didn't want him to know I liked him so much. I couldn't believe it myself. I was really falling hard for this guy. "Okay, I'll be right back with your order." I placed his order then went out the back door for a breath of fresh air. I knew I only had a minute before the next tables ordered would be ready.

As I leaned up against the wall *–I needed it to hold me up*, I thought, does he like me as much as I like him? He couldn't possibly, after all look at him; he's a God, and look at me-plain old Jane. I started to have a lot of doubt. He was probably just being nice. I told myself that it's probably customary in Britain to be so nice to people; something to do with their up-bringing. I went back inside. Three other orders were up, surprise, surprise... so I went ahead and served the tables accordingly.

When his order was ready I took it over to him. As I turned to leave he stopped me. "Avery," he called, "I was wondering if you would like to get together on your next night off?" I didn't hesitate. "Sure, that sounds great. I'll check my schedule to see when I'm available and get right back to you." Who was I kidding, I was available for the rest of my life... my next night off work was Monday. "Actually, I think I'm off this Monday." I said calmly. "Then it's a date." He announced quite excitedly.

I left him to eat in peace, as I continued to serve the other customers. And seat new ones that seemed to be pouring in still, like half starved zombies. Funny thing... an unusually large amount of orders for rare steak that night... I wondered if maybe the moon was full, or if Jack's (that's the chef) steak dinner had a following of sorts.

The Darker Side of Light

Before he left, I gave him my address and phone number. "I'll pick you up at 9 pm then?" He said with confidence. "Okay, see you then Liam." I said as I cleared another table. He left and I was feeling like I had forgotten something.

On my walk home that morning the sun was very warm. It felt wonderful against my skin. I thought about my future date with Liam on Monday, I just couldn't wait. Then it hit me- like a ton of bricks…it was my twenty-first birthday on Monday. Oh my God! That's the day Jen and I are going to the concert. She is going to kill me. I had no way of contacting Liam. Stupid me didn't even get his last name, let alone a phone number. I prayed he would come back in before Monday. I could explain to him that I had plans with my girlfriend and make the date for another night. No such luck.

The cat came back

It had been raining off and on for the last two days and when I headed home Monday morning it was pouring out. When I got to my front door the black cat was sitting there. It meowed at me and rubbed up against my pant leg hastily. As if to say, hurry up and open the door already. "What are you doing out in the rain? Cats don't like the rain, didn't any of your other cat friends tell you that?" I questioned. It meowed loudly and sounded kind of pissed off.

Once again it scampered in as soon as I opened the door. "Smart" I thought, it ran right into the kitchen and waited by the cupboard where I kept the tuna. "You're in luck." I told it. "I went out and bought some more tuna just in case you came back." As I opened the can it meowed like crazy and rubbed up against my leg like it knew me. "Relax" I told it. I'm going as fast as I can. I noticed the cat's fur. "Wow you dry really fast, what's your secret?" It purred softly. "Not talking ah?" I said as I put the food down on the ground for it to eat. Then I patted its back to make sure. Yes, it was completely dry. "Amazing," I said out loud.

I wanted to get to sleep right away. I had my big date with Liam in the evening and I wanted to get my beauty sleep – if you know what I mean.

The Darker Side of Light

Entering my bedroom, I noticed the cat sitting on the chair in the corner. It just sat there staring at me. "Not hiding under the bed this time cat?" I commented. I felt like it was disapproving of me somehow. "I know, I know… I'm a terrible person. But Jen would do the same thing if she were in my situation." I said to it like it knew what I was talking about. It made a funny sound confirming the way it felt then curled up into a ball and went to sleep.

I hadn't seen or heard from Liam, and I had been avoiding Jen's calls. My plan was as follows; I would call Jen about two hours before we were supposed to be leaving to go to the concert. I would fake like I was sick- really sick, too sick to leave the house, let alone go to a concert. I knew I would be able to pull it off, because I used to do it all the time when I was a kid. *Well not all the time, only when I really needed to.*

She would have time to find someone to go with her. She had lots of friends and I knew she would have no trouble finding someone to go with her at the last minute. After all it was 'The Arkells.' Lucky for me she kept the tickets with her seeing how she bought them as a birthday present.

The concert was starting at nine, the same time Liam was supposed to be picking me up. This would work out in my favour because Jen would already be at the concert hall, and there won't be any chance of her seeing me with him. I would just have to make sure we went to a place where I didn't know anyone. That wouldn't be too difficult…

Nine o'clock came and went… and there I sat all dressed up and no place to go.

I felt like a piece of you know what…I'll say it- shit. It was my twenty first birthday, I had lied to my best friend, I was missing the concert of a life time and for what? Some random guy who talked to me nicely? Not to mention I hadn't been on a real date for years… How could I be so stupid?

I sat on the couch, cat by my side. Turning on the TV, I thought about Jen; she must be having a blast at the concert. The concert we were going to, to celebrate *my birthday*. The cat rolled on its side touching my thigh. I started to feel really sorry for myself, and as I patted its belly, it purred softly. "What is wrong with me?

Why am I such a loser?" I asked the cat. It didn't answer –go figure… it closed its eyes like it didn't want to listen to me anymore.

Around eleven o'clock, I decided to go to bed. Not that I was tired, I just didn't want to sit there anymore thinking about how stupid I was. As I turned the TV off the cat jumped up and off the couch. It started making this real funny sound like it might be going into heat or something. It hissed and the hair on its back stood straight up. It ran into my room and hid under the bed. "I think you need to go outside cat," I said. Just as I squatted down to look under my bed, the doorbell rang. "Oh my God, it's him!" I said frantically. I got really excited. I ran to the front door, smiling all the while, I took a deep breath in to calm myself then opened the door slowly. It was Liam!

Looking very distinguished in a sharp navy-blue suit, a bouquet of long stem roses in hand, he stated, "Sorry I'm so late love, business, you know. Don't want to bore you with the details." I could smell the sweet aroma of the breath taking red splendour as he passed me the flowers. "Oh, thank you Liam, they're beautiful."

I invited him in. "Would you care for a glass of wine – red or white?" I asked. "Yes, that would be lovely Avery. Whatever you're having will be fine." He said with that sexy voice.

I poured two glasses of red wine and we sat on the couch in my living room. We sat for a moment in awkward silence then he made a toast. "Here's to a wonderfully delicious night together." As we clicked glasses together, I wondered at his choice of words. Then quickly came to the conclusion that he was probably very hungry because all of a sudden, I was. "So, what's the plan?" I asked excitedly

He looked at me intensely, moving closer, he gently touched my hair with his hand. "Oh, I don't know, I thought maybe we could dine in tonight? After all it is rather late." I felt all funny inside, like I was about to pass-out. My heart pounded hard with passion and I started to breath heavy. Moving closer still, he reached over and kissed my lips softly. I closed my eyes and for a moment drifted off to paradise. It was nice… I hadn't felt like this since…

The Darker Side of Light

well I had never felt like this before. At that very moment, I would have done anything he wanted.

He moved away from me and I slowly opened my eyes. I didn't know what to say. I was speechless. Still holding my glass of wine, I downed it. He smiled warmly at me and asked. "What would you like to do Avery? Do you want to go out, or would you prefer to stay in?" He looked towards my opened bedroom door.

There was no question in my mind as to what I really wanted to do at that moment. But the good girl in me said, no. "Let's go out for a bite to eat, I'm kind of hungry, how about you?" "I'm famished." He said as he looked seductively into my eyes.

When we went outside to get into his car, I almost fell over. He drove a 2018 candy apple red Austen Martin. "Is this your car?" I said surprised, and as I did I felt like a total moron. Obviously, it was his car. No one in their right mind would let someone borrow such an awesome car - Unless it was his dad's or something. "Yes love, sorry, my Porsche is in the shop." He said laughingly, but I think he was serious.

We drove for about twenty minutes and ended up in a part of town I had never been in before. Which was not surprising because I really didn't get out much. Pulling up in front of a very ritzy restaurant called The Belle Loom; a young man about my age opened my door to escort me out of the car. Liam handed the keys off to another young man to park it for him.

Entering this classy bistro, it felt like I was entering another world. One I could only dream about. "Good evening Mr. Montgomery," said the maître d' as he took us right to a private table for two. The room was beautifully decorated. Slender white tapered candles adorned royal blue silk clothed tables. Soft music in the background; a violinist played a beautiful concerto, under a massive ice sculptured bridge. Liam told me it was a replica of the Tower Bridge that stands over the river Thames in London England. I hadn't notice until this moment that there was a river covered with Plexiglas making its way around the entire room. From where I sat I could see an old picture of a blue knight that looked a little like Liam. Exotic plants strategically placed gave the place a warm welcoming feeling. And as we sat there I wondered how I got so lucky?

Everyone who worked there seemed to know him. "You seem pretty popular." I said jokingly. "There only being cordial because I sign their pay cheques." He said matter-of-factly. I was taken aback. What did he just say? He signs their pay cheques? He owns the joint? I tried not to act surprised or confused in anyway. But I was... I started to think – why on earth did he ask someone like me out? Why on earth would he have even set foot inside the place that I worked at? I mean look at this place. It was amazing. It didn't make any sense to me. I started to feel uneasy and out of place; anxious to the point of wanting to get up and run. Liam sensing my fears quickly put my mind at ease. Without uttering a single word, he placed his hand on top of mine. It felt warm and inviting. My fears melted away. I felt like he really liked me...just me. He was incredible.

A somewhat nervous looking waiter came over to the table sporting a fancy bottle of red wine. He stood there waiting for instructions. Liam disapproved and told him to bring something from his private stock. "A bottle of 1945 Chateau Mouton-Rothschild Jeroboam" he ordered. "Nothing is too good for my guest." He said warmly as he looked deeply into my eyes.

I really must confess, I don't know anything about wine, it sounded expensive. And the taste definitely confirmed it. I felt embarrassed, all I had given him to drink was a glass of cheap ten-dollar wine; that I purchased with a dollar off coupon.

During the meal, we talked a little, small talk mostly. We really didn't have anything in common, just this hot mysterious lust for each other. We drank a lot of wine, and I ate very little. I don't' think Liam ate at all. We knew what we really wanted. It's just too bad we didn't want the same thing...

When we left the restaurant, he asked me if I wanted to go dancing or if I just wanted to go home. I wasn't fooling anyone. I really wanted to go home – with him. "I'm a little tired." I told him. "I wouldn't mind going home."

When we reached my place, he walked me to my front door. "Well good night Avery." He said slowly and ever so seductively. I don't know what came over me? Maybe it was a combination of the wine and my liking him so much, but I did this really stupid thing. Something I had never done before. I grabbed on to him tightly and kissed him hard on the lips. He returned my kisses and as I unlocked my front door we both kind of fell in.

Before I knew it, I was partly undressed on my couch, Liam on top of me. My eyes closed tight, consumed by passion, we kissed each other with absolute lust; with desire, I didn't know existed. He was all consuming; it was almost like he could have swallowed me whole... and at that moment I would have let him.

Then something strange happened.

I started to feel dizzy and faint, thinking for a moment that the wine had got the better of me. But then there was this terrible smell in the air. A horrible, awful smell that made me want to hurl. I didn't know where it was coming from. I started to cough, and choke a little. "Sorry Liam," I said as I opened my eyes.

"OH MY GOD!" I screamed. "GET OFF ME! It was the most fowl creature I had even seen. It looked like it was at least a hundred and fifty years old and its yellow eyes- evil, pure evil. Eyes that were filled with lust and hatred. I felt so lost and hopeless as my heart sank into a deep, dark place to hide from the shame and disgust.

I didn't understand what was going on. How could I? Liam was gone, and in his place, was this depraved creature. "Liam," I cried foolishly. It felt like my shoulders were in some sort of vice-grip. It pressed down hard on them and I could feel its nails tear into my flesh. Screaming out in pain, I pleaded with the beast to let me go. It didn't budge. Instead it pushed down harder. Grinning at me, revealing a mouth full of blacken decay and rot, it spoke with a familiar voice. "Well my lovely Avery, can you guess what I fancy?" Thick putrid, greenish-black saliva ran out of its mouth and fell all over my face. I started to barf. But this didn't seem to deter it. "Please let me go, you're hurting me!" I begged. It didn't care...

It started to rip at my flesh, I screamed out for help as I fought back with all my might. Under all my screaming and fighting back, I could hear a faint, low hissing sound, and then a death-curdling howl. The Cat... then everything went black...

The Darker Side of Light

I awoke the next day sometime in the late afternoon. I was in a lot of pain and had great difficulty sitting up. My chest was badly scratched and I had a deep laceration across my lower abdomen. I started to feel sick to my stomach and wanted to cry when I looked around the room and saw all the blood, my blood…

I couldn't remember what had happened. The cat meow from across the room. It was staring at me as if to say – "Foolish girl, you're lucky I was here to save you." …and I started to remember. Holding my stomach, I forced myself to my feet and walk with great difficulty into the kitchen. I would need to go to the hospital, but not yet. The cat followed close behind me and sat by the lower cupboard that contained the cans of tuna. "I guess you're pretty hungry?" The cat meowed at me and rubbed gently up against my bare, blood-stained leg. I took out the last three cans of tuna and started to open them. "Okay, relax, cat," I said, "I'm going as fast as I can…"

A cold breeze ran up my spine and out of the corner of my eye, I could see my front door swinging wide opened. Fear gripped at my heart. I began to shake uncontrollably. My judgment clouded and my thoughts confused- was it still here, was it back?

My friend my savour
"Avery? Avery, where are you?" I heard the concerned voice of my friend Jen. I saw her face, she looked so sad. It's okay I told her. It's going to be okay. I reached out for her. Then she was gone… "Jen," I screamed. Stepping backwards, I slipped in my own blood, hitting the wall behind me and slid down it. Too weak to carry on I passed out.

When I awoke, I was in the hospital. My mom sat in the corner and stared out the window at the night's sky. Rosary in one hand, Kleenex in the other, she silently wiped away the tears. "Mom," I began to say. She looked at me, and then back out the window. I don't think she heard me. Clearing my throat, I repeated a little louder, "Mom." Still no response. Was she mad at me, I thought? Somehow found out about my scandalous ways? My mom was a devout Catholic and did not believe in any form of pre-marital relations –if you know what I mean. "I'm sorry mom." I told her as I started to cry.

The Darker Side of Light

My father came into the room; his face was grey and solemn. Placing a fresh bouquet of flowers on the table beside my bed, he gently kissed my forehead and then turned to my mom and said. "Any changes?" She just shook her head, no. He took a seat beside her and held her hand in his. "I know it's hard Cathleen, to see her this way." She looked at him, tears welled up in her eyes, holding the tissue up against her mouth she looked over at me and shook her head in despair. "I don't know what to make of it Mike. I've tried talking to her, reading to her from the Good book – she's too far gone now."

I sat up in the bed. "Really mom? Too far gone?" She still didn't listen to me- she never does. "Mom why are you doing this? I said I was sorry. I know what I did was wrong, but haven't I suffered enough without you shunning my existence?" She didn't answer, didn't acknowledge me in any sort of way. "Dad, can you talk some sense into her? I mean come on, I'm twenty-one. I have a life you know." He ignored me too. "Mom, this isn't the dark ages… its natural to be attracted to the opposite sex, to have those feelings. Just because you're all up-tight about it, doesn't mean I have to be." I spouted in a defiant sort of way. She just looked at me and shook her head despairingly. I knew I was a great disappointment to her.

"It's late Cathleen, we should go." He told her. My mom and dad got up and walked out of the room. "Wait, come back! I didn't mean it. I'm sorry." I shouted after them. I got up and followed them out into the hallway. Surprisingly I felt great. The terrible pains I had from my act were gone. And as I walked down the corridor behind them, I continued to question them. "Why don't you look at me? Turn around, I'm right here. Am I so awful that you can't even look at me mom - dad?" They seemed to be talking amongst themselves and I couldn't make out what they were saying. "Why do you always do this mom?" The elevator door opened, I stood and watched as my parents entered. They turned to face me. Blank vacant stares; on the faces of the two people I loved more than anything in the entire world. And as the shiny, cold metal door closed, I slid down the wall that was behind me. Crumpling into a pitiful blob on the hospital floor, I wept. "They hate me, my own parents… they hate me…"

After a while I got up and walked back to my room. I was getting out of there, I would just have to get my clothes.

Weird and Wacky Tales & Other Such Nonsense
Linda Noble-Cordy

The Darker Side of Light

I opened the narrow closet door that was situated behind the room door. Shit I spouted, when I saw it was completely empty. Then I had an idea; I'll call Jen and ask her to bring me some clothes. Walking around the privacy curtain to get to the phone, I noticed some poor soul was lying in the bed. "Dame, I'm in the wrong room." I could see under the oxygen mask her face was badly bruised and the assortment of tubes coming out of different parts of her body made me think she must have been in one nasty accident. I felt really sorry for her, and as I went over to pick up the receiver to call Jen I got a closer look. Wow she looks really familiar... how do I know her? Then it hit me like a ton of bricks. "No, that can't be me... this isn't happening! I'm tripping out! I must be tripping out... I'm having a nightmare, that's what I'm doing. That makes perfect sense. That explains a lot...Wake up Avery, you're having a bad dream!"

I wasn't dreaming.

When I finally came to my senses and calmed down, I decided I would have to make the best of it. I would go home in the hospital gown if I had to. What difference would it make, no one could see me anyways.

When I reached my front door, it was clear that something terrible had happened inside. The door was blocked off with yellow police tape that repeated 'caution crime scene' in big black letters. As I crouched down to go under the tape, I heard the voice of a woman. "You don't have to do that anymore silly girl." I stood up. "Who's there?" I questioned. "I don't have to do what?" Looking around I noticed my saviour the black cat prancing towards me. I continued to look around for the body that went with the voice. "You can go right through Avery, you are not restricted by the boundaries of a mortal life." "What?" I said very confused. Looking down at the cat, the source of the voice was clear.

"But are you sure you want to go inside?" "What?" I repeated. "Stop saying 'what' foolish girl," she demanded. "Are you really talking to me cat?" I questioned. "Of course, I am, you're the only one here aren't you? And stop calling me CAT, it's extremely rude. I have a name, and you may call me by it – it's Pearl."
Pearl... my black Pearl... my heroine had a name... how fitting, I thought.

The Darker Side of Light

What is the truth?

There was blood all over the walls and floor, not only in the living room were the thing attacked me but in the kitchen and bedroom as well. Confused, I sat cross legged in a corner of this house of horror. "What happened Pearl, what really happened?" In my mind, I thought that there was a good possibility I passed out, Liam left and that is when the beast attacked me. "Is Liam... okay?" I asked with some degree of uncertainly.

"Is Liam okay!" she hissed at me. "What's wrong with you? You have left your body, but have you lost your mind too? What care have you for a Sankta, he almost killed you. If I hadn't been here, you would be dead right now. And your loved ones would be visiting your grave instead of your hospital bed." Sitting on the blood-stained arm of the sofa, staring me down she questioned, "You don't remember what happened?" I lied a little and told her no.

Casually licking one paw and then the other she surmised aloud, "Interesting, very interesting..." As her attention focused back onto me again she asked with some hesitation. "Do you want to know the truth or do you want to keep on believing that this Liam is an innocent?" Firmly I told her, "I want to know the truth!"

"Very well, from the beginning then," she began. "The fiend, the one you call Liam, crossed over – escaping from Tekram's Helm; it's the only place that could possibly hold the evil ones. That is until this one came along... He was the first to escape. And on my watch, my very first watch...

It was my duty to guard his cell, and I failed my position. Nowhere in my training did they equip me for what lay ahead of me. I followed him to the realm we call the Gant Terrain. This is where his trail went cold. I knew eventually he would need to feed again, it was just a question of when and where. Then he struck - carnage lay in the wake. And as luck would have it, he made a vital mistake; left one of his victims barely clinging to life. It was in those last few seconds, I was able to meld minds and see him, know where he was heading- the fifth realm."

"You mean here, earth?" I pointed to the floor. "Almost, just on the other side of here." she told me. "I saw him enter your subconscious. I could tell it was your reality that would be in

The Darker Side of Light

jeopardy. He invaded your thoughts, slowly stealing your energy, your life force. By making himself appealing to you – he first gained your trust and then your approval. The beast is perfecting his craft. An illusionist of sorts with deadly consequences, he baits the spirit with sexual gratification and when the spirit is at its most vulnerable, he jumps in for the kill. Destroying the spirit, he then feasts on the flesh. That is why you awoke when you did. He wanted you to feel the pain and experience the terror. Then and only then can he thrive. And it is not only your body he devours it is your soul as well."

I fear you may still be under his spell." "What do you mean 'his spell' Pearl?" I was trying to understand what she was telling me but it just didn't make sense, none of it.

With some compassion, she said. "Everything you experienced was a fantasy Avery, not real."

"But he took me to his own restaurant, the Belle Loom. That had to be real." I mentioned with some degree of hope. She continued, "Sankta's are immoral by nature, I have never met one that could be trusted and this one is no exception. Then she let me have it, "*Avery, you never left this room.* "What!" I said, overwhelmed with the things, she was hitting me with. "Are you sure? Are you sure you're not making a mistake? I went in his car. There were other people, a giant ice sculpture and a man playing a violin… I can still hear the music. Are you telling me none of it was real?" "That's what I'm trying to tell you. With your desire for him, he was able to enter the world in which you walk and talk –but as a dream. You have fallen victim to his advances. If it's any consolation, you're not the first to be fooled and you won't be the last…" She announced. "But how did he do it Pearl, When? I just don't get it. How could one person do this to another?" I questioned.

"He is not a person Avery! He is a Sankta, a cold, calculating killing beast." She explained further, "He used your world – your subconscious world to seduce you. In this world, he could become real, real enough to eventually achieve a physical form. This is where we must catch him and hold him forever. He must not be allowed to escape again."

The Darker Side of Light

"As much as I hate to say it, his reign of terror has just begun on this plane. Your kind – you are weak and easy targets, much easier than the beings of Gant. I can see why he had chosen you Avery to begin his reign of terror," she interjected with a cooled air of smugness. "Your innocence is *rare* indeed. And as you are fully aware – that is how he likes his meat!"

I should have been upset with what she had just told me but for some reason, I didn't really care. "So now what?" I asked out of curiosity. "How do you plan on stopping him Pearl? I mean...no offence, but you're... you're- well you're small..." I said quietly, hoping not to upset her in any way. After all, she was a cat with an attitude.

"You still don't remember what really happened do you Avery?" I shook my head no. And started to think that maybe I really didn't. After a long pause, she told me, "It is vital that you remember what really happened to you if you are to help defeat it." Somehow sensing my apprehension, she questioned, "You do want to stop it, don't you? Look what it did to you. How it tricked you, playing on your human weaknesses. Do you want that to happen to others?" "No, of course not." I answered. But in my heart, I wasn't sure I could help.

"Well… what is your position? Will you help me trap the beast? Or shall I just leave you to your fate?"

My fate...I had no idea that my whole existence depended on my answer.

Unsure of myself I answered, "What can I do? I can't." I still had feelings for him –Liam, not the beast. A longing, a desire for his touch still haunted my soul. She was right, he did have a hold on me. And I convinced myself it was not him that attacked me. It couldn't have been.

All of a sudden, I grew frightened. I felt like I was in danger. It was coming for me again. "No! I won't do it! Leave me alone, leave me alone." I screamed. I began to cry and she said very coldly, "Very well then. We are done here."

Instantly I was back in the hospital room, and all my fears were gone. My mom was sitting looking out the window again. I walked over to her and touched her hair softly and kissed her cheek. "I love you mom." I whispered in her ear. She kissed the crucifix on her rosary then made the sign of the cross over her chest. Did she sense me there? I wondered. Lying down on the hospital bed, my mind went blank –not a care, not a worry in the world… I quickly drifted off into a deep blissful sleep.

Awake or not

The next time I awoke I was all alone and in a different room. My mom was not sitting by the window; there was no window; and the walls would have been completely bare if not for the large crucifix directly in front of me. A high-pitched noise pierced the air with a dull echoing sound. It seemed to go on forever. Eventually a nurse came rushing in, followed by two other nurses. She said something to one of them and the noise stopped. I felt heavy and stiff, not like the first time I had woke up.

"Good morning Avery," she said pleasantly. "So, you've decided to join the land of the living again." The three smiling faces looked down at me. My throat hurt and I could barely get the words out. "You can see me?"

"And just in time for her birthday." One of the other nurses announced. Did I hear her right? - my birthday. "The concert, I have to call Jen." I said in a whisper as I tried desperately to sit up. I didn't know how I got there or why, just that I had to get in touch with Jen and tell her where I was. The nurses looked at each other and then the first one spoke. "It's been cancelled. They've cancelled the performance." For some reason that made perfect sense to me and I believed her, besides, why would a nurse that doubles as a nun lie?

"Where's my mom?" She didn't answer. I said it again, "Where's my mom?" "Try not to talk Avery, I bet your throat is really sore," she told me. "Yes," I said as I tried to nod my head. Which I found I couldn't do very easily. "Sister Karen could you please page Doctor Chapmen, Sister Liz could you please call Mrs. Martin and give her the good news?" she instructed the Sisters. "I'll stay here with Ms. Martin, until her parents get here." "Yes, right away Sister Fay." They spoke one after the other.

I was so happy to see my parents again. They looked different somehow- tired or something. I couldn't quite put my figure on it.

The Darker Side of Light

Two police officers showed up at the same time as my parents. The one called Officer Harris introduced himself and his partner Officer Waite. And after a little time had passed he asked my parents to leave the room so they could talk to me in private.

Officer Harris asked me how I was feeling and if I was willing to talk to them about what happened. I told him I felt horrible. I knew I would have to tell them the truth; how I was supposed to go to the concert with Jen and how I stood her up to go out with this guy called Liam – Liam Montgomery- about how I felt so sick, about the smells and how I was attacked. But wait… the nurse said the concert was cancelled. I was so confused.

I blurted out, "I left the door unlocked. It was raining; there was a black cat sitting in the rain. I let the cat in. Where's Jen…?"

Then I had a vision of a black cat lying mutilated on the floor in my bed room. It's blood, guts and fur all over the place. I remembered this cat from my childhood. It was my cat. Everything was mixed up and out of order and didn't make any sense.

Then Officer Harris asked "How long had you known Jen? When did I see her last?"

I was getting more confused and started to have different memories. *I could hear concern music – The Arkells… I thought about Jen. I remembered laughing with her. Happy Birthday she said.* Then I felt tremendous guilt.

"I don't know, I can't remember." I started to cry. "Can I see Jen? Will you ask her to come see me? I need to talk to her." They looked at each other strangely, and I had a feeling they didn't believe what I was saying. And why would they – I didn't believe it myself. They told me if I remembered anything to call them right away.

By the next day, I felt so much better. It could have been the drugs I was on, but it didn't matter - I couldn't wait to go home. I wanted to call Jen, ask her to come and bring some clothes and make up. I also needed to call my work and tell them I won't be showing up for my shift that night. To my surprise, I had no phone in my room. I went into the hall to ask the nurse were the phone was. "Who do you want to call?" She asked. "Just a friend," I replied. "Sorry

The Darker Side of Light

doctor doesn't want you making any calls." "Why not, it's just a phone call? Oh ya, I have to call my work too." That's been taken care of. Your work has been informed." "Well I want to call them myself." "No, no phone calls, that's the doctor's orders." "You have got to be kidding! What is this, a prison?" "They'll be none of that talk in here young lady. Off you go back to your room. You should be resting, anyhow."

I didn't want to rest, I wanted to go home. When no one was looking, I slipped down the hall to the visitors waiting area. There on a table up against the wall was a telephone. I dialled Jen's number. The phone rang and rang. Finally, her mom answered. "Hello." "Hi, Mrs. Talbit, is Jen home?" "Who is this!" she demanded. I had an awful sense of dread, but I didn't know why. Slowly I said. "It's Avery, Avery Martin." There was a cold silence. For a moment, I could hear her breathing into the receiver. "Mrs. Talbit… could I talk to Jen please?" then she hung up, she just hung up on me.

What a bitch, I thought. I was about to call back but then I remembered something… the concert. I told Jen I couldn't go because I was so sick – I remembered that! I started to feel really dizzy. I sat on a chair and searched my brain for answers. Why did the nurse tell me it was cancelled? For a moment, I thought I was losing it. Maybe she didn't say that. And maybe the other one didn't say it was my birthday. My parents never mentioned it; you would think my own parents would have wished me a happy birthday.

There was a teenager sitting on the other side of the room with headphones on. "Excuse me…" I waved at him to get his attention. He pulled one of the earpieces out. "What's the date today?" I asked. "It's the twenty first." "April?" I confirmed. He looked at me like I was crazy, and nodded his head yes. "That's what I thought." I felt a moment of relieve. "Tuesday, right?" "No Friday." He answered. "No, I'm, pretty sure it's Tuesday," I told him. "Well I'm pretty sure it's Friday." He looked at me as if I had lost it. "It's Friday April 21nd." I looked at him confused. And he continued, "2017," he laughed a little and shook his head again. "Where have you been lady?" He spouted as he put his earpiece back in.

Oh my God, I've been out of it for two years! Why didn't anyone tell me?

The Darker Side of Light

My mind started to race. I needed to call work; for sure I was fired. And my apartment... I would have no place to live? I certainly didn't want to go back home to my parent's place. I had to talk to Jen, explain what really happened to me. She deserved to know the truth, even if she would hate me for it.

Her mom answered again. "Hello," her voice sounded distant and very sad. Hello, Mrs., Talbit, please don't hang up on me again." I said quickly. I know Jen is probably really mad at me, but could I *please* talk to her." I pleaded.

Silence again... "Mrs. Talbit, are you there?" Her voice cracked and it sounded like she was crying. "Oh Avery, I didn't want to be the one to tell you this." "Mrs. Talbit, what's wrong, is Jen okay?" "No, she isn't..." her voice drifted off. "Where is she? Is she there?" "No, she's... she's dead." "Dead! "What happened to her?" After a long silence, she said quietly – "We were hoping *you* could tell us what happened, Avery." I held the phone out and looked at it. "What?" I felt a knot in the pit of my stomach slowly tighten. My mind raced and at the same time did not move. I could hear the voice of the teenager. "Hey are you okay?" My body trembled and shook. I could hear the concert music again. I was laughing, singing...I saw Jen. She was singing, laughing... then fear, all consuming, paralyzing fear.

The room felt like it was closing in on me, and I couldn't breathe. The teenager asked me again if I was okay, but I couldn't answer him. I wasn't okay, far from it...

Dropping the phone, I raced out of the room and collapsed on the floor. My mind filled with images –horrible, terrible images. I could smell that same foul odor, I started to throw up as my body went into spasms. Fear gripped my soul and I could not escape it. It was happening again! It was on top of me, tearing at my fresh. Then I saw Jen's bloody form. Her face twisted, distorted with pain, she reached out with two blood soaked hands. "Stop!" she cried, "stop...!"

Not just a dream
I didn't want to think about what happened to me or to Jen. Officer Harris and Officer Waite took turns calling me to see if I remembered anything. But I didn't and I didn't want to.

The Darker Side of Light

The week later I was allowed to go home with my parents. My mom insisted that I talk to someone. "It's important Avery, you got to talk about what happened to you." She insisted. She went ahead and made an appointment for me to see a psychologist, after she found me one night, opening up all the cans from the kitchen cupboards. Apparently, I was feeding my imaginary cat. She told me. "I'm fine mom really." I told her. But who was I kidding I was far from fine. I was falling apart inside. I was constantly forgetting things, losing track of time and now it would seem – sleep walking. I convinced myself that what I really needed was to go back to work. Put all this behind me and get on with my life.

I made a decision. I would apply for my old job.

I stood on the sidewalk, across the road from Gill's grill and steak house; the place I used to work. Funny it didn't seem that long ago, but I guess it was… "Cross the road Avery, go on… you can do it." I told myself. I was afraid. I don't know of what – just afraid.

A woman walked towards the place. I could tell by her movement that she was happy. As she opened the door she turned to look at me. Smiling warmly, she gestured me to follow her. Jen? Jen! It was Jen. I raced across the street.

I flung open the door and looked around the room for her. The place was packed. Gill saw me before I saw him. He came racing over and wrapped his arms around me. "Avery, it's so gooda to see you!" Kissing both my cheeks he then squeezed me again. "You wanta to come back to worka now? You know you always have a jobba here," he said in a thick Italian accent. I looked at him for a moment then focused on the rest of the room. "Did you see Jen come in here Gill?" I questioned.

"Jen? You mean your gooda friend Jen? No, no… you sit down Avery, I make you a nice cup o coffee and something gooda to eat." There was no place to sit. My eyes filled with tears. I thought about what my mom had said, I wasn't ready to leave the house yet. "I should go, thanks anyways Gill." "No, Avery you sita down, don't go." "But Gill the place is full, and I want to go home. I'm not ready yet." I told him. His voice changed and as he screamed "I said sit down!" He pushed me towards a seat that someone was already sitting in. "What are you doing Gill?"

The Darker Side of Light

Looking at the person, to apologise, I noticed they didn't have a face. Just blank white flesh surround by long dark brown hair. I started to panic, a sense of dread gripped my heart. "This can't be happening? I must be dreaming!" I looked at Gill for answers but Gill was gone and in his place, was something foul and putrid; it was the beast that attacked me. He was back! My worst nightmare was coming true. Grabbing my arms, it twisted my body towards it. I couldn't move, couldn't escape. I tried to scream. But nothing came out.

Knocking me to the ground, I landed on my living room floor. Before I knew it, it was on top of me; it clawed and tore at my flesh like a dog digging up a juicy bone. Finding my voice, I whimpered, "Stop, please, you're hurting me! Please let me go." But it was too late... I was dead.

As it ate up my flesh like a delectable appetizer; with my soul the main course, I looked at the body lying there on the hardwood floor. It wasn't me he was devouring, it was Jen.

I woke up in the hospital bed. I had never left it in the first place... It was all a dream, *all* of it. The nightmare continued... every time I fell asleep or maybe I was waking up, I really couldn't tell. I couldn't tell what was real and what was not. Because nothing and everything was real...

One thing was for sure - it always ended the same way – badly. The only difference was the faces of the victims and there were many. They changed, but not the monster that killed them, he was always the same.

I remembered the black cat- Pearl. Or was that just a dream too? I remembered the conversation I had with her. Was it true, was I under the spell of the creature that acted me? I needed answers, I needed to find her. I was ready, I had to be, this nightmare had to end.

Ready or not...
Fear assaulted my senses, and I awoke to the carnage that had taken place only moments earlier. Sitting in the same bloody spot, on the same bloody floor, up against the same bloody wall, I looked over at the clock just above the kitchen stove. Ten after one. How could this be? Then I remembered *everything*.

The Darker Side of Light

"Oh my God! Jen!" Holding my guts in with one arm, I pulled myself across the blood-soaked floor with the other to where she lay. "Jen," I shook her arm. "Jen, wake up." I cried. Then I heard a familiar voice. "She's gone Avery. I'm sorry, I couldn't hold on to you both." I lay face-up on the floor beside my best friend. I wanted to join her. Go wherever she had gone but I couldn't.

"Why is this happening? Why am I still here?" Let me go, please just let me go. I don't want to be here anymore."

"You have no other place to go. You will always be here Sankta." *Sankta...* The word echoed in my head. It was false, a trick she was playing. It had to be.

I begged her again. "Please let me go." "I'm sorry Avery I can't." She said with some remorse. I felt myself slipping away again. I closed my eyes. Hoping, praying this would finally be over. "No! Not this time." she screamed, as she pulled me back, I could feel my body healing itself.

Opening my eyes, a dark shadow came into view. It seemed to be all around me – touching me, caressing me gently, wanting me. A deranged longing came over me and I felt dirty-disgusting. "Pearl are you there?" "No, love it's me." I heard my own voice say. Wait, it wasn't my voice it was Liam's. "No." I cried out. "No, please stop." Overwhelmed with sadness, I was ashamed at how it made me feel. I just wanted to die. And knowing that's what this beast wanted too, given the option, I would have gladly obliged it.

It was trapped in me. Not in my body, in my mind, I could feel it. Like a big fish in a small bowl in the middle of a vast ocean. The only visible way out was my death and Pearl was not about to let that happen, not yet. Not until she had a permanent holding cell for this beast. In the meantime, I would do…

No one would believe me. Why would they? I would be held responsible for all those murders. After all it was my DNA they found at the crime scenes. I told them over and over again what really happened. But no one would listen. They said I was crazy, mentally and criminally disturbed. That's their opinion and they're welcome to it... I know better.

The Darker Side of Light

So here I sit in this prison within a prison. Not allowed to die and not permitted to live. A beast within a beast —that's what most call me. As for my friends… well they just call me Liam.

Liam, he was so dreamy, I couldn't believe he was actually interested in me… the plain Jane; the one nobody wants to ask out or even talk to, plain Jane (well not anyone half decent anyways). But Liam did, boy did he - he swept me right off my feet…

Angel of Misery

I once asked May's angel- Wouldn't life be great if all negative emotions were gone... no more sorrow or hate; no more regret or shame?

Her reply...

I like to feel she said to me
Anger, sadness...
It sets me free
It fills the longing in my heart
As much of me, it is the part
It shields and comforts all my needs
As words bring forth the strangled weeds
Then turns to joy and pleasure there
As emotions form pathogens of despair
To take away my need to feel...?
How can this be right or real?
And what would be left of me?
I'm afraid I do not see
Nor do I understand
The reason for the perfection of man
Don't get me wrong, to abolish hate
Would be great
To stop the evil would be grand
A legacy fit for mortal man
But at what cost to me?
What part of me must I set free?
And what then will fill the hole?
I'm not ready to let go

The answer is no

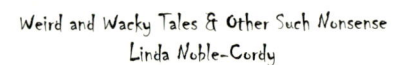

The Darker Side of Light

The Seed and the Wind

Weird and Wacky Tales & Other Such Nonsense
Linda Noble-Cordy

As autumn rested its tired head, a tiny seed lay on the cold, uncaring ground. Her fine, fragile, feathery pappus lay limp – almost expired. Sleep would come soon, it was just a question of time. And as she embraced her destiny, a warm, tender wind caressed her gently. How lovely his embrace, how caring his touch. Responding to his affections she freed herself from fate and allowed herself to fly.

The wind admired greatly his tiny friend and as he carried her higher and higher, she flourished in his embrace. He kept her close to his heart and she, him. It would seem nothing could separate them. Taking his new found affection to places she didn't know existed; she saw things she didn't know were possible. How perfect their life was - how perfect and complete. And as he pushed her forward and back, up and down, around and around, she didn't seem to mind. They had each other, they were alive and they were free... that's all that mattered.

Time, having hold on measure would see all good things come to an end...

Alas, the wind, sensing his own fate, knew the time had come when he could no longer sustain his lovely little companion. The time when he, himself would soon expire. He would have to place her back down on the cold, uncaring ground and leave her to her own fate. He didn't understand it, how could he? And how could he possibly explain to his love that he could no longer support her? That he could no longer care for her. And as he gently ever so caringly placed her on the frosty, winter's soil he faded away...

She couldn't understand why he had left her so; without a reason, without a word – goodbye. Heartbroken and forsaken, sadness wrapped in a blanket of sorrow, covered her as she drifted off to sleep; she cared not for what lay ahead in her next life - how could she?

Time, having held direction, would see all good things begin...

With the warmth of spring came new life and so too came a new life for the little seed. Growing taller and larger than most, her spiky green stems and leaves were a testament of not only strength but also protection. Even her beautiful purple flowers displayed a shell of thorny armor. No longer a tiny, fanciful seed, this Thistle was grounded with a vitality matched by few. Roots planted deeply in the rich, fertile soil nourished and supported her every need.

One warm, sunny day the gentle wind whispered softly to her with his embrace, but she could not feel him there, not anymore… and although in her heart she still dearly loved the wind, she could not allow herself to be vulnerable to his charm. With a sadness of his own making, he left her there and then; knowing he could never change her spirit.

Time having felt change, marched on.

Thistle was dying; she knew this was to be her fate. Her rich green foliage, however faded, possessed an exterior harder and stronger than ever. She held on tightly to her seeds and she would until the very end. And as the last of summer wended from view, she let go and was gone. All that remained was her legacy. The gentle wind circled around the foundlings with care. How lovely his embrace. How caring his touch. They embraced his affections –the likes of which they had never experienced but somehow knew. Released from their guarded chambers, he carried them high up into the cold autumn air and they flourished. As he pushed them forward and back, up and down, around and around, they didn't seem to mind. They were alive and they were free.

…and That was all that really mattered.

Dandelions Bloom

Dandelions bloom in spring
Yellow grass beneath my feet
And as far as the eye can see
Dandelions blooming in spring

Lovely yellow, fields of gold
Lighten the heart and warm the soul
Colours rich and full of life
A palette of God's pure design

Rolling hills of brilliant light
Fashion fancy summer's sight
Here where earth and sun are one
A life time cycle just begun

Dandelions bloom…

For as far as the eye can see
What beauty…A gentle breeze
Warm and mild
Slows the pace for a while

It gladdens the heart and makes one feel
Like a lovely dream that is made real
Not a care, not a worry in the world…
As dandelions bloom in the spring

The Cheating Heart

Becel Noel if truth be told was
brought up well
Experiencing all the finer
things in life
Her parents knew one day
she'd make someone
A real fine young wife
Trained and molded by the best
—the cooking, the cleaning and
all the rest
Her days were filled with duty
And nights were filled with
dreams
Of the perfect marriage – pure
and white and clean…
Then the day arrived
She gladly welcomed fate
And couldn't wait to meet this
man
Her very own first date
(it had been all arranged)
A handsome chap five-foot ten
He kissed her hand and softly
said "My name is Ben"
To know love is to be in love
that is how she felt
And although she didn't really
like old Ben
She thought with time she
would
So, she agreed to his courting
and ideally, she stood
The wedding followed shortly
Her wifely duties she began
Her lot in life to please her man
Days to weeks and weeks to
months
I think you know the rest
Years and years of loyal
service, this was Becel's quest
And although she never bore
him any young

The Darker Side of Light

She felt she did her part and with time she loved him
Despite his cheating heart...
Yes, she knew of all the women that came and went with ease
She put up with all the phone calls, he claimed was just another niece
The late nights, the no shows, the disappointing sex
Her life – to sum it up was a complete and utter wreck
Then one day she'd had enough – no more would she stand by
He was going to leave her
She thought – 'he has to die'
Twenty years of loyal service
Twenty years of all his shit
And now he was going to leave her?
Not if she had a say in it
And when they found him late last year
To everyone's surprise
Not a mark did they find on him
Not a hair out of place
Suit neatly pressed –not a wrinkle, not a trace (of foul play)
He sat there at the kitchen table
Handsome and smart-looking too
And the paper in his cold dead hands
Was dated December 10th, 1982

Who am I mocked the turtle

Awake, awake the diligent cried
My good friend, let not the day go by…
Let not the sun alone do shine
For it is time, it is time…
Once again it is time

But the turtle not a move did make
Not a sound or faction fake
Again, the diligent cried awake!
Awake, awake, it's getting late
And you must face your fate

A small voice carried with it sound
As four feet planted on the ground
And slowly did the head appear
And questioned why time was near
And why the diligent shed a tear

As the black pot boiled hard
The diligent tossed in a pound of lard
Onions do affect me so
So, question not your time to go
But the turtle just said –no?

Who am I that fate must bind?
A life to which a cannot find
Any reason, cause or ground
To which a fate I must be bound
Who am I mocked the turtle

Who am I that time does beckon
And the sun alone can't reckon
Or see too clear alone do shine
This reason for its fate –not mine
This reason for its course with time

Wanting to avoid the dread
The diligent bowed his head and said
You are wanted by those who need
And that is why I wake your breed
The others they must feed

The Darker Side of Light

Very well the turtle sighed
But know that before this day goes by
It is not my soul that fate does steal
It is not my fate that time does seal
Nor will I go with great appeal

With a hatred in my heart so bold
The story of the hopeless will unfold
A bitter taste of justice fine
A want of sorrow's fruitful wine
Mocked the turtle now it's time…

The black pot boiled with a fury
But the turtle he did not worry
I will leave this life of dread
Point dueling noted the diligent said
A knife in hand not meant for bread

Weird and Wacky Tales & Other Such Nonsense
Linda Noble-Cordy

My Solitary Wanderer

My solitary wanderer
Oh, how I miss you so…

In dreams, I wonder where you are
And sometimes journey where you go
But where you've gone…
I do not know

In a field of eternity, I look for you
And sometimes call your name
It always echo's back to me
Like a quaint refrain

A melody of days gone by
Of memories and such
My solitary wanderer
Oh, how I miss you, oh so much

The Darker Side of Light

The Sea Raven's Barnacle

Canada Day
July 1st 2043
8:45 a.m.

James Noble-Broodbauer stood outside his mother's front door for what seemed a life time. He wanted to go in but something was holding him back. "You can do this Jim. You've got ta do this." He told himself.

Shadowy clouds began to gather in the sky above and the air grew thick with humidity making it difficult to breath. He entered the security code into the key-pad that was just above the door-knob. A gentle breeze caressed the back of his neck; causing him to shiver despite the heat. The rushing sound of rain surrounded him as he took a deep breath in and then let it out. "You can do this." He repeated.

Slowly he turned the knob and as the door unlatched a strong gust of wind flung opened the door causing him to lose his grip. "Wow, there must be a really bad draft in here." He thought as he walked over the threshold. He would have to remedy this before he would be able to sell the house.

It had been just under a year since he had buried her. In his mind there was still a slight lingering odor of death in the air. It would take a while longer before it would completely go away he surmised. You see James' mother had been dead three hot summer weeks before he had found her lying lifeless on the old brown couch. There were no warning signs, the old girl hadn't even been sick. It was quite a shock for James to find out she had a weak heart. She never complained once or told James about it. It wasn't until after her death he discovered she had been on three different medications for it.

Walking into the living room how empty it felt, and with good reason, for all the furniture, pictures… everything had been taken out and disposed of. James of course kept a few pictures and items his mother treasured, but everything else was either thrown out or given to charity. Looking at the dull bare walls he uttered, "It definitely could use a good coat of paint."

The Darker Side of Light

As he continued to walk around the empty shell that once held so much life, memory took him back to happier times. He recalled bringing his first girlfriend home. He was fifteen, and the girl, Emma... he remembered her name, was sixteen. He envisioned the old brown, conventional couch that once sat up against the now naked, paint chipped wall. He laughed to himself when he recalled his mother walking in and catching them kissing on the couch. What a fury his mother had when the mood suited her. "What is going on in here?" she screamed. "Get that piece of trash out of my house at once!" She took off her shoe and threw it at the two of them. James could almost feel the breeze of her shoe as it flew past his face, as his memory recalled the moment. Poor Emma didn't know what to do. She jumped up and made a mad dash for the front door. He laughed out loud again and smiled at a memory that at the time was so devastating.

The house was completely empty except for the attic. He would need to go up and have a look at what was actually up there. He was strongly considering calling in the same company that disposed of his mother's belongings, just have them take everything away.

He was always leery of the attic as a child but for the life of him, he couldn't remember why... Maybe it was because the house was very old or that his father once told him a grief-stricken woman hung herself on a rafter-beam up there, and her ghost walked around looking for a way out. James' father had a way of keeping him from doing something he didn't want him to do by scaring the pants off him. Like the time when James was eight years old; he told James not to play near the canal (*which James had a habit of doing*).

His father Bill, sat at the kitchen table waiting for his supper. His large spatula-like hands soiled and callused, tapped impatiently upon the table top as he looked over at James. "Your mom tells me you were playing in the river again? How many times do we need to tell you...?" He stopped, he was angry but mannerism didn't show it. He took a long drink of his beer, finishing off the bottle. Then placing it on the table he spouted, "Abby get me another beer, will ya hun?" A face tanned, and well-weathered from construction work, stared intently across the table at a frightened little boy. He didn't like being upset with James, but at the same time he knew the dangers of playing near the canal. They had both told him repeatedly not to go there. They had tried grounding him, taking away privileges and still he went there to play.

His mother Abigail placed a beer in front of Bill and as she turned to go back to the stove she said, "Will you please talk to him, it's got to stop before something bad happens, he just won't listen to me." Bill took a gulp of his beer, and placed it on the table. Pondering his thoughts, he looked towards his wife with a gleam of concern in his sparkling pale grey eyes.

"I didn't want to be the one to tell you this," he began, as his gaze fell upon James once again. "But it looks like I'm going to have to. You know Jimmy; if you fall in the river, that'll be the end of you…, you'll get eaten by the monster that lives at the bottom of it. And not all at once… he'll eat you a little-bit at a time… first your fingers then your toes, then a leg… that way he can survive until the next stupid little boy comes along and falls in, because *he* didn't listen to his parents either. Remember that girl that went missing last month?" He stopped and waited for a response. James nodded his head yes in acknowledgement. "She was last seen walking along Canal Road wasn't she? Well, what do you think happened to her?" he said firmly.

Abigail sighed deeply, as she shot 'the dagger look' at old Bill. "Never mind your father Jimmy, just don't go near the water, that's all." Yes, his father did have a way with words. All in all, he believed him, and stopped playing by the river after that. As a matter of fact, he still didn't like going near the canal… too many fatal, unexplainable accidents over the years.

James climbed up the long narrow staircase that led to a long narrow hallway which contained two closed doors on either side. At the end of the hallway to the left was his mother's bedroom, and to the right his old room. Directly in front of him now was a large window which was the only source of natural light in this dismal passageway. "This whole place needs a good coat of paint." He thought to himself. "So, dreary…"

He looked towards the ceiling. There was a small rope hanging down about two feet from his reach. He jumped up and grabbed on to it, but missed. He tried again, this time he got it. The weight of his body opened the latch and released the folded stairs. He was careful when pulling them down, and was worried he might fall through them as he began to climb up slowly.

The Darker Side of Light

He flicked on the light switch, to his surprise it worked. A dim light lit up the room to reveal a neat, yet very dusty, cob-web infested, yet very well organized, collection of boxes and small pieces of furniture. As his eyes glanced around the room he decided he would have the movers come in after all. There really wasn't anything he needed or wanted, and besides even if there was; it hadn't been used for so many years... what use would he have for it now?

Outside the thunder cracked, and the rain that had started when he arrived, pelted down on the rooftop with great force. It was very loud up in the attic and James wanted to get out of there quickly. Turning to climb down the stairs, just as he flicked the light switch to the off position, a thunderous clap shook the entire house. It somehow lit up the windowless, dust-ridden attic in such a fashion that he stopped dead in his tracks; hand still on the light switch; he stood frozen on the folding stairs. Not quite sure if it was out of fear or curiosity that made him stand there, but he did nonetheless.

Turning his head, he looked eye-level across the attic floor. The room was still aglow, and he thought it must be some kind of electrical storm. Why else would the room be lit-up? He realized his hand was still on the light switch so he removed it quickly, not wanting to get electrocuted. Then he noticed a box directly in front of him, up against the wall, it seemed to be glowing. A box marked 'Dad's things for James: December 2002.' "That box must have been put there sometime after grandpa died," he surmised. He had passed away over forty years ago; James was only eleven then, so he didn't really remember a lot about it. He did however, recall that his grandpa had come to stay with them two years prior, shortly after his father was killed in a car accident.

James flicked the attic light back on, as the electrical storm began to fade. He climbed back up the few folding stairs he had just gone down, walked over to the box, and picked it up. The box wasn't that big, nor was it very heavy. James found a chair and sat on it with the box on his lap. The tape across the top peeled off with ease and as he opened the box he felt a little excited.

On top, under a piece of old newsprint was a journal that belonged to his grandpa. On it was the title: 'The Omnibus of James Alexander Noble.' It was neatly hand written, and in perfect condition. James leafed through it then put it to one side and continued to go through the box.

Wrapped in old newspaper then again in a tea towel was an old wooden framed, black and white generation photo of his Grandpa as a little boy; his father was standing behind him, his grandfather to the left, and his great grandfather to the right. James had never seen this picture before. He stared at the picture for a while then put it gently down on top of the journal.

Next, he picked up a little oval container that looked like it was made out of wood but somehow, he knew it wasn't wood. It had swirly lines all over it, making it look a little like a brain. Turning it over, he felt something inside it move. He looked for a way to open it but couldn't find one. And after a quick study he placed it alongside the photo and journal.

Reaching into the box he picked up an old grey woolen sweater. James held it up and looked at it for a moment. He remembered it. He remembered his grandpa wore it all the time. It was in fine shape for such an old garment. It looked new and it had to be well over a hundred years old.

Then his thoughts took him back to the time when grandpa came to live with them. Tears welled up in his eyes as sad feelings attached to his childhood entered his thoughts. Wiping away a tear from his cheek, he told himself, "Stop being so foolish. It was so long ago… get over yourself Jim."

He placed the old keepsake next to his chest. He thought about the day his grandpa arrived from Scotland. It was just before Christmas, he and his mother picked him up by car. It was a new car, one she had just bought with the insurance money. The Toronto airport was a good hour's drive from their home in Bradford. When they finally arrived, and found grandpa, he was sitting there in his eminent grey sweater.

Mom rushed over to him. "Sorry I'm late dad." She told him, "The traffic was horrible, and the parking… Don't get me started on the parking…" "That's okay love, don't worry about it." Grandpa responded in his thick Scottish accent as he hugged his daughter. Then he took notice of James, "Hi ya Jimmy! Come give your old grandpa a big cuddle will ya?" James wrapped his arms around grandpa and squeezed him as hard as he could. He was so excited to see his grandpa again and happy he was going to be living with them now.

The drive home was not as long, for one reason the traffic was not as bad and for another reason, grandpa was there. James recalled vaguely his grandpa telling them about how he sold his house in Scotland, and the price he got for it and where he stayed for the last two weeks until he would travel to Canada. What James remembered most about the car ride was grandpa's thick Scottish accent. At times, he couldn't understand a word he was saying, but this changed over time, and once grandpa started telling him "*the tales*," he understood every word. "Ah yes… grandpa's stories… they were grand… as grand as the old man himself." He thought aloud.

James could tell that outside the storm which carried such rage had stopped. This would be a good time to leave and head for home, he thought. He picked up his grandpa's few meager belongings; taking care to wrap the photo back up neatly in the dish towel and then newspaper; then he carefully put everything back into the box. He would take them home to his own place and have a better look at these precious keepsakes. As he was leaving the old attic he decided he would not call the movers right away, he would go through the boxes first himself. After all there was really no rush. Maybe he'd bring his son William with him to help.

William was his only child, and every year since the divorce three years ago, he and his ex-wife Paula agreed to joint custody. This seemed to be the one thing they could agree on completely. "Yes," he thought. "That's what I'll do… I'll stop here first, before we head up to the cottage."

At home, he placed the box on his kitchen table, then walked over to the fridge and opened it. As he searched for something to eat, he could hear his grandpa's voice in his head. *"How about a nice cheese & jam sandwich Jimmy?"* Cheese and jam… he hadn't had one of those since he was a kid… "Oh, what the hell…" He chuckled to himself when he remembered -it was the only thing his grandpa even made.

When he was finished eating, he decided it was good a time to have a look at the old man's journal. Reaching into the box he took out the photo and unwrapped it again. "Wow" he thought surprisingly, "William really looks a lot like his great-grandpa."

He walked into the living room and placed the photo on top of his fireplace. Returning to the kitchen he took out the rest of the items - placed them on the table and draped the vintage sweater over one of the chairs.

Sitting at the kitchen table, strangely he felt like he was not alone, he felt the presence of his grandpa all around him. Memories faint, too far away to recall, clouded his thoughts for a moment then quickly disappeared. "Nonsense," he thought, shaking the notion from his mind. He would not allow his imagination to get the better of him.

He opened the book, there was an inscription on the inside cover that read: This journal is intended for my grandson James Noble-Broodbauer. December 1st, 2002. Mere weeks before he died, James thought. There was a small sealed envelope tucked securely inside the first page. James carefully opened it and took out a thin, neatly folded single sheet of paper which read:

Dear Jimmy, I wish we could have spent more time together. Life is very short and I know mine is almost up. I wanted to let you know before I go that I love you very, very much, you are a bonnie lad (my favorite... but don't tell your cousin Bob... Ha, ha, ho, ho).

I have told your mother not to give you this letter, or the items I will be leaving for you for wee while. Don't be upset with her for not giving you the sweater or Delwin's box right away. I know you are keen about them both.

I finished writing my journal, and I want you to have it. In it are some of the stories from my childhood that I have told you and others I have not. Well Jimmy, I will say Bye, bye for now... one day we will meet again, until then...

May you always find wisdom in your thoughts, strength in your belly, and love in your heart.

Love,
Grandpa Noble

The Darker Side of Light

James carefully folded the letter back up and placed it tenderly back in the envelope. He laughed out loud at the notion of framing it and conveniently showing his cousin Bob when he saw him next. Placing the envelope on the table, he opened to the first page and began to read, and as he did the words written formed a vision; a vision that took him to another time and another place…

It was the autumn of 1940; I remember it as if it were yesterday…

Mother sat at the kitchen table crying hysterically. Father had just told her he had received a letter from King George the VI. Father was needed to fight the good fight, as it were. He, along with a sizable number of other good, strong Scotsmen, was needed on the front lines to do battle.

He received the letter in the post a week earlier but he didn't want to tell mother, for fear she would be upset, and she was. He would be leaving in two weeks, he had no choice, and he didn't want one.

Mother was so very sad…

War was a terrible place to find ones' self in, it didn't matter whose side you were on. Mother had lost her father and two brothers in the First World War, and now it was fathers turn, she thought. "Don't worry love… it won't last long. I'll be home before you know it." Father said as he tried to comfort her. She just sat there shaking her head no, and crying, almost screaming it seemed. "Why do you have to go Jim? Can't you say you're no well?" Then she added, "Bess Aims' man Frank didn't have to go because of his bad feet, maybe we can get the doctor to say you've bad feet Jim?" "No Mary, I don't have bad feet. It's my duty to fight, and I am no coward…" he added. "I'm a man, and I will fight to protect not only my family but my country from those Nazi bas…!" He stopped himself! Mother looked at me and then at father. I could tell she wanted to say more, but she didn't. "Dry your eyes Mary, it's not the end of the world." Mother got up and started to clean the house. She didn't talk much for the next few days.

It would be up to me to find a way to keep mother's eyes from crying and father from dying… I knew just the place to go and who to see about it.

The Darker Side of Light

At the end of Blacklaw Lane there lived three sisters, Rose, Jean, and Annabel Green. Rose and Jean both considered old-maids, worked as seamstresses at the garment factory three miles outside of town. Annabel didn't on account of her blindness.

My best pal Stevie Jones told me that his granddad, who was chummy with Mr. Green (their father); told him that when Annabel was just a wee baby, she had the most beautiful and unusual sky-blue coloured eyes anybody had ever seen. Folk from miles around talked about how beautiful she was and how lovely her eyes were. She was even featured in The Paisley Daily Express our local paper; not only for her lovely eyes, but also because her mother was sixty-three years old when she had her. Both her parents were aged and her sisters were twenty-seven and thirty-two when she was born. She was apparently quite the celebrity in are wee part of the world. That is until a terrible incident happened…when wee baby Annabel was only three years old.

A mogully, nasty creatures they are… hideous monstrous beasts that would steal your very soul if they only could. Well one that went by the name Mortimer Mogully (I only know this because Stevie's granddad told him), caught wind of Annabel's eyes and had to have a look for himself. Turns out he was in search of new eyes, and took a fancy to poor baby Annabel's. One night he crept into her room and stole the poor ween's eyes and replaced them with shiny blue glass ones. Of course, nowhere as lovely as her own eyes and she couldn't see out of them like a normal person. But she could see… oh yes, she could see much more than you or me. It frightened most folk, those shiny marble eyes, so her mother and father put black glasses on the wee lass so that no one could see her eyes again.

When she was nine her mother died, and shortly after that her father also passed away. It seems she told them both not only the day but also the hour it would happen, and by what ailment.

Some called her a witch, for she could see things and knew things other folk didn't. Some folk went to her for cures and love potions, others for advice and others still, not so nice things…

Speaking of not so nice things… that brings me to Dora Flinch; she was the meanest, most ill-tempered hag you will ever meet. She lived two doors down from our flat on Forbes Place. My father once told me she was quite the looker when she was young, and that she had won several athletic awards in school. I couldn't tell if my father was serious or joking, for he was laughing a lot and my mother as well. I didn't get the joke... I think my father wasn't telling me the whole truth. Anyhow, I found it very hard to believe. She was no 'looker,' she was six feet tall and just as wide and was as ugly as mud-pie. Her old man Dave Flinch was a tall man too, but beside Dora he looked scrawny and brittle like he was about to break in two at any moment.

The two of them fought all the time. I had actually witnessed firsthand her chasing him down the road with a big cast iron frying pan in her hand. She waved it wildly in the air like a crazed lunatic. I could see what Da meant about her being athletic, it must have weighed a good two stone and when she tossed it at him, she hit him square in the back of his head. Knocked him out like a light. She carried him home and they stopped fighting for a long time. Dave wasn't much good for anything after that happened, but he did still have an eye for Annabel Green ...or so it was rumored.

This leads me back to Annabel Green's home. It seemed that a few of us had need of Annabel's attention on this particular day. A lady I had never seen before with a wee lassie was just leaving when I arrived. She thanked Annabel graciously as she passed her a 5-pound note- which by the way was a lot of money back then.

I had just sat down on a chair at the kitchen table when Dora Flinch came storming in. She didn't even knock. "You keep away from my Davie, you hear me you tottie...you're nothing but a no-good hussy!" Then she noticed me, a shocked look upon her face. She swiftly picked me up by my shirt collar and threw me out the front door, slamming it behind me. Well you could hear Deadly Dora Flinch (that's what we nicknamed her) screaming at poor Annabel all the way down the street. People came out of their homes to see what all the fuss was about. A crowd gathered outside the Green's home. There were big bangs and smashes, and then it was silent...

Mrs. White who was trying to peek in the window said quietly, "I think Dora must a killed her." Then the front door opened and Dora Flinch calmly walked out. Not a word did she speak. Everyone just stood there in utter shock. Had Dora killed Annabel Green? No one questioned her, no one dared, they were all too afraid. Dora Flinch went home and we didn't see much of her after

The Darker Side of Light

that. She never yelled at any of us kids nor did she chase us with her broom. Even Urey Steed felt it was safe to walk past her door again.

About Urey; he was one of my school pals. One day he came over to our street to play ball with some of us. It was his ball that landed amongst her clean linen and made some muddy stains on the white sheets that were hanging on the line. So, it was Urey who would have to go fetch it. Besides we were all too afraid to. Well, when Urey went to get his ball back he was in for a big surprise, we all were. She was so angry that she picked him up a tossed him clear across the river that ran beside our row-housing; he landed in a tree, fell out of it and broke his arm. His parents, of course went to her door to have a few words with her, but when they saw the size of her and that big mud-pie face, they were too afraid to do anything about it. Mr. and Mrs. Steed kept Urey away from our street and he was not allowed to play with us after that. Yes, she certainly earned her nickname 'Deadly Dora Flinch.'

I rushed back into the house and found poor beautiful Annabel crying. She sat at the kitchen table, her black glasses in two pieces on the floor. I picked them up for her and put them on the table. She looked towards the opened window as she called out loud, "Nothing to see here Mrs. White, go home to your wee-yens, and that goes for the rest of ya teh!" She looked over at me; it was the first time I had ever seen her eyes. I have to admit I was a little frightened. They were definitely stunning… and as black as coal.

As she started to calm down the blackness left her, changing the hue as I watched; her eyes turned to sapphire blue, and then crimson-violet. If an angel had walked on earth it was named Annabel Green. How lovely she was… her skin as soft and white as eiderdown, her hair a shiny mahogany-red that flowed over her shoulders like shimmering satin lace; and her eyes now bluer than the clearest blue sky… oddly enough there was no pupils in the middle, just shades of effervescent blue that seemed to move and shift forming cloud shaped images. And as she spoke the shapes changed to suit her mood. It was at that very moment I fell in love with her. I would marry Annabel Green when I grew-up, if she'd have me. Oh, what fanciful thoughts inspire the young…?

I noticed on her left cheek just below one of the mystical eyes was a large red welt. Deadly Dora had right hooked Annabel. Her glass eyes still filled with tears, I went over and gave her a cuddle,

The Darker Side of Light

but nothing could console her. I went over and put the kettle on. I thought a nice cuppa tea might be just the thing she needed.

We sat in silence for a long while as we drank our tea. Then Annabel stopped crying and confided in me. "I told the wench she was going to die Jimmie, and not in a nice way… I told her she would soon meet with a disastrous ending…" In my head, I was thinking "Good… she's a mean, old, crabby lady anyhow." But in my heart, I knew I didn't mean it. It must have terrified Dora to no end to see those black eyes…then to be told her fate… well that would have scared the britches off the bravest of men.

We sat for a while longer in silence then Annabel spoke again. "You are very kind Jimmie, thank you…" She dried up the last of her tears and asked me, "What brings a lovely wee laddie like yourself to my house today of all days? Don't tell me, I know… a love potion for a lassie ya fancy?" She smiled at me as she pinched my cheek. I could feel my face growing red. "Noooo!" I said quite embarrassed. "You needn't be so serious Jimmie; I was only given your leg a pull. I know what you're here for lad, and I know just where… I mean… I have just the thing."

She got up from the kitchen table and walk toward a closed door just off to the left side of the wood stove. "I'll be right back," she announced as she closed the door behind her. I'm not sure where the door led to, but I somehow had a feeling she had left the house. She was gone for a good ten minutes, maybe longer. Wondering if she was ever coming back, I got up to open the door as she was coming through it.

"Oh, what are you doing there Jimmie? You startled me." She said somewhat out of breath. "Where did ya go Annabel…? China?" "Em… something like that Jimmie," she replied laughingly. We both sat back down at the kitchen table. "It's good to be back," she said under her breath. She was sweaty and still breathing heavy. "What do you mean Annabel?" I questioned. "Oh, nothing Jimmie, pay me no-mind. How about you fix us another nice cuppa? And I'll tell you what I have for you." She said smiling at me.

I jumped up without hesitation and put the kettle on. "Where did you go?" I asked again. I was so excited. I knew she had something very special for me. She sat there quietly for a wee while then she spoke, as she did she reached into her shirt pocket

The Darker Side of Light

and took out a wee black velvet bag, and placed it in front of her on the table. "I have obtained a charm like no other Jimmie."

I quickly sat down and stared at it. "What kind of charm Annabel?" I questioned with anticipation. I reached out to touch it, but she put her hand over it to stop me. She looked at me with great concern and said, "What I am about to tell you Jimmie must never be shared with any folk from around here, they will not understand; do you understand what I'm telling you? You can't even tell your pals."

I shook my head in agreement as I stared at the hand that hid the treasure from sight. "I have your word then?" I looked at her, right in her sky-blue, glass eyes and said, "You have my word Annabel, I will never tell another living soul, I promise."

She looked deeper into my eyes, then deeper still; she seemed to be seeing things. She smiled gently at me with a look of knowing I can only surmise and stated. "There will be ones you can tell, you will know when the time comes, and by the right means you will reveal what I am about to reveal to you."

She continued to cover the mysterious sachet with her left hand as she gestured towards it with a nod of her head and a glare of her eyes, "In this wee black bag there is a powerful protection. The keeper of it is safe from all harm. Even Death itself cannot claim or take the man who carries this treasure. He is invincible as long as he carries it on or near his person. Do you understand?" I enthusiastically nodded my head yes. The excitement was overwhelming, I shouted out loud, "What is it Annabel? Please tell me before I bust!"

"I have searched out its source in another realm, one that is a far-flung distance from this one. It is a rare and unusual find, and I was very fortunate to come across it the way I did." She announced, "It is a barnacle off the magnificent Sea Raven."

I was so excited and had so many questions. I didn't know what a Sea Raven was, let alone what its barnacle was. How could it protect a person, and where had she gone in ten short minutes to get it? I didn't need to speak she would have the answers to my questions...all of them, even the ones I didn't know I had.

Nodding her head towards the wood-stove, "The kettles boiled love, let's have a wee cuppa tea before I tell ye more, I'm awfully parched."

There I sat, tea poured, waiting for Annabel to take her first sip. "Oh, that's lovely, just lovely Jimmie." She took another sip then sighed deeply. I was on the edge of my seat. In my head, I was screaming, "Well... tell me more I'm waiting! What is a Sea Raven's barnacle, can I see it now, can I see it now?" She looked at me and with hesitation, she said, "Aye, okay then, I'll tell ye, but remember not a word, right?" I shook my head frantically, "No, no, I won't tell a soul Annabel, I promise!" She slowly removed her hand from the desired treasure and as she continued to speak a strange and unusual view I did see.

I was witness to a somber land where nothing moved, not even a breeze blew, for the air itself deadened the space. The vision took me across an endless escarpment, where seagulls hung like immobile wind-chimes desperately waiting for a gentle wind to carry them home. Gigantic waves like crystal statues of foreboding doom hung in the air, while the rocks below waited in vain for their descent.

Then crossing a dead sea, I reached a colossal city. There were very little trees or greenery to speak of, and the streets were aligned with an assortment of tall ebony buildings stretching up into the sky like gigantic mirrored monuments. Contraptions that appeared to be forms of transportation littered the streets in a tangled mess of lifeless confusion.

And then I saw the people... Mannequins, they appeared to be, for none motioned not even to breath... An era frozen in time and space - like a final snap-shot taken. It was really quite frightening to see and my mind filled with horror when I thought about how much they looked like us... people of earth.

"In this place time does not stir, it can't..." I heard her voice; it seemed to be all around me. "It was stopped by a force understood only by the one who commanded its stillness. We call this force KYEN, and this is the reason for the Sea Raven's reign here. It has cast its protection over this world so that no further harm can come from it. This world was once a place of great achievement and prosperity; growth and development not only

The Darker Side of Light

of the race you see before you but also the universal core; the source of all source...KYEN.

A seed of corruption was planted in their minds by the evil ones; the ones we call the Boshney. It has been festering for a long, long time. And now there is no future here, only a past to be corrected. It is very disheartening to witness such loss, as advancements of a great pursuit has turned against itself.

This world - where time does not motion had only twelve hours left before it would be no more... all that exists in this realm would also be no more and never would again. That is what the Boshney hope to accomplish here. They are thieves and assassins - the evilest creatures you will ever meet.

KYEN sent the Sea Raven to this planet to protect it by holding it in a state of limbo. It circles high above the atmosphere where time still motions. It only comes down to rest on this doomed existence every, one hundred thousand light years. It was at this juncture that I was fortunate enough to make contact with this majestic apparition."

I too travelled to where this magnificent bird came to rest. Viewing it firsthand; its legs scaly like tall oak trees and just as thick, clung onto the sharp rust-colored rocks of the mountaintop. It was a creature beyond my wildest imagination. It stood at least ten stories in height, as obsidian waves of jet-black brilliance shimmered with florescent light, capturing every colour of the rainbow. The eyes of the deity were like enormous seer's stones that mirrored a solemn vast landscape. A beak of speckled granite opened slightly to release a melodic melody that touched my heart with blissful contentment. How safe and secure I felt in its company.

I saw Annabel approach it. How small she looked beside its greatness. She stood close to it and spoke words I did not understand. As it responded to her I felt its gaze upon me. She placed a hand on one of its coarse legs and pinched off a small flake of its skin. She spoke to it again and then ran down the mountainside as fast as her legs could carry her. The vision ended... and I was back in Annabel's kitchen. "Wow that was amazing!" I shouted.

The Darker Side of Light

"Okay you may have a look." She said gesturing to the mysterious package. I reached out my two hands and picked up the tiny black velvet bag. It was incredibly light, and for a moment I thought it might be empty. I opened it up and looked inside. To my surprise there was an object within. I reached into the wee bag and took out a small black shiny feather shaped stone. I held it in my fingertips, it was heavier somehow, and had the weight and feel of a metal like iron about it. It felt pleasantly cool and smooth to the touch, and I had a strong need to rub it. When I did, it made a faint familiar sound, like a tune I knew but couldn't remember the words.

"Don't be doing that! Don't' be rubbing it." She grabbed my hand to stop me. "We don't want to be drawing any unwanted attention to ourselves, now do we?" Then she warned me, "You must never rub it Jimmie, it is a very bad thing to do; and will only lead to danger. There are things, awful nasty creatures that would kill for what you hold in your hand. If they hear the sound they will surely find it, and they will kill anything or anyone who gets in their way. They are very tricky and cunning too, and will find a way to steal it from you or whomever you give it to, namely your father... so they must never find it."

"Okay," I said. She added, "There is something else you need to know... this part is most important. You cannot tell your mother or father about what you have seen. And you must somehow hide the charm from sight; sew it into a piece of clothing he owns and will be taking with him. It has to be something you know he would not leave behind like a shirt or a jacket. But make sure he doesn't find out, for if others find out he carries it, they could easily over-power him and take it from him. His life would be in great danger as would be your mother's and your own." I nodded my head in agreement.

"Now for payment..." She looked at me with a very serious look upon her face. "You will come here this Saturday and do chores, agreed?" I agreed whole heartedly. "Thank you, Annabel." I wrapped my arms around her and hugged her with all my might. "Way you go now, my sisters will be home any minute."

No sooner did she say it, when they came barreling through the front door. I put the Sea Raven's barnacle back into the wee black sack and placed it in my front pants pocket. I dodged around the

The Darker Side of Light

two old maids and as I walked out the front door Rose spoke to Annabel with great concern. "What has happened Annie, we heard on our way home about that Dora Flinch... are you all right love?" As I turned to close the door behind me I shouted, "Thank you Annabel, see ya Saturday."

On my way home, I thought about what I had seen and what Annabel had told me. I was in awe and at the same time bewildered. The vision I had just witnessed was one I had never experienced before. It was as if for that very moment I was actually there, in that strange world. I played it over and over again in my mind. How I wished I could tell Stevie about it, boy would he be impressed. Alas, I was not to tell anyone, not even my best pal, I gave my word and a man is only as good as his word... so not a word would I speak of it. Well that is until the time was right...

I felt so happy that father was going to be safe. I ran through my plan of action in my head. Where could I hide the wee velvety black sack with the protection charm inside, so that father could not find it? And what did he carry with him all the time? Yes, that's it! His woolen sweater! He always wore it morning and night. Mother had bought it for him on his birthday last January. He said it was the best present he had ever received. You see my father had a condition were he always felt cold, and caught the chills often. Even in the nice weather he rarely felt warm. He told my mother that since she had given him the sweater he never felt the cold. Surely, he would be taking it with him to keep him warm.

It was settled, I would go home and when father takes it off to give himself a wash, I would take it and quickly sew the sack securely to the inside seam. I was fairly good at sewing, even if it was women's work.

Mission complete, Father would be safe, and although mother would still worry, I would assure her that father would come home to us.

James sat for a moment and wondered about the incredibly vivid imagination of this storyteller. He wondered what caused his grandpa to invent these stories in the first place. He was so young, and to have such an active imagination was beyond James' understanding. All in all, it was a lot to take in. He took the journal and went into the living room to sit in comfort and continued to read.

***

The following Saturday, I went to Annabel's home just as we had agreed. I spent the good part of the day chopping wood and piling it up beside her house. When I was finished, she invited me in for tea and biscuits. "Did you find a safe place to hide what I gave you?" she asked me. "Oh yes," I told her, "I found the perfect place. I sewed it inside the sweater mother gave him for his birthday last year. He always wears it, and just about never takes it off on account of his condition." "Oh yes", she said coyly, "I know just the one you mean." I think my mother bought the sweater from Annabel, but she never did say.

I was dying to know more about the world Annabel had shown me, and just as I was about to question her about it, she answered.

Staring at me with great focus, her glass eyes filled with tears, and somehow, I could feel her sadness. It was as if it were a part of me too. "Long ago the evil Boshney set their sights on another world; one that is most dear to me. It is a world called Meltehmare. It is a great distance from here. You can only achieve entry by way of portal; a doorway that takes you there in the blink of an eye."

I looked deeply into her magical glass eyes and as she continued to speak the vision of this world came into view. "You must venture far beyond this realm's boundaries; beyond mortal reality, beyond time as you have come to understand it. Here you will find Meltehmare, place of my birth."

"Wow! That's amazing" I said excitedly. I could see it as clear as day. It was absolutely beautiful, and unlike the other world this one was alive and vibrant. As I continued to view a land of great splendor, we traveled with some speed across the opened terrain. The scene was one of beauty, utterly breath-taking; I imagine this is what heaven must look like. The colours were brilliant, animated shades of illumination that seemed to reach out and touch my senses. I felt such joy and pleasure here. It seemed to be in the air itself. Never before had I ever seen or felt such loveliness… I was at home here, not only welcomed but safe as well. And in that moment if I could have stayed – I would have.

"Why did you leave it Annabel? Why would you leave such a beautiful place?" I questioned. "I didn't have a choice in the matter. My life was in great danger as was the life of all Melts, so my parents along with the parents of other wee yens, had us all sent away before it was too late. I was sent to earth, while others were sent to destinations unknown."

As she continued to reminisce she warily said, "We should have listened to the warnings of the Myomancy, but alas we did not. It would prove to be a dreadful mistake." I looked at her confused and she continued. "The elders were warned about the evils that were about to come, but they did not heed it. Instead they welcomed the wicked Boshney with opened arms, the fools... and no help came to us - not like they did with the frozen world you witnessed."

Then she took a deep breath in and then moaned a deep lonely sigh of sadness. "Meltehmare is no more..." Before my eyes was a land without colour, dreary and bleak. A hopeless waste land where nothing motioned, nothing existed. "The Boshney have destroyed our world; raped it of its essence and stripped it of its power." Even though she spoke of such atrocities she did not allow me to view the actions that caused the devastation.

"The ones that stayed behind were slowly drained of their life source as was the land itself. Used as food to feed their horrific appetites. But even this has an ending." She gave me a sad wee wink and we sat in silence for a long while surrounded by a virtual wasteland, a world dreary and desolate. "No more will they covet my folk or my land for it alas is no more..." She stated.

Then it was over, the vision stopped and although we were back in Annabel's kitchen the sadness was still with us.

She continued to speak, "They need to feed on life's pure essence or they will die. When they realized their food source was depleting quickly on Meltehmare, they tried in vain to breed us like cattle, but only met with failure at every attempt. Too weak to reproduce, one by one, the Melts that remained met with a tragic ending as well. Now the sinful Boshney are forced to search the universe for the remaining few of us; all the while sourcing out other forms of provisions. Other sources that are not as rich, but when you're starving, ham hocks are as good as steak.

The Boshney not only need our power to survive, they crave it as well. The few of us that remain throughout the endless universe

The Darker Side of Light

grow stronger in substance and the Boshney know it. They can sense it like a thirst that will never be satisfied; or a smell that will never have the satisfaction of taste upon its tongue. They hunger for our power and grow weaker as we grow stronger. We will use this forthcoming to bring an ending to these monsters and those that do their bidding." She looked at me with the most serious of somber looks and said, "That is of course, if earth is saved before the Sea Raven's reign is complete."

Flabbergasted beyond reasoning I questioned. "Are you tell'n me that the frozen planet is earth? That it's my planet that's doomed?" She took my hand in hers and spoke softly, "Aye Jimmie - earth. Not the earth you know, but the earth of the future.

"How did this happen, how can we fix it?" I said in a panic. It seemed more important now that I knew it was my home in danger of extinction. "Don't fret lad, events have started to take place that will change history. We still have time; time to heal the mistakes made." She assured me.

We just have to deal with the nasty mogullies in the meantime. They are relentless and very tricky beast. "Do you mean like the one who stole your eyes Annabel?" I questioned. She laughed at me, "No mogully ever stole my eyes lad. Where did you get a crazy notion like that...? Wait don't tell me, I know. That Stevie, remind me to have a wee word with him." She chuckled and said, "Oh look at the time Jimmie, its half past five, you'd best be on your way home, your mother will be worried if you're late for supper. "Can I come again next Saturday, and do more work for you Annabel?" I asked. "Aye, I'll see you next Saturday love, if not then, another time and we can have another chat."

She hugged me for a long time and then kissed my cheek. What was that all about? I wanted to ask, but I could see Annabel was still very sad, for her eyes were filled with tears again. She walked me to her front door. I thought she must still be thinking about her planet and the family she had lost. I thanked her for the tea and biscuits, and headed home for supper. I just couldn't wait for next Saturday to come…

James stopped reading at this point and decided he would make himself another cup of tea before continuing. It was so interesting… his grandpa's journal. He vaguely remembered this story. He thought that more than likely his grandpa had left out some of the details he was now reading.

He went into the kitchen to make the tea. As he did he noticed the little oval box on the kitchen table was vibrating. Was he imagining things he thought? He went over and picked it up, then shook it. "Delwin's box…" He said out loud. Running his fingers across the grooves of its smooth finish he wondered what it could possibly have inside. He recalled the words that were written for him: 'So don't be upset with her for not giving you the sweater or Delwin's box right away. I know you are keen about them both.'

Why was he so 'keen' about them both? He wondered. He put down the perplexing item and picked up the pale grey sweater and decided to try it on. It buttoned down the front, and had seven nickel-sized, charcoal-grey buttons firmly attached. He guessed that perhaps the sweater was originally the same color as the buttons.

To his surprise, it fit perfectly, and better yet it didn't feel dirty or old. As a matter of fact, he felt comfortable and amazingly cozy… he could understand why it was so well worn.

The tea made, James headed back into the living room to continue reading. Still wearing his keepsake, he sat down and took a long sip of hot tea.

***

Father's train was leaving at 6 a.m. Friday morning. He was on his way to the Czech Republic with his regiment 439th brigade. Oddly enough mother didn't cry when we arrived at the Glenfield railway station. She just squeezed him tight and told him he'd better come back in one piece or she'd kill him. As she continued to hold him tight she made him promise to write every chance he could, and keep her posted on his whereabouts. Mother didn't want to let him go, but she finally did.

I could see in my father's eyes he was very sad to be leaving us. He squeezed me tight and patted my back firmly. He told me to be brave, and take care of my mother. I smiled at him, and gave him a big hug and kiss, knowing full-well he would be safe from harm.

I never did make it to Annabel's as planned. Saturday morning at 2 a.m. the first bomb dropped. The sirens went off all night long and mother and I took refuge along with a lot of other folk in the basement of Paisley Abbey. It was a terrible, awful noise, those sirens. I covered my ears to block out the noise, but it didn't seem to help; and then the bombs… a horrible whistling sound just before they hit the ground…BOOM! It felt like the whole planet was under attach and soon we would all be dead.

I thought about the frozen earth, and wished we were frozen now. All of a sudden, I was there. But this time the people were moving, carrying on as if nothing was wrong. I stood in the middle of a street and everything moved around me very quickly. I tried to call out to them, to warn them of the danger they were in; I tried to move, but alas I could do neither. Then I saw it- the Sea Raven. As it gracefully glided down into earth's atmosphere all motion stopped and I was freed from whatever force held me still.

Even though the noise and panic had stop in my world, and we were allowed to go back home; my mother and me, had great trouble sleeping at night for fear a bomb would drop right out of the sky and kill us in our sleep. And as fate would have it, we weren't far off the mark. Sadly, this would be the fate of one Dora Flinch…

Three weeks had passed since the first attack, and it had been five days since the last siren warning. It was 6 p.m. I remember this because mother had just put supper on the table; a nice big scuff of liver and onions, with mashed-tatties and gravy, my favorite! I couldn't wait to start eating. Mother had just sat down with me to say our prayers.

There was no warning sounded, no explosion, but we knew something terrible had just happened. Mother and I looked at each other as we sat frozen on our chairs. "Did you feel that Jimmie?" she finally said to me. I nodded my head yes, as we both quickly got up and ran out the front door. We weren't alone, our neighbors were all coming out of their homes as well.

The Darker Side of Light

A small group of us gathered on the street. All of a sudden Mr. Johnson yelled out. "Look at the Flinch's roof!" We all turned our attention to it. Smoke was bellowing out a large hole in the roof. Mr. Johnson and Mr. Thomson entered the house while my mother ran back into our house to call the fire brigade.

No sooner did Mr. Johnson and Mr. Thomson go into the house when they came running back out. "Clear the area! Everyone get back!" They both shouted one after the other. "It's a bomb, clear the area, get the children away!" Mr. Johnson grabbed his wife and children and headed towards the water. Mr. Thomson did the same and the others were close behind. I, of course ran back into my house to get my mother. We all waited on the other side of the river for the fire brigade to arrive.

As we watched and waited we saw Dave Flinch come out the front door. He looked perplexed, almost stupefied, which was really not an unusual look for him. Mr. Thomson called out to him. "Dave, get away from there!" Dave stood and stared at us, he didn't know what to make of it all. Mr. Thomson ran to the bridge, that was as close as he was about to get. "It's a bomb Dave! Run...!" He shouted at the top of his voice. Dave still didn't know what was going on. But he did heed the warning and ran towards Mr. Thomson as fast as he could.

It didn't take the Strathclyde fire brigade long to get there for they were located less than a kilometer away on Gordan street. Before I knew it, our little street was filled with all kinds of strange folk. The police put up barricades so curious on lookers couldn't get too close. The whole block and the houses around it were evacuated and we were all sent to Paisley Abbey for shelter again.

While we were there, I overheard my mother as she stood outside talking to some of the other ladies. "It's a terrible tragedy what's happened to Dora Flinch. God rest her poor wicked soul." My mother said to Bess Aims and Mrs. Thomson as they nodded their heads in agreement and made the sign of the crucifix across their chests. "Aye, but if you ask me, she had it coming." Responded Mrs. Thomson, who lived right next door to the Flinch's. "Everyone knows she's an awful brute, and the way she used to treat poor Dave... Well we've all seen Dave walking around town sporting a black eye on more than one occasion. Mind you, any man who would put up with that - really isn't much of a man." "And the way she'd boss him around; yelling at him like he was

The Darker Side of Light

a child...." Mother said as she sorrowfully shook her head back and forth.

"Poor man..." Bess Aims started to laugh. "Mind the time he hung her fancy silk knickers on the line? The ones she bought in London at that fancy posh shop." "Aye," Mrs. Thomson added, "and one of the Johnson boys tried to use it as a kite? Foolish lad... He could have made a four-man tent- he could have housed the lot..." They all started to cackle. I started to laugh myself, for it was me and my pal Stevie who put him up to it. Boy was Deadly Dora ever mad when she saw her good drawers flying high in the sky and then to see all the kids on the street laughing... well let's just say we all stayed clear of her for a good fortnight.

Just then Dave Flinch walked past and hush fell over the gossiping gaggle. "Oh, I'm so sorry about your loss Dave." Mrs. Thomson quickly said. "It's just awful, and you were so lucky to be in another room when it happened."

Dave didn't say anything he just nodded at the ladies and kept walking. The three busy-bodies stared at the back of him until he was far off, and then Mrs. Thomson whispered, "Did you see his eye? That's what I'm talking about." Mother and Bess Aims both nodded their heads in agreement. Then Bess Aims added quietly, "I heard after giving him that shiner she sent him to bed with no supper, and that's why she was sitting at the table alone when the bomb went through the roof and landed on her head." "I heard the same thing," my mother said agreeingly.

"We should count our blessings that no one else was killed. If that bomb would have gone off it would have taken out the whole block. Your place for sure Mable, you're right next door." Mother said mournfully as she put her hand on Mrs. Thomson's shoulder. Mrs. Thomson responded, "I don't want to think about it..."

She made a gesture by nodding towards the direction Dave had just taken. "I bet he's on his way over to that Annabel Green's..."

Mother added, "You know what I heard..." Then she noticed me sitting quietly on the stairs behind them. "What are you doing there Jimmie? Away you go now!" The three of them shoed me away, and as I ran off down the street I yelled, "Annabel wouldn't have anything to do with Dave Flinch! He's a coward and a Pansy-boy! She's too good for the likes of him." Mother yelled at me.

"This is not for your big lugs Jimmie Noble; away you go play with your pals. Mind you don't go near the house though..."

I followed after Dave, I wanted to make sure he wasn't on his way to Annabel's home. I soon caught up to him just as he was about to enter Mulligan's Tavern. I waited then walked in a few minutes after he did and sat down beside him at the bar.

He ordered a pint of ale and a shot of scotch. He threw back the scotch then wrapped his two hands around the pint. I stared at him as he sat hunched over on the bar-stool, looking like a man who carried the weight of the world upon his two chipped shoulders. I kind of felt sorry for the bloke.

He took a big gulp of his ale and then looked over at me. "Jimmie, what are you doing here lad, have you come to gloat?" "No, I said firmly. I just wanted to ask you about Annabel." "Annabel... Annabel Green?" he said surprisingly. "What about her?" "Is it true what they say about you and her?" I couldn't finish the sentence. He smiled a little and chuckled under his breath. He took another big gulp finishing off the rest of his ale. "Another round Bill," he ordered the bartender, "and a cider for the lad." I waited for him to answer. The bartender brought over the drinks and once again Dave threw back the scotch. "Ahh, that is lovely," he signed and licked his lips. I took a sip of my cider and continued to wait for him to answer. He didn't...

"Well is it true?" I asked again. He looked at me somewhat puzzled, like he didn't know what I was talking about, or as if I was speaking another language. "Is what true?" he asked. "What are you going on about Jimmie?" I think he must have suffered brain damage with all the knocks to the head he had endured at the hands of Deadly Dora.

"You know... about you and her... I was there the day Dora came to Annabel's house. She came barging in, threw me out the front door and started fighting with Annabel." I could see by the look on his face he didn't know anything about it or maybe it was because he just didn't care.

He continued to drink as I spoke. "I want to know if there is any truth to the rumor because I plan on marrying Annabel Green when I grow-up." He started to choke on his ale and spat out a large amount that was still in his mouth. Laughing hard and coughing at the same time he said. "You're fixing to marry that wench are ya lad…make an honest woman of her?" He patted my shoulder, "Good luck to ya son."

I didn't see what he found so amusing, I was quite serious. He turned to Bill who was at the other end of the bar serving another customer and shouted at the top of his voice. "Did ya here that Bill, there's going to be a wedding, our Jimmie is fixin to marry Annabel Green." Bill walked towards us with a big smile on his face. "You don't say… and does your mother know about this Jimmie?" The man at the end of the bar started to join in to by humming the wedding march.

A couple of ladies that my mother knew, who were sitting at a table in the corner piped in with their two bits. "Oh, a wedding, I can't wait…I hope I get an invite?" the one said to the other. "Aye, me too," said the other. "Have ya picked the date Jimmie?" They all started to laugh and carry-on. "It looks like you've some competition Dave." said one of the nosey ladies. "Aye it looks like it," he responded.

I was so embarrassed. I could feel my face growing beet-red. I ran out of the place yelling, shut-up, shut-up…" Dave called to me. "Come back lad, we're only having a bit of fun with ya." I didn't stop, I just kept running until I arrived at Annabel's house.

I needed to see her to ask her about Dave. I knocked upon her door, no answer… I knocked again…still no answer. That was strange because Annabel was always at home. I went around the back of her house to see if she was there. No sign of her. I went back around to the front of the house and tried to open the door. It was locked. I peeked in the window. The place was empty…

Annabel and her sisters were gone. As my breath hit the window pain, the glass fogged up. I took a step back, and just as I was about to wipe away the condensation, I notice something written on the glass. It said, "I will find you." Had Annabel left this message for me I wondered?

Still, I was very sad, where could she have gone? Maybe she went home to her planet I thought. I wish I could have said goodbye. I went back to Paisley Abbey and hoped that mother didn't catch wind of my shenanigans at Mulligan's Tavern. She would be really upset if she were to find out I had followed Dave into the pub and really angry if she knew what I had said.

It was two days before they were able to safely remove the bomb. They flew in a man from England to de-fuse it. He informed a few of the adults that we were very lucky, because apparently, the bomb was no dud. It was still active, and he couldn't explain why it hadn't detonated when it hit the ground. Me and my mates figured it was because of Deadly Dora… it was too afraid to explode.

The adults all stood across the river and watched as they carried out the bomb and loaded it onto a flat-bed lorry. Some of the women, my mother included, were terrified, thinking it might still go off, they yelled at us boys to stay back. Of course, we didn't, we wanted to see it up close. It was huge and reminded me of a big shiny, metal fish.

A wee while later they carried out the remains of Dead Dora Flinch. They had placed her in a large wooden crate and put her on the same lorry as the bomb. I don't think there was much left of her, how could there be?

James remembered parts of this story and a little rhyme that his grandpa had told him that went; 'Deadly Dora Flinch, she never gave an inch, and in the end, it was her that got the pinch…'

***

One night I had a strange and unusual dream. It was as real as real can be. In my dream, I was floating in a big glass bubble above my home town. Somehow, I could see for miles and miles. Annabel was there with me, (she had found me) her exquisite outline glowing against the night sky with majestic shimmering, radiant light. I was seeing her true form for the first time. How utterly divine she was, and perfect in every way.

She was telling me about the war. How it had been orchestrated by the Boshney; that they were using war as a means to destroy mankind. The violent actions of the human race were being used as a cover to hide their evil deeds. I didn't quite understand what she was trying to tell me for I was not wise to these deeds, but soon I would be witness to them.

As Annabel looked out over the landscape she continued to speak to me. "The Boshney know that some of us are here on earth, and they know that war is the perfect cover to seek out and capture us. They have sent Dodgesons and Dugties to earth to invade the body of mankind in the hopes to gain the knowledge needed to find us. In this attack, they corrupt the mind to the point of madness. And if the madness doesn't claim ya, the lethal assault on vital organs surely will." She turned to me and as her gaze met with mine, her lovely glass eyes revealed a vision of the danger. "Take warning with me Jimmie, for you must protect yourself against this threat.

James stopped reading, he could picture in his mind's eye the whole scenario, and it actually frightened him a little. He remembered clearly the story his Grandpa had told him about these creatures. In his head, he could hear the old man's Scottish brogue as clear as day and could envision his actions as he described these bizarre entities.

"Dodgesons are these tiny wee microscopic creatures made out of what appears to be dust. They are attracted to fire; which makes them strong and changes them into Dugties; a powerful underworld creature. The Dugtie can enter the body as smoke, so mind that you never smoke Jimmy. Dodgies are very dangerous wee beasties, they were sent to earth to not only find the Melts, but also to wipe out mankind. The only way to destroy Dodgies or Dugties is to get them wet before they enter the body. They hate water and keep away from it at all times, for water kills them instantly. So you'd be wise to keep a glass of water by your bedside to protect you while you sleep.

What they do is when you are breathing; as we all do… they travel up the nose, or if you're a mouth breather, down the throat. Now you might think that the wet in your nose or mouth would kill them…and you'd be right, however, there might be that one in a million- that smart one that goes straight down the middle, and wreaks havoc with your insides. They cause all kinds of nasty business once inside. It's a terrible thing to witness. I always keep a wee bag of pepper in my pocket for luck and just in case…"

The old storyteller reached into his pants pocket and pulled out a little plastic bag of black pepper and shook it at him.

The Darker Side of Light

"It's your only defense against them. If one of those nasty little buggers gets through, you'll have to sneeze him out. Here Jimmy you take this bag, and keep it in your pocket at all times. They don't stand a chance against a good sneeze once they're in. Now if by chance one gets to fire, well that's a whole other kettle of fish my boy. Bloody Dugtie, I saw one once... turned a good Christian man into a horrible, wicked monster. It was a terrible frightening site to see. Oh, the evil deeds he did carry out... But that's a tale for another day. I just heard your mother's car door slam."

He looked towards the front door, "Shhhh! She's here... not another word lad!"

Grandpa quickly took the mute off the TV and pretended to be asleep on the couch. James recalled being terrified for weeks on end, and his mother telling his grandpa, no more stories. James chuckled to himself; he carried a little plastic bag filled with pepper in his pocket for years after that. And a fresh glass of water fashioned his night table at bedtime, even still. He always thought it was there just in case he got thirsty in the night. Funny thing...he never seemed to drink it, never did get thirsty in the night.

Flash-backs to the doctor's office and visits to Sick kid's hospital pierced his memory for a moment then were gone. The fear and the feelings attached to those days seemed too far away too surreal; nonsense, he told himself. It was foolish to be afraid, after all he was no longer a child, and besides, these were just the tales of a very imaginative old man. After a few minutes, James continued to read from where he had left off. As he did he pictured once again in his mind's eye the scene as if he were actually there.

"Take warning with me Jimmie, for you must protect yourself against this threat." As clear as day they appeared, there must have been over a million of them. They swarmed the open sky searching for their victims. "They must never enter your body Jimmie; for if they do they will surely kill you. They will then destroy every living thing on earth, and they will not stop until they get results. Do you understand Jimmie?" She questioned. I didn't completely understand, not at first.

She continued, "A bounty hunter who travelled across the Temissqual quadrant, twenty odd years ago to examine a wee lassie that might be a Melt, somehow disappeared. Over time suspicion grew when he did not report back. They eventually found out his last stop was earth. Their prophets devised a method known by some as Spodomancy; Divination by way of fire... Which told them he arrived in a place known as Poland; that is where they began the search." As I continued to gaze into her seer's eyes she showed me the most horrifying sight I had ever seen, and hope to never see again.

There were hundreds of folks being herded into train- cars like cattle. Men, women and children alike were being hit, punched and kicked for no apparent reason as they were forced to board these large, windowless wooden crates. Ones that refused to go were shot dead, or beaten until they cooperated.

I witnessed one woman crying desperately as a soldier took her wee baby off of her and carelessly tossed her on the ground like she was a piece of trash. Even though she spoke a different language from my own, I could understand every word. "Noooo", she screamed. "Please let me keep my baby! Please don't take her away." She dropped down on her knees as she groveled at his feet. "I beg you please kind sir ...I'll do anything you want, please don't hurt her, please give her back to me." But the heartless soldier just took the butt-end of his riffle and rammed it into side of the women's head. She fell over and never moved; she just lied there lifeless.

The wee lassie that was no more than one-year-old cried and cried, and then she too was brutally silenced. I screamed out "Nooooooo!" I felt so helpless. Covering my eyes, to shield me from the iniquity, I pleaded, "Take me away from here Annabel, I don't want to see anymore."

James envisioned the whole thing and he could hear her heart wrenching cries as they pierced through to his very soul. He felt her sadness and her fears as tears poured down her little soft rosy cheeks. He wanted nothing more than to hold her and comfort her; take her away from all this injustice. He saw the heartless soldier; he saw the evil within his soul; the look upon his face as he sadistically shook and choked the little child to death. As if she was less than nothing, without importance or significance; just a noise that needed to be silenced.

His body jerked violently as he tried to force himself back to reality. Questioning his own sanity, he felt he needed to stop reading for a while. He would need to digest what he had just experienced, so that he could put it into the proper perspective. Besides it was late and he had work in the morning.

He went into the kitchen and placed the journal down on the table. Running his hand over its cover he thought about his own son, he was just about the same age that his grandpa was when he made-up these stories. He wondered about the terrible things his grandpa must have witnessed as a young boy to have fabricated the stories the way he did.

He took off the sweater and hung it over the chair again. Strangely he felt a little cold and naked when he took it off. He went over to the temperature controls and turned the thermostat up, in hopes to turn off the air conditioner and warm the air a little.

James got up at 7 a.m. the next day and got ready for work, it was business as usual. He was still very tired as he had great difficulty going to sleep the night before. He tried to put the events of yesterday behind him, but found it very difficult to do. Although he found the journal to be very interesting, he had to remind himself that it was a fictional story he was reading, and should be viewed only as that.

He somehow managed to get through the day, and then made his way back home at 4:15 p.m. When he entered his condo, from the doorway he spied the kitchen table. There lay the journal just as he had left it the night before. A part of him wanted to continue reading, but the other part told him no, not yet. He went in for a shower then had something to eat. Walking the short distance into the living room, journal in hand he sat down and opened to the page where he had left off.

When I awoke, I thought about what I had witnessed. Such hatred for another person, I never knew existed until that moment. I wondered if the cold-blooded soldier was ever just a man, and if so, had he a wife and child of his own, and if he did… how could he commit such a heinous act? If nothing else, he must have had a mother… or someone in his life that he loved at one point. I just could not understand such hatred, and to this day of writing and remembering, I still do not understand. The only explanation for these actions would be put upon the Dugtie… For no man or soldier in a sane state could commit such horrific deeds.

The Darker Side of Light

It had been a month since father had left; finally, Mother received her first letter from him. They had been stationed in the Czech Republic in a place called Novo Mesto, which bordered with Poland and Germany. They would be moving into Poland in a few days, and then making their way along the border into Germany. He told my mother he hadn't seen any combat yet. She was very happy about that.

This would turn out to be the only letter my mother would receive from my father. Months and months passed and she feared the worse, for my father, like her own father and brothers were infantrymen; frontline foot soldiers, sent into the heart of Satan's den...

I knew she was thinking about the loss of her father and brothers in the First World War, she didn't need to say it. There were no words that would ease her worries. I still could not tell her about the protection charm father had with him for I had made a promise to Annabel.

Then it happened...

It was a lovely winter's day, very unusual weather in Scotland. The sun was shining for the first time in a fortnight. A warm breeze blew gently and began to dry-up the wet ground. After school, my mates and I got together for a wee game of footie. By the time the game was finished, it was almost supper time, so I ran home, not wanting to be late. I threw open the front door and yelled, "Ma, I'm home, what's for supper?" No response. "Ma!" I yelled again. Still silence. I went into the kitchen only to find my mother in tears. Her face was red from crying, and her eyes were nearly closed from the swelling. When she saw me, she burst into tears. She was clutching a piece of paper tightly in her hand. "Oh Jimmie, I've got bad news to tell ya son, it's about your Da..." She could barely get the words out. "He's been killed..."

I ran over to her and wrapped my arms around her. "No Ma, it's a mistake, it's a mistake, he can't be dead!" "I'm afraid it's true pet..." She held on to me tight, as she sobbed uncontrollably. I would have to tell her about the Sea Raven's Barnacle, I would have to let her, father was protected and that even bullets could not harm him. I loved my mother so much, I couldn't stand to see her in so much pain...

"Don't be sad Ma, he's alive I tell you, he's alive... Before Da left, I went over to Annabel Green's home and got a very powerful protection charm for him. I sewed it in Da's sweater because I knew he would be taking it with him on account of his condition. It's a barnacle off the Sea Raven. Annabel told me it was the most powerful charm anyone could possess; you can't die as long as you have it with you. So you see Ma, it's a mistake, they made a mistake." "Oh, Jimmie that's just nonsense, you don't believe that, do you?" She gently touched my cheek, and looked deeply into my eyes with a compassion that only a mother can own. "There is no such charm Jimmie, no magic that can elude death." She paused for a moment. "...And besides, your father never took the sweater with him. It wouldn't fit in his carry-on; it's still hanging up in his wardrobe."

My heart dropped down to my feet. I couldn't believe what my mother was saying. "No Ma!" I screamed and raced into my parent's bedroom and flung open the wardrobe door.

There it was, hanging neatly on a hanger, my father's only shield against the war.

"Noooo!" I screamed at the top of my lungs. I ripped it off the hook and clung on to it in desperation. Hugging it tightly, wishing my father was still in it I cried, "I'm sorry Da, I'm so sorry..." I felt so empty inside.

I fell onto my mother's bed; my salty tears stained her nice clean white pillow case as I cried and cried... It was all my fault; I should have made sure my father had it with him when he boarded the train. I should have checked first, asked mother if she'd packed it for him. But alas I did not, and now my father was dead.

James closed the journal. He took a deep breath in then let out a long mournful sigh. He looked over at the photo on the fire place with tears in his eyes. "My poor grandpa..." He couldn't begin to imagine how devastated he must have felt; to have such overwhelming responsibility and guilt about losing his Dad. For a second he thought the boy in the picture smiled and waved to him. He rubbed his eyes, got up and walked towards it. "I must be going crazy, now I'm seeing things." He turned and looked in the

The Darker Side of Light

direction of the kitchen. *"The Sea Raven's barnacle... Could this be the very sweater that belonged to great-grandpa, the one grandpa stitched the charm into?"* He wondered.

Then it came back to him in a faint and faded memory. He remembered how important this particular piece of clothing was to his grandpa. He recalled a time when his grandpa was in the hospital just before he died. James was very upset because they had taken the sweater off the old man. "Where is grandpa's sweater mom? He needs it; he has to keep it on!" "Don't be silly Jimmy, he doesn't need to have it on in here and besides he's asleep." She told him. James started to yell at his mother. "Yes, he does mom, he told me he can never take it off, that he would die if he did; that the Dugtie would find him!" "Don't you take that tone with me, young man!" She said quietly yet crossly at him. Then she softened her voice, "Oh that's just nonsense; he was just telling you a story, he doesn't need to wear it in bed."

He looked everywhere for it, then he found it neatly folded in the bottom drawer of the hospital dresser. He placed it over his grandpa's sleeping body and whispered into his ear. "That was a close one grandpa." He patted his chest lightly and kissed his whiskery cheek.

James turned to the nurse who had just come into the room and spoke. "Please make sure grandpa keeps his sweater over him, or he will be really mad at you, and probably sue the hospital if he finds out you've taken it off of him."

"Jimmy! What has come over you?" His mother spoke firmly again, "Go wait out in the hall for me." She ordered as she shoved him out through the opened door, she turned to the old, well-weathered nurse and said, "I'm sorry about that, he's just very upset about his grandpa." "That's okay, I understand, I have grandsons of my own."

Smiling she turned to address James. "Don't worry, I promise to keep your grandfather's sweater over him, okay Jimmy?" His mother instructed him to sit on a chair outside the room and wait for her while she spoke to the nice nurse. She was in the room for quite some time, and when she finally came out, James could see she had been crying.

The Darker Side of Light

James picked up the sweater to examine it more closely. He couldn't see any pockets or pouches on the inside. If there was one, it must have been removed he thought. He ran his hand along the inside seam, lightly pinching the material as he did. Then he found it. A small hard lump on the left side seam near the bottom, it was sewn right into the wool. How cleverly disguised, he mused.

Dare he open it? Dare he look to see if there really was such a charm? "No, not yet… I'm going to wait." He decided. He put the journal and the sweater away in a drawer in his bedroom and placed Delwin's box on the fireplace alongside the photo.

The next few days passed very quickly for James. He found himself bringing work home as the final numbers needed to be matched and balanced. It wasn't that James was unorganized; on the contrary, he was extremely meticulous when it came to his job. The fact of the matter was that James had to collect the financial information from all seven department heads and make it all relate to one another and in the end balance.

Some expense receipts were questioned and then either accepted or rejected. All invoice slips would be matched and accounted for. A lot of emails were sent back and forth to the key players of each department. Data was collected then filed accordingly. Hard copies of finalized reports were downloaded onto disc and stored. Even though it was considered a paperless system, a final report for each department was printed and physically stored, just in case…

He was glad when it was all over and felt a great sense of accomplishment. He was looking forward to picking William up on Friday to start their summer holidays together.

Thursday evening around 6 p.m. after having eaten supper James went into the living room and poured himself a class of red wine and put on an ambient radio station to help him relax. He sat comfortably in his reclining chair and took a sip of his wine. He felt great; no thoughts of work crossed his mind; no numbers needed to be scrutinized; he was free… He closed his eyes and stretch out in his comfy chair. The background music was soft and soothing. Rhythmical notes that calmed his soul, like a lullaby to a baby. At first, he didn't notice the ting, ting sound as it was hidden by instrumental sounds of the electrical beat. It wasn't until

The Darker Side of Light

the DJ came on to introduce the next melody did he notice the sound. "Ting, ting, ting..." It went right on going as the man on the radio continued to speak. It sounded somewhat hollow and far-off. The next song started, and James turned the volume down. There it was again... "Ting, ting, ting, ting." "Where is that noise coming from?" he thought.

He stood up and looked around. It seemed to be all around him. "What the...!" he said out loud. Walking into the kitchen the sound grew louder. He followed it into his bedroom, it became louder still. The sound was coming from his dresser drawer. He opened it quickly and the sound instantly stopped.

There, before him, was the journal and the mysterious gray garment. He hadn't forgotten about it, but at the same time he didn't remember it either; he was simple too busy over the last few days. He picked up the sweater and decided he would put it on again. Returning to the living room - journal in hand, he sat back down on his chair, took another sip of his wine and started to read where he had left off.

I should have checked first, asked mother if she'd packed it for him. But alas I did not, and now my father was dead... and it was all my fault. I was so ashamed of myself. ...how could I have been so foolish?

I eventually cried myself to sleep. When I did I had another amazing, insightful yet heart-rending dream. Once again, I met with Annabel high above my town. She sat beside me and spoke comforting words as she wrapped her arms around me. "I am sorry about your father Jimmie, know that it was not your fault; you are not to blame." I just sat there in silence. I didn't know what to say, for it was my fault. How could I tell her how foolish I had been?

"Some things in this world we cannot change, no matter how much we want them too. This was the circumstance that surrounded your father's part." I looked at her with tears in my eyes. "Why Annabel, why did my father have to die?" Sadly, she replied, "That's just the way it must be love."

She looked towards the ocean, and I could see she was deeply troubled. Her radiant glow was dreary and carried with it a silent melancholy that I understood somehow; for I felt it too. Then she

The Darker Side of Light

turned to me and spoke. "I have something more to show you before I leave this realm. It is the place you once viewed, that horrible, evil place where the wee lass was brutally murdered. I want to show you what happened next. Are you willing to see?" I didn't want to go back there but felt that it must be something very important, or else Annabel would not have wanted to show me. "Yes," I said hesitantly. "If you feel I should."

A strange feeling came over not only my mind but also my body. It was as if I was moving forward and backward, fast and slow all at the same time. When the feeling stopped, I was situated at the same point I had last viewed. Her crying silenced, it was business as usual for the heartless soldiers.

Without words Annabel pointed towards a wooded area just above the encampment. I followed the direction of her gaze; it was my father and his regiment! They were hidden along the tree line just out of sight. "Da!" I yelled. But of course, he couldn't hear me. I watched as my father and his men attacked the soldiers that so brutal took life without mercy. Soldiers whose actions mimicked cruelty and hatred; not one of a human race but one of lawless beasts and monsters…

Annabel spoke to me in a voice as pure and sweat as any angel. "You see Jimmie; there is a purpose for all action and an action for all purpose. Your father and the men who fight alongside him, stand for justice and freedom. Even though they may not like or otherwise care for these people, they know they have the right to be free, and to live free…. It is for the greater good that they carry-on, even though loss is certain. If I can bring you any comfort Jimmie, it would be in the knowing that your father's death is not in vain." I understood what she was trying to tell me. I didn't like it but I understood.

Then she brought me to him. "Jimmie is that you son?" Father lay on the ground clutching at his chest. "Yes, Da it's me." I wrapped my arms around him and hugged him tight. "Don't go Da… Don't die…I love you Da, and I miss you, Ma does too." I cried. "I love you too son, tell your mother I love her, and not to fret, right?" "Okay Da, I will." I didn't want to let him go. I wanted to bring him home with me, walk right through the front door and say, "Look who I found wandering the streets, Ma!"

The Darker Side of Light

Father stopped breathing. I looked at Annabel, she was crying, crystal tears ran down her lovely cheeks. "Can't you do something, can't you help him?" She just shook her head no. I got very angry. "Why, why can't you help him…? You have magic don't you Annabel? Use it, use it to save my Da…" I ordered. "I can't love. I've caused enough damage here already. I can't interfere again." What are you on about Annabel, what damage?" She just stood there silently crying. No more words would she speak to me, no matter how much I questioned her.

I looked all around hoping there was someone else who could help my father. There were people all about; the ones that were forced into the cars were running for the woods, trying to get away from this hellhole. I stood up and screamed at the top of my lungs. "Help, help!" No one came…

I felt something gently touching my shoulder, I turned around it was my father. I wrapped my arms around him and cried, "You're okay Da!" I squeezed him with all my might. "Will you come home with me now? Ma will be so happy to see you." He didn't answer me. I released my hold on him and looked up at his kind face. He looked over to Annabel, tears welled up in his eyes. I had never seen my Da upset or sad before. He was always strong and courageous. Even when his own mother died I never saw him cry.

He took a step towards Annabel and hugged her gently. Taking a step back, he took her hand in his; he gathered up his thoughts and spoke. "I remember Annie, I remember everything now. Thank you for what you've done for my family. I know now what sacrifice you have made, and I understand why you've done it. This must be very upsetting for you. I want you to know it means everything to me, what you've done not only for me, but for mankind… And for what it's worth… you will always hold a special place in my heart." Annabel never spoke, she acknowledged my father's words, but she never replied to them, she was just too sad.

Turning to me, Da gently took hold of both my shoulders and looked fondly into my eyes. "I won't be going home with you, son… have to go. Take care of your Ma and give her a big kiss and cuddle for me and tell her I love her. You won't be seeing me for a long while. Know that I love you, and a part of me is with you always." He placed his right hand lightly on my chest and smiled warmly at me. I could feel the warmth of his love touch my soul

The Darker Side of Light

safe and secure. In that moment, I knew I had nothing to fear. I would never really lose my father. Death was but a mere transition in life's great mystery.

"Away you go home now, mind your Ma, and do well in school." "I will Da, good bye." "Good bye Jimmie." Father turned and walked away. I watched him go for as long as I could. I wanted to go with him, to run after him. "Wait Da! Take me with you!"

Annabel took me by the hand. "It's time to go back Jimmie." Then it was over, and I was home again; lying in my mother's bed, I awoke just as the sun was starting to rise. I felt different, more at ease. The weight of overwhelming guilt that had attached to my spirit was released and I was freed from sadness and grief. I took comfort in knowing that my father's death was not in vain and that one day I would get to see him again.

I looked to my left, mother was still as sleep. "Ma," I said as I shook her arm. "Wake-up Ma, I've something to tell ya. It's about Da!" She slowly opened her eyes and looked at me. "What is it Jimmie?" I kissed her cheek and gave her a big cuddle. "What's all this about then?" she questioned still half asleep. "Ma I just had the most amazing dream about Da. He's okay, he told me to tell you he loves ya and not to fret, and that he would see us again... so don't be sad Ma." My mother turned on her side to face me and gently stroked my cheek with her supple hand. I could see she was still very upset, as her eyes started to fill-up with tears.

"Please don't be sad Ma. Da is okay I saw him, I really did." She looked lovingly into my eyes. "I know you did son...it's going to be all right." She kissed my cheek and got up. "I'll go fix us breakfast..."

I never dreamt about my father or Annabel again for that matter, no matter how hard I tried.

Life went on and in the winter of forty-one mother started working for a company that made bullet casings. One night she came home from work and told me she had met someone she wanted me to meet. It was a gentleman she worked for. "You'll really like him Jimmie, he's a real gentleman and he has a good job; he's the head Forman at Bell & Wright. He's coming by for dinner so you're to be on your best behavior."

She made me wash up and put on my best suit. "Why all the fuss Ma?" I asked. "I want to make a good impression Jimmie." She responded. I didn't really understand why I had to dress-up in my Sunday best for some bloke. I thought my mother must fancy this man and when I saw her all dressed up in her good frock, I knew she did.

"But what about Da? He's not going to be too pleased Ma!" "Oh, Jimmie your fathers been gone now for over a year and he won't be coming back." I was very angry with her and started to yell. "Yes, he will Ma! He told me we would see him again and he won't too happy if he knows you're inviting strange men into the house." "Jimmie your father has gone to heaven. We won't be seeing him for a long, long while."

I told her again about my dream, the whole dream this time; about Annabel and about how I saw father when he died. She listened but I don't think she believed me.

"Jimmie, I know you miss your father and love him dearly, I do as well. But life goes on, so must we all. I have to think about our future Jimmie and he's a good man..." I could see I had upset her so I stopped making a ruckus and helped set the table.

When the knock came to the door I answered it. I opened the door and there stood before me with a bouquet of flowers and box of sweets in hand was the chap my mother had invited into our home. I stared at him for a long time. "You must be Jimmie." He finally said. I just kept staring at him. I didn't like the looks of him. There was something not right about him but I couldn't put my finger on it. I could hear my mother calling from the kitchen. "Who's at the door Jimmie... Jimmie who is it?" I didn't answer. I wanted to tell this fella he had the wrong house but my mother was suddenly right behind me.

"Oh, Joseph come in, come in," she said excitedly as she pushed me aside. "It's so good to see you." She turned to me and gave me 'the look.' He handed her the gifts he had brought for her. "Oh, thank you Joseph, you shouldn't have. This is my son Jimmie. Jimmie this is the nice man, I was telling you about, Joseph Quay."

He put his hand out. "Nice to meet you Jimmie." I just stared at it; I didn't want to shake his hand. My mother cuffed the back side of my head. "Mind your manners Jimmie Noble. I shook his cold, clammy paw and when my mother wasn't looking I wiped my hand on my pant leg.

"Take Mr. Quay's hat and show him into the parlor Jimmie while I set out dinner." My mother was acting strange, and was putting on airs. "What parlor Ma?" I asked, knowing full well what she meant. I also knew she wanted to choke me but she couldn't. She gave a little nervous laugh and shook her head at me. "Right this way Joseph." She instructed him as she smiled warmly.

"Is the boy a little simple?" He asked. "Oh no, he's just having us on…" she said as she laughed again. She turned to me and gave me a stern look of disapproval. I knew I was in for it when he left but for some reason I didn't care.

All through dinner mother and Mr. Quay talked with one another. Mr. Quay tried to tell a joke, but he wasn't very good at it. My mother laughed much harder than was called for. It kind of made things seem even more awkward. She tried to get me to tell one of my jokes but I wasn't having it. And besides why waste a good joke on the likes of this Mr. Quay? I really didn't have anything to say to either of them.

All the while it was eating me up inside. What was it about this bloke…? Something just wasn't right. Maybe it was the way he looked. He was not very handsome or charming in any way. He was rather short and very hairy and wore thick black rimmed milk-bottle glasses. Even though he wore a very nice suit, he smelt of turpentine and saw-dust.

I was glad when the evening was finally over. Mother insisted that I fetch Mr. Quay's hat and show him to the door while she prepared a carry out for him.

I handed him his black felt hat and as he took it, he grabbed my left arm hard. Pulling me close to him, he bent over and whispered into my ear with the most dreadfully sinister voice. "We know all about you Jimmie, we've been watching you." I was terrified but won't show it. I stared right through his milk-bottle glasses, right to his two black beady eyes and hissed, "Mogully!"

The mogully in his true form

Quickly releasing the hold on my arm, he started to chuckle then patted my head. "Ah, such a fine lad..." Mother was approaching from the kitchen. I moved back and pushed his greasy paw away. "No need to be rude Jimmie." My mother scorned. She passed Mr. Quay his carry out and walked him to the end of the lane. As I watched from the parlor window, I could only imagine what my mother was telling him about me. What that conniving snake was capable of getting her to reveal. Then I remembered I had told her about the charm... about Annabel. We were in grave danger my mother and me.

James got up to pour himself another glass of wine. He didn't ever remember his grandpa talking about his mother or this man Quay. For a brief moment, James experienced a memory buried deep in his subconscious. It was cloudy and distorted, and somewhat surreal. Like a flash of lightening, it was there and then it was gone... He started to feel oddly strange and out of place. Maybe it was the wine, he thought. He decided he didn't need another glass after all. He went over to his comfy seat and sat down. Before picking up the journal to read, his thoughts ventured back to his own childhood.

He recalled a time shortly after his dad died. He was getting bullied in school. He kind of felt the same way he did way back then. The boy's name was Benjamin Conway... Ben was in the same grade as James, and before the accident James and Ben were very good friends, best friends. Their father's Bill and Dean had been friends for years; good friends... drinking buddies as a matter of fact. And on that unfortunate night it was Dean's car that slid off the road and landed in the icy river. Both men drowned, unable to escape the chilly water conditions. Ben's father Dean had been drinking heavily. For insurance purposes, they had fixed it, so to speak, to make it look like it was Bill who had been behind the wheel when in actual fact it was Dean. Mrs. Conway, having a relative or two in the right places; namely the police department and the coroner's office, took care of the whole ordeal. No one would be any the wiser, including the boys.

It got to the point where James was afraid to go to school. It wasn't just the physical bulling that upset him so much as the verbal abuse. "... Your dad killed my dad because he couldn't drive! If my dad was driving it would have never happened! Your dad is a loser, he shouldn't have been driving my dad's car in the first place."

Other children started to pick on him too. He was having great difficulty trying to cope with it all, and soon it was very clear to his mother something was going on. When he finally confided in her and told her the problems he was having at school he felt much better, and soon after that it stopped all together; the pushing in the hallway when the teacher wasn't looking, the horrible little notes past back and forth between class mates, the accusations… all of a sudden it just stopped.

Grandpa gave James a charm—a black, shiny stone to carry in his school bag. "Here you take this Jimmy, I guarantee your enemies won't bother you ever again." "What is it grandpa" he asked inquisitively. The old man placed a round golf-ball sized stone in James' right hand and then took James' left hand and placed it over top. He clasped his own large rough hands around James' small agile hands and held them there. "It's called an Apache tear." He said as he looked warmly into the eyes of his grandson. "I understand what you are going through… you are a very brave lad. Only the bravest of the brave carry a stone such as this." Then he removed his hands from James' and started to tell the tale of the Apache's tear…

It was a long, long time ago. Things were a lot different then but in some ways very much the same as now."

He gave a gesture to James to let him know that he was referring to what he was going through with his friend Ben.

There lived in this vast continent many great and noble red-men known as the Apache Indians. They were many in number and great in strength. They were a proud people who lived in peace with all of nature and worshiped mother earth and all that resided therein. Now there were these folk…Christian folk, the majority of them were good folk. Not much different than you or me. But there were some of them that were just too big for their britches, something like your mate Ben… They called the Apaches savages and wanted to convert the lot of them to their beliefs and moral standings. What the Christians believed to be true was not necessarily what the Apache believed to be true. The Apache couldn't understand why folk, who said they were good, could be

The Darker Side of Light

so controlling and manipulative. Why folk who spoke so openly about free-will and freedom of choice wanted nothing more than to tell the Apaches' how to think and what to believe in. War broke out and many good Christian and Apache folk alike were murdered senselessly. It was a bloody battle and when it was over there was no victor...

The old story-teller stopped and took a long, deep breath in and held it. His eyes glazed over as he seemed to have drifted off somewhere faraway, and long ago. "Grandpa, grandpa... are you okay?" James questioned as he shook the old dreamer's shoulder. He cleared his throat, "Aye, I'm okay. Where was I, oh ya...?" Slowly he continued.

The Good Christian folk that had forced their ways on to the Apache and in turn instigated war, would have to face their actions before God and be accountable for their deeds.

The slain Apache warriors looked down from the heavens at the devastation and were very sad... they were sad not only for the loss of their own people but also for the loss of the Christians as well. And as they cried out their sadness, tear drops rained from the heavens. When the tears met with earth's atmosphere they poured down across the whole continent and turned to black stones as a reminder of the loss of life.

James opened up his hand to have a better looked at the solid black stone. "Hold it up to the light Jimmy." The old man instructed. "I can see through it grandpa." "Aye, with this stone one will always see through to the truth... things aren't always how they appear, even though things seem dark and hopeless, when you shine a little light in, you can see through to the other side...to better days." James remembered holding the stone in his hand with the pure enthusiasm, all his worries ended at that very moment. He trusted his grandpa and believed in him completely.

It wasn't until years later that James would find out the real truth about his dad's car accident and why the bulling stopped all of a sudden. It wasn't because of the magical Apache stone his grandpa had given him as much as it was his grandpa's confrontation with the Conway family. Just before he had given James the stone he went over to Mrs. Conway's home and threatened to expose the whole cover-up if the bulling didn't stop. He also insisted that Ben apologize to James and then be removed from the school immediately. They did one better... Mrs. Conway took Ben and her other three children and moved out of Bradford within the month.

He picked up the journal with both hands, holding it with tender care he stared at the hand-written cover with great admiration. He felt an overwhelming sense of pride that his grandpa had entrusted him with this treasure; a family heirloom of sorts.

How different things were for him now. And when was it exactly - that he stopped believing? He wished he still held that same undaunting trust; to believe in someone so completely, without question. But regrettably that was not the real world.

He pondered how he really felt about words written with such onus. His grandpa told a good tale that was for certain, but did he really, truly believed it? Could he possibly have dreamt it and thought it was real? James couldn't take it seriously or believe there was any legitimacy in it, as much as he wanted to. How could he? It just could not be true...

He could understand why his mother had not given him the box with his grandpa's keepsakes right away. She had always been very practical and never understood grandpa, even though he was her father. She was just trying to protect him from what she liked to call 'his flights of fancy.' But why did she never give it to him, and if she didn't want him to have it, why keep it up in the attic for all those years? The questions he had, would remain unanswered. And as childhood memories faded once again, he opened the journal and continued to read...

***

I would need to act fast; I would need to get help. Annabel was long gone and the only other person who would be able to help me was Stevie's granddad Mr. Jones. There was one major problem... he was very, very old; he had to be in his late sixties. I would talk to Stevie at school the next day and find out if his granddad still lived with them. He was my only hope; I had nowhere else to turn.

When my mother came back into the house, she never said two words to me about the way I was acting towards Mr. Quay. She simple told me to wash up and get ready for bed. That was not like my mother. She would have normally ripped down one side of me and up the other. It was if she was under some kind of spell or enchantment. For a split second, I thought this could be a good thing… Then I remembered who or what put the spell on her; that nasty mogully!

The next day on the way to school I met up with Stevie. I told him about Mr. Quay and what he had said to me; and about the way my mother was acting. He was very concerned about mine and my mother's safety and took everything I said very seriously. We agreed to meet up after school and go over to his house to talk to his granddad about it.

When we arrived at Stevie's house, his granddad sat asleep on a rocking chair in the parlor beside the hearth. Reading glasses at the edge of his nose and a book lying across his lap; his white hair and pale thin frame gave the impression of one very fragile and timid. This, I would soon find out, couldn't be further from the truth.

When we entered the room, he woke-up immediately. "Hi granddad," Stevie said. "Do you remember my pal Jimmie from school?" Stevie's granddad was very old but he definitely had his wits about him. He gave a little cough to clear his throat. "Of course, I do! How are you, lad?" He said in his thick British accent with an underlining tone of Bulgarian brogue.

He could see by the look on our faces, we had grave business to discuss with him. "Grab a chair lads and tell old Granddad what this is all about." Stevie pulled two chairs over from against the wall and we sat facing the old man.

You could tell by looking at his weathered face he was a man of great knowledge. His hazel eyes sparkled with a kind, understanding wisdom that only came to those of meaningful years.

Behind him just to the right of the hearth were a number of pictures hanging on the green and blue striped wall-paper. One photo, I found quite impressive was one of Mr. Jones as a young officer. He sat on top of a Belgian Sopwith Camel; one of the first fighter planes of World War One.

The Darker Side of Light

"Well lads, what's this all about?" he repeated as took off his reading glasses and placed them on the table along with his book. He reached over and picked up his pipe and lit it. Stevie looked at me, and gestured towards his granddad. "Go on, tell him, it's okay." I remembered my promise to Annabel. 'I promise, I won't tell a living soul.' Then I remembered how she looked at me and said. 'There are ones you can tell, you will know when the time is right.' Now was as right a time as any...

I told him the whole story right from the very beginning. He sat there in silence puffing on his pipe and nodding his head in acknowledgement. He listened to every word I said and when I was finished he still sat in silence for what seemed a very long time.

Then he spoke, "This is quite the state of affairs you've gotten yourself into my lad. The mogully is not one to be taken for granted. They are extremely dangerous and conniving; I know...I've seen my fair-share of them. And if he knows what I think he already knows, none of us are safe; hell, the whole town is in danger. ...I'll have to take care of it right away." He got up and put on his shoes, coat and hat. I was curious to know where he was going, but I didn't want to ask.

"This little rodent problem will be dealt with swiftly and without mention...right?" Then he gave me a wink. "Away you go home now Jimmie and don't tell anyone what you've just told me." I could see this well-seasoned Royal Naval Airman already had formed a plan of action and he had every intension in carrying it out.

I was so relieved, that is until I got home... The mogully was there... in my mother's kitchen sitting in my father's chair at the table. He and my mother were having a conversation when I walked in on them.

"What is he doing here?" I said out-loud. Mother noticed me first; she spouted out, "Where's your father's sweater Jimmie?" I played dumb. "What sweater Ma?" She began to get angry. "You know perfectly well which sweater I am referring to Jimmie Noble; your father's grey sweater, the one I bought him for his birthday." "I don't know Ma, isn't it in Da's wardrobe where you hung it up?" She stood up and came towards me fast. "I've looked there... you have some cheek, you do!" The look on her face was

The Darker Side of Light

frightening and I wanted to run but I knew I had nowhere to run to. She grabbed me by my shoulder and shook me hard. "Where is it Jimmie, what have you done with it?" "I don't know Ma!" I started to cry, not because I didn't know where it was — because I did. But because my mother was scaring the trousers off of me.

"Why do you want Da's sweater Ma, you're not given it to the likes of him are you?" I looked over at the mogully who sat comfortably on my father's chair. He smiled barefacedly at me and my blood ran cold. How disgusting and despicable he was in his mortal form.

He continued to stare at me with his evil ugly face and said, "Have you not told the lad that we are to be married and that I 'm to be his new father?" The look of self-righteous satisfaction was all over his revolting mogully face. I looked at my mother in total shock, I didn't see that coming. "What's he talking about Ma? You aren't really going to marry him are ya?"

I couldn't help myself, I turned to him and yelled out, "You stupid, ugly, hairy mogully! Get out of my house and leave my Ma alone. She's too good for the likes of you!"

He got up to come after me but my mother stopped him. "Are you going to let the brat talk to me like that?" He questioned. "He needs to be taught a lesson." "Aye, he does, but not by your hand." Thank goodness, my mother was coming to her senses, I thought.

Then she smacked me hard across my left cheek. I don't know what was more hurtful, the sting of the hit or the action of my mother. She always yelled a lot but she was never one to act violent. "Now where is the sweater Jimmie I need it! I didn't answer her, I clamed up like a captured spy. She kept smacking me across my face and head. I just stood there and cried. I wasn't about to tell her where it was. For I knew this was not the actions of my real mother, well I hoped it wasn't...

She soon grew tired. "This is useless... he's not talking." She told the mogully. "Go to your room Jimmie." She insisted. "I'll deal with you later." "Wait, what are you doing?" I heard him yell. "He didn't tell us where the charm was. Come back here Jimmie!" I ran to my room and slammed the door shut. I blocked the door with a chair so that the nasty beast couldn't come in even if he tried. I took out my father's sweater that I had hid under my mattress and held on to it tight. As long as I had it that horrible mogully couldn't harm me.

A little while later my indifferent mother came to my bedroom door. She couldn't get in so she just shouted at the door. "I'm going out with Mr. Quay for a while I'll be home late, don't wait up, and if you know what's good for you, you'll find that sweater and put it on my bed for when I get home. You hear me Jimmie?" "I told you Ma, I don't know where it is!" I screamed back.

When I was sure they had left, I put on my father's sweater and headed to the kitchen for something to eat. I would need to find a safe place to hide until morning. I wasn't about to stay at home knowing that once I fell asleep they might break in, pinch the sweater and kill me. I knew just the hiding place, the Flinch's condemned flat. Dave never moved back in on account of not only the damage to the place, but also the bad memories. They had fixed the hole in the roof but no one would rent the flat, said it was haunted. Haunted or not it was safer than my own flat. I would rather face the ghost of Dead Dora Flinch then the mogully or my mother for that matter.

I packed a bag of things, I thought I might need, like a flash-light, a blanket and pillow, some comic books, my homework and a cheese and jam sandwich. It was dark out by this time and no one was out on account of the rain. I headed two doors over, jimmied the lock and went inside.

I had never been inside Deadly Dora's flat before. It was the exact same shape as ours expect it was completely empty. I passed by the kitchen and couldn't help but look inside. I shone my flashlight all around the hollow room, and gave myself the heebie-jeebies. I could see exactly where the bomb had landed. Instead of putting down a new floor they just patch up the hole with bits of wood. It was no wonder no one wanted to rent the place…

I slowly walked down the hall to the master bedroom and shone my light inside before I entered. It looked safe…no ghosts to speak of. There was a big walk about wardrobe in the corner that must have belonged to Dora. I cautiously opened it up and as I did, I closed my eyes tight; half expecting something to come flying out at me. Nothing did… I opened my eyes and saw that the

The Darker Side of Light

wardrobe was completely empty. I went inside and closed the doors behind me. I would be safe here until morning.

The next day I quietly snuck into my house and got ready for school. Lucky for me, mother had already left for work so I was safe for the time being. I hurried off to school to look for Stevie. I wanted to tell him what had happened to me the night before.

Just as the bell rang Stevie came running up to me all winded. At first I was worried something was wrong. "Are you all right Stevie," I asked concerned. "What happened, is your granddad okay?" It took a minute for him to catch his breath. When he finally did he whispered, "It's done... granddad told me to tell you not to worry it's done."

I was so happy I wanted to wrap my arms around him and thank him but he had this faraway look in his eyes. "What's wrong then Stevie?" "Nothing... I have to go. I'll talk to you about it later. Just be careful okay? And if anyone asks you anything, you don't know nothing... got it?" Aye, okay, but..." That's all I got out. He nervously looked around and left me standing there wondering what troubled him so.

I went into school feeling somewhat confident and safe. The mogully had been taken care of, and I had on my Da's sweater securely under my own clothing. It wasn't even a little bit bulky, so no one noticed. It seemed to fit me perfect, hugging my body as if it were a part of me.

I didn't see Stevie all day. Even after school he was nowhere to be seen.

I went home to face my mother. I really didn't know what to expect. As I walked in the front door, mother's friend Bess Aims was just leaving. "Right then Mary, I'll see you tomorrow. Oh, hi Jimmie, my you are getting bigger every time I see ya and so handsome just like your father." She made the sign of the cross across her chest and commented, "God rest his soul... Bye now." "Bye Bess, see ya." mother replied from the kitchen.

I walked slowly into the kitchen and sat down at the table. "Is everything alright Ma?" "What do you mean Jimmie, why wouldn't it be? Oh, did you hear about the accident at my work... about that poor Mr. Quay?" "What about him Ma, what

The Darker Side of Light

happened to him?" I asked her warily. "Well," she started. "He was working late last night and somehow got his head caught in the press. The police figure he had his head in there to fix it not realizing that the machine was still turned on. It came down and crushed his skull in… poor old bugger. It's just terrible."

My mother didn't sound all that upset so I questioned her further. "So, what'll you do now Ma? I guess the weddings off?" "Wedding… what wedding?" She questioned. "The one between you and Mr. Quay." I answered. "This is no time for your jokes Jimmie, the man is dead, and besides I wouldn't marry the likes of that hairy little man…he smelt awful and… oh never mind he's dead now, God rest his unfortunate soul."

For some strange reason, my mother and her friends had a habit of saying "God rest his or her soul" if they'd been talking about somebody who had died. For the life of me I don't know why. Maybe out of respect or maybe because they were afraid they might hear them and come haunt them in the night.

"Where would you get a silly notion like that anyhow?" She asked. "I'm only joking Ma, my pals at school told me how ugly he was; I'm just pulling your leg." "Really Jimmie, I just don't know where you get that sense of humor from. Certainly not me…"

She didn't remember a thing, I knew my mother was under some kind of enchantment and now it was broken.

That night, I lied in my bed awake for a long while, for some reason, I just couldn't sleep. I was happy that the mogully was dead and that my mother was back to normal. Then it hit me like a ton of bricks… the mogully's words— "We've been watching you… 'We'." Did that mean there were more of them around? Were they watching me now? I wondered if that was what Stevie was so nervous about; and why he said to be careful. If my mother and I were still in danger, I would need to go see Mr. Jones again. I was suddenly very frightened. I went to my mother's bedroom and climbed into bed beside her. "Can I sleep with you tonight Ma?" She was already fast asleep. I cuddled up beside her and prayed for morning to come soon. It was always safer when the sun was out I figured.

Weird and Wacky Tales & Other Such Nonsense
Linda Noble-Cordy

The next day at school Stevie was nowhere to be found, so after school, I ran over to his place. I knocked on the door and a mysteriously beautiful lady answered it. She was tall and incredibly thin, her eyes were ice blue, as was the eye-shadow that covered them. What was really the most striking about her, were her full, bright red, painted lips which stood out against her pale skin and bleach-blonde hair that was neatly tied up in a bun. She was very pretty and looked like one of those fancy ladies from the catalogues my mother gets delivered to the house.

"Yes, love can I help you?" she said with those ruby red lips that curved into the loveliest smile, revealing a set of perfectly straight white teeth. Her voice, a calming wave of perfection that could lull a colic-babe to sleep.

I stared at her for a long while before I was able to speak. "Is Stevie home?" I asked. "Stevie? There's no Stevie living here lad, you must have the wrong house." I looked at the number on the house - 14. That was Stevie's number all right.

"Is this 14 Sherburne?" I asked. "Yes love, but there's no Stevie here." Where could Stevie and his family have gone so quickly and why? Were the Jones' so afraid of the mogully that they went away for fear of their lives? Maybe Stevie just told me not to worry to give him a chance to run away. It just didn't make sense we had been best mates since first grade.

I looked around her slender form into the hallway. It looked different somehow. I wanted to get in and have a look around. "Do you have a telephone?" I asked. "Yes" She responded slowly. "May I use it please to call my mother?" "Yes, come in." she said without hesitation.

She took me into the parlor; the same parlor that only forty-eight hours earlier I was in. It was completely different! The Jones's furniture was gone... the old man's rocker and table, even the blue and green stripped wall paper had been removed. Instead the walls were a pale blue and there wasn't a photo to be seen. A large black leather couch sat where once stood a curio cabinet filled with Stevie's mother's knick-knacks. Beside it on the small black wooden table was the telephone. I was starting to think something was wrong with me. Then I noticed the old man's pipe sticking out of the ashes in the fireplace.

The Darker Side of Light

"The phone is over there Jimmie, you may use it to call your mother." She pointed to the phone and I walked over to it to make a fake call home. My back to her, I picked up the receiver but kept my finger on the button, and then I pretended to dial my number. All the while this elegant lady stared at me from the parlor entrance.

"Hello Ma, can you come get me...I'm at 14 Sherburne...ya, okay, thanks, bye..." I hung up the receiver and looked over to her, she was gone. This would be a good time to leave. As I walked towards my exit she appeared again. A big smile on her face, "Would you like a cup of tea while you're waiting for your mother Jimmie?" "No thanks," I answered. Then it hit me... how did she know my name? "Thank you for letting me use your telephone Miss, I should be on my way now; I'll wait for my Ma outside." I announced.

I went to leave but she blocked my exit. I could hear footsteps coming down the stairs from behind me. I turned to look; it was a man...a little ugly hairy man that looked a lot like Mr. Quay. As he reached the bottom of the stairs she stated, "Jimmie this is Mr. Bunting." He gave me a nod of his head.

I turned to her. "How do you know my name Miss?" "Well you told me of course silly." "No, I never." "Mr. Bunting and I have a few questions we'd like to ask you Jimmie." I wasn't having any part of it. This Mr. Bunting was definitely a mogully, I didn't know what she was, maybe a temptress of sorts.

"I have to go now Miss, thanks for letting me use your phone," I repeated. "Oh, please call me Martha," she insisted. ...the temptress had a name.

"Did you get hold of your mother Jimmie?" she asked. "Yes, she's on her way to get me. I told her I'd wait for her outside." The nice spoken lady changed all of a sudden, she grabbed me by my arm and forced me back into the parlor. She had quite the grip for such a slight bit of a woman. Then she did the strangest thing. Turning to me, just before closing and locking the parlor door; she blew a kiss at me with those lovely ruby-red lips.

Before I knew it I was sneezing madly. It was Dodgesons, thousands of them; they were trying to get me. I let out a little scream as I ran about the room trying to dodge them. I needed to get to water... wet the wee buggers, but how? Then it hit me - or should I say something I would normally get hit for. I gave them the good old Bronx cheer. That's right – I blew big wet raspberries at them. And it worked. I was safe again for the moment.

Outside the parlor door, I could hear Miss Martha and Mr. Bunting arguing. I ran over to the phone to make a real call this time. I picked up the receiver and started to dial the operator. I was horrified to find the line was dead... She must have known all along, the sneaky wench. I started to panic and was just about to start screaming when I heard a little tap at the window. It was Stevie; boy was I happy to see his sorry mug.

I tried to open the window but it was locked. "I can't open it" I whispered to him. I turned around nervously hoping my foe didn't hear me. "What should I do?" Stevie pointed towards the fireplace. "The flue... there's a passageway out." he mouthed. I heard the key in the lock. "They're coming hide." I whispered through the window.

I ran over and sat on the couch just as she entered with a tray of tea and cookies. "My mother will be here any minute to fetch me." I told her. "Yes, I'm sure she will," she smiled brashly, "In the meantime, you may as well have some tea." I would have to play along. "Thank you," I said smiling back. "That is very kind of you." She looked at me puzzled, turned around, and left, locking the door again. Even though I was hungry and thirsty, I wasn't about to drink the tea or eat the cookies. They were probably poisoned or enchanted with some kind of spell.

I raced back to the widow. Stevie was nowhere in sight. I went over to the fireplace. I didn't know what I was looking for but I knew somewhere there was a secret door. Then I heard the key in the lock again. This time they both came in. Miss Martha sat beside me on the couch and Mr. Bunting sat a good distance away on a matching leather chair. Even though this menace of a mogully sat yards away I could smell his odor drifting towards me... saw-dust and turpentine what a horrible gut-wrenching smell.

"Jimmie, I'm afraid I haven't been completely honest with you." She began sweetly. "Mr. Bunting and I are detectives that work for Scotland Yard. We are investigating the death of Mr. Quay, do you know him? We know your mother did, she worked with him,

The Darker Side of Light

didn't she?" "I don't know, why don't you ask her?" I replied brazenly.

She cast a glare at the smelly mogully, and then back at me. As pretty as she was she had a terrible wickedness about her. And as she spoke my heart filled with dread. "Oh, I plan on doing just that Jimmie. I have every intention of asking your mother a few questions; and believe me, I will get results."

From across the room Mr. Bunting piped in. "We have reason to believe that Mr. Tomas Jones may have murdered Mr. Quay, so he is being held for questioning as we speak." "What about Stevie, what have you done with him?" I asked knowing full well he was somewhere outside. "And why did you lie to me when you answered the door?"

They looked at each other then she spoke. "I had to be certain it was you and not one of Stevie's other chums. Stevie, his mother and sister have been placed in protective care until further notice. I can take you to see him if you like; he's not far from here. We can leave right now. I have a car parked around the corner. Have you ever been in one? They go really fast, you'll love it" Smiling coyly at me, she flaunted her good looks in the hopes of winning me over.
"No thanks, I'll wait here for my mother." "Not to worry Jimmie you're safe with us." Safe...? That was a joke and a half. I didn't know such a lovely face could tell such wicked lies.

"And what happened to the Jones's stuff, all their furniture...?" "Evidence," spouted the mogully. "Since when is wall paper evidence?" I contested. "You need not concern yourself with such trivialities lad, what's important is that you co-operate with us fully and tell us everything you know." He added.

I played the victim, and looked into her eyes with sincerity as I spoke. "So, what's all this got to do with me anyhow? My mother told me the police said it was an accident; Mr. Quay got his head stuck in a press; that the bloke didn't know the machine was turned on. That's all I know." "We don't think you are being completely honest with us lad. You know more than you're letting on." Sweetening the pie, she added, "There is a big reward for anyone who can give us information that will lead to the conviction of Mr. Jones." I looked over at Mr. Bunting and questioned. "How do I know yous two are really from Scotland Yard?"

She looked at the mogully and gestured to him with a nod of her head. He got up and walked towards me hand in his pocket. He took out a badge with his photo on it. It looked real enough, but I wasn't sure, I'd never seen a real police ID before. I would play along anyhow. "What can I do?" "You can start by telling us everything you know Jimmie." She said softly. The mogully put in his two bits, "Yes, you are in grave danger, I'm afraid to say... It is of utte most importance that we have your full co-operation in this matter." "Why am I in danger, I haven't done anything wrong." Miss Martha took my two hands in hers and held them tight. "We know what you have done Jimmie, we know exactly what you have done. You may as well come-clean."

I pulled my hands away. "I don't know what you're on about, I haven't done anything... I want to go home now. You have no right to hold me back." I yelled. "Drink your tea lad." She insisted. Nodding to the mogully, the two of them left the room and locked the door again.

I could hear the two of them outside the door. I was curious to hear what they were saying, I ran over and put my ear to the door. "I say we stick the little bugger in the Fachet with the Dugtie, he'll soon talk." Miss Martha spouted. The mogully replied, "Yes, but we can't move him until after dark. We can't take the chance of anyone seeing us with him. I can't afford to be seen with the lad, not after what happened yesterday." "Get the needle ready, I'll have to knock him out myself..." She ordered.

I started to panic again; I was running out of time. I raced over to the fireplace and searched frantically for the secret door. While I looked, I quickly picked up Mr. Jones' pipe, half brushed of the ash and stuck it in my back pocket.

It had to be here somewhere; Stevie did say there was a secret passageway in the 'chimney'. I searched frantically. Eureka! I found it on the right-hand side, two feet up, inside the lum. And as I gave thanks to God and Stevie, I pushed it opened and crawled through it. It was dark and dusty inside but I didn't care. I was on my way to freedom. I saw a dim light ahead and shortly after that I heard Stevie's voice. "Hurry up, what took you so long, I was beginning to think you were getting pally with that Martha wench." "Oh ya," I commented sarcastically, "we were having a great party, too bad you couldn't join us mate." Stevie helped me out and closed the flap behind me.

We ran off down the street as fast as we could, until we could run no further. Out of breath and at our wits end we sat on the park bench by Glen Abbey station. There were quite a lot of folk about so we felt safe for the moment. I turned to Stevie, "Boy was I ever glad to see you."

I told him all about what the temptress and the mogully had said to me. Stevie informed me that she was no temptress but in fact a Boshney. "They know about Annabel and the only reason they haven't killed ya is because they think you know where she is. That, and the fact you possess the charm they're after. Those are the only reason your alive pal."

Still nervous and anxious Stevie looked around just to make sure we hadn't been followed. "They know granddad is partly to blame for killing Mr. Quay. They want the others involved and that's the only reason why my granddad is still alive. We have to save him and find out where they have taken my mother and sister." I had no idea what we should do, and was strongly hoping Stevie had a plan.

Like I had already mentioned, Stevie and I had been best mates since first grade. Even though Stevie was a full year older than me, on account of them holding him back a year, and for the life of me I don't know why. He was the smartest twelve-year-old I knew, smarter and more quick-witted than most adults as matter of fact. And over the years, we had gotten ourselves in trouble on more than one occasion, but nothing like this, this was serious stuff.

"They're holding granddad in the bunker under our cellar. There is a secret passageway to it hidden in the foundation of the outhouse. We'll have to sneak back after dark and depending on how watchful they are… I might need you to distract them long enough so that I can free him." He told me.

"Wait a minute… what exactly do you want me to do?" I was starting to have second thoughts. "You might have

The Darker Side of Light

to go back in. You might have to stall them upstairs while I get granddad out." He informed me. "Then how will I get out? No... there has to be another way. I don't want to go in there again. They're going to sic the Dugtie on me this time, I know they are." "Just don't tell them anything important and whatever you do don't tell them where the Sea Raven's Barnacle is." He insisted.

I grabbed on to my chest. "Don't tell me you're wearing it!" he stated somewhat annoyed. "I had too; it's the only safe place. They'll be looking for it at my house. Besides you couldn't tell I had it on, so neither will they." "True, they won't think you're fool-hearted enough to be carrying it around with ya, smart plan mate." He said laughingly.

I always dreaded night-fall, and this one was particularly fearful. I really was hoping I won't have to go back into the house at 14 Sherburne. There was another half-hour before it would be completely dark so Stevie and I went over to my house to let my mother know I was okay. When we got there Stevie waited outside to keep a look-out.

Inside the house looked like a tornado had gone through it. My bedroom was in a terrible the state. They had turned everything upside down, including my bed. It was a good thing I had kept the sweater on after all. I started to worry about my mother, for she was nowhere in sight. I feared the worst. I called out hoping she was hiding somewhere. "Ma are you home, Ma where are you?" No answer. I went into the kitchen that is where my mother usually was. There was a note on the kitchen table which read: 'We have your mother and if you want to see her alive again you will bring the charm to 14 Sherburne tonight.' Signed 'Mr. B'.

I would have no choice. I would have to give-up the Sea Raven's Barnacle to save my mother. Of course Stevie thought I was crazy. "Don't do it Jimmie, they'll kill her anyways and you too. You can't let on that you have it. There has to be another way." He thought for a moment. "I've got it... You tell them, you'll make a trade - they let her go and you'll tell them where they can find it. Make up something, like you hid it at Deadly Dora's or at school. I know... tell them you hid it at Annabel Green's. They'll have a hell-of-a-time trying to get in there. That way they will release your mother and buy us some time to free granddad. Once he's sprung he'll know what to do. He has friends in high places, and

The Darker Side of Light

they hate the Boshney as much as we do." It sounded like a good plan and besides it was the only plan we had.

All I could think about was saving my mother. I was afraid they might try to hurt her or put her under another spell. Just before we got to Sherburne Street, Stevie went around the back way, down Dune Avenue. I kept walking until I got to the house; I walked right up to the front door and knocked on it as hard as I could. The door opened and there stood a tall, thin, red-headed lad about sixteen years old. Funny, I didn't remember seeing him around the neighborhood before. I knew just about all the kids around town, even the teenagers, because we all played footie at one time or another together.

"Ya, what do you want?" he asked abruptly. "I'm here to see Mr. Bunting." "Dad, there's a wee bloke at the door for ya!" He yelled looking over his right shoulder. Turning his attention back at me, "What's your name mate?" "Jimmie, I'm here to fetch my Ma." "You're Ma? You're Ma?" He repeated. What's her name?" He asked. "Mary, Mary Noble." "Are ya daft...? There's no Mary Noble here, you must have made a mistake." "She's here, get Mr. Bunting!" I screamed, as I moved forward trying to see past him. He put his hand out to stop me. "Alright pal, take it easy. Dad..." twisting his body around as he yelled. "He says his name is Jimmie and he's here to fetch his Ma, Mary Noble...."

I heard foot-steps coming up from the basement, and they grew louder as Mr. Bunting reached the top of them. He came barreling around the corner. "I'll take it from here son, you can go back home now." He informed the oblivious red headed lad. "Tell your Ma I won't be home for supper, will ya?" "What about the package you wanted me to deliver?" he questioned. "That's okay, I'll have one of my men fetch it later, it's not ready yet." "Suit yourself then, bye Jimmie, hope you find your Ma." He said half laughingly. He grabbed his coat, left the house and hopped on his motorbike that was parked on the road.

I was starting to wonder if Mr. Bunting was really a mogully or if he had been invaded by the Dugtie and that was the reason why he was so mean. His own son riding safely off down the street, he grabbed me by my shirt collar, and the stench that came from him confirmed his true identity.

The Darker Side of Light

He took me into the kitchen. "I wasn't expecting you 'd be back this night lad. You're a brave one after all. I take it you got my note?" he questioned. I pulled it out of my pants pocket, "Aye I got it all right, now where is she, you wanker. You'd better not have hurt her, or you'll end up like your old pal Mr. Quay." I was afraid but at the same time I was so angry. All I could think about was getting my mother home safe and sound.

He started to laugh, "Sit here and don't move," he instructed. Walking over to the stove he put the kettle on. "Miss Martha will be back at any moment, we'll wait for her."

"Where is my Ma?" I asked again. "Don't worry, you play your cards right and you'll see her soon. Did you bring the charm?" He asked hastily. "I'm not saying another word until I see my Ma." He stopped what he was doing and sat down across from me at the table. He looked at me with these dark-brown, almost black looking, beady eyes. I could tell he was kind of nervous by the way he was looking at me, but the intensity of his stare still seemed to reach in and grab my soul. "Tell you what...you give me the charm and I'll take you to your Ma right now. I give you my word; I'll let you both go." Then he whispered. "I'll tell Miss Martha you escaped. I'll fix it to look like it." Then he winked at me. "Well what do you say lad, is it a deal?" I didn't trust him. "No, no deal!" He started to get anxious. "Look lad, you're running out of time, at least with me you've got a sporting chance." Then he let it slip. "With the Boshney you and your mother are dead either way." "Boshney?" I questioned pretending not to know. "What's the Boshney?"

I heard the front door open, Mr. Bunting got up and put his finger to his lips. "Shhhh," he whispered as he looked slyly towards the direction of the sound. Either this sly mogully had his own agenda or he was trying to trick me into giving him the Sea Raven's Barnacle for the Boshney. Either way I still didn't trust him.

A few seconds later Miss Martha entered the room. She looked distraught and her white skin was a pasty grey. Mr. Bunting got up, took her by the arm and led her into the parlor across the hallway. "Stay here lad...remember your mother's life is at stake..." He threatened.

I was praying that Stevie had found his granddad, and that they were getting help. It felt like a long time had passed since I last saw him, surely they had escaped by now. I stood up and walked towards the parlor. I wanted to get a listen to what they were talking about. Miss Martha was definitely in some kind of trouble. I couldn't make out what they were saying, but I could tell by the tone of their voices something was wrong. The parlor door opened and I ran back over to my seat at the kitchen table.

Miss Martha came in first. "Right, no more games, hand it over Jimmie." She demanded as she sat down across from me. "Where is my Ma? I want to see her first." "No... I demand you hand over the charm. You did bring it with you didn't you?" I remembered what I was supposed to say. "No, do I look like a fool to you? I'll tell you where the charm is on one condition. You let my mother go unharmed." She started to laugh; a wicked, sinful laugh.

She got up and came across the table at me, grabbed me by my shoulders and threw me across the room. I hit the wall and slid down it. She came at me again and before I knew it, she was over top of me. She wrapped her two hands around my neck and picked me up off the ground like a rag-doll. Lifting me high off the ground she tried to shake the life right out of me. Mr. Bunting just stood there watching the whole thing. He had this self-righteous mogully look on his face as if to say, 'you had your chance lad.' I tried to scream but she had quite the choke-hold on my throat. Then she let me go, she just released her grip and I fell a good distance to the floor.

"He's got it with him! I don't believe it." she said excitedly. "Who's the fool now Jimmie?" She picked me up by my ear. Right then, hand it over." "No... I'll never give it to you ... you scabby look'n wench! The hairy, ugly mogully with his head smashed in is better look'n than you are! And you smell like an old fisherman's wife!" I told her. She let out an awful noise as her anger escalated to hatred. If she could she would have killed me on the spot. She pinched my ear even harder and picked me up into the air as I kicked my feet at her wildly. Luckily for me, I didn't feel a thing for I was under the protection of the charm. I grabbed onto the arm that held onto my ear and screamed. "Let me go, you hideous smelly hussy! You, ugly old cow! You smell of cow dung and codfish..."

You will never see a Boshney wench so angry as when you insult her attractiveness. I hit her right where it hurt; her vanity. Her face grew red as her anger escalated even further. "Strip-search the rascal-yen," she instructed the mogully as she tossed me towards him. I started to feel anxious. They would surely find the sweater under my clothes and rip it off of me.

"No!" I screamed. "What about my Ma, you said if I brought it you would let us go." "I said no such thing, you and your mother are as good as fish food!" she said mockingly. "Wait, I'll tell you everything I know…I know about Annabel…" She cackled a hideous sound, "Too late lad…" What did she mean 'too late'? Had they found her and if they did was she alright? I had a horrible feeling that if this Boshney witch had any part in it, she wouldn't be. "Strip him!" she ordered again. She sat on the kitchen chair and watched while the wicked mogully fought to tear off my clothes.

There I stood down to my skives. No one was more surprised than me, to find out that the garment that contained the charm was not visible on my person. It had vanished somehow, turned flesh-tone. "I told you I didn't have it." I lied; I could feel it next to my skin.

"That's impossible, what magic is at work here? What spell are you under lad? Could it be that of a despicable Melt?" She looked over to Mr. Bunting who was still catching his breath from fighting with me and my clothing.

She wanted to get even with me somehow. "Go fetch his mother, it's time we put an end to this once and for all. You might not feel any pain Jimmie, but your mother certainly will." "Bring her down Mr. Bunting and bring the Fachet as well." She smiled a wicked grin like a she-devil about to do an evil deed.

"No, please don't…" I pretended to cry. I'll tell you everything you want to know. I'll tell you where the Sea Raven's barnacle is if you promise not to hurt her. "Please…" I squeezed a few tears out. "I think he's telling the truth this time." The mogully looked at me and then towards Miss Martha who was not so sure. I would need to be more convincing. "I'll take you to it myself, it's at Annabel Green's place and only I know the way in." The mogully piped in, "I can believe that, after all he did escape from us once before, the sneaky little bugger… How did you get out of the parlor anyways?" I wasn't about to tell. Looking at him dimly, I shrugged my shoulders like I didn't know, and whispered magic. "You'll need to show me that trick lad." As he nodded his head in approval, she spouted, "That is of no importance you fool... Yes, you will take us there and retrieve the charm. But be warned Jimmie, if you're lying, or deceiving me in anyway, I will not only torture your mother until she begs for death but you will have the pleasure of watching it. Do I make myself clear?" She was indeed as evil as they come. I nodded my head yes.

She looked somewhat out of sorts, like she was about to pass-out. "Put your clothes back on," she instructed. Gesturing to Mr. Bunting, the two of them left the room, went into the parlor and closed the door behind them. It was very quiet and I wondered what they were scheming. I had really got myself in a muddle. I would have to take them to Annabel's place to stall for more time. I prayed that Stevie had rescued his granddad and they were on their way back with reinforcements. My mother was in the house somewhere, probably tied-up in one of the rooms upstairs. I hoped with all my heart they had not harmed her, but I had no way of knowing.

I heard a low knocking sound coming from behind me. I turned around; the sound was coming from the kitchen's back door. I looked through the wee window, it was Stevie and he was smiling at me. Half dressed, I opened the door slowly, so not to make too much noise. "What are you doing mate?" he smirked. Wee bit of an orgy going on, ya cheeky devil ya..." "Very funny... ha, ha you're a right laugh you are." I whispered. He gave me the thumbs-up. "I found granddad and your Ma too, they're both in the auto, come on let's go, blue-boy." He didn't need to tell me twice.

Mr. Jones had a 1936 Ford hard top parked at the side of the house. We got in and quickly drove away to safety. "Ma," I wrapped my arms around her and hugged her with all my might. She smiled at me and said. "Oh Jimmie, it's good to see you, son, where have you been?" My mother still didn't know what was going on. I thought maybe this was for the better. "Nowhere Ma," I told her. I covered her up with the blanket that was on her lap and she closed her eyes and drifted off to sleep.

We hadn't got more than a block away when I heard the most earsplitting sound. It sounded like a siren going off, but it was

The Darker Side of Light

worse. I covered my ears to shelter myself from the noise. "Do you hear that?" I yelled. No one else seemed to notice it. "Come on! You can't hear it?" Stevie looked at me strange and shook his head no. I couldn't even hear myself think. "Awe! What is that?" It stopped. "What is it Jimmie? What's wrong lad?" Mr. Jones asked as he continued to speed down the road. "Can't stop, we need to get as far away as possible before they know you're gone." He stated. "I think they know Mr. Jones." I had a strong feeling Miss Martha was not too pleased...

Travelling north we came to a little town called Aberfeldy and stopped at a Smoke shop off of Burnside Lane. Both Stevie and I went inside with Mr. Jones, my Ma on the other hand, was still fast asleep. "Don't' wake her Jimmie, let her rest, she's been through a lot." He said compassionately.

Mr. Jones introduced us to Mr. Ferguson the shop owner; who was a rather stout man with a big fat belly that stuck out from below his dirty white shirt. He had a larger than life black handlebar mustache below a bulbous red nose. And as he puffed away on his pipe he yelled at us in a deep intimidating voice. "Hey, don't be stealing any sweets, right? I'm watching yous two..." Mr. Jones started to laugh. "I'll not be a minute lads, help yourselves to whatever you want, it's on the house."

"On the house?" Mr. Ferguson repeated crossly. I don't think so; you'll be paying for whatever the wee scalawags take Jonesy." And as they disappeared into the back room we could hear his deep booming voice fading off. "I have account of every bit of merchandise and if anything is missing it's on your tab Jonesy..." We looked at each other and started to laugh. There were a lot of sweets to choose from but both Stevie and I had one thing on our minds- Turkish-delights; and as we both quickly scoured the shop for the best sweets known to man; we found them and proceeded to fill not only our mouths but our pockets as well.

When we had our fill, Stevie grabbed four sodas and went over to the back of the shop and yelled through the opening. "We're going to wait in the auto for you, granddad." We didn't want to take the chance of Mr. Ferguson coming out and seeing the majority of his Turkish-Delights missing. He would probably cuff our lugs.

The Darker Side of Light

We travelled further north to an industrial area by the train tracks, in the town of Inverness. Mr. Jones drove the car right inside a big empty storage building and from there we got into another auto and continued to drive north. It was very late by this time. It had gotten very foggy and it was pouring rain. My mother and Stevie asleep and I too would soon be on the nod. We drove for a long time, and when I awoke we were in a place called Thurso; X marked the spot, so to speak…

Mr. Jones helped my mother out of the car and proceeded to grab hold of her arm to help her walk towards the cottage. She was coughing a lot and I thought at first she must have caught a cold. "Are you alright Ma?" I asked her as I grabbed her other arm. She looked at me for a moment as if she didn't know me and then she said. "Aye, Jimmie, I'll be fine, don't worry son."

The first person we met was Mr. Campbell. A very cheerful man, in a nervous sort of way; he welcomed us into the cottage that he called the Myer, as he tried to engage Mr. Jones with idle chatter. "How was the trip Mr. Jones? The rain didn't keep you back did it?" Mr. Jones gave a grunt and walked past him swiftly, pushing him off to the side. Still holding tight to my mother's arm, he stated, "I'll tend to your Ma. Stevie, why don't you show Jimmie around the place?" "Aye grandad, I'll give him the two-bit tour." He replied.

Mr. Campbell waited for us to walk past then followed in behind. We were met in the parlor by an odd-looking man. He was tall and thin, with thick wiry white hair, and big fat lips; he kind of looked like a hairy fish. I guess what was really strange about him was the fact that he had no ears. And the big black glasses he had on were attached to a black band that went right around his head. The first thing that came to my mind was that he was a Melt – an odd, fishy type of Melt.

Stevie smiled at me and winked – "I've never seen this bloke before." He went right up to him and said hello mate, I'm Stevie Jones. Looking straight ahead he spouted, "I know who you are lad." I turned to Stevie; I knew he was thinking the same thing I was thinking… 'This bloke is weird…' I walked up to him and offered him my hand and said. "I'm Jimmie Noble." He shook it and not surprisingly, it felt a wee bit scaly. "I am Fenton Chale, nice to meet you." He said politely.

The Darker Side of Light

He started to breath heavy, and his briny hot breath hit my face head-on. Looking straight ahead still he spouted, "So glad you made it, we were all a little worried you might not be joining us." I waved my hand in front of his face and looked over at Stevie who was snickering under his breath. I started to laugh too, I just couldn't help it.

My Ma's condition came into my mind. I straighten myself up, "Right then... Oh ya, that lady that was with Mr. Jones is my Ma, Mary Noble. She's no well, at the moment. Is there a Doctor around these parts?" "Your Ma...?" He questioned. "But... very sorry, very sorry indeed..." He looked towards Stevie then back at me, bowed his head again and walked off.

"What the ...?" I started to laugh a little and under my breath, I quietly said, "and I thought the mogully was thick in the head. Did you see that Stevie, the bloke didn't have any ears, and I don't think he heard me ask about the Doctor?" "Aye, his race doesn't have lugs like you or me. But don't kid yourself, the bloke can hear and see too. Isn't that right Fenton?" He stated softly. Then from the other room Fenton yelled, "Aye." I smirked at Stevie, "still thick though..." "I heard that lad," came his voice again." I couldn't help myself, I started to laugh as did Stevie. "Aye, that he is... just joking Fenton, we're only having a go at ya."

I followed Stevie down the hallway to a set of stairs that led to the cellar. "So where is the fine-hearing Fenton from then?" I asked out of curiosity. By this time nothing would surprise me. "He's from here, just not around these parts." "Ya okay then pal, I believe ya, even though thousands won't." He put his figure to his lips to let me know he had more to say but not until we were well out of Fenton's hearing range. This turned out to be a pretty far flung distance.

The cellar smelt of mold and mildew, and had the appearance of practically any other cellar you would find in Scotland with one exception; it had a secret door that led to a metal lift.

We travelled downward a good distance then stopped. Stevie informed me we were well below sea level. I started to get a bit panicky. "Don't worry, we're safe." He assured me.

When the doors opened, we walked into a massive underground dwelling, the likes of which I had never seen before. Stevie told

The Darker Side of Light

me it was called the Myer's Refuge. It was a large octagon shaped room and along five of the eight walls were screens – at least 20 feet wide and 10 feet high. I felt like I was at the picture show and was about to watch a Brick Bradford or Flash Gordon movie.

In the middle of the room at opposite ends of the floor sat Mr. R and Mr. M, two dispatch officers who ran the communications. After the introduction, I asked Stevie, "Why the letters, don't they have real names?" He just looked at me straight-faced and said, "No." They sat dutifully at their stations watching glass screens in front of them and listening to radio waves that flashed on the big black screens against the walls. And every now and then they made strange noises and spoke into the air as if they were commutating with invisible people.

On the desk were much smaller screens and keyboards that they touched continuously with great speed even when they were talking into the air. What was really odd was the assortment of different languages they spoke. Most of which I didn't even recognize.

It didn't seem to bother them, us being there. They nodded accordingly then continued with their tasks; which really seemed kind of boring if you ask me.

I walked over to Mr. R, "Hey, what are you doing there? Can you get the game on one of those big screens mate?" I asked jokingly. He looked at me as if he didn't know what I was talking about. "Game, what game would you be referring to James?" Why the football of course, where have you been pal?" "I think that is obvious, don't you?" he said kind of uppity. I could see he didn't have much of a sense of humor, so I left it alone.

Fenton came in and handed Mr. R. a package then walked over to Mr. M and did the same thing. As he walked over towards us I asked jokingly, "Hey ya Fenton, heard any good stories lately? "Aye, lad I did…I heard the one where you were running about in your skives…" I guess the bloke wasn't that thick and to top it off he had a sense of humor. I liked that. "Ya," I responded. "That Miss Martha couldn't get enough of this…" I flexed my arm muscle as Stevie burst out laughing. "Aye a proper Charles Atlas you are mate. …and he used to be so skinny…" Fenton smiled and nodded his head at the joke.

The Darker Side of Light

Yes, it was true, I had sent away for the 'Dynamic Tension' course on how to face down your bullies, so did Stevie. We just didn't work at it enough for either of us to have any real muscles to speak of. So, I don't know what Stevie was on about he was just as skinny as me.

"I can't help it if the women find me irresistible." I said with confidence. Referring to my swollen ego, Stevie commented. "I can scratch your head from here pal...who loves me...? I love me..." "Anyways..." I stated.

Wanting to change the subject, I turned to Fenton and said, "Fenton why the dark glasses, are you sporting a black eye under there that you don't want anyone to see?" Although I couldn't see his eyes, I knew he was looking at me. "Something like that." As he replied his big jelly fish lips quivered and shook. "Can I see it? You don't need to be embarrassed, we've all had our share of shiners mate." I told him. "No, I never take them off. I need them not only to see but for protection." I looked at him strangely. "You never take them off, not even to sleep, not even for the ladies...? Why not?" Stevie piped in "Just show him Fenton, it's the only way you'll get him to shut-up about it." I think Stevie was just as curious as me. "Ya, come on Fenton." I encouraged.

After some thought, Fenton took his two hands and placed them on either side of his head where his ears should have been, and then froze. "Go on Fenton, just for a minute, it won't be all that bad." Stevie coaxed. Fenton took a step towards me then slowly pushed his glasses down the rim of his nose. I pretended not to be surprised or shocked in anyway. His eye was black alright...both of them. They looked like two gigantic shiny marbles. He had no eyelids, just two big holes with these shiny black balls sticking out of them. And as he put the glasses back in place I asked him, "So where abouts are you from exactly, Fenton?"

He looked over at Stevie, who nodded his head for him to tell me. "I'm from earth, just like your friend there has told you. But I am from another part of earth, a deeper place than this." I didn't understand what he was talking about. I shook my head in disbelief and shrugged my shoulders. "I am from inside the earth. My realm is exactly five thousand three hundred and sixteen, point three miles straight under a land mass called Greenland." "You're Danish then? That explains a lot." I said jokingly.

The Darker Side of Light

"No, I am a Kelwright," he said seriously (I don't think he cared much for the Danish). "I am here like the others; like the good gents Mr. R and Mr. M to help correct that which has gone so terrible wrong." I had a feeling he wasn't just talking about the war and what was going on between the Boshney and the Melts. Something in his tone suggested a much grander dilemma, a much greater predicament. I would eventually find out, I was not far-off the mark.

Looking around the room, I could see it was quite empty. Stevie called me over to the back corner where a solitary chair sat. In the center hovering about two feet above it was a small crystal contraption that kind of looked like a glass brain. The only interesting thing about it was that it didn't seem to be attached to anything. It just hung in the air and spun around slowly in the one spot. Fenton spoke up as he exited the room, "don't be messing about over there, boys."

I looked at Stevie as much to say, "What is it man?" Volunteering the information, he pointed at the floating apparatus and said, "This machine can take you to any place in the universe and to any time as well."

"That's no machine." I started to chuckle sarcastically. "Yes, it is - it's the real-deal." He informed with conviction. "Ya okay... whatever you say. *That's* just a chair and *that's* a glass-brain-looking thingy-majiggy."

"Not the chair, not the chair!" He insisted as he pointed at it again. "I'm serious," he insisted. "It's called a Quantum Major Factor or Q.M.F for short." "Do I have gullible written across my forehead? I'm not fallen for your shenanigans pal."

"Right then..." I spouted as I jumped into the seat and laughingly said, "Okay take me to that Boshney wench." In that instant, a strange feeling came over me and I felt really dizzy. Stevie grabbed me by the arm and yanked me out of the seat. I screamed out in sheer panic as I felt myself leaving where I was. "What are you doing man? Are you crazy? Do you have a death wish?" he questioned.

"What just happened?" I was confused and disorientated. And felt like I was about to throw-up.

The Darker Side of Light

"What just happened? What just happened?" He repeated. "If I hadn't of grabbed you, you'd be at the mercy of that Miss Martha – that's what just happened."

After a few minutes, he calmed down and the sick feeling left me. He then told me the little bit he knew about it – that in the wrong hands it could be a very dangerous weapon but that only a few people were able to use it – I guess I was one of them. I listened and more importantly I took him very seriously. I still had trouble believing it was some kind of time machine. But I wasn't about to tempt fate again. Not without a sensible and solid plan – that is...

"I'm starving, how about you Jimmie?" Stevie exclaimed. I wasn't really but I wanted to get out of there – I was starting to feel claustrophobic – despite the large size of the room. "Ya, me too." I told him.

Stevie and I made are way up to the kitchen. There I met a little French woman named Edith, who if you asked me, looked like a female version of a mogully. Stevie assured me she was just born that way. All in all, she was a fine cook. I never tasted such lovely steak and kidney pie, and the pastries and sweets were out of this world.

Just as we were finishing up Mr. Jones entered the kitchen. I could tell by the look on his face he was worried about my mother. "Is she alright?" I asked. "Can I go see her?" "It's best you let her rest Jimmie. She's a strong woman, but I'm afraid only time will tell if she will be able to fight off the infection completely."

Stevie looked at me very seriously, and commented, "You should know it could take a long, long while for your mother to get better, she might not ever be right again." "What are you talking about Stevie, there's nothing wrong with my Ma, she just needs to rest that's all. What are you on about?" I was angry at him for talking such rubbish. I was really starting to get worried about her. I hadn't realized what a heavy toll my mother had endured until that moment. I mean, I knew she was held against her will, and that the Boshney might have infected her with the Dodgesons. But she always seemed invincible to me. Like nothing could harm her. Boy was I ever wrong...

I would soon find out that she had suffered greatly, not only at the hands of the mogully Mr. Quay with his enchantment spell;

but also Mr. Bunting who had inflicted her with the Dodgesons not once but twice. And both times she fought off the intruders with all her might.

A few days had passed and her condition seemed to be getting worse. She lay in a white room, covered with white sheets, with no pleasantries around her to speak of. I knew how much my mother loved flowers so that morning, I went out and picked some wildflowers and brought them to her.

I was taken aback when I first viewed her, and for a moment I thought it wasn't her, how could it be? Mr. Jones sat by her bedside, and nodded to me as if to say, it's okay to come in. And as I slowly walked towards her sleeping form I could hear her struggling to breathe. Her raspy breath seemed to choke and smother her.

Mr. Jones shook her arm gently, "Mary you've a visitor." She was so gauntly in appearance. Her eyes glazed over, were dark and sunk-in; they had a faraway look to them, as if part of her wasn't there. She could barely speak, but her face lit-up a little when she saw it was me. "Oh Jimmie, it's good to see you pet. Help me sit up a wee bit will ya Tomas?" With the help of Mr. Jones, she slowly sat up; she was as pale as the white wall behind her and just as stiff. She continued to breathe heavy then started to cough uncontrollably. Mr. Jones helped her by holding a bucket by her head so she could throw-up into it. I could see she had very little strength left and I felt so helpless. I wanted to cry but I held it in, I wanted to hug her tight but I was afraid I might hurt her.

She finally stopped coughing and lay back down again. "I've brought some flowers for ya Ma, brighten up the place a wee bit. Look your favorites, Harebells and Cowslips." She smiled at me and with a lot of effort said, "Thank-you love." Tears rolled down the side of her face as she lied there unable to move it would seem.

Mr. Jones spoke up, "Good news Jimmie, I've made arrangements for your Ma to go to Culloden House for treatments. We'll be leaving after breakfast. He turned to Ma, "You'll be better in no time at all Mary, don't you worry." She didn't say anything, she just lied there. "Don't you worry either Jimmie, I'll stay with her. I'll see to it she gets proper care." "I'm not goin'...?" He shook his head no. "I am going with my Ma! I'll not let you take her without me." I was very upset, worried that I might not ever see her again.

Ma gestured for me to come close to her; her stare fixed on me with intension, she pulled my arm over to her and I bent down close to her face. She whispered in a raspy lifeless voice, "I know you want to help son... but you wait here for me, it's better that way. I love ya son." I gently kissed her boney cheek. "Okay Ma, if that's what you want." I wasn't about to argue with her. "Away you go have some fun, and don't worry about me, I'll be okay, right?" I turned and walked away. "I love you too Ma, get better... so we can go home."

Stevie and I spent the next few days exploring the little village of Thurso and also questioning the gents in Myer's refuge about the Q.M.F.

It was the most fascinating device I had ever seen. Its arrival in Scotland was somewhat of a mystery however, and after much coaxing, we persuaded Mr. M, into telling us about its origin; which we found out to be alien in nature.

It had been invented by a being who went by the name of Delwin. But even Mr. M, didn't know how it actually worked, so we weren't to bother him about it. I got the impression he didn't want to know how it worked. He told us it was not his concern and that he had other pressing matters at hand. What could be more important than travelling through time? I thought to myself.

My curiosity was getting the better of me and I wanted to explore what the Q.M.F. could do.

I think Stevie was a little curious too, because he was willing to let me try it again – he called it a controlled experiment.

He instructed me to stand under the crystal brain-thingy and not to move or speak. "And keep your mind blank too!" he said at the last minute. "Oh great, now you tell me." I said in a panic. "shhh" he insisted. "Now think of the kitchen upstairs – now go there." I closed my eyes for one seconded and when I opened them I was in the kitchen. "Wholly cow!" I screamed. I felt fine, and was only a little disoriented by the change of view. I hurried back down stairs to tell Stevie it worked.

The Darker Side of Light

I did many little trips to different rooms of the house. Nothing too far for my only way back was by foot. And I dared not go to a different time, for free I would never have a way back.

"I bet the Boshney would love to get their grubby hands on this machine." I commented to Stevie. "Aye, they have been trying to find it for centuries; the devils don't even know it's here."

Stevie seemed to know a lot more than he was letting on. I figured it was on account of his granddad being so involved with all that was going on. I just didn't know what my part was, and why I was able to use the Q.M.F. and why I was given such an important task as to have in my possession the Sea Raven's charm. I was just a kid - a nobody.

Mother seemed to get better at Culloden House and was back to her old self in no time. She wanted to go home to our own flat, but we soon found out that we could not go back until it was safe. My mother and I were given safe passage to London, and our few meager belongings that were still at our flat on Forges Place would remain there, as we were not allowed to return or have any of our things brought to us. We were set up in a nice furnished flat on the posh side of Downing Street. They had secured a wee job for Ma, and I was already registered in a private school; everything was taken care of for us.

Ma was not permitted to contact any of her friends or family members. Out of all my Ma had gone through, I think this was the hardest part. She was very depressed and sad most of the time although she tried to hide it from me; I could still tell.

Things slowly returned to normal, well, if you can call my life in 1942 normal.

It was my 12th birthday. I was very excited because my mother said she had a special present for me. I raced home after school and waited patiently for my surprise. After supper, my mother brought out two parcels from her bedroom. "This one is from me Jimmie and this one came in the post for you today. It was hand delivered by a very nice young man." We were both very surprised because only a few people knew where we lived. Who could it be from, we both wondered?

The Darker Side of Light

I didn't know which one to open first. "Well go ahead open up your presents…" I picked up the one from my mother and opened it up. It was a camera! "Thank you, Ma! It's just what I wanted." I had been wanting a camera since I was eight but my Ma said we couldn't afford one. "Wow, a real camera! Are you sure about it Ma?" "Yes, Jimmie don't you worry, I've been saving up for a long time." I got up and hugged her tight, "Thanks Ma, you're the best." "Happy Birthday son, now mind you read the instructions so you know how to work it."

I left the other present on the kitchen table, I was too enthralled with my new camera. I got up to go to my room so I could study the handbook. I wanted to get started taking pictures right away. "What about your parcel Jimmie?" She asked. "I'll open it later Ma, this is more important." "Come back here Jimmie Noble, I want to see what's in the box even if you don't." She demanded.

"Okay Ma" I sat back down and picked up the parcel wrapped in Kraft-paper. Ma was more anxious than me.

"Well open it… who's it from?" It's from Annabel Green," I said excitedly. "Oh," she said kind of disappointed. There was a sealed envelope on top of a small dark brown wooden box. "What is it Jimmie?" "I don't know." I shook the box, it looked familiar but I couldn't place it. "There's something inside it I think but I don't know how it opens. There's no lid or top Ma."

She took it from me to examine it. "I have no idea on how it opens, love? Oh, I've seen the likes of this sort of thing before." She exclaimed, "It's one of those fancy, mystical boxes magicians use in magic shows. There's a trick to opening it." Then she handed it back to me. "Here you go love, you'll have to figure it out.

Maybe Annabel wrote it down in the letter she wrote you. Why don't you let me have a look?" I handed my mother the letter. She opened it, took a moment to read it to herself and then out loud to me.

"'Dearest Jimmie, I wanted to wish you a happy birthday. And let me just say how sorry I am that I couldn't help you with all that you have gone through. Know that it was the way it had to be.'"

My mother made one of her- who are you kidden faces and continued to read. "'I have enclosed a very special birthday

The Darker Side of Light

present for you. It is called Delwin's box- I do believe you are familiar with it?' I started to get really excited and a little afraid for I knew what Delwin's box was.

'It originates from a galaxy one hundred thousand light years in every direction from earth; it is called Ultalmalia; this cosmos marks the border between the Temissqual Vista and the plane of KYEN.

I bestow this treasure on you Jimmie, for it is your destiny that will change the future. When the moment is right you will know what to do.'

Mother stopped reading and started to laugh, as she shook her head in disbelief. "What a load of gaff. Only that Annabel would make up something so ridiculous. She couldn't just say it's a magician's box…no, she has to make it sound all important, and toff."

Mother let out a deep sigh of displeasure and continued to read. 'It is very important that you keep it secret and safe from all harm, and under no circumstance should you try to use it before you are ready and know the right action to take.'

"Wow, I screamed out loud. "This is the best present ever…" "You know what this is then?" My Ma asked sadly. "Oh boy do I…" In my excited state, I forgot about my mother's feelings. "It's almost as good as my new camera…almost Ma!" I couldn't tell her it was the most fantastic gift in the entire universe. I hid my enthusiasm and said. "It's just a silly magician's box Ma. It's nowhere as great as a camera. I like my new camera much more." I went over and gave her a big cuddle. "Thanks Ma, I love ya."

She folded up the letter and put it back in the envelope. "That's about all it says. Right, away you go play with your camera. And mind you read the handbook first."

I took my camera and Delwin's box into my room. All the while I wondered why Annabel would give me such an important device. After all, I wasn't anybody of importance. And the Q.M.F. was the most amazing machine ever invented; it was the most remarkable instrument in the entire universe and beyond for that matter.

I hid Delwin's box in my room so that no one could find it. But not before taking a picture of it with my new camera.

Later when I wanted to read the letter Annabel had sent me it had mysteriously disappeared. Then Ma told me she accidently dropped it in the fireplace.

Time waits for no man... it marched on and so did we all.

We lived on Downing Street for the next three years; until the war was over and we were notified by the post of all things- that it was safe to go back home to Scotland. The letter basically thanked my mother for staying in the accommodations provided and that she had served her country well; but no longer would they be footen the bill, so to speak, we were on our own now.

Ma wouldn't have been able to afford such a nice flat or continue to pay for private school. And although we had both made new friends and liked the city very much, we both wanted to go home right away. So we did…

The year was 1947, the war had been over for two years and we were home and safe from adversity. After all those dodgy years my mate Stevie still resided at the Myer.

Sadly enough, he had lost his granddad to illness the year before, his father was missing in action and his mother and sister - well they were still missing and at the mercy of the Boshney.

He had just turned eighteen in May so it was off to the service for him. He planned on following in his Dad's and Granddad's footsteps by becoming a Royal Naval Air Force Pilot. He and I both knew it was a great cover for a much grander mission.

I told him I would be joining him next year when I turned eighteen as long as my mother was alright. Life had taken a heavy toll on my mother that was for certain. I don't think she completely recovered from the initial attack, and for the last six months she lay bedridden. She was dying of consumption - the same illness she was originally inflicted with. There wasn't anything the doctors could do to save her. She refused to get treatment like she had got before. She made the excuse that we couldn't afford it. I told her she didn't need to worry about the money, it would be taken care of.

I went ahead and made arrangements for her to be treated at Culloden House but she simply refused to go. "I can't go through that again Jimmie," she told me in her weaken state. "I'd rather die... You have no idea the hell I went through back then. It was terribly painful, just thinking about it... No Jimmie, I'll no go, I' rather die, and I mean it."

I wanted nothing more than to relieve her of the terrible disease that was swiftly killing her body, but I respected her wishes and cancelled the appointment.

I tried to stay strong for the both of us, it wasn't easy. I paid Mrs. White to check in on her during the day and make her a bit of lunch while I was at work. When I got home at night, I tended to her needs, I tried to make her final days as pleasant as possible, and often read to her to help ease her mind.

Her lovely face aged beyond her young-years told a tale of one deeply troubled. It wasn't just the disease that was ailing her; it was her conscience as well...

"I've something I need to tell you Jimmie." Her words came out winded and filled with sorrow. "It's been weighing heavy on my mind for years and years. It's something your father and I should have told you years ago, but the time was never right. And then we lost your father to the war.... I didn't want to lose you too. But you do have the right to know."

Tears swelled up in her soft brown eyes. "Oh, Jimmie, I'm sorry I didn't tell you sooner, please don't be mad at me, you're all I've got. I couldn't leave this world knowing you were angry with me." She started to weep. In her weakened state, it was even difficult for her to cry, she just didn't have the strength. "It's okay Ma, don't be sad. What could possibly upset you so much? Tell me, it's okay, I'll understand." I assured her.

She looked at me very seriously and said. "Just before your father and I met he was in love with another woman. Even though she loved him too, she could never marry him. He came here to Paisley, where we met and fell in love. We tried for years to have a child, but I couldn't carry to term. I lost three sons over a four-year period and your father was overwhelmed with grief." She stopped talking and tried to catch her breath as her wheezy, phlegm-filled chest continued to choke the life out of her. A good five minutes passed before she had the strength to continue.

"I have always loved your father Jimmie, and would do anything for him. He wanted more than anything to have a son of his own." She looked towards the window as she drifted off for a moment. I could tell it was killing her to carry on, but she did nonetheless. Looking towards me she spoke. "What I'm trying to tell ya is I'm not your real mother Jimmie…. You were born to your father's first love." She started to shake uncontrollably. Please don't be angry for not telling you sooner son."

A part of me didn't want to believe what she was saying; and I hoped it might be the illness talking through her. However, the sincerity of her confession was one I could not deny.

I bent over and gently wrapped my arms around her tiny, fragile frame. "It's okay Ma… don't fret. You are my only mother and always will be."

It didn't matter to me that Mary Noble wasn't my biological mother, I loved her with all my heart and I told her so. She looked deeply into my eyes with a passion only a mother holds and a conviction only a parent can claim. I saw before me the woman who raised me to be a man, the mother who I loved with all my heart and soul.

She spoke slowly, "I have always loved you Jimmie, right from the first time she placed you in my arms; you were only three days old, oh you were so, so lovely. I finally had my wee baby boy…" "So, you knew her then, this woman? Who is she?" I questioned.

She started to choke, and her wheezy breath rattled as it suffocated the life right out of her. Every second counted…

Her face grew red as the pressure in her head mounted. She grabbed my forearm with her frail hand bringing me in close to her as she pointed towards her dresser. "What is it Ma, do you want something out of your dresser?" I questioned. She shook her head no as she began to cough uncontrollably. Still pointing she uttered the words, "The box, look in the box…the letter…" "Aye, okay Ma, I'll get it for ya." I assured her. She held on to my arm a little tighter and shook her head no at me again. "It's for you…"

Her eyes filled with tears as she whispered. "I'm so sorry son, I shouldn't have kept it from ya." "It's okay Ma, you rest for a while, we'll talk about it later, you need your rest okay." "No son I need to tell ya…" she gasped for air, her gaze faint and fading; words came out sketchy but precise; "Annabel… Annabel Green… she is your natural mother Jimmie." Then she was gone… and I was left alone and wondering… "How could this be?"

***

James sat for a long while and stared at the photo of his grandpa on the fire place. He really didn't know what to think. "Okay" he finally decided, "Maybe his grandpa was adopted and maybe his mother told him on her death bed. But come-on… his real mother had glass eyes, and better yet… was from another planet? He laughed out loud and spouted, "Damn aliens…" It amused him to think about the idea of having alien blood travelling through his veins. Of course, it was complete and utter nonsense, all of it, he decided. He closed up the journal. "I need to get some sleep," he thought.

He would be picking up William in the morning and leaving all this nonsense behind him. He decided he would finish reading the journal, but not until he got home from holidays. He didn't want to take the chance of William finding it lying around and reading it, after all he didn't completely understand it enough himself to explain to his eleven-year-old son why his grandfather wrote such far-out tales. William would surely question him about it; he was a very sensitive, very inquisitive kid. James felt William didn't need to be involved with his grandpa's stories. "Hmmm… mom must have felt the same way," he realized.

He still planed on going to his mother's house before heading up to the cottage. He didn't want to be there for more than an hour or so. He planned to go through the boxes in the attic quickly to see if there was anything of any importance then make the call…

He picked up William at 8:00 a.m. Friday morning. It always amazed James how little William had packed for himself. "Are you sure you have everything you need Will? We'll be gone for three weeks at least. Did you remember to pack a tooth brush this time?" William still half asleep; his strawberry-blonde curly hair matted and un-brushed fell slightly over his eyes as he flicked it back he yawned. "Yes dad, I packed everything." James questioned. "Did you want to get dressed first…?" "I am dressed dad, these are my clothes." William replied as he looked down at his zebra-striped shirt and faded black flannel-looking shorts that fell to just below his knees. "Oh… okay, I thought you were still in your p.j's." "Whatever dad," he replied as he got into the front seat passenger-side of his dad's bright yellow 2040 Moedel Atome.

Once in the moving car, William drifted off to sleep. James didn't disturb him; he thought it was best just to let him sleep. He would need to stop and recharge the car's engine before heading onto the highway. He pulled into an ION Solar-station and replenished the energy supply, it would last for at least three weeks before he would need to recharge it again.

He didn't want to think about the stories his grandfather wrote, but for some reason they kept creeping into his thoughts. He turned up the radio to drown out his thoughts. It helped for a little while, and then they were back, dogging his thoughts with visions of another time… another life.

He looked over to William who was still asleep. He was tempted to wake him up so that he would have someone to talk to; to distract him from his present dilemma, but decided at the last minute it was better to just let him sleep. Besides they would be there soon, Bradford was only a few kilometers way now. His thoughts then returned to his last trip to his dear departed mother's home and the strange electrical storm that took place.

Profound thoughts of a sound fate entered his line of reasoning. "If it weren't for that flash of light, I would never have noticed that box. And I wouldn't be going back to look through mom's junk." It kind of freaked him out to think of it as some kind of sign.

"We're here," James announced. "What, already?" William stretched and looked out the car window. "Huh, where are we?" He looked over at his dad. "What are we doing at grandma's house dad? I thought we were going to the cottage?" "We are, we just have to do a little work here first. You and I need to go through the last of grandma's things in the attic. Then we'll go for

The Darker Side of Light

breakfast and then head to the cottage okay?" He added, "It won't take long, half-hour at the most."

"The attic… we have to go in the attic? Are you serious dad?" William quickly woke up and felt a terrible sense of dread enter his mind. "Can I wait in the car?" James was surprised at William's response. "What…? No, you can't wait in the car." He laughed, "Why do you want to wait in the car?" William looked towards the house and uttered, "I don't know, just do."

William didn't want to go in the house let alone go up into the attic. But he couldn't tell his dad. He was still confused about what had happened the last time he was there. Just before his grandma went crazy… just before she died. He never did tell either of his parents, he didn't know how. "Alright, I guess, I'll help you." He said complying. All the while hoping her ghost didn't haunt the place or that any of those creatures she was terrified of were still lurking about.

As they entered the old house William covered his mouth and nose with his hands and turned to his dad and said with a muffed voice. "Did grandma really die here? I mean did she go to the hospital or something?" James looked at his son surprised. "Yes, she did die in this house." James noticed William was covering his face with his hands. "It's not that bad, don't worry." He assured him. "It's not that dad." He replied, still covering his face. William didn't know if this was a good time to talk about it, he wanted to but he was still not sure.

Taking his hands away from his face he continued. "Did you notice anything strange about grandma before she died? Any weird stuff she might have said to you about… creepy things?" James didn't know what William was talking about. "What do you mean Will? What kind of creepy things? What did grandma say to you? You can tell me it's alright." "Nothing, never-mind, it's not important anyhow." He said unsure of himself.

James stopped in his tracks and gave his full attention to William. His own apprehensions faded in that moment as he looked on in anticipation waiting for William's reply.

William really didn't want to be there. He asked his dad one more time. "Are you sure I can't wait in the car dad?" "What's up Will? I think you need to tell me." He said with great concern. "It's just that I think grandma was possessed or something." He whispered. "She was crazy the last time I saw her. No offence dad, but she was acting really strange." He paused for a moment. "What if her ghost is still here?" James didn't know how to take in what William was saying. He would never have guessed William would have had such thoughts of her. He never knew his mother to act strange or peculiar in any way, she was quite the opposite; always level headed and sensible.

What would cause William to say such things about her? "Your grandmother was a good woman, she would never hurt you Will. She loved you, and if her spirit is around… somewhere, she would never do anything to harm you, you don't have to be afraid of her." He said convincingly. "Oh, it's not her I'm afraid of as much as the *creatures* that were after her." William stated.

"Dad, remember last year when I went to stay with grandma?" "Yes…" he said as he recalled it in that moment. It didn't seem to hold any importance, but he felt soon he would find out it did. "That was just before she died, wasn't it?" he questioned. "Ya dad it was. That's what I'm talking about, she was acting really weird. It freaked me out, I didn't want to tell you because by the time I saw you it was too late. She was already dead. And I didn't know what to say. So, I just tried to forget about it. But now that we're here… I kind of think you should know."

William had gone to stay with her the last week in June. William didn't know it, but he was literally the last person to see her alive. Normally he would still be with his mom but she was called into work unexpectedly and was unable to take care of him. His dad was also busy with work, and there was no point in sending him to a sitter when his grandma was more than happy to have him come to stay with her for the week. It started off as a regular visit. His mother dropped him off at 7 p.m. Sunday night. Grandma had his room ready for him and his favorite food in the refrigerator. His grandma let him do pretty much anything he wanted to do. All pretty normal stuff… until it got really weird.

William began, "It all started Wednesday night, late Wednesday night. I awoke to the sound of grandma talking to someone. It actually sounded like she was arguing with someone. But I could only hear grandma's voice, and no one else. I got up and quietly headed down stairs. I didn't turn on any lights because I didn't want anyone to see me. I followed the sound of her voice which

The Darker Side of Light

was coming from the kitchen. I saw this dim light coming from the kitchen. I looked in and saw all these candles lit. I thought for a minute that maybe there was a power failure and that was why grandma had all the candles lit. I couldn't see her anywhere so I called to her. 'Grandma are you there?'

In the corner beside the fridge I saw a shadow, it was her, and she was just standing there staring up at the ceiling. 'Grandma... what are you doing?' I asked. She came at me quickly, with her index figure to her lips, and waving the other hand back and forth in front of her like a crazy person; her clothes were soaking wet like she had just come out of the pool or something. It really scared me dad."

William parroted his grandmother's voice and gestures as he spoke. "Then she said, 'Quiet, they'll hear you.' 'Who, who will hear me? There's no one here grandma.' I told her. I asked her why all the lights were turned off? But she didn't answer. I went over to flick the light switch on. And she yelled, 'Don't turn the light on. They'll see us for sure.' 'Who grandma, who will see us?' I asked. 'There's no one here but us.' She looked at me with this really strange look in her eyes and said, 'The Dodgies are all about!' She looked really wacked-out dad. She started to get all panicky and all messed-up. She kept saying, 'there here, there here I tell you.' and something about them coming for her. And you're not going to believe this dad, but she must have had every single bowl she owned on the table and counters filled with water. Even the sink was filled with water."

James didn't know what to say. He was speechless. He could only assume that she had read the journal and somehow got caught up in the story. And with her heart condition it was probably too much for her. Or maybe she was suffering from some form of dementia and no one knew about it. That could be the only reason for her strange behavior.

"That's not all dad," he added. "This is the really messed-up part. I went and turned the light on anyways and as soon as I did there was this strange high-pitched noise; the kitchen light popped and went out, and then all the candles went out too! I was so scared... Then get this... grandma grabbed a bowl of water and threw it at me. I screamed at her. 'What are you doing grandma?' She grabbed me by the arm and insisted we go upstairs to the washroom. She said we would be safe in there.

We stayed in there the whole night dad. She even had blankets for us and pillows and the sink and bathtub were filled with water. She said if she needed to jump into the water not to worry, and that I was to jump in too! I tell ya dad it was really strange. I wanted to cry but I didn't. I asked her why she threw the water at me in the kitchen, and she said it was for my own protection! My own protection… She lit more candles and said we would be safe as long as we didn't leave the bathroom. I asked her how long did we have to stay in there? She told me until the air in the rest of the house cleared. I didn't know what she was talking about. I wanted to call mom but it had to be three in the morning by this time, plus she wouldn't let me leave the bathroom."

James was in shock. He couldn't believe what he was hearing. "Wow, I am so sorry Will, I had no idea. I wish you would have told me." James felt terrible that William had to go through such a scary experience. "You should have told me, you can tell me anything. James wrapped his arms around William to hug him. "I wish you would have told me. I am here for you no matter what… remember that." "I know dad, it's just… well I didn't think you would believe me, you know, with her being your mom and all and then she died." He added after some consideration, "If someone said those things about my mom I wouldn't have believe it."

James wondered how far this fantasy-world of his mother had played out before William felt the need to get out of there. "Did you call your mom that morning and ask her to pick you up? She would have come and got you, you know. Or you could have called me, I would have come right away, no questions asked."

William was silent for a moment. He wasn't sure how to answer because he wasn't exactly sure himself. "No dad I didn't. I think maybe because that morning, even though I woke up on the bathroom floor, I felt okay; I mean I wasn't scared or anything like that. And grandma was in the kitchen making me something to eat like nothing ever happened. All the mess was gone and she seemed back to normal. Well sort of normal." William paused for a moment as if he were collecting his thoughts and sorting them out into some kind of sequence.

He gestured his speech, pointing to his own body parts as he confirmed his observation. "She had on these huge red rubber rain boots, a furry pink house-coat, one oven mitt on her left hand and a red winter hat on her head to match the boots I think. I started to laugh when I saw her, she really looked funny. I didn't say anything, well not right away. I sat down and ate first, and when I was finished and about to leave the kitchen I asked her, 'hey grandma what's with the get-up, are you expecting it to rain in here?' She came over to me and practically touched her nose on my nose and said. 'One never knows, it just might. You'd be wise to follow suit... it never hurts to be ready, for it's a wise man who knows his fate and follows it.' Then she said something like 'If you're not ready you'll be left behind with the lot.' Whatever that means... she was definitely not herself dad, but I wasn't afraid, I actually felt safe with her. She seemed to know what she was talking about."

James continued to listen to William, he still could not fathom his mother in such a state. Maybe she had been drinking, he thought, and lost all sense of reality. "Anyhow," He continued. "Mom called later that day, I told her I wasn't feeling too good, so she picked me up after work. I watched for her, and when she got there I said goodbye to grandma and ran out the door before mom got out of the car. That way mom won't be able to see grandma and her red rain boots ...ya she still had them on dad, all day, the hat too."

There was silence for a moment then James spoke to his son. Well William, I don't know what to say... Grandma had a weak heart and was very ill near the end. If I had even known she was sick, I would have got her some help, and we definitely would not have let you go to stay with her. But she didn't tell me, I had no way of knowing. I am so sorry you had to experience that... I mean I would have preferred that you had fonder memories of her than you do." "Oh, don't worry dad, my memories of grandma are good." William assured his dad.

James and William stood at the base of the staircase that led to the second floor and to the waiting attic. James had second thoughts about continuing with his original plan. He turned to William and just as he was about to say let's forget about it, I'll do it another time. William spoke up. "Okay dad, let's do this. Let's clean out that attic!" Reaching into his pocket William pulled out a little clear plastic bag of what appeared to be greyish sand. He waved it in front of his dad. "What on earth is that Will?" James said surprised. "It's pepper dad, grandma gave it to me for luck. Then

The Darker Side of Light

she told me these far-out stories about creatures from other planets, and how they were sent to earth to search for some other aliens." James looked at the little bag William hung in front of his face. "You didn't believe her, did you?" He asked concerned. "No, but I figured it couldn't hurt. It's only pepper... plus I promised grandma, I would carry it with me always."

"What else did grandma tell you...?" he asked half-jokingly. "Well dad, she was going on about some lady named..." He had to think about it. "Oh ya, Martha, and how she stole some other lady's baby. I think she said the baby's name was... Starling or something like that." "Starling... Starling...?" James repeated as he began to remember. James felt dizzy and confused. "It was Starlet. 'Ya that was it – Starlet." William agreed.

Suddenly, James was filled with grief. "We named her Starlet." He said sadly. How could he have forgotten about her. His little baby girl. Up until this moment he had no memory of her. Why had he forgotten her?

He felt very weak and out of place. Turning around he sat on the second step of the staircase. "What's wrong dad? Do you know what grandma was talking about? Did she tell you about it too?" James sat in silence and slowly looked towards William. Lost in the moment, he shook his head back and forth and muttered, "This isn't right, this just isn't right. It can't be real." "What dad? What isn't right? What's going on?" William began to worry about his dad and thought maybe he shouldn't have told him anything.

It was so long ago but he remembered. Paula had gone into labor six weeks early. The baby was born prematurely and ended up living only a few days before she died. It was a terrible time for them. They knew something was wrong with her but they didn't know what. Even the doctors couldn't explain it; she seemed healthy enough at first, even though she had what they called 'Corneal Opacity.' They said it was a genetic defect but not life threatening.

He cleared his throat and then spoke, "We named her Starlet because of her eyes... they were pale blue...they sparked like they had little stars dancing around in them. Starlet was your sister William; she died shortly after she was born. The doctor told us if she had survived, she would have been blind - no pupils..." As he spoke the words he remembered. ...How could he have forgotten such an important coincidence as this? What did it mean?

His eyes filled with tears and he covered his face to hide his sadness from his son. "It's okay dad." William sat beside his dad and wrapped his arm around him. They sat in silence for a long time and then James spoke. "Let's get out of here." He stood up and walked towards the front door. William was right behind him.

James decided, he would tell his son everything he knew. As crazy as it was - he would show him the sweater that contained the Sea Raven's Barnacle and he would show him the mysterious Delwin's box and the photo. He would tell him everything he had read in the journal – they could finish reading it together. Maybe they could make sense of it. Maybe together they could find the truth…

The Predator and the Prey

Come into my home, gestured the spider to the fat, tasty fly
I will make you beans and pie… and anything you wish, I've got
A tasty bit of dead maggot? Or maybe you'd prefer some flesh
As you can see, I'm finished with the rest
And as the spider eyed his claim, he gathered up his final stance
Come in my friend, come in…

The hefty fly in all her wisdom fair
Circled high, to clear the air
I will not… she did reply
I will not fall victim to your will
Then she laughed and laughed more still
Crying out, I've seen death before
For I was born upon its door
And I know it lies in the words you spout
So, I will not come in – I will stay out

Bravo, the spider clapped. You are smarter than I thought
Too bad, oh yes, he sighed, now you won't get what I've got
And then with more ham than pig
The spider cried goodbye wise friend and turned to go back in
Wait, the fly did call, I have something to confess
And as the large fly landed softly, the spider he did grin
For soon to dine, he would begin
I will take you at your word, for I want what you've got
You see, I'm not at all what you had thought
The spider knew he'd meet his match and raced to clear his door
And as the tyrant plunged her stinger in, she cried
Oh, I am so much more…

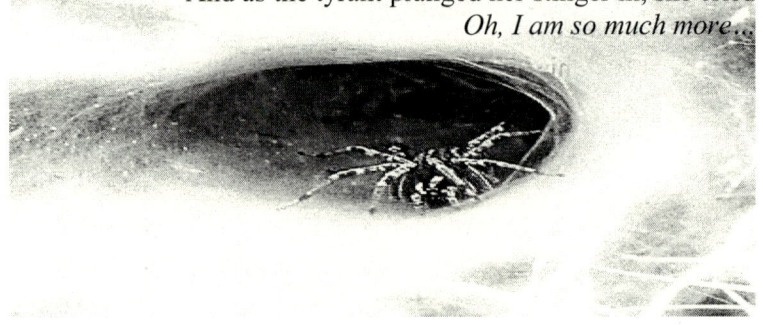

Let me in

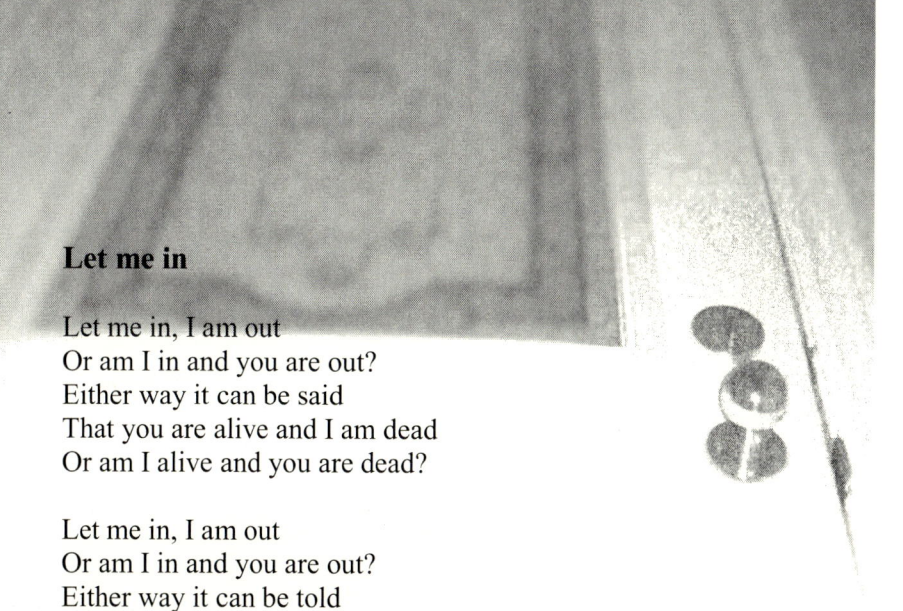

Let me in, I am out
Or am I in and you are out?
Either way it can be said
That you are alive and I am dead
Or am I alive and you are dead?

Let me in, I am out
Or am I in and you are out?
Either way it can be told
That you are young and I am old
Or am I young and you are old?

Let me in, I am out
Or am I in and you are out?
Either way it can be thought
That you are friend and I am not
Or am I friend and you are not?

Let me in, I am out
Or am I in and you are out
Either way it can be that
We are either this or that
We are neither this or that

The Darker Side of Light

Frail bars bind this beautiful beast so burdened.
Dreams alone, will satisfy a heart that longs for flight
And death alone, will bring about a life of freedom
Or so the story goes...

The Will in Love
A Will that is truly strong and stern
Has been broken down by
One glance, one turn
And i that looks but does not see
Beyond a blind fine symmetry
And i that sits with gilded wing
Will fly again one day in spring
When summoned by a power higher
Determined Will become a flyer
For the most determined, the most betrothed
Have fallen down, hard fast by love
Broken spirit, mend ye not so fast
Confined by natures new found grasp

Our trip to the Metro Toronto Zoo
(1994)
We went to the Zoo
The children and I
One beautiful spring day

We walked all around
The parks of the grounds
Visiting a few of God's fine creatures
The splendid, the wondrous
The amazing features

The Bats, the Cats
And even the wombats
Slept the whole day through

The Polar Bears and seals
Had great appeal
Playfully frolicking in the cool
Of their pool

The giraffe tall and slender stood
On the grass beside some wood

The Elephants Grand
Roamed their land
A large opened area of rock and sand

The highlight of our trip happened when
We visited the apes in their glass pen
The little apes were jumping and swinging
From rope to stoop
Attacking each other
And eating some-kind of goop

The great mother ape
Was feeding and cleaning her young

All this, I admit seemed perfectly normal
Until alas looking up
I spied something quite formal

It was the great father ape sitting up high
Looking at him I wanted to cry

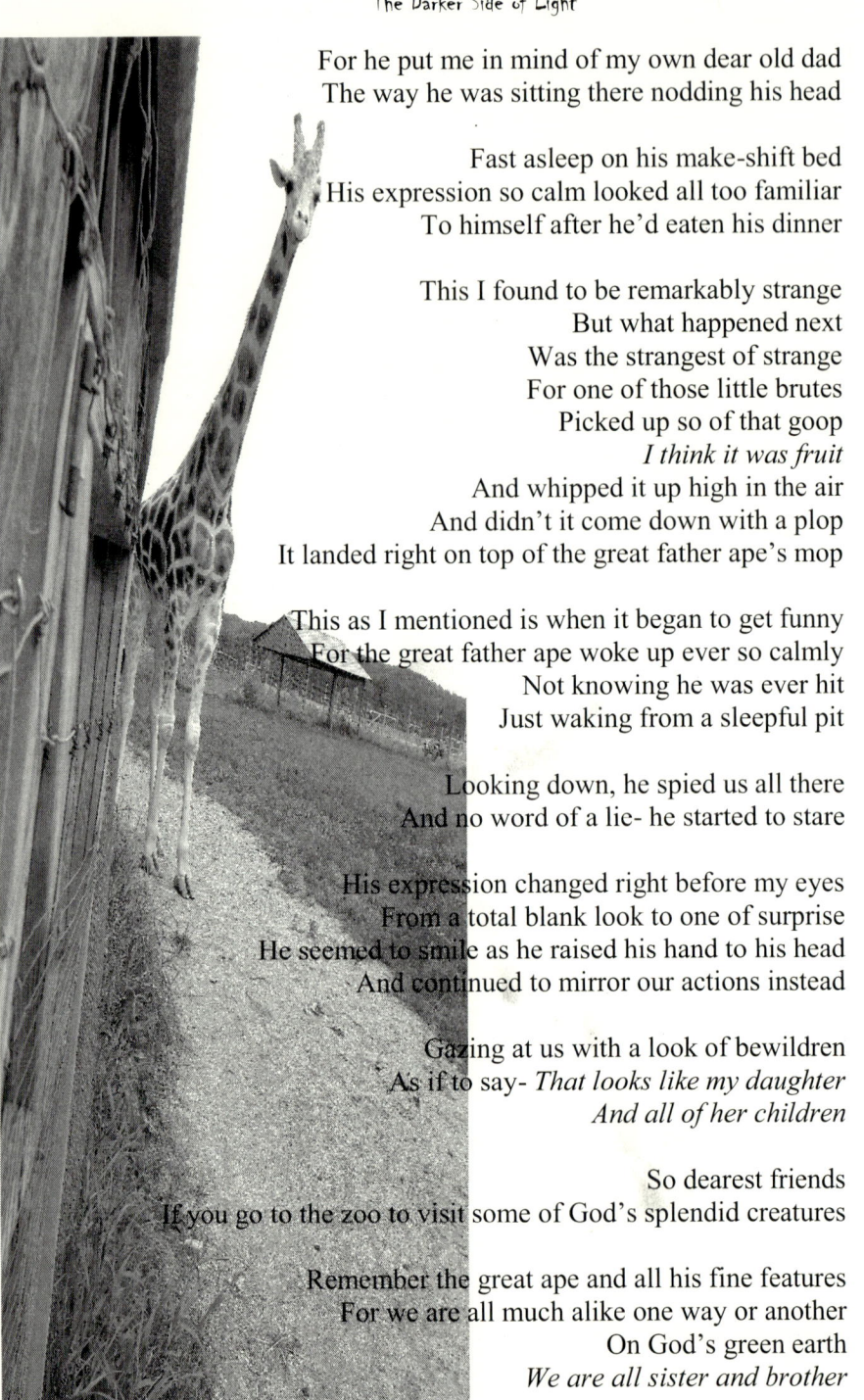

The Darker Side of Light

For he put me in mind of my own dear old dad
The way he was sitting there nodding his head

Fast asleep on his make-shift bed
His expression so calm looked all too familiar
To himself after he'd eaten his dinner

This I found to be remarkably strange
But what happened next
Was the strangest of strange
For one of those little brutes
Picked up so of that goop
I think it was fruit
And whipped it up high in the air
And didn't it come down with a plop
It landed right on top of the great father ape's mop

This as I mentioned is when it began to get funny
For the great father ape woke up ever so calmly
Not knowing he was ever hit
Just waking from a sleepful pit

Looking down, he spied us all there
And no word of a lie- he started to stare

His expression changed right before my eyes
From a total blank look to one of surprise
He seemed to smile as he raised his hand to his head
And continued to mirror our actions instead

Gazing at us with a look of bewildren
As if to say- *That looks like my daughter
And all of her children*

So dearest friends
If you go to the zoo to visit some of God's splendid creatures

Remember the great ape and all his fine features
For we are all much alike one way or another
On God's green earth
We are all sister and brother

The Seasons
The fellowship of spring's surprise
Will warm the depths of summer's eyes
And like the one who talks the game
Summoned up will act the same
Then to sleep, rest in view
Begins the end of fall anew
Colour's rich does begin
A freedom she will never win
As winter buries that which it hides
Brought to life by frozen tides
And as I relish in the thought
Of lessons learned and to be taught
I wonder how it comes about
That seasons pass without a doubt
And change persists to flourish there
Without a worry or a care
Without a whisper of regret
Of time to pass and time to get
And how we change as seasons do
Sometimes old and sometimes new

My Write

Sometimes we lose before we begin
The light that is born within
Forsaking all that binds us tight
Embracing all that which comes by night
Living on a breathless whim
Somehow filled the emptiness within
Then drawing strength from yesterday
Drawing strength from miles away
Religion peeked in times then…
Drifted away with yesterday's wind
The complete nature of my rhyme
Will all make sense in yesterday's time
For like a tear that falls to earth
Quickly cherished, cuddled, and nursed
A saddened angel
A gift from God
A tiny ray of light…
For I feel there is Hope in everything I write
As sad and melancholy, it may seem to be
It holds a special place in my heart to me
For it is mine

And I write on…

The Darker side of Light

Acknowledgements

I would like to thank those who let me use or take their photo to enhance this book:

A special thanks to…

Daughter Meaghan – "crossing the bridge of uncertainty" (front cover), her artsy photo (page 152) and pic on page 90.

Son Jordan for *letting* his friend Taylor - sit while I took his picture at the *(haunted)* Wilson's Hill Cemetery – thanks for your patience Taylor (page 15).

Daughter Amanda for letting me take a picture of her with her sister Meaghan when they were young – *this did not happen often* (page 90).

Grandson Demar, A.K.A: 'Demar Extreme Volcano' (front cover and pages 26 & 99).

Granddaughter Champagne, whose picture I used at the end of the poem *Betsy Bouncy Doll* (page 96).

Son Colin for posing for a picture at the end of *Once Upon a Sorry Time* (page 122).

Cousin Angie who inspired me to write *Lonely Heart* with her photo by the seaside (page 123)

Aria Breeze, for letting me use a photo she took, thus inspiring poem My *Solitary Wanderer* (page 161)

Miriam King, Editor of The Bradford Times- thank you for your insight -helping me to re-think the title of this book.

Also, I would like to make special mention of the following pages: 157-Grandmother Violet, 167-a generation photo of my dad, James with his father and grandfathers, 195-Grandmother Muriel, 203- a sketch my husband Brent did in high school.

Other photos in this book, I took myself or got via the internet and formatted.

And thank you Chris for taking the time to read this book.